The Way Home

ALSO BY AMANDA PROWSE

Novels

Poppy Day

What Have I Done?

Clover's Child

A Little Love

Will You Remember Me?

Christmas for One

A Mother's Story

Perfect Daughter

The Second Chance Café

Three and a Half Heartbeats

Another Love

My Husband's Wife

I Won't be Home for Christmas

The Food of Love

The Idea of You

The Art of Hiding

Anna

Theo

How to Fall in Love Again: Kitty's Story

Kitty

PRAISE FOR AMANDA PROWSE

'Amanda Prowse reflects society in our times in her gripping novels'

—Katie Fforde

'A moving, romantic tale about finding your place in the world and the people who can help you get there'

—Libby Page, praise for *Swimming to Lundy*

'An utterly compelling and exquisitely crafted read. I loved it!'

—Heidi Swain, praise for *All Good Things*

'A candid, moving and inspirational book. I am blown away'

—Jonny Benjamin, bestselling author of *The Stranger on the Bridge*, praise for *The Boy Between*

'Amanda Prowse is the queen of family drama'

—*Daily Mail*

'A deeply emotional, unputdownable read'

—*Red*

'You'll fall in love with this'

—*Cosmopolitan*

'Captivating, heartbreaking and superbly written'

—*Closer*

'Uplifting and positive but you may still need a box of tissues'

—*Cosmopolitan*

'Warmly accessible but subtle . . . moving and inspiring'

—*Daily Mail*

The Coordinates of Loss

The Girl in the Corner

The Things I Know

The Light in the Hallway

The Day She Came Back

An Ordinary Life

Waiting to Begin

To Love and Be Loved

Picking Up the Pieces

All Good Things

Very Very Lucky

Swimming to Lundy

This One Life

Ever After

Life As Planned

Novellas

The Game

Something Quite Beautiful: seven short stories

A Christmas Wish

Ten Pound Ticket

Imogen's Baby

Miss Potterton's Birthday Tea

Mr Portobello's Morning Paper

I Wish . . .

A Whole Heap of Wishes

A Wish for Forgiveness

Fifteen Minutes

Children's books

The Smile that Went a Mile (with Paul Ward Smith)

Today I'm in Charge (with Paul Ward Smith)

Non-fiction

The Boy Between (with Josiah Hartley)

Women Like Us

The Way Home

Amanda Prowse

LAKE UNION
PUBLISHING

Published by Lake Union Publishing, Seattle

www.apub.com

EU Product Safety Contact:
Amazon Media EU S.à r.l.
38, avenue John F. Kennedy, L-1855 Luxembourg
amazonpublishing-gpsr@amazon.com

ISBN-13: 9781662515248
eISBN: 9781662515231

Original cover design: Jo Myler
Cover adaptation: Will Speed
Cover image: © Ihor Biliavskyi © Yoko Design © Edge Creative / Shutterstock

Printed in the United States of America

For Ben and Kate – setting out on your greatest adventure together, newly married. Know that wherever you are, whenever you need us, we will always guide you all the way home. We love you more than words can say . . .

Present day – aged 70

Lilly-Bob Cooper drew the curtains and smiled at the spring-blue morning light. The surface of the water was calm, still like mirror glass, solid, as if she could walk right across it to where buildings lurked, and alleyways sat in shadow. As was her habit that had become ritual, she lifted her hand in a wave to the bank on the opposite side of the river.

It was a fascination, even after all this time, how the wide stretch of water could present in this way, and in a matter of hours, in the face of a squall, might become agitated, pitted, catching raindrops like tiny bombs that dented and distorted; resounding with noise, a protest almost at the chaos on the surface. Right now, however, it offered the perfect conditions for painting. She felt the usual fizz of excitement at the prospect of setting up her easel.

With the sound of Debussy's *La Mer* filling her apartment, she almost danced to the front door, lifting the hem of her teal silk caftan to reveal gold pumps, before stooping to pick up the mail from the welcome mat. Her thick grey hair fell over her eyes, and she shook it from her face. The usual fodder for the recycling bin: pizza flyer, a glossy brochure for a conservatory company, a letter marked 'NHS' which as ever sent a shiver of concern through her seventy-year-old bones. NHS – something medical. She wasn't very good with medical. This she opened first, ripping the envelope and scanning the contents, which she read aloud.

'*We would like to invite you for a routine examination* . . . Well, how lovely! I would of course be delighted to accept, rarely get asked anywhere nowadays. What should I wear, I wonder?' She drummed her be-ringed fingers on her mouth, as if giving it real consideration. She did this – chattered to herself for much of the day, even enjoyed the one-sided conversations. She'd got used to it. It was just the way she was. It was that or live large chunks of her life in silence, and that would never do.

Silence was, she felt, the gateway to loneliness. Not to be confused with welcome moments of quiet contemplation or peaceful reflection in a hushed space, but the kind of silence that had sound, echoing all that was missing from her life. The self-chatter and background music helped keep it at bay. It was one thing being an older lady, but a lonely older lady? No, that wasn't for her. I mean what would follow, the acquisition of cats?

The second letter was in a brown envelope with the capitalised word 'URGENT' stamped on it in red.

'Booo!' she hissed as she pulled out the insubstantial sheet, her dad's instruction loud and clear: *Always booo before you open a brown envelope, just to let them know you're on to them. Brown envelopes are never good news. Do not give them the upper hand!*

'*Dear Mrs Cooper* . . .' She lowered the paper and gasped. 'Flippin' heck! I got married and didn't even know it, congratulations to me! I do hope he's a nice fella, a handsome fella! I wonder if I wore white?' It made her laugh, the assumption, even in this day and age. This letter, too, she scanned. '*I am writing as a representative* . . . *this the fifth letter* . . . *blah-di-blah* . . . *the block* . . .' She looked over her shoulder and out of the kitchen window. 'Block? *Block!* Urgh, we are not a block, we are a low-rise development! Nine apartments, over three floors, hardly a block! We are a bijou development! Not that this person, who no doubt wears a polo shirt to work, would know or care about the difference.' She tutted, returning her attention to the letter. '*The block*' – she pulled a face – '*in which you reside is the subject of a regeneration order.* Sounds fancy.' She laughed. '*. . . moved to suitable alternative accommodation, should you meet the criteria eligibility . . .*' Lilly sighed. A letter sent to her in error. She would call them tomorrow. Or maybe the day after that. Admin wasn't really her thing, either.

The front door bell rang and her proximity to it made her jump.

'Morning, darling!' She stepped back to allow Clodagh entry and popped the mail bundle on to the hall table next to a bust of a woman's head on which she had placed a crown of woven willow. 'Did he go in okay?'

Clodagh, her twenty-seven-year-old neighbour and single mum to four-year-old Apollo, who lived in the flat above, sighed heavily. This girl, her son and their visits could wrap even the gloomiest of days in sunshine. Lilly treasured them, these interactions that made her feel part of the human race and not someone merely observing it from the wings. They had opened up her horizon, allowed her to be part of a bigger conversation as she was given insights into their world. Another vital facet to her life that helped keep the silence at bay.

Clodagh shook her head. 'It was a crowbar kind of morning. They had to practically wrench him from me. He was crying, I was crying, and I remembered what you said, about giving him the exact number of hours and minutes until I was coming back to pick him up, in case it was a fear of abandonment that was upsetting him. It was all very fraught. I was shouting, *It's school, not prison! Only six hours, which is actually three hundred and sixty minutes!*

Apollo went crazy! I think three hundred and sixty of anything seems like a lot when you're four.'

'Darling, it's a lot when you're seventy, if that thing is unanswered emails, dirty Martinis or press-ups.'

Clodagh nodded. 'Yup. Anyway, Mrs McNally, the head teacher, was being stern, telling him not to cry and that he had lots to look forward to as today they were going to play with the dinosaurs—'

'Real ones?' she interrupted with enthusiasm, quite enamoured by the idea.

'No, pl— plastic.' Clodagh stared at her, as she was wont to do, still, despite being friends for over a year, a little unsure of her humour. 'Anyway, Milar's mum was tutting and shaking her head as if I was doing something wrong, or as if Apollo was. That kind of disapproval just makes me feel worse. Makes me drop things, lose my keys, and get my words flustered.'

'Of course it does. Would you like me to go and punch her?'

This time there was no mistaking the humour and Clodagh laughed loudly.

'Yes. Yes, I would. I just find it so draining, Lilly, starting the day with this battle. It's exhausting.'

'I can only imagine. Tea?'

'Please.'

As was their habit, the two made their way into the kitchen, where the square table sat pushed up against the wall, with a vast oil painting of a Renaissance nude hung over it. The chap who had brought it from the gallery had, upon arrival, turned his nose up a little when she'd met him in the wide communal first-floor hallway. She had watched as he took in the slightly fragrant stairwell of the 1950s interior. The sweep of the elegant metal balustrade, an open design with a contemporary feel, metal Vs in a row that were currently a shade of pea soup. She remembered them being black for most of their life, then blue, then orange, which became red and now this green. She rather liked it.

The polished concrete floor of the communal hallway was a myriad of colours, with tiny crushed stones and the odd sparkling crystal all uniquely captured, and it was just as vibrant as it had been on the day it was laid almost seventy years ago. Lilly knew that if the man delivering the painting couldn't see the beauty in the place, then it said a lot about him.

Her home: flat six, Waide House, on the east side of the building, middle floor of three, had a secret. She liked to watch people's faces as they walked in via her solid wood front door with its small rectangle of glass in the middle. Took joy in studying them as they entered the surprisingly spacious square hallway where wooden doors led to two large bedrooms, the lounge, bathroom and kitchen. The hall was a little dark when all the doors were closed, a little drab, maybe. Here, too, the polished concrete floor that she so loved and the original wooden panelling that lined the walls, unchanged since her childhood.

She could guess what visitors were thinking, *spacious but could do with brightening up,* and it made her smile, as they missed the point entirely. It was classical, of its time, untouched, and echoed loudly of the era in which it had been built. Lilly was quite convinced that if you listened very carefully, you might be able to hear the craftsmen who had laid the floor, constructed the stairs, cut and fitted the wood, chatting during their tea break, discussing how they felt about the new prime minister, Mr Eden, rejoicing over Chelsea winning the league, and whether or not they were going to see that new film, *The Dam Busters*. Some probably declining the outing, only ten years since their war had ended, unsure if they wanted the reminder . . .

Then came the good bit, the secret revealed, as visitors entered the generously proportioned rectangular lounge. Drawn like moths to a flame, walking quickly to the wide, wide window.

Wow!

Jesus!

Wowsers!

I did not expect that!

And she would smile a little smugly, knowing that *Wow! Jesus! Wowsers!* They had most definitely not expected that!

Yet there it was.

The river.

Old Mother Thames.

Flowing in all her glory.

The height and breadth of the window meant the view was uninterrupted. The proximity to the riverwalk, previously a narrow towpath that she could wander towards the docks and the industrial heartland of Vauxhall, but now, following investment, upheaval and, she was sure, more dust than it was healthy to consume, a wide, smooth path. A popular place on which to promenade, rollerblade, cycle or walk hand in hand with your intended, while marvelling at the sunsets that were nothing short of utterly spectacular! From the window, it seemed as if the flat was perched, almost hanging over the river itself, which it was, practically.

A secret indeed.

Even the delivery guy's face had broken into a grin at the sight of it, and she'd sucked in her cheeks and nodded, as he smiled at her knowingly.

The flat above hers saw more sky, certainly.

The flat below looked out on to the walkway.

The flat to her right had a similar view to hers, bisected by a Victorian lamppost and with one of the towering new skyscrapers plonked to the side. A great, hulking, shiny white building that put her in mind of a stack of Polo mints, part blocking what used to be an uninterrupted view of Lambeth Bridge, then Westminster Bridge, with the Houses of Parliament in the background on the opposite bank, and of course, *Grand Benjamin*, which was what her dad used to call *Big Ben*, just to be different.

Her view was a pearl. A hidden something right there in plain sight. A breathtaking, ever-changing vista that she had marvelled at every day of her life since she had been tall enough to stand and look out over it.

Clodagh screwed up her face.

'Your music is . . .'

'Beautiful, isn't it! I can almost smell the sea, can feel the motion of the waves!' Lilly closed her eyes and waltzed to the tap with the kettle held aloft, conducting the invisible orchestra with her free hand.

'I was going to say "very loud".'

'Oh!' Lilly laughed and picked up the remote control, lowering the volume. 'Aren't remote controls the most magnificent of inventions!'

'I guess.' Clodagh took a seat at the table and removed the white corduroy scrunchie from her slender wrist, winding it into her thick blonde hair to form a pineapple on top of her head, revealing a band of dark-brown roots.

'Back in the day, we used to have to jump up from the sofa to turn over the channel or lower or raise the volume, and the idea of controlling music that was playing in another room – this would have been seen as witchcraft or magic, depending on your view.'

'I can think of better inventions.' Clodagh smiled.

'Name me three,' Lilly suggested as she took the handmade pottery mugs from the shelf and popped teabags into them.

'Defibrillators.'

'Oh God, please let's not go down the medical and worthy route. I can imagine your other two, dialysis and chemotherapy?'

'Good shout, yes.' The young woman pointed at her.

'No, Clodagh, no! We all know they are the best things, along with transplants, drugs, anaesthesia, and the concept of washing hands pre- and post-surgery, of course we do! I'm talking about the frivolous things, the marvellous, everyday things like an egg slicer – all that time we save by just popping the little boiled thing into a plastic recess and pushing down the cage-like lid instead of having to chop, chop, chop with a bloody knife – wonderful! Or . . . or . . . headtorches! The headtorch, what a thing! I can now walk along a darkened pavement, cross a river or run from the law with my hands free!'

'I don't have a headtorch.' Clodagh yawned, something Lilly noticed she did a lot, understanding that looking after a live wire like Apollo, while working part-time and studying for her degree, all without help, must be a lot.

'Well, let's hope you never need to run from the law with your hands free.'

'I'm more likely to encounter a darkened pavement when I head to the bins.'

'Dull but true. I shall order you one from Amazon.' Lilly poured the hot water and agitated the bags with a spoon.

'I think you must be one of their best customers.'

'Quite possibly. It's the novelty of it! I still find it remarkable that I can clickety-click on all manner of things from nail scissors to washing powder, and poooof!' She made an exploding sign with her fingertips, touching them together then fanning them apart. 'A man hands it to me on my doorstep.'

'You are funny.' Clodagh smiled at her.

'I always think you mean "old" when you say "funny", as if you find my ways funny because I'm old. Amused by the things I find amusing.'

'I am most definitely amused by the things you find amusing, but I don't think it's because you're older. I bet you were just as bonkers as a child, weren't you?'

'Oh, none taken, darling.' Lilly removed the teabags, sloshed in milk and handed her guest a mug, before taking the chair opposite her. 'I don't know if I was bonkers as a child, but I was certainly a little odd, preoccupied almost. I realised quite early on that our set-up was a little unusual, understood that *I* was quite unusual.'

'Unusual how?' Clodagh sat back in the chair, her head tipped to one side, curious. It was the thing Lilly liked about her most, their lovely ease of conversation.

'I suppose the whole dynamic. I was quiet, a little anxious, maybe, when I wasn't at home, more interested in watching, taking it all in. But my dad was full of noise, but the best kind of noise. I remember being given a lift in a car by the father of a girl in my class. A car was a novelty, and I was delighted to be driven home, felt like the Queen of Sheba!' She noted the flicker of confusion on Clodagh's face, clearly not an expression she was familiar with. 'I knew if it was my dad driving, I'd have had lots of questions about the car, the speed it could travel, how you actually drove it, all kinds of things, but what fascinated me the most was that the girl – I think her name was Cathy, can't recall exactly – anyway, she and her parents sat in silence. I mean, absolute silence! Not a word. Her mum and dad barely interacting, not how I'd imagined it to be at all. And not just quiet like me, observing, but all staring out of their respective windows in their own little worlds. As if they couldn't chat, didn't know where or how to start. My dad talked to me constantly, and if he wasn't talking, he was whistling or singing along to music. It was lovely.'

'What did you do?' Clodagh sipped her tea and closed her eyes as if it were nectar.

'What did I do? Nothing! I didn't do anything. I found it excruciating, but I didn't talk. Didn't feel like I could, as if there was some unspoken rule that car travel meant no talking, worried that maybe any questions might distract the driver, who wore cream string-backed leather driving gloves with a little keyhole press stud on the side. The leather bit was tan in colour. I remember every detail about those gloves, the way the fingers squeaked when he gripped the steering wheel.' She heard the sound in her mind's ear. 'I think in hindsight they might have been a bit wary of driving around here – this wasn't the most salubrious of areas, dimly lit, more industrial than fancy, with the odd towering block of flats thrown in for good measure. I remember arriving here, being dropped off at the back of the flat' – the wide concrete apron was just the same – 'just a small road in those days.' She harumphed to think of the four-lane A-road that it had developed into. A main thoroughfare into and out of Westminster, where buses, cabs, lorries, vans, cars and those infernal buzzing mopeds that reminded her of mosquitoes, and were about as irritating, all sat nose to tail for much of the day and a lot of the night. 'I remember feeling quite sad. Quite unable to imagine living that kind of life, a silent one. My lovely dad was keen to hear about the trip. He didn't own a car, never owned a car, in fact. He didn't see the point, not when we could always jump on a bus or Tube with such ease, and that was before we considered the expense and the parking of said vehicle. Yes, Dad wanted the detail, but all I could say was that the journey had made me sad.'

'That doesn't sound like a good memory,' Clodagh sympathised.

'It wasn't good or fun. Would you like some toast?' It bothered her, how thin Clodagh was, her skin so pale, the veins on the underside of her wrists purple and prevalent. Sometimes Lilly felt cold just looking at her. She liked to feed her, wondering if this was one of the primal urges a mother might feel, that desire to provide sustenance.

'Yes, please.' Clodagh smiled at her. 'If it's no trouble.'

'No trouble at all!'

1962 – aged 6

Her dad whistled as he polished his shoes. Lilly-Bob liked everything about her dad. She liked the fact he had seen fit to shorten her name, Elizabeth-Roberta Cooper, to Lilly-Bob. She liked his stupid jokes that no one else seemed to find that funny.

Lilly-Bob, I was going to tell you a joke about time travel, but you didn't like it . . .

She liked the way he then laughed heartily as if it were the first time he'd heard it too. She liked the fact he whistled all the time. *All the time!* A vast repertoire of hymns, tunes, ditties and songs that left his 'oooh'-shaped lips and brought him joy! His eyes were always bright and smiling as he whistled. She knew he was home long before the telltale sound of his key in the lock or his rhythmic, bespoke *one-two-one* knock on the front door, like a code, letting her and her mum know it was him. It meant that she never felt scared in the flat, even at night when the river cast moving shadows over the ceiling that made it seem as if she were underwater, as she could always hear him and was able, depending on volume, echo and pitch, to determine which room he was in. He would practise his violin by the window, a mournful sound that had the power to make her mother weep, but beautiful, nonetheless. Still a mystery to her that he could make that shallow thing made of wood produce such notes.

He always played with his eyes closed, as if lost entirely to that music, as if he and that old violin were one.

Most of all, Lilly liked to sit and watch him, liked the proximity of the man who was often out; at the music shop in Bloomsbury where he worked during the day, playing concerts at night, hauling his violin in its battered case on and off the Tube. And on a Sunday, with his pale-green and leather canvas rucksack slung over his shoulder, containing a rolled windcheater, a Thermos full of tea and a wrapped cheese sandwich, he went rambling.

Where he rambled she wasn't quite sure, but he always came home with a sunburnt face, a ravenous appetite, sweat stains under the arms of his shirt that made the fabric a little stiff and yellow, and with grass and mud clinging to the soles of his clumpy old army boots. He'd leave them upended by the front door, waiting for the little slices of compacted countryside that had hitched a lift to the big city to dry, before lifting the boots in both hands a couple of days later, and banging them together over the bin, watching as the dried clots tumbled into it. It was fascinating to her, trying to imagine a place where such stuff was abundant, green stuff and brown stuff. Very different to this little slice of grey-paved paradise in Vauxhall, Lambeth, which they called home.

The absence of him always made the flat seem a little colder, colours not quite so bright, food not as flavourful, as if everything was subdued and not nearly as exciting. No matter how she occupied her time, a small part of her was always on high alert, waiting for his safe return. He was, quite simply, a rainbow over her world, and she adored him. As he did her, his face lighting up at the sight of her; it made her feel special, made her feel loved.

Her mum was great, more than great. Lilly liked it, too, when they did things together, like making cookies ready for her dad's return, crocheting squares that her mum would deftly sew together to make a blanket, or when her mum taught her how to put on lipstick.

'It doesn't seem that hard!' she had laughed when her mum had brandished the shiny gold Max Factor Ruby Red capsule in her hand.

'Ah, but there's an art to it, Lilly-Bob, not that you will be wearing lipstick for some years yet, but you can practise if you want. Would you like me to show you?'

'Yes!' Excitement didn't cut it, she was ecstatic!

She watched, fascinated, as her mum first powdered her lips with the flat sponge from her compact, then, holding her small mirror in one hand, slowly traced the outer edges with the almond-shaped end of the lipstick, before filling in the gaps. With her lips coated she then plucked a tissue from the box and kissed it firmly, transferring the shape of those full red lips on to the white surface.

'Now, here's the trick: another coat!' She winked at Lilly and again stared into the small mirror as she repeated the process, and when she had finished made a dull thudding sound with her lips as she kissed the air.

'This would last all day, unless you ate spaghetti or kissed boys!' Her mother laughed.

'Eeeuw!' Lilly pulled a face, and it wasn't at the thought of eating spaghetti.

'You won't always feel that way.' She winked. 'One day the thought of kissing boys will be quite delightful!'

Lilly was glad when they changed the subject, hating the way her cheeks flamed and her skin felt a little itchy with embarrassment.

It was when her mum jumped up from the table to grab her cigarettes from her handbag that Lilly took the tissue with the kiss and carefully folded it, before tucking it into her cardigan pocket.

Yes, her mum was great.

She just wasn't her dad.

If her dad was the star, her mum was the support act.

It made Lilly feel happy, to be close to him, to have him smile only at her, as if she were his very best thing. Waggling her foot in time to the beat, as The Drifters' '*Up on the Roof*' filled the room. It was something that bewitched her, how a little circle of plastic could so change the atmosphere, make her happy, make everyone happy! Simply by the lowering of the stylus on to the disc, listening to the crackle in anticipation and waiting for the music to change their lives.

And change their lives it did.

As the music played, their whole flat and the people in it were transformed, no longer living under the shadow of industry in Vauxhall, where a post-war boom saw ugly residential and commercial buildings springing up all around, but instead somewhere warm and sunny, living in a world of possibilities and laughter with nothing but good times ahead!

Her dad, like everyone else, sometimes had bad dreams, and on the days after a night disturbed by his calling out, the thumps and bumps that echoed through the wall as her mum calmed him, the atmosphere in the flat was always a bit tense. Countless were the times she had witnessed her mum, a little surly, a little lost in thought, a little grumpy, bashing pans in the sink. Squirting too much Fairy Liquid on to a plate, which was both wasteful and alarming, an indicator all was not well, before slamming kitchen cabinet doors in an act of defiance. Her dad, similarly alerted, would sit up straight, and with his cigarette between his fingers lower the map, newspaper or book he was reading, and listen for a second or two to the clues that her mum's mood might need pepping up.

He'd walk over to the record player, taking his time, as if choosing which song or tune was best for the job, trying to find the right lyrical combination to unlock his wife's happiness.

Sometimes it was Chubby Checker, and he'd rush to the sink, grab her arm, and with her mum still in her frilly-edged pinny and rubber gloves, they'd do the Twist right there on the kitchen floor. Other times it was Ella Fitzgerald's '*More Than You Know*', and he'd slowly pull her close, tucking her head under his chin as he smooched her around the hallway, the best floor for smooching apparently, allowing for a slight glide underfoot. She didn't like it so much when they smooched. Not only did her very presence feel like an intrusion, but when they had finished dancing her mum always had two dark, inky-black streaks of mascara down her cheeks. Lilly-Bob couldn't understand how a dance so beautiful and gentle could make her mum cry, but it did. When this happened, it made *her* feel helpless, made her feel like squirting too much Fairy Liquid and slamming the door of a kitchen cabinet.

Her favourite by far was when he chose Bill Haley & His Comets and she'd curl up on the sofa, with the beat jumping in her chest, watching her parents shake, rattle and roll their way around the apartment, jiving, according to her dad, in the way they had when they first met. Moving quickly over the parquet flooring, her dad pulling her mum in close before twirling her away from him, like she was a spinning top. Seamless moves that they executed perfectly, as if they'd practised a lot or as if it came naturally, so in sync were they. Her mum's skirt rising to reveal the lace hem of her petticoat as she spun, feet tapping, knees bopping, faces red from exhalation and wide grins that made them look younger. Yes, this was without doubt her favourite.

Lilly trailed her fingers over the advertisements in the newspaper with which her dad had covered the tile-topped coffee table. An advert for *'Van Heusen – the shirts with the Savile Row touch . . .'* and another for *'Benson and Hedges – when only the best will do . . .'* Her dad smoked *Player's*.

One of his hands was deep inside a tan brogue and in the other sat a soft-bristled wooden-backed brush which he used to work the polish on to the leather in circles, dabbed on the brush from its little round container that gave off a strong and distinct smell. The shoe-polishing kit he kept in an old toffee tin under the sink, the lid of which had rust spots.

'Shiny shoes are important. It's all about standards, Lilly-Bob. A well-made bed. A clean-shaven chin. An ironed shirt, and shiny shoes. Standards!'

He used to say this often. She'd nod, wanting to show she was listening, but never really understanding how this might be valuable advice for her. Her mum made her bed, she had no shirt to iron, no chin to shave, and as for her shoes – she was more often than not in navy Mary Janes, and the need to polish them was, thankfully, minimal.

His cigarette dangled from his bottom lip as he worked; the smoke rose and covered his face in a grey, misty veil through which he had to squint. His shirtsleeves were, as ever, rolled neatly and evenly above his elbows, his top button undone, white vest peeking from underneath. Burgundy braces sat snugly over his skinny shoulders, and his hair moved as he worked, shaking free of its Brylcreem bonds and falling in a curtain over his forehead. Her dad was a distinct combination of smells and movements that meant she could identify him by sound and scent alone, even with her eyes closed. She didn't like that he had bad dreams, and thumped about in the night, didn't like that *anyone* did, but especially her dad.

'Now, this big old river, right here in front of our flat—'

'The Thames!' She shouted her interruption; it always felt good when she knew something, and she delighted in sharing it with him.

'That's right, the Thames.' He beamed. 'People might think it's just a body of water, but it's so much more than that, she's the beating heart of London. The *reason* for London! The Romans established the city and called it Londinium, and they built the first wooden bridge over the river, can you imagine? How clever was that, with so few of the tools and machines that we take for granted?'

'My teacher says all rivers start as a trickle, and if they are lucky, they become this huge river! Even the Nile, just a tiny trickle!' She threw her arms wide open, entirely in awe of this fact. Who could envisage such a thing: a trickle that after a while was able to support huge boats and had bridges over it and people living on the edge of it! It was miraculous!

'That's right. Just a trickle, and how lucky are we that a tiny trickle became this silver ribbon that winds its way through our city. *Old Mother Thames.* And if ever you get lost, Lilly-Bob, just make your way to the river, find *Grand Benjamin* or any of the landmarks that you know, follow it along, and eventually you'll find your way home. She'll always help you, she'll bring you here – all the way home.'

'Tea's ready!' Her mum's voice carried through the flat and found them by the window, interrupting the moment, but with good reason. Tea was tea and needed to be eaten when it was hot. That was the rule. If the tea went cold, her mum would stare flatly at them both, as if they had let her down, sometimes brandishing her fork, as if at her wits' end, as if it mattered far more than it did. As if she had something else on her mind, something else to worry about.

'I don't spend half my life peeling potatoes, cooking meat, boiling veg and whipping up sponges only for you two to pitch up late and leave it ruined. Bloody selfish is what that is!'

She'd then push her chair away from the table and go for a lie-down, abandoning the congealing plates of food and leaving Lilly-Bob and her dad at the square table, her without an ounce of appetite on her tongue and a feeling of guilt in the base of her stomach. It wasn't Lilly-Bob's fault they had become engrossed in a map, or her dad hadn't stopped reading to her, or that they'd been staring at the water through the window, convinced they'd seen the scary head of a leviathan briefly pop up in a swell, waiting to see if it might re-emerge. But it always felt like her fault, all of it, and she nearly always cried. Her dad would cup his hand over hers and say, 'Mum's tired. I'll go take her a cup of tea.'

She wanted to understand, figuring it must be exhausting, all that peeling, cooking, boiling and whipping. Sniffing up her tears, she would watch as he boiled the kettle, filled the teapot, wiped the cup and saucer and poured the brew that seemed to fix just about everything, winking at her as if to say, *everything's all right,* before walking slowly to their bedroom and shutting the door behind him. Shutting her out or shutting them in, she was never quite sure.

The end result was just the same.

Lilly would sit quietly then, staring at food that no matter how vibrant it might have started out always seemed a little grey when cooled. Forcing fried eggs, minced meat, boiled spuds, soft carrots, chips, tinned peas, smoked haddock, mash, suet pudding, tinned peaches and the other meals from her mother's limited menu down her throat. Sometimes her parents would re-emerge quickly, both smiling as if nothing was amiss, instantly igniting a flame of happiness and relief inside her.

Sometimes they'd come out of the room and her dad's eyes were red, like *he'd* been crying. But that could not be true, it wasn't possible, because dads did not cry!

Other times they'd be silent, and she'd sit long after she'd finished eating and the flat had turned dark, before accepting they were not coming back to the table any time soon. At those times, she'd put her empty plate in the sink, quietly push her chair in and go to bed, where she'd lie, listening, hoping for the sound of music, her dad's violin or his familiar whistle. Usually she heard nothing until the morning, when she'd find him in the bathroom, shaving at the sink in his vest and trousers, braces hanging down over his hips. Her mum would be in the kitchen, humming along as eggs boiled, to the radio playing '*Love Me Do*', her hair set, mascara thick, red, red lipstick applied in a double coat, and a smile that was wide and forgiving, confirming her dad's wink that everything was indeed all right.

'Your tea's ready!' her mum called again. Her dad put the shoe and brush down and they moved comically quickly, as if racing. Her tummy rumbled with hunger and her mouth watered at the prospect of corned beef hash with baked beans, one of her favourites.

'How was your day, darling?' her dad asked his wife. He always calling her darling, never Jean or Jeannie or dearest. She was his darling.

'Good!' Her mum giggled. 'Very good, in fact!'

'Oh?' He beamed. 'Did you lose a farthing and find a sixpence?'

'Nope.' Her mum picked up her cutlery but held them still as she took a deep breath. 'I went for a lovely walk, a long one.'

'Careful, you'll be joining me on a ramble next!' He pulled a face, his eyes shining with love.

'It was definitely not a ramble, more of a stroll.' Jeannie Cooper took a dainty forkful of beans and put them in her mouth.

'Where did you walk, Mummy?'

Lilly-Bob was curious, hoping her mum might have interesting tales of her adventures, like her dad did of his, which were too numerous to recount. Her favourites, however, were probably the curious cow who had once snaffled a sandwich right out of his hands, an exploding bottle of pop that scared a flock of sparrows, an unfortunate mix-up with a map on a foggy day that meant he ended up almost back where he had started, and an alarming encounter with a scarecrow at dusk that had made him scream like Great-aunt Winnifred when she found a mouse in the tea caddy.

'Where did I walk?' her mum repeated, staring at Lilly-Bob as if she had momentarily forgotten she was there, as if roused from a daydream. 'Where did I walk . . .' She took a long, slow breath. 'I walked up and down the Tottenham Court Road.' She smiled and took another small mouthful of beans.

Present day

Lilly left the table and grabbed the bread knife and seeded sourdough loaf that she bought every other day from the artisan bakery on the Wandsworth Road. A dark-crusted work of art that was dense, tasty, and so moreish she knew that if she were let loose with a pound of butter, a sharp Cheddar, a jar of spicy pickle and a breadboard, she could quite easily demolish the whole thing! Her friend, Glenda, spoke of her own waning appetite, picking like a bird at her food and abandoning more than she ate on the plate. But not Lilly. It had once been a source of shame, her desire to gorge, her love of food, her delight at the prospect of a good dinner, but not now. She was seventy, healthy, broad of hip, had bags of energy and was doing her very best to entirely banish the feeling of shame over anything! Not always successfully. But when it came to food, she now rather liked her appreciation of fresh pasta, thick gravies, golden-crusted pastry, plump, iced patisserie, fresh bread, warm cheese and a really, really good glass of red. I mean, why not? Life was too bloody short! That much she did know.

The toast popped and she slathered it with butter and Clodagh's preferred chunky peanut butter. Placing the plate on the table, she watched the girl tuck in.

'Thank you, Lilly. I love it when you make me toast.'

'Oh, it's nothing!' Lilly batted away the compliment, knowing it was actually something. It was showing love. It was building a community. It was family.

'I'm not used to anyone looking after me. My mum was bloody useless,' Clodagh blurted as she chewed her breakfast. 'I still miss her though.' It was the first time the girl had made such an admission, and Lilly, unaware of the circumstances of their estrangement and with a bloom of kinship in her chest, trod carefully.

'That must be hard.' It was tricky to offer sympathy and support without appearing to pry. 'Did your mother, erm, did she . . .' Lilly spoke hesitantly. The last thing she wanted to do was ask a question the answer to which might make Clodagh feel uncomfortable.

'Die?' Clodagh suggested, seemingly without nerves.

'Yes.'

'Oh, no.' Lilly felt her shoulders sink with something close to relief. 'And this is a controversial thing to say, I know' – her friend swallowed her toast before going in for a second bite – 'but I often thought it might have been easier for me if she had.'

'That's . . .' Lilly was a little lost for words. Clodagh was right: it was a controversial thing to say.

'I told you it was controversial!' Clodagh exhaled. 'But I think if my mother had died when I was little, that would have garnered sympathy, you know the look: head pulled back on shoulders, eyes narrowed, lips tucked in, gaze downcast and usually accompanied by an "aww, dear" or a "poor lamb". I mean, yes, I would still have been different, my life not so easy, but different beyond my control, different because of fate or sickness or an unfortunate incident with the number ninety-seven bus.'

Lilly gave a slow smile of understanding and felt her mouthful of tea take form in her throat, making swallowing difficult.

Yes, she more than understood that not-so-easy life because your home situation was a little bit different, because your mum was bloody useless.

'But instead, you were different because . . . ?'

Clodagh put the remainder of her toast on the plate and took her time.

'Because she wasn't a great example, hasn't really been there for me since I was small. More interested in going out than staying in with me. I bored her stupid, I could tell, even when I was little. I don't think she ever answered a question without putting a sigh at the front of it. She'd meet a bloke and forget about me, like literally!' She shook her head as if such a thing, when relating it to Apollo, was impossible. 'I'm not even joking; she once went on holiday with a cab driver she met in a nightclub one Saturday night, and I just got on with it! A whole week of letting myself in and out of the house, eating cereal and heading off to school. I didn't know where she was, didn't tell anyone' – Clodagh looked up at her now – 'but I knew I was in trouble if she didn't come home soon. I was embarrassed, and even though I was a kid, I knew it was shitty behaviour.'

'How old were you?' Lilly could not imagine being so negligent, so unappreciative of a gift like Clodagh, and there it was: the smell of strong bleach in her nostrils.

'Twelve.'

'You must have been scared.' Lilly kept her voice low, aware that this was uncharted territory and, again, not wanting to pry.

'I wasn't scared of being by myself, I was used to that, but as I say, I was worried about what might happen if she didn't come back. I'd seen friends in and out of care, and I dreaded it.'

'That's rotten.' Lilly's heart flexed for the twelve-year-old Clodagh.

'I was starting to panic, thinking about who to tell and what to say. There was a teacher at school I thought I might be able to confide in. I was working out how to approach her, practising what to say in my head, but that night, Mum came home. All tanned and giggly, with her new bloke, who moved in for a while. Can't even remember his name. They didn't mention the fact they'd been gone for a week, and so I didn't. They bought me a little plastic doll, a woman in a flamenco dress with a fan in her hand and a veil on the back of her head. I've still got it somewhere.' Clodagh coughed. 'So yeah, even though she was rubbish and I hardly ever see her now, I still miss her, or more accurately, I miss what a mum should be in my head. A mum who reads you bedtime stories and makes you toast.' She lifted the slice and grinned. 'Does that make sense?'

'It really does.' Lilly smiled at the girl, enlivened by the compliment more than she could say, feeling such an affinity with her young neighbour. 'I guess all of us have an image in our head of what the perfect family looks like, yet I doubt it really exists. And I expect that what we think of as a perfect family probably isn't once you scratch away the gilt.' In her mind's eye she saw her parents dancing, laughing, loving . . .

'Maybe. I just want things to be nicer for Apollo. I want him to feel safe.' Clodagh shuddered a little as she double-blinked, suggesting she, too, didn't always feel safe.

'I guess there are only two choices when you become a parent, aren't there, you can either do as your parents did or do differently?'

'Yep. And I definitely do differently!' Clodagh gave a short, wry laugh as she stated the obvious.

'I also think that the perfect family is the one that's right for you. They come in all shapes and sizes, right?' Lilly didn't want her friend, who tried so hard, to feel less than.

'Right.' Clodagh smiled back. 'It was a rotten childhood, but at the time, like everything really, it was just how it was! It wasn't easy being different, but it never occurred to me that I could change anything, so I just plodded on.'

'I remember feeling the same, just plodding on, until I started at art college and realised that I could change *everything!* And so I did!' Lilly clapped.

'You made good friends?'

'My first friends, actually! Or friend, more specifically: Glenda.'

'Glenda? *Your* Glenda?' Clodagh had of course met her right here in the kitchen.

'Yes, my Glenda.' Lilly smiled too. She supposed it was some kind of achievement that the two were still buddies, having faced more than their fair share of ups and downs, disagreements, and the moment that had threatened to split them for ever. Lilly remembered the day, so long ago, yet still with the power to floor her, when her friend's actions had nearly shattered their friendship. She was grateful they'd got through it.

The incident was not something she spoke about to anyone, not wanting to cloud their view of Glenda or to relive it. She gathered herself and continued.

'Up until then, it was like I spent my childhood with my nose pressed up against the wide glass window of life watching all the goings-on; children playing happily with each other in the playground, teenagers laughing as if they were all in this fabulous club, boys at school quoting to each other lines from *The Navy Lark*, "Ooh, nasty . . .", "Oh lumme!"'

'What's *The Navy Lark*?'

'Oh.' It was a reminder of the gulf in their ages. 'A radio play, a sitcom, really. Everyone had a radio, everyone listened to it. And I would watch them all interacting, chattering to myself but not knowing how to be more normal, more invitable, more like them.'

'Were you lonely?' Clodagh asked with a notch of concern at the top of her nose, and Lilly suspected that this was one of her biggest fears for Apollo, who even at the tender age of four seemed a little non-conformist too. And Lilly more than understood, as loneliness was one of her biggest fears.

'I was. But not at home, never lonely at home, and that was by far my preference: to have a haven, a safe space, somewhere I could laugh and be myself, somewhere I was so loved. That is always the preference, Clodagh, for every child, to have peace at home. I am sure some of those kids who appeared to find life easy didn't have what I did when they put their key in the door. It's what saves you, ultimately.'

'Yes.' The girl blinked her understanding. Lilly hoped it helped.

'At school it was as if my peers spoke another language, one I didn't understand. And even if I'd wanted to learn it, at the Dame Margaret Nichols Academy we could only study French; there was no mention of this other mysterious language of popularity. That might, had I been able to master it, have given me access to groups of friends.' She finished her tea and instantly rose to re-boil the kettle. 'My dad used to tell me not to take it to heart, the fact that I wasn't invited anywhere, ever. "*Take no notice, Lilly-Bob*," he'd say. "*Take no notice! They're idiots, the lot of them. They'd give anything for your brain.*" And I'd stare at him. Knowing they probably would not give anything for my brain.'

It was true, the younger Lilly-Bob was quite convinced the popular girls in her school were very happy with their brains, which let them know all the lyrics to every Beatles song. Their brains that knew what clothes went with what shoes, how to put on eyeliner, style their hair, the right thing to say . . . Their brains that meant boys would like them. Their brains that meant they didn't travel alone on the bus wishing they were invisible, and wishing, most of the time, that they could hide – only wanting to read or paint. As these were the only two things that brought her joy. And when she was immersed in either, it didn't feel like a consolation, far from it – they made her happy! So happy! Still did. Her art bag was stuffed with notebooks, canvasses, brushes and paints; the piles of books teetering in corners and on surfaces, some read, some tantalisingly awaiting her attention, testament to this.

The kettle rattled to a boil. Lilly sluiced the mugs under the tap before adding new teabags for a refill.

'It wasn't until I got to art school that my oddness became currency. I was cool because I *didn't* know the words to pop songs, because I didn't look or sound like everyone else! It was a revelation, like being able to take a full breath for the first time, like removing a too-tight corset, like walking into a warm, welcoming space when before I had been left out in the cold.'

'You found your tribe, Lilly.'

'I did, Clodagh, I found my tribe.' She smiled to think of her old friend Bertie. 'Anyway, back to the topic. What are we going to do about Apollo hating school?'

'I honestly don't know.' Her neighbour looked a little crestfallen. 'I'm not sure he hates it. I think he's okay once he gets inside, at least that's what his teacher said. It's having to leave me that's the problem.'

'Having never been a mother, I can only offer subjective advice.' The picture filled Lilly's mind as clearly as if it had happened yesterday, and there it was again, the smell of strong disinfectant.

That's a good girl, count backwards from ten for me . . .

Ten . . . nine . . . eight . . .

Then nothing.

Nothing.

'I understand, and please do!' Clodagh looked up, giving Lilly her full attention.

'What if someone else were to take him to school, someone who isn't giving off an air of anxiety that might make him anxious?'

'You think I give off an air of anxiety?' the young mum asked, giving off an air of anxiety.

'I think it's possible,' Lilly responded, tactfully.

'Who can take him in?' Clodagh reached for the fresh mug of tea that Lilly was offering.

'Me.'

'You'd do that?' she asked, eyes misting, which was all the thanks Lilly needed.

'I'd give it a go. Because sometimes I find a different person, offering a different perspective, can help you see the world differently. Now, finish your toast.' She nodded at the plate.

'Thank you, Lilly.' Clodagh sniffed. 'Have you had any letters about a regeneration order on the flats?' she asked as she took a bite.

'I have, darling, only opened one, but didn't read it all. Sent to me in error. I own the flat, so, sadly, for me, whatever plans they have for fancy new windows or painting the front doors, I will be very obviously excluded!'

'I've been too scared to open them. I'd hate to have to move. Apollo loves it here. We both do; we're settled.' Clodagh swallowed the toast as if it were a big lump, clearly frightened by the prospect. 'His haven, his safe space . . .' she echoed.

'You don't have to worry about that.' Lilly sipped her hot tea.

'Are you sure?'

'Quite sure.' She winked at the girl, who was yet to understand that the council were slow, inept and broke. There would be no regeneration, no matter how many letters they sent out.

1967 – aged 11

'Hel-lo!' Lilly called out as she let herself into the flat and, using her toe on the heel of the opposite foot, freed her tootsies of her brown lace-up school shoes. Leaving sweaty foot marks as her end-of-the-day feet padded up and down, she took a moment to savour the feel of the cold concrete on her soles – quite blissful!

'I'm ho-ome!' she called again, dumping her heavy bag, which was loaded with exercise books, on to the floor. Her homework was to cover them in wallpaper or similar and to write her name, subject and year on the front. She didn't mind the thought of it; her dad would help her. He was a dab hand at anything craft- and glue-related.

'Hel-lo!' she tried once more, having fully expected her mum to call out her usual 'Yoo-hoo!', as she liked to do, while peeling something at the kitchen counter, mopping the floor or folding clothes fresh and stiff from off the airer.

She stood for a moment, listening.

No sound of her dad's violin.

No whistling.

It was more than the quiet that now alerted her senses, rather a feeling that crept over her, the thought entering her mind, based on nothing more than intuition, that something wasn't quite right.

It was like lighting a fuse, waiting, heart in mouth, as the spark travelled painfully slowly along the cord.

Swallowing the uncomfortable boulder of concern, she walked towards the lounge and popped her head inside. It was empty. She noted the tide on the river was high and lifted her hand in a wave to the other side, as was her habit. Then the kitchen, where the sight of her dad, his back towards her, shirtsleeves rolled, elbows planted, head hanging forward slightly as if he might be reading, filled her with something very close to relief. It was sweet and instant. No need to feel worried. Her daddy was there.

The radio was on, volume lower than usual. She could just about make out The Beatles' '*Penny Lane*'.

'Hi!' She smiled, humming as she walked to the fridge, pulled out the bottle of milk and fetched a glass from the draining board. 'We lost our netball match, twenty to thirty-five.' It had been a shock; their team, the second netball team of the Dame Margaret Nichols Academy, were very good. 'We played a school in Chiswick. They were a bit snooty. Miss Darnell said we played well, but we were all a bit quiet, because I think we knew we could have done better. The trouble is when the other team scores quickly and they're shouting *Yes!* and jumping up and congratulating each other, it's as if they've already won. It makes you feel a bit rotten and it's hard to come back from that. That's what I think, anyway.'

She sloshed the cold white stuff into the glass before downing it in one, making no attempt to remove the wide milk moustache that felt cool on her top lip, knowing it would make her dad laugh when he eventually spotted it. Still he hadn't looked up. This was not unusual, as often he was lost to a page, a word, a description, a picture, a thought, a memory. So much so that often her mum, who might have called his name once or twice already, would have to say it louder and louder until he responded. 'Robert . . . Robert! . . . ROBERT!'

Once she had even banged a saucepan with a spoon to get his attention, and he had practically jumped in the chair, as if he had been miles and miles and miles away. This happened quite a lot.

Lilly wanted him to comment on her dire netball match. It was bad enough that all the girls had gone off together to the Wimpy, no doubt for some post-match analysis over their Pepsis, and she hadn't been invited. No shock there. She was never invited. She wondered if it was because she lived in the shadow of the vast concrete monolith that was the Nine Elms Cold Store – it had a creepy reputation and she wondered if that made her seem a little creepy, not that there was a darn thing she could do about that! It wasn't like they had the money to relocate to the other side of the river where the pretty streets of Pimlico lurked.

Her dad's lack of response only became unusual when she put the bottle back into the fridge and walked towards him, realising he was not reading, not looking at anything other than the bare tabletop. Slowly tracing shapes with his fingertip, as it moved in a figure of eight over and over on the surface.

'Are you okay, Dad?' she asked softly, and just like that the sense of foreboding returned.

'Huh?' He looked up, eyes widening, as if only just noticing her, as if he had been so engrossed in whatever occupied him that the sight of her was a complete surprise.

Realising he was in no mood for laughter, she pulled the sleeve of her jersey over her thumb and used the woolly cuff to wipe away her milk moustache, which suddenly felt far from funny.

'I said, "are you okay?", where's Mum?' The two questions were strung together.

The clock was marching towards five, and that was when they ate their tea and there was no sign of any food prep in progress. No sulphureous scent of cabbage boiling, no sound of sausages spitting under the grill, no hiss of eggs hitting the fat of a skillet, no smell of bacon that clung to her hair and clothes, no mouthwatering waft of vanilla as a soft sponge domed inside the oven. There was only the barely audible beat echoing from the transistor on the tiled windowsill, as Jimmy Ruffin now sang '*What Becomes of the Brokenhearted*' . . . a beautiful ballad that would loop in her head all evening, no doubt. What was missing was her mum as she stood with her arms in suds or brandishing a spatula or spoon.

Everything was still. Disconcertingly so.

Lilly felt the smallest flicker of concern. Tea was at five, always. Her body anticipated it, her mind looked forward to it. She hated the thought of being hungry.

'Sit down, Lilly.' Her dad leaned over and pulled out the chair to his right, even though she was entirely capable of doing so.

She sat.

'Erm . . .' He opened his mouth. There was the longest pause, which allowed her heart rate to increase and her worry to flare. His lips sounded sticky, as if he'd lost his spit.

'Erm . . .' That word of indecision again. This was not what she wanted, indecision, dithering, and dramatic pauses, not from her dad. He was the person with his hands gripping the reins, he was the one who steered the ship, and if *he* was floundering . . .

'What is it, Dad?' she prompted, as her leg jumped up and down under the table with a potent mixture of concern and impatience.

'Mum has moved out.'

Lilly-Bob laughed out loud. A sharp burst of giggles that disappeared as quickly as they'd arrived. It was funny because mums didn't move out. Mums made the bed, cooked the tea, sang along to Jimmy Ruffin, and danced with your dad when the mood was right. They knew where to find things in jumbled drawers and the dark confines of cupboards, they knitted you jumpers by the electric fire of a winter's night, they brushed your hair when it was ratty, they ran your bath and warmed a towel for you by the fire. They told you that you looked pretty when you wore a frock, they showed you how to put on two coats of lipstick, and they gave you a leaflet about menstruation on your eleventh birthday, 'just in case'. They made you a birthday cake and covered the top with sprinkles and tiny pink, twisty candles bought from Woolworths that melted in drips quicker than everyone could sing or you could blow them out. Mums made sure you had your mittens in the cold and your sun hat in the warm. They made you soup when you were poorly, dabbed calamine lotion when you got chicken pox, read to you from *The Wind in the Willows,* and let you rest your head on their shoulder and fall asleep on the bus.

What they didn't do, not ever, was move out.

'Where has she moved to?' she asked in a voice that sounded echoey in her ears, watery, a ridiculous question for the most ridiculous of scenarios.

'To a flat above a shop on the . . . the Tottenham Court Road,' he stuttered and whispered.

'How long has she gone for?' she asked, trying to piece together the puzzle, to figure out how and why.

'I don't know, but I think' – he sat up a little taller, even managed to find a fake, brief smile – 'I think that if we assume it's for ever then we won't be disappointed. And if it turns out not to be the case, then we'll be extra happy when she comes home.'

Lilly-Bob stared at him, waiting for the punchline that never came. It was at this moment that the spark reached the dynamite and her whole world exploded, falling about her in flaming fragments that she would, for a lifetime, try to gather and put back together.

Her mum had gone.

Gone!

Her mum!

The two of them sat at the table in silence, allowing the news to settle, each looking up briefly towards the washing-up sponge resting by the sink, the Marigolds paired, folded and hung over the taps, the frying pan on the stove, the sticking-out handle of the grill pan, the pinny on the back of the door, the compact mirror by the kettle, the peg bag hanging on the door handle; all these things her mum's domain, her toolkit, carrying traces of her presence within this room, this kitchen . . . Traces of a life that would, from now on, be changed, because deep in her heart, Lilly knew that her dad was right. It was for ever.

'What's for tea?' she asked eventually, as if understanding that the hands of the clock weren't going to stop just because Jeannie Cooper would be residing in a flat above a shop on the Tottenham Court Road. It would soon be five o'clock, and that was when they ate their tea. Because life went on. It had to go on.

'I don't . . . I don't know,' he replied, as tears filled his eyes.

This was when she understood that dads did cry! Although she wished they didn't. And a moment she knew she would never forget and never forgive. The sight of his tears, falling quickly over his ruddy cheeks and chin, quicker than he could swipe at them, his eyes brimming and spilling as if he were filled right up with tears. It was odd and unnerving to feel the flare of something close to hatred towards her mum, who she loved. Knowing she would never forget the sight of him so broken and never forgive the one who had made him cry. Her mum, who had moved out. Her mum, who would not be there to tuck her in and say goodnight.

She was glad, then, of the lipstick kiss that sat on a tissue, folded over and nestling in her bedside cabinet drawer. A goodnight kiss captured that she could press on to her cheek, not as good as the real thing, not nearly as good, but it was something. Despite the growing feeling of resentment towards the woman, it was conflicting, as Jeannie was still her mummy. And she would miss her more than she was willing to admit.

Her dad laid his arm on the table and rested his head on it. His shoulders shook as he cried some more. It was as if he had already lost, no doubt making *him* feel a bit rotten. And Lilly understood that it was hard to come back from that.

Present day

'So how long is this arrangement going to go on for?' her friend Glenda asked with a distinct air of disapproval. Not that Lilly had expected anything less. She rolled her eyes and gripped the bulky phone tightly under her chin.

'What *arrangement,* exactly?' She couldn't keep the edge of irritation from her question. It was how it was with Glenda, friends for so long that they fluctuated between love and hate, nothing was sugar-coated, no need for verbal filters or self-censorship.

'You having to get up and drag the kid to school every morning! I don't like the idea of it, Lil, not at your age. I wouldn't even do that for my boys, and their kids are my grandchildren! I mean, every single morning!' She sighed.

'Well, luckily for Clodagh, I am not you. I'm also not a hundred, not incapable and not decrepit – not yet! And I shan't be dragging him. We have a pleasant commute, and we get on rather well.'

Glenda tutted, ignoring her reasoning.

'I mean, it's all right when the weather is nice, but what about when it's snowing? What if it's icy out, or raining? You need your sleep.' Lilly was trying to work out the connection between foul weather, sleeping and her ability to drop Apollo off at school, while Glenda hardly drew breath. 'I don't like it. I know Nicola and Cheryl wouldn't dream of asking anyone to take their kids to school, especially not an elderly neighbour.'

'They might have to if you won't do it! Besides, I'm not elderly! And I never intend to be elderly!' She was shouting now, caring less what her mate's rather lacklustre daughters-in-law would or would not do.

Again, Glenda ignored her.

'Well, I'm only saying what's on me mind, and I think she's taking liberties, that girl who's just moved in.'

'She's not a girl, she's a young woman with a child who is doing her very best, and my goodness, what kind of world are we living in if I can't help out a neighbour in need? And she hasn't just moved in. You've met her several times. She's been here for over a year now.' It irritated her how she felt the need to justify her relationship with Clodagh, wondering if Glenda was suffering from the old green-eyed monster. With this in mind she decided not to confess to just how much she loved walking Apollo to school.

There was something therapeutic about the routine and rhythm of it, seeing the same faces, looking out for the black cat who sat on the lid of the same wheelie bin, Mr Lycra the cyclist who always shouted *Good morning!* as he left his front gate, their schedules obviously colliding. Two weeks in, and she had no desire to stop. Besides, it seemed to have done the trick. The little boy was calm and chatty, walking into school without drama, yet to shed a tear. Clodagh was beyond thankful and had caught up on her coursework. She was striving to get her degree in sports therapy while working half-days in a fancy new coffee shop near the American Embassy along the river in Nine Elms.

'That's the trouble, you have the very best intentions, but as I said, I'm just worried someone might take advantage of you. I mean, he's not your grandchild, is he?' Her friend's words, no doubt coming from a place of concern, landed in Lilly's chest like tiny, poison-tipped daggers. As if she needed a reminder that she had no grandchildren, something she would have quite liked. More than quite liked. This was immediately followed by a flare of unease as her self-confidence dipped; had she overstepped the mark, did Clodagh think she was muscling in, trying to make more of their relationship, trying to take the place of a grandparent or, God forbid, a mother? That would be the worst thing! Just the thought of it was enough for Lilly to feel her heart race a little, for the rising tide of humiliation to lap at her ankles, and for her to lose a little of her faith that she had done the right thing.

'I am aware, Glenda. And I thank you for your concern. I don't feel remotely taken advantage of. It was me who suggested it. Clodagh has never asked me for anything.'

It was true. If anything, the young woman had been healthily suspicious when they first met. Their friendship had bloomed in spite of their less-than-auspicious first meeting, which had occurred as Lilly sat on the path in front of Waide House with her paintbrush in hand. Alerted by the child's presence, she had looked up in time to see him lean on the wall and throw a plastic lolly wrapper into the river.

'What are you doing, dear? You really shouldn't do that!' She had raised her voice a little. He had turned to face her, his dark, dark hair falling over his face, expression nonplussed, lolly wedged into his mouth, the white stick protruding from his lips.

'Please don't bark at my son!' the boy's mother had called from behind. Lilly turned to see the young woman, who clapped her hands together twice and reached out her arms, calling for her son to come to her. He ignored her and turned back towards the water, the toes of his little trainers digging against the brick to hold him in place.

'I don't think I barked. The thing is, he threw rubbish into the river – plastic! He threw *plastic*!'

'And I said, don't bark at him, or me!' The young woman doubled down, blinking as if this confrontation didn't come naturally to her.

'I'm not barking! But he really can't throw things in the water. It's a terrible thing to do. We have a duty of care, I believe, to the river, but also to kids. They need to understand the consequences of their actions, so that, hopefully, they think twice before doing it again.'

'Apollo, come away from the lady!'

This had bothered Lilly. The words and tone suggested she was a danger, someone to be avoided. It was hurtful.

'Well, if I barked, I didn't mean to.' She tried out a closed-mouthed smile of apology. 'I feel strongly about the river.'

'No shit!' The woman took a step closer. Young, very young, eyes wide, skin pale. She looked like she needed a hot meal. They took a beat and Apollo's mother spoke. 'I'm sorry I wasn't watching him more closely. I never let him litter. It's the worst, I hate it. It's hard to watch him every second.'

'I can imagine. Apollo? That's a wonderful, strong name. Son of Zeus, no less, twin to Artemis and the god of archery, dance and music, to name but a few.' Her dad had loved to read excerpts to her from his book of ancient Greek and Roman mythology.

'I always liked it. I wanted him to have a name people would remember, hopefully for all the right reasons and not because he commits ecological crimes . . .' The girl pulled a face.

Lilly laughed.

'I wanted to see it float!' Apollo, who had climbed down now, stood facing her, his stare unapologetic, his explanation sincere.

'Hmmm. I used to make boats out of twigs and sticks and throw them in when I was not much older than you. I figured that twigs and sticks might have fallen into the river anyway, plus they'll break down, but plastic' – Lilly shook her head – 'it's really nasty stuff.'

'Why is it?' the little boy asked, pulling his lolly momentarily from his mouth.

She looked briefly towards his mother, who smiled, an expression of encouragement, permission to explain.

'Plastic hangs around for years and years, and if fish swallow it or get trapped in it—'

'Are there fish in here?' he interrupted, pointing excitedly at the water. It was thrilling to have captured his attention, to be making her point.

'Yes, over a hundred and twenty species, in fact.'

'Really?' This question came from his mother.

'Yes, really. We even had a dolphin a few years back, swimming between Putney Bridge and Hammersmith, only visiting, I'm sure, but a dolphin, nonetheless. Can you imagine the excitement?'

'I can, actually!' The girl stared at the water, as if picturing the pretty creature.

'I'd like to go on a boat.' The boy spoke with enthusiasm.

'Well, there's lots of them about.' She liked the pluck of the little chap.

'What are you doing?' Using his cherry-red lolly as a pointer, he angled it towards her easel.

'I am painting. Painting the river.'

'Can I see it?' Without waiting for a response, he walked closer and came to stand alongside her. Paying no heed to the rules about personal space, he stared at the picture in its infancy, taking in the broad stripes of pale colour that she was building up, waiting for it to take shape so she could add in the depth, detail and movement.

'What do you think?' Lilly asked.

'I don't think it's very good. I like dinosaurs.'

'Apollo!' His mum shouted her mortification, her hand against her brow. 'I am so sorry!'

'No, no, he's absolutely allowed to express his opinion. I love honest feedback, especially when it comes to art, and besides, he's probably right. I mean, is there any painting in the world that wouldn't be made better by the addition of a dinosaur; the *Mona Lisa* with a triceratops peering over her shoulder?'

'*The Hay Wain* with the head of a diplodocus emerging from the lake?'

Lilly liked both the woman's enthusiasm and her imagination.

'Warhol's tomato soup cans in the claws of a pterodactyl!' Lilly added.

'Oh!' The young woman snapped her fingers. '*The Last Supper* with a T. rex taking up the fourteenth spot!' They both laughed loudly at the thought of it.

'I'm Lilly by the way. Lilly-Bob.'

'Lilly-Bob? That's quite a name too.'

'Yes, but far better than Elizabeth-Roberta, which it was before my dad shortened it. I'm just called Lilly nowadays. No one has time for a long-winded double-barrelled name. We're all in too much of a hurry.'

'I'm Clodagh.'

'Hello, Clodagh.' She held the young woman's gaze for a second and felt the connection forming. It was lovely.

'We've just moved in.' Clodagh pointed behind her, to the top floor.

'Ah, in that case we're neighbours. I'm flat six, middle floor. Call in any time if you need anything.'

'Really?' Clodagh asked, as if checking whether this was an offer with substance behind it, suggesting help might not be on tap for the young mum. 'That's so lovely.' Her joy was evident. 'We haven't been here that long, and I don't know anyone.'

'Well, you know me now, and yes, really, just knock on the door, any time.'

And so it had begun: they'd built a bridge.

'I just think you have to be careful.' Glenda pulled her back to the present. 'You have a lot of money squirrelled away.' And there it was: Glenda's fascination with Lilly's savings account. 'Doesn't sound like the girl's got a pot to piss in, and you're far too generous for your own good.' Lilly never understood what this phrase actually meant, *too generous for your own good . . .* 'It's not like you've got a husband to keep an eye on your finances.'

'True, it's a wonder how I manage at all!' Lilly knew her sarcasm would be lost on Glenda, who had a husband, a Norman, to be precise, who was a quiet soul but a good man, who *clearly* kept Glenda, who hid her money in her bra when she collected her pension, on the straight and narrow. It made Lilly smile, this advice from her friend, the assumption that a man, *any* man, would be better at handling her finances. It was as outdated as it was insulting. It wasn't the first time Glenda had mentioned her money, and she sure as sugar knew it wouldn't be the last. It was an unpleasant truth that she felt the interest came with a certain smack of envy. Not that it was Lilly's fault; her dad had bought the flat when offered the chance by the Tory government's Right to Buy scheme in 1983. And when he died, he had left it to her, meaning she lived mortgage- and rent-free. The dream for most, she understood, and with minimal bills, Lilly certainly lived comfortably on her income from the art gallery where she worked.

She pictured him: sweet Norman, quiet Norman, who had on the darkest of days so long ago shown her nothing but kindness, but that said, he was hardly Richard Branson.

There was a loud knock.

'Oh, that's the front door, Glenda. See you later!'

In truth she was glad of the excuse to end the phone call.

Lilly opened the door and smiled at the bespectacled young man with the shock of auburn hair. She took in his tight-fitting blue suit that emphasised his slim build, his shiny shoes and his open-necked shirt, immaculately pressed. *Shiny shoes – standards!* The man looked to be on a mission, if she had to guess, from one of the churches that preached the importance of such a presentation of shirt, shoes and politeness, alongside an intolerance towards anything that deviated from the heteronormative teachings of the good book. A curious and confusing dichotomy, and only one of the reasons she steered away from organised religion of all types.

'Mrs Cooper?'

'No. I'm not Mrs Cooper.'

'Oh!' He immediately referred to a leather-bound folder in his hand. 'This is flat six?' he queried, nervously.

'It is, but I am Miss Cooper. *Miss.*'

'Oh, right! Oh, good!' He smiled with an expression of relief. 'I'll get the paperwork changed.'

'What paperwork?' She was curious; this was not what she had expected at all. Usually, the spiel began with a message of light, love and redemption, brought to her door by none other than a representative of the big man himself.

'Oh yes, yes, right.' He coughed to clear his throat. 'Might I come in?' He pointed towards her hall. 'We have an appointment.'

'We do?' she asked quizzically, wondering what appointment, and how she might have missed it. It wouldn't be the first time she'd got in a muddle, turning up on the wrong day for dentist visits and often getting confused over the fortnightly recycling schedule. She might have told Glenda she wasn't old but she blamed these thought fuzzles entirely on her age.

'Yes! I emailed but didn't get a reply.'

'Well, that explains it; I don't open emails. I used to but found it jolly confusing trying to figure out how to reply, and that in itself was quite stressful. And even if I did know how to reply, the whole idea of being that accessible, it's not for me, dear.' She shook her head.

'I see.' He stared at her with a look of utter bewilderment. She supposed it was a little alien to him and his generation, the idea of being out of contact by choice. And as for social media – she had very little interest in pictures of people's lunches or builders in hi-vis doing a dance as they lip-synced in heavy boots.

'I re-sent it, but still didn't hear back, so thought I'd pop in on the off chance, and here you are!'

'Here I am!' She smiled. 'And who are you?' She stood firm in the doorway, folding her arms across her chest.

'Sorry, yes! I should have showed you my ID; I'm from Portland and Montague.'

'And who are they?' she persisted.

'Ah, yes, sorry, Mr A. Portland and Mr P. Montague, the developers who are taking over the block.' Lilly felt her hackles rise. 'We've sent a few letters, too, but not had a response from you, so . . .' He let this trail.

'So . . .' She rolled her hand.

'So, might I have five minutes of your time to . . . to discuss the, erm, the . . . the proposed timeline for the regeneration and the appropriate course of action for all residents?'

With tiny beads of sweat on his top lip, he sounded very much like he was reciting a script.

'I didn't catch your name?' she asked with a softer tone, not wanting to make him any more uncomfortable than he already was; the young man seemed a little prone to apologising. He was, after all, only doing his job.

He indicated a lanyard around his neck and held it up for her to inspect. 'Vaughan. Joshua Vaughan.'

'I think you can tell me all you need to here on the doorstep, Mr Vaughan. We can get this cleared up quite quickly, I'm sure.'

'Right.' He swallowed, lowered his folder and pushed his glasses up his nose. 'Have you read the letters we have sent, Mrs – *Miss* Cooper?' he self-corrected, as his face coloured in that way that it does when someone is trying really hard to get it right but still gets it wrong.

'Not really. You see, it doesn't apply to me, dear. It often causes confusion, not your fault, but I am not a council tenant. This flat, number six' – she pointed to the silver number on the front door – 'is privately owned by me. This has been the case for decades, and before that it was my dad's. So, any work being carried out; the painting of communal areas, replanting of the raised beds at the front, the installation of bin sheds in the basement' – she paused – 'I'm trying to think of all the wonderful improvements that have been touted and reneged on in the last few years; they don't and won't apply to me. Oh, and if you are going door to door, can you please not disturb Mrs Veerswamy on the top floor, flat seven. She works nights at St Thomas's and will be asleep.'

'No, I've' – he stared at her – 'I've already spoken to Mrs Veerswamy. In fact the only people I haven't spoken to are you and Miss Clodagh Newman.'

'I see.' She wasn't about to give him any information on Clodagh, her routine or whereabouts.

'The thing is' – again he swallowed and pushed up those specs – 'it's not about painting or bin sheds.'

'Right. What is it about, then?' She wished he'd get to the point. She needed the loo, an unpleasant consequence of her age, the frequent need to pee.

'Portland and Montague are undertaking an exciting new project to regenerate this land, this place, this block.' There it was again, that word. She grimaced, still keen to hear all about it, amused by his use of the word 'land'. They were, on this little slice of riverside, without acreage. 'I have plans and images that I am happy to show you.' He lifted his folder.

'Images?' She was curious.

'Yes!' Seemingly motivated by her interest, he opened the folder and pulled out a shiny A4 sheet showing a brand-spanking-new stack of Polo mint-style apartments. There were even tiny people on the curved balconies, some sitting on those inadequate bistro sets that seemed enticing when you considered morning coffee in the sunshine but were in reality uncomfortable and usually left to rust outdoors in the damp British winter due to a lack of available storage. 'Two hundred and twelve apartments of the highest specification,' Mr Vaughan enthused, 'granite countertops, marble tiling, state-of-the-art sound systems, climate control, a rooftop pool, gym, cinema room, sauna, underground parking, twenty-four-hour concierge, the works!'

'A rooftop pool? Wow!' It certainly sounded very impressive. 'It looks . . .' She paused, not wanting to burst his bubble, but also a little confused as to where he was suggesting there might be space to build such a modernist monstrosity! 'I can't see where there's space along this little stretch of the river?' She narrowed her eyes at him, still wondering why the need for such close consultation. When the last tower had been built, there had been a public notice shoved up, a meeting in a hotel conference room that she had failed to attend, and an apology in advance for all the noise, dust and disruption, but this . . .

'It's going to be here, Mrs Cooper.' This time she didn't correct him, because his words were of such magnitude they echoed in her ears and made her knees feel a little weak.

'Here?' She was having difficulty in understanding. 'What do you mean, here?' She actually laughed.

'I mean that we are knocking down Waide House.'

'Knocking it down?' she whispered. Behind her she heard the faint echo of '*Shake, Rattle and Roll*', could hear the thump, thump of her parents' feet on the parquet flooring of the lounge.

'Yes, to build *The Fortescue* – that's the name of the new block.' He pointed to the shiny picture again.

Lilly leaned on the doorframe. 'That's not' – she took a breath – 'that's not possible. I own this flat. It's my home.'

'I'm afraid it doesn't quite work like that.'

'Doesn't it?' Her confusion was genuine, because it jolly well should!

'Not when it comes to developments of this nature. There was a multi-stakeholder benefit analysis run on the project long before it got the go-ahead.'

'I see.' She nodded, even though she had no idea what he was talking about; she didn't want to appear stupid.

'The council are going to make a lot of money from the development, money that will be ploughed into much-needed, vital services for the community. All the tenants we have spoken to have agreed to relocate. All the tenants that responded to the letters and emails, that is.'

'But this is what I am trying to explain to you, Mr Vaughan, I am not a tenant! I will not be relocated! I can't be shoved this way and that like a pawn on a chessboard. This is my *home*.' She wondered which of her words he was having difficulty grasping.

'It's not that straightforward. As the property owner, you will be subject to a compulsory purchase order. At a fair price, don't you worry. The way it normally works is that Portland and Montague will get three valuations from trusted local estate agents, the process will be entirely transparent, and we will then come to a settlement figure that suits us both.'

'So you've done this before?'

'Once or twice.' He smiled in a way that suggested confidence, and that it had been more than once or twice. Instantly, she liked him a little less.

'My flat is not for sale, Mr Vaughan. It's not for sale.' She wanted to raise her voice, but felt a little weakened, and more than a little afraid, unaware if what he was proposing was legal or possible and what she might be able to do about it. Unsure even how she could find out.

'I understand that there are emotions at play here, Mrs Cooper, so what I propose is that I give you a few days to have a think, let it settle in, maybe read the letters we've been sending you, and then I'll pop back to answer any questions you might have.'

Joshua Vaughan zipped up the leather folder, leaving her with the shiny artist's impression of *The Fortescue* in her shaking hand. And for the first time in as long as she could remember, Lilly-Bob wished she had a man, a partner, a husband, a Norman, to talk to as she stumbled into the kitchen and fell into a chair at the little square table.

She pictured the numerous buildings, homes, many of them, that had been bulldozed over the years to make way for the redevelopment of her beloved postcode. Home now to shiny glass blocks that reflected other shiny glass blocks. Entire structures, symbols of her childhood, gone overnight and the people who lived in them shunted out to live goodness only knew where. The most significant changes in her lifetime had been the erection of the SIS Building, home to MI6, right by Vauxhall Bridge, and the knocking down of the vast monolith that had been the Nine Elms Cold Store to make way for St George Wharf – a huge futuristic clump of fancy flats that cost an arm and a leg and were only, in her opinion, marginally nicer to look at than the concrete cold store they'd replaced.

'Surely they can't do that to me, can they?' She put the question out into the ether and felt the knife of loneliness twist in her breast at the lack of response.

1970 – aged 14

It was a warm day. Lilly's body, as if moulded out of shape by the heat, felt too soft to galvanise into action. In her denim cut-offs and halterneck vest, she lay flopped, covered in a blanket of lethargy that pinned her to the velour-covered sofa. The air, thick with heat, meant her desire to do anything other than read was absolutely zero. Even raising a hand to move her long fringe, stuck to her forehead with sweat, felt like too much effort. Despite having all the windows of the flat open wide there was barely a breeze. The river was usually a wonderful regulatory source of wind, as any waft seemed to gather on its surface and whistle through the rooms, but not today.

The ancient clattering electric fan that they'd perched on the coffee table offered little by way of relief. In fact it only served to irritate with its clunking whir and frustrating lack of oomph. It was the summer holidays, and Lilly had so far devoured three books in ten days. *A House for Mr Biswas, The Prime of Miss Jean Brodie* and *Are You There God? It's Me, Margaret.* Each one was 'the best book ever!' . . . until she finished the next and declared the same.

She was now looking for a new distraction as she loped into the kitchen. Not for the first time, she wondered how different her life might be if her mum was still here, thinking of summer holidays past when they had baked together, crocheted together, taken trips to the Parliament Hill lido and ridden the Tube back, her damp swimming costume rolled inside an equally damp towel. Her hair wet, skin clammy, stomach full of the hot Bovril they had consumed as a treat after swimming, and a feeling in her core as if her body were singing with delight, limbs just the right amount of tired after her swim.

In truth, she simply missed the way it felt having her mum around, with her soft voice, delicate pastel-coloured blouses, floaty skirts and petticoats. A lovely feminine element of fragrant warmth. A bright thing. She had liked it very much, and missed her mum's humming habit, and her ability to whip up biscuits and scones in a jiffy that filled the flat with the most glorious of scents. Yes, Lilly missed her still with an ache in her bones that she didn't mention, not ever. As pining for her mother was marginally outweighed by the anger she felt towards her, that and the fact that Jeannie Cooper had hurt her dad. Her wonderful, wonderful dad. That was quite possibly the most unforgiveable aspect of all, and the hardest for her to comprehend.

Her mother leaving marked Lilly as unusual, another reason for her to be considered persona non grata when it came to popularity in the playground. It was quite a rarity; certainly everyone she knew had a mum and a dad, and at least one brother or sister. Jeannie leaving reduced them to a family of two. Odd.

The moment she had realised her mum wasn't coming home was still there for perfect recall, and with it the same bloom of sadness in her throat. What made the whole dire situation even worse was that she had left them for a man called Derek Manners. *Derek Manners!* Even at her tender age, Lilly was convinced that if Jeannie had done a moonlight flit with someone smart, successful, someone that could, to the untrained eye, be considered an upgrade, she might have been able to understand it a little more. Not that she would ever have been approving, not that, but *Derek Manners!* Nothing about him was an upgrade.

Her mother's new man was so very average, so boringly beige, and her dad was vibrant! Clever! Funny! It was undoubtedly her mother's choice of man that was as hard, if not harder, to fathom than her actions. Her dad was a poet, a musician, a cultured man. Derek repaired and sold televisions from his shop on the Tottenham Court Road. Her dad wore a neat pair of slacks and braces; Derek wore a cardigan! Her dad drank whisky from a cut-glass tumbler and studied maps; Derek liked football. Her dad made pasta, having been taught by the *nonna* of his flatmate while living in Sardinia after the war. He would bring home delicacies prepared by other musicians in his orchestra: baklava, preserved lemons, fat, milky olives, fattoush, tapenade, spiced paneer, all kinds of wondrous world foods that made her tastebuds dance, and which they ate greedily with their fingers at the kitchen table. Her mum had told her in a half-conspiratorial, half-amused way that Derek Manners ate the same things every day of the week. A roast on Sunday, leftover roast on Monday, sausage and mash on Tuesday, mince and rice on Wednesday, cold meat, chips and beans on Thursday, fish and chips on Friday, bacon sandwiches on Saturday, and then back to the roast . . .

The same things.

Every day.

Of every week.

The same!

Lilly could not imagine the absolute hell of a life that was so ordered, so predictable, so dull! She wasn't sure what she wanted to be when she grew up but knew that she'd rather be anything other than dull.

Her gran on her dad's side refused to allow Jeannie's name to be mentioned, and as she used to pop in after her mother had gone, arriving in her polyester tabard to clean the house and dollop grey food and overboiled tinned carrots on to plates, they almost stopped talking about her mum altogether. Her gran had died quite suddenly a couple of years ago, but still they didn't mention Jeannie, not really. It had become a rule that nobody set, and one Lilly was personally too afraid to break, not wanting to upset her dad further. Her gran had been a tough old bird who had survived two world wars, the loss of her brothers and parents, and had not a tooth in her head. Lilly could still recall the way she had spoken in the immediate aftermath of her mum's departure, her hair in curlers nestling under a pink net, cigarette held aloft between her fingers, one arm clamped under her ample bosom, mouth thin.

She's no good! None of them are, them women who have no regard for the vows of marriage, who mess up the lives of kids without so much as a by-your-leave! She's selfish, brazen and morally slack, that's her! A terrible, terrible person!

A harsh assessment, yet her dad had kept his head down, choosing not to offer comment or rebuttal; neither did he wink at Lilly to show it was all in jest. Lilly took his lead, unwilling to admit that she still, at night-time, liked to retrieve her copy of *The Wind in the Willows* from the drawer of her bedside cabinet, watching as the pages fell open to reveal the now-smudged lipstick mark on the tissue that was as precious to her as any jewel. Running her fingers over it, she'd whisper 'Night night' out across the river, secretly hoping it would travel over the London rooftops and land in her mother's ear, where her head lay on a brushed-cotton pillowcase in a flat on the Tottenham Court Road.

Lilly saw her on the odd occasion; the first time had been the hardest. She was invited for tea a couple of weeks after her mum's departure, and her dad had ironed Lilly's blouse and handed it to her with a small smile. It was approval of sorts. She had visited out of curiosity, desperate to see her mother's new set-up, to understand what was so great about her new life that had made it so easy to throw away her old one.

'Do you like plants?' Derek Manners had asked, as she sat on their squeaky leather sofa in the narrow sitting room that Lilly found to be quite claustrophobic. There was a wide shelf around the top of the room from which tumbled long, trailing leaves and which went some way to explaining the smell of soil that lingered in the air.

'No, I *hate* them.' Her quick and steady reply, letting him know that whatever he liked, she hated. Hoping that he decoded her words and understood that what she really hated was him.

'Which would you prefer, darling, orange or lemon?' Her mother had held aloft two bottles of squash as she stood in the doorway.

'Neither,' was her immediate reply.

'Oh, milk, then?' Her mum's next suggestion.

'Nope.' Lilly had then folded her arms across her pressed blouse.

'Well, I've . . . I've made sandwiches, ham and tomato, and I've cut the crusts off, just as you like them.'

'I'm not hungry.'

'What would you like, love?' her mum had asked softly.

'Err . . . to go back to my dad?' She fired verbal spikes.

And so it went on. As eleven-year-old Lilly-Bob protested in the only way she knew how.

The whole encounter had felt forced, awkward and embarrassing, leaving her skin covered in a sticky film of unease, as with one eye on the clock she'd longed for the hands to move faster, and her mum had cried while beaming behind her tears. It was as if Jeannie believed that if she smiled widely enough, Lilly might not notice the cascade of sadness that streaked her face and trickled over her two coats of red, red lipstick. But Lilly did notice, and her heart lifted a little to see such sadness. *Serves you right!* was her mean and conflicting thought, knowing she, too, would cry later, picturing her mum's distress, and angry all over again because it was her own fault! Jeannie had chosen to leave the flat, her husband, her child, chosen to leave it all and swap it for this beige life with Derek Manners in a grotty, noisy top-floor flat without a view.

'I'm so booooored.' Lilly walked into the kitchen now with the lumbering gait of exhaustion, arms hanging down, hair over her face, head to one side as if even her neck had not the will to support its load. Not that she was even tired, but it was a reflection of her current mood.

Her dad's cigarette, smouldering in its little dip on the edge of the chunky glass ashtray, filled the room with its familiar scent, as the sound of Gordon Lightfoot's song '*If You Could Read My Mind*' filled the air. Her dad closed his eyes occasionally and moved his head as if conducting or playing, she wasn't sure which. Retrieving his cigarette, he took a long, slow drag, before removing a fleck of tobacco from his bottom lip with his thumb and forefinger. She watched the end flare red hot and the thin paper snake away, leaving a sausage of ash. She liked to guess when it might fall, watching it, fascinated. He lowered the tiny paintbrush that he had only just dipped into the thumb-sized metal paint tin containing a rather lovely shade of yellow and rested it on a chopstick stand he used for the purpose. About to add details to the fuselage of the Vulcan Bomber Airfix model airplane he had patiently constructed and painted, he paused his efforts.

'Sorry, Lilly-Bob, I think I must have misheard you.' He rubbed his forehead.

'I said, "I'm so booooored."'

'Do you know, that's what I thought you said. If your gran, my mother, was still alive, she'd whip your hide.' He winked, confirming what she knew to be true: that he'd never let anyone whip her hide, or anywhere else for that matter. 'The reason for my confusion is that you live in the greatest city in the whole wide world. You live in the middle of London – *London!'* He laughed, head shaking as if in wonder. 'This is the city where you can sit by the lake in Kensington Gardens, go boating on the Serpentine in Hyde Park, swim in Hampstead Ponds, take a bus ride and marvel at the finest architecture in the world: Westminster Abbey, St Paul's, the Royal Mint, the Royal Albert Hall! Go marvel at the uniforms and headgear on display at Horse Guards Parade, wave to Her Majesty through the gates of Buck House! Or . . . or . . . take a gander around the British Museum, be dazzled at the V&A! Visit Covent Garden Market and find the reddest, shiniest apple you can. Take a picnic and idle an hour by the canal in Little Venice! We have countless theatres, cinemas, coffee shops and cafés. And art, my little one, oh, the art . . .' He closed his eyes briefly. 'The National Gallery, the Tate! All of it there and awaiting discovery, no more than a hop, skip and jump away.'

'I guess . . .' She was aware that she was on shaky ground and decided not to reiterate the point that she was bored and couldn't be bothered. Plus, Vauxhall was hardly the arty side of London; stepping outside, she was more likely to see tower blocks, abandoned docks, rusty ships and dog poo than art! She didn't think it prudent to point this out.

'Do you know how many people right now, all over the world, are looking at the four walls that encase them or their very dull landscape and are dreaming of coming to a city like this? *Our* city?'

'I don't,' she admitted, running the pad of her thumb over the fraying hem of her shorts.

'Lots.' He reached out and ruffled her hair, a habit that irritated her, made her feel like a baby. 'Lots and lots, and they will be working hard to scrabble together the fare, putting coins in a jar that holds all their dreams and wishes, and you have it all right here on your doorstep. Never take it for granted, Lilly-Bob. Find the joy in it every day. This city is ever-changing. Growing in some places, shrinking in others, but always changing, and what you see today you will never see again, never the exact same! If that's not a wonder, then I don't know what is.'

'I think I might go and sit out the front and read another book.' She had *Jonathan Livingston Seagull* teed up.

'Good idea! Or you could take one of my old easels and paint what you see? There's something quite lovely about sitting on the towpath, getting lost in the river, the sounds, the sights . . . Give it some thought.'

'Thanks, but I think I'll start my new book.' Decision made. He was always trying to get her to paint. She didn't have the heart to tell him that just because he loved it, didn't mean she did too.

'Bored!' He shook his head, made a 'tsk' sound and retrieved his thin paintbrush. It was as she left the room that she caught his expression: one of sheer disappointment or something close to sorrow. She felt a physical jolt in her gut. It was her very worst thing, the thought of upsetting or displeasing her dad. She was on his side, fervently on his side. Her mum had chosen Derek Manners and so Lilly chose him, always.

Sinking back down on to the sofa, she knew she had learned a great lesson. It wasn't that she could, if she so wished, visit any number of London landmarks in the pursuit of boats, soldiers, artefacts, apples, coffee, films and paintings, but rather that the next time she was bored, she must not, under any circumstances, mention it to her dad.

With her book in her hands, she looked up through the window at the bright blue sky and felt a wave of emotion and an inexplicable desire to weep at the beauty of it, and at the awful fact that her dad had looked so let down. The appeal of her book was somewhat diminished. Keen to make it up to him, her thoughts turned to the river and the idea that maybe she might quite like to paint it, if nothing else to make him smile.

Her dad was, unsurprisingly, where she had left him, nose millimetres from the Vulcan Bomber, his hand steady as he made the tiniest of strokes.

'Do you know, I think I might have a go at painting the river, Dad. Can you help me set up your easel?'

He looked up at her, his eyes glistening as if to hear these words had moved and delighted him in equal measure. Abandoning his project without hesitation, he almost jumped up from the table.

'With pleasure, my love, with absolute pleasure!' He clapped, actually clapped!

And so it began.

Present day

'Mummy said I might have to go to a new school,' Apollo stated quite matter-of-factly, as they made their way along the Wandsworth Road.

'Did she?' It was a rotten thought, knowing how he had finally settled and was a lot happier to go into school – not once had a crowbar been required. Lilly thought it best to act dumb, for fear of inadvertently giving the little boy any information or confirmation of a discussion had with his mum.

'If I go to a new school, will you still be able to take me?' He turned to look up at her now, his nose already, at this early hour, with a smudge of something dark on it, his eyes big and hopeful.

'I don't know, darling!' she trilled, fighting the swell of emotion in her breast at the possible ending of this extraordinary privilege, and the fact that he sounded less than enamoured with the idea of her not chaperoning him. She was not, as Glenda had pointed out, his grandma, but it felt so nice. This tiny peep into motherhood that she would always relish. A gift, no less.

That's a good girl, count backwards from ten for me . . .

Ten . . . nine . . . eight . . .

Then nothing.

Nothing.

‘Did you have a dad?’ This question she had not expected, understanding enough from Clodagh’s lack of detail around the topic that it most likely wasn’t a rosy relationship that had produced this fabulous kid.

‘I did, yes. I had a wonderful dad.’ She smiled to think of him, as was always the case. Today, however, it was tinged with the tight pull of emotion in her throat at the thought of her meeting later with the shiny-shoed Joshua Vaughan, wondering what her dad would say about the whole carry-on.

What’s he talking about? It’s our home!

I know, Dad . . . I know . . .

She had seen the young man twice now. The second meeting, he had stood on the doorstep and again urged her to catch up on all previous correspondence, read the emails, the notices and the letter from her local MP, Mr Passmore. She had indeed read the letter, and had felt nothing but disappointment at the words, which were openly admiring and supportive of this *‘exciting new opportunity’* for their postcode.

Lilly supposed he was right. It meant money flowing in and a boost to all the services and leisure activities that would be required to support the influx of people. It made only the briefest mention of the social housing provision, which in her view was minimal and inadequate. Neither did it reference the wants and needs of an older woman who was about to lose her home, or acknowledge the wonderful community that existed at Waide House, which would be lost for ever. Having discussed the possibility of dispersal with Mrs Veerswamy on the stairs, her neighbour had simply sighed wearily and shrugged, saying, ‘What will be will be, Lilly.’ She didn’t blame the woman’s lack of energy for retaliation, understanding that when you were tired, it made for an easier life, going with the flow . . .

It was, however, the first time she had felt the soggy blanket of defeat smother her enthusiasm for the fight ahead. Having carefully crafted an email to the MP, it was a bitter blow to find that the same MP had almost pre-empted her communiqué with a glowing endorsement that spoke of opportunity and progress. Her counterarguments in the face of such support sounded like small fry, inconsequential, petty and personal. '*Since I was a child . . . the only home I've known . . . an homage to 1950s architecture and design . . .*' Not that she was about to roll over, no siree. Mrs Veerswamy might be happy to pack up and move out, hand her life over to fate, but not Lilly. She vowed to write again immediately, to remind the member of parliament that she was his constituent, not some fancy investment company who promised much and couldn't care less about how they achieved their aims but a woman who had lived here her whole life, paid tax here her whole life; did that count for nothing?

'What was your dad's name?' Apollo picked up a stick and brandished it like a sword as he walked, thwacking at invisible thickets to clear their path, for which she was grateful. An act most chivalrous.

'His name was Robert.'

'Robot?' Apollo yelled his delight; she laughed out loud, too, at the suggestion, quite sorry to have to correct him.

'Robert.' She smiled. 'And I was named after him. Part of my name is Roberta.'

'I don't see my dad any more.' The little boy continued to thrash at the invisible undergrowth as they walked, his movements vigorous.

'Well, I know what that feels like. I didn't see my mum.'

This she said to let Apollo know he was not alone in the missing-parent stakes. It wasn't, of course, strictly true; she had seen her mum, not only on the odd occasion Lilly visited the grotty flat on the Tottenham Court Road, but also the couple of times that Jeannie had turned up at Waide House.

We were just passing . . .

The sight of her in the kitchen, sipping tea at the table, the most confusing and conflicting thing. It had taken all of her strength not to run into her mother's arms and weep her relief that Jeannie had finally, finally, come home! It was only the sight of Derek Manners in tow that helped her understand that it was only ever a flying visit, this in turn enough to send a fresh flare of fury through her veins. That beige man in their home! How dare he! And worse still, the fact that her mum had chosen Derek Manners all those years ago and continued to choose him.

Reconciling this never got any easier.

Her mother, throughout the years, lurked like a shadow in Lilly's peripheral vision, making the odd attempt to build a bridge of reconnection. Every time felt like starting over, and always, always, with Derek Manners in attendance. The sight of him hovering in the background in his big-buttoned cardigans and soft-soled shoes made Lilly's flesh crawl. It bothered her that Jeannie never quite figured out that if he hadn't stood there like one of his pot plants in the corner, talking to her mum about what really mattered might have been a tad easier. As the years passed, Lilly, taking her lead from her dad, was consciously never overtly rude to her mother or Derek Manners, but was always intentionally indifferent, cool; never quite able to forget the sight of her dad crying at the kitchen table. This was enough to strengthen the welds of the cage she'd constructed around her heart. And still she carried out her secret ritual each night, thankful for that kiss on a tissue, a thing most dear.

Aged fifteen, she had flatly refused the offer of being a bridesmaid at their eventual wedding. Her mother then made the decision to elope, and she and Derek Manners had, apparently, married at Gretna Green before honeymooning on the Isle of Mull. They had brought her back some shortbread in a tin.

Lilly had binned it, unopened, some months later.

'What's your favourite dinosaur?' Apollo asked.

This was quite standard when it came to their morning commute, the verbal zigzagging from topic to topic.

'Hmm . . . I would have to say T. rex. Fierce, yet also cute, with those tiny little arms. How do you suppose they scratched their noses or brushed their teeth?'

Apollo's loud laugh was her reward.

'Someone would have to do it for them!'

'I think you're right.' She winked.

'My first favourite is a triceratops, and my second favourite is a diplodocus, and my third favourite—'

'How many favourites have you got?' she interjected.

'Lots!' He smiled up at her and she realised his question had been no more than a wonderful ruse to share his knowledge of the beasts. Smart kid.

'Well, you'd better speak quickly. I can see the school gates up ahead . . .'

'Can you take my stick home and keep it safe for me?' He handed her his trusty sword.

'I will. I promise.' She took it from him, again feeling such joy that she could even play the smallest part in this boy's life, quickly followed by a gulp of sadness that it might all be about to change.

She walked briskly home, stick in hand, caring less about the odd looks she got as she made as if to thwack away the invisible thicket.

Clodagh met her in the stairwell as she returned.

'Oh, Lilly! Thank you for taking him, you're a lifesaver – how did he go in?' Clodagh folded the apron for the coffee shop into her tote and pulled her hair into its pineapple on top of her head.

'He was great, no crowbar needed. There was lots of dinosaur chatter and he asked me to keep this stick safe.' She held the thing aloft.

'God, not another stick! We have quite the collection already. Feel free to accidentally lose it.'

'I wouldn't dream of it! A promise is a promise.'

'So, you're seeing the developer guy again today?' Clodagh sighed, clearly aware that it was a delicate topic.

'Yes. Later this morning. I'm conflicted. I want to get it over and done with and let him say his piece, keen to say mine, too, but I'd rather not have to see him at all.'

'I understand that.' Clodagh reached out and placed her hand on the arm of Lilly's floral kimono, the belt of which she had wound around her head and wore as a kind of turban to keep her grey locks at bay.

'I'm also going to write again to our useless MP, Mr Passmore, if nothing else to keep in his conscience, to let him know I'm not just going to roll over.'

'Good for you, Lilly.' The girl hesitated, as if nervous to speak openly. 'They've offered us a flat in Kennington. I have thirty days to decide.'

'Kennington? Not too far away,' Lilly added with optimism, knowing that a twenty-minute walk might as well be another country when it came to daily habits and routine. Wherever they went, it would never be as good as hearing them laugh on the stairs, having Clodagh pop in, or the sound of her knock on the door when she was in search of tea and sympathy.

'I guess not. But if I say yes, it means Apollo can stay at his school.' The young woman spoke with a certain reticence, as if she might be letting the side down. Not that Lilly viewed it in this way, not at all.

'Well, that's a good thing.' Lilly hated the thought of everyone moving on and moving out. Not that she had any intention of doing either. Equally, she knew that a lack of housing security for Clodagh and Apollo meant it was probably smart to take what was on offer and make it permanent. The best thing to allow them to settle.

Mrs Veerswamy had, unsurprisingly, already accepted a move to Bromley to be nearer her son and his wife. And Mr Chaplin in flat four was apparently being moved into residential care at a place in Walworth. Not that she saw much of him any more. Various carers popping in and out gave her updates. He was the second-longest resident of Waide House after herself. She remembered with fondness his late wife, Alma, who used to smoke out of the window, and their daughter, Judy, who moved to Canada decades ago. Alma had bought Lilly a paperweight for her birthday one year. She still had it somewhere. And the kindness of the Chaplins on that day when she had almost fallen apart . . .

'Do you want me to change my shift at work? I can try and wangle it so I'm here for the meeting?' Clodagh's offer was touching. She wished Glenda could have heard it.

'Goodness, no! I can handle Mr Vaughan. Off you pop. Come in for a cuppa later and I'll fill you in.'

'Yes, I will. I'll bring unsold cake!' Clodagh called as she reached the bottom of the stairs.

Lilly placed the stick in the corner of the hallway, propped behind the door. The brochure for *The Fortescue* was on the table. It was impossible to imagine: the shiny kitchens, fancy bathrooms, spacious open-plan living rooms, floor-to-ceiling windows, communal spaces with velvet sofas, the vast chandeliers, and a bloody rooftop swimming pool! All on the footprint of this little development. Were it not her home that was at risk, it would have been nothing but impressive. She put the kettle on to boil, then was drawn by a knock at the door.

'Hello, Mrs Cooper?' a voice she recognised called through the letterbox.

'Mr Vaughan!' She stared at the little metal flap, now raised and through which he spoke.

'Yes.' He seemed a little out of puff. 'I'm aware I'm horribly early.'

'Two hours early,' she pointed out.

'Yes, I know. Thing is, I now have to be in Romford this afternoon and wondered if it might be possible for us to chat now, so I can fit it all in.'

'You see, that bothers me, Mr Vaughan. The assumption that I am simply at home waiting for you to turn up. I might have plans, places to be, people to meet!'

'Do you – have places to be, people to meet?'

'That's not the point!' she snapped. 'I don't have to let you in!'

Lilly Cooper knew her rights.

He stood his ground. 'I am not asking to come in, Mrs Cooper—'

'For the umpteenth time, it's *Miss*!' she interrupted him, riled by so much more than his inability to address her properly and the fact he was in her space, upsetting her morning, bringing this horrible, horrible possibility of having to move out to her front door.

'My apologies, *Miss* Cooper,' he enunciated. 'What I'm proposing is that you let me in so we can talk face to face. Things are tricky enough without us having to converse through the letterbox.'

'I agree, so let's not converse at all!' she suggested, pulling her kimono close around her body, leaning on the wall of the hallway, feeling the bite of the defunct storage heater against the back of her legs. It happened this way sometimes, when she got up too quickly or hadn't eaten; she felt a little light-headed, a bit chilly in her bones. Her eyes sought out the dent in the wainscot where her dad had once chased a visiting mouse with a hockey stick.

Don't kill it! she'd screeched with an emotional teenage sentiment that hadn't really left her, as he lunged towards the tiny furry creature who seemed to be cowering, all wide-eyed and cute. No doubt due to her diversionary shout, he had missed the target and whacked the wood, hence the dent.

I'm not going to kill it, but I'd rather it didn't move in with its fifty siblings! They'd both laughed at another absurd tale that, like so many other memories, became part of the fabric of this flat, this building . . . all lost for ever if it were to be razed to the ground.

'The only way to resolve this issue is to talk about it, Mrs – *Miss* – Miss Cooper! Miss!'

'No, the only way to resolve this issue, Mr Vaughan, is for you to leave me alone! I am not moving, and I am not selling!' she fired. 'Or you could write me another of those threatening letters. I have so many I might wallpaper my kitchen with them!' She smiled at the thought and wondered if she had any wallpaper paste, liking the visual as a way to protest.

'So, you've read them?' His tone suggested this was a win.

'Some of them,' she admitted, unwilling to confess that she had found most of them down the back of the unit in the hallway, gathering dust where they must have toppled.

'You seem like a nice lady. I am only doing my job, but I would like to say that this development is going ahead. We have gone through all the correct legal channels and notified you accordingly. The fact that you have not responded within the time frames allowed for response is not really our fault. Your obstinacy at this stage in proceedings is only making things harder for everyone.'

'I disagree. I think my obstinacy at this stage in proceedings is making things decidedly better for me. If I wasn't obstinate, I'd be preparing to go like Mr Chaplin, Mrs Veerswamy, the lovely Polish couple on the ground floor, and Miss Newman and her son.' She stared at the stick Apollo had given her for safekeeping and briefly imagined poking young Mr Vaughan through the letterbox with it. 'I don't want to be whisked off to a bloody newbuild in the suburbs. I don't want to leave my home! My obstinacy is the only reason I'm still here after all these years and why I will remain here. I'm not going anywhere!'

'So you've said, but the thing is, you can go wherever you want to. No one's suggesting a newbuild in the suburbs. We will honour the market value of your property, which I can tell you is coming in at a very attractive price, well over a million.' It was, she knew, a lot of money, but it wouldn't buy her this flat anywhere else, because there was no other flat like this one and certainly not with the view, her memories, her childhood footprints on the floor, her dad's scent in this hallway, her history in its walls. 'You could even buy a one-bedder in *The Fortescue!*'

She wasn't sure if he spoke in jest, but her anger boiled just the same.

'I don't care about market value. This is my home, it's always been my home, this is where I want to live! I have no intention of selling! And if I ever did, it would be because I had decided the time was right, and not because some upstart developers with a shiny brochure were harassing me and trying to force my hand!'

'We're not harassing you, Mrs Cooper. We just want to talk. Mr Portland himself has said he'd be happy to come and see you, if you would prefer that?'

'Sweet Lord above! I don't want to talk to anyone about it! Don't you ever get bored of going around in circles, Mr Vaughan?'

'Actually, I do. Yes.' He sounded resigned, tired, fed up. It was hard to tell which. 'I have a bad back and having to walk up and down your stairs and bend to holler through this letterbox is doing me no favours at all.'

Lilly smiled. It was funny, human and too bloody bad!

'How did you hurt your back?' She was nosy, curious. He was only young, early thirties if she had to guess.

'I got roped in to play cricket in Greenwich Park last year, fielding. My lack of prowess on the sporting field was no match for my overconfidence. Someone lobbed a ball and I overreached, skidded on wet grass and landed in a heap. I was in agony, and when I looked up my teammates were crowded around me, screaming at me for dropping the ball. I felt like a right chump. I never played again.'

'There's a lesson there, I suppose: don't drop the ball.' She smiled.

'Good advice.' She heard the echo of amusement in his tone.

'Doesn't sound like cricket is your thing.'

'No, I prefer football. Watching it, that is, not playing.'

'Who do you support?'

'Millwall.' She noted the man's silence, as if waiting for her response. 'You not a Millwall fan?'

'No. Not a football fan at all,' she admitted, thinking of Derek Manners . . . *You heard about Lineker?*

'Look, Miss Cooper . . .' Hurrah! He'd got it right, this momentary joy tempered by the fact that they had very quickly, it seemed, got to the 'look' stage, suggesting he might be running out of options and patience. *Look* . . . we need you to comply. *Look* . . . everyone is getting a little sick and tired of your shenanigans. *Look* . . . you're only going to make it harder for yourself in the long run. Well, everyone could sod off! 'I want this to be as straightforward as possible for you,' he continued. 'Once the compulsory purchase notice is issued, things change, and sometimes they change quite quickly.'

'Change how?' The idea of having no legal say and being forced to sell made her feel sick.

'I'm probably telling you more than I should, but we have a project plan that is policed by a kind of traffic-light system. All aspects of the build are either green for go, amber for in train, or red, which indicates a problem. You are red, Miss Cooper. You are one of the only reds and, right now, the project managers, developers, builders, investors, relevant government bodies and local authorities that have okayed the multimillion-pound project are all keen to make the problem go away.' It was odd to be thought of as a problem, although she rather liked the idea of being a thorn in their side. 'This means they will throw money and resources at it, at you. On top of the market value of your property, you are entitled to other compensations to allow for the upheaval, the disruption, the cost of moving—'

'Yet again, Mr Vaughan, it is not about money!'

'But it *can* be about money!' he countered, to her surprise. 'It can be if that amount is so life-changing or it allows you to start over in a perfect place without financial worry.'

'I have the perfect place where I live without financial worry!'

Lilly heard him sigh.

'Please let me in, to talk to you properly, or if not me, then someone from the council, or one of the social welfare team, one of our accountants or one of the project managers for the build, or, as I suggested, Mr Portland himself, any number of people who want to see this . . . this stand-off brought to a swift and mutually satisfactory conclusion.'

Stand-off! It made it sound like the Wild West, like she was some gun-toting renegade holed up in the saloon while the townsfolk quaked and cowered, waiting to see who'd shoot first. This, too, she rather liked, knowing if her old friend Bertie Barnes were here right now he would love her for it! But it wasn't the Wild West. It was SW8, Vauxhall, London. The place where she had been born. The flat she had been born in and the only home she had ever known. And it wasn't the townsfolk who were quaking in their boots, but rather the local authorities and the huge organisations who wanted to get their grubby mitts on the money they'd trouser once the deal was done.

'Look,' he repeated, 'it's not that we don't have sympathy for your situation, nor that I, personally, don't understand your affection for this place—'

'It's not about affection!' Again she interjected. His words made it sound trite. Emotions were a part of it, yes, but it was so much more than that. The people were gone, the stories of her childhood along with them; all that was left was this flat, the bricks and mortar that represented her entire history. 'And it's not about money, not for me anyway. It's about someone, a stranger, coming along, taking a fancy for something that doesn't belong to them, something that has never belonged to them, and deciding to take it away. And that doesn't strike me as right! How can it be right? People should not be able to take anything without permission! What next, taking watches off the wrists of others because they take a liking to them? Grabbing computers from someone's bag rather than saving up to get their own? Forcing people to hand over the keys to their snazzy cars because they'd rather have a Porsche than ride a bike?'

Joshua Vaughan laughed; she heard his throaty chuckle. 'That's exactly what happens all over this city, every day!' he said. 'People get their watches, laptops and cars taken.'

It was her turn to laugh. 'Exactly, Mr Vaughan, *exactly!* Finally it seems we might be on the same page!'

'Miss Cooper, I . . .' He paused, and then seemed to think better of prolonging this discussion. 'We will be in touch.'

She saw the flap of the letterbox fall shut, and then came the sound of his shoes tip-tapping down the beautiful polished concrete stairs as he made his retreat.

'I think I won that one.' She smiled at her reflection in the small mirror by the front door, knowing it was a story she would relish telling Clodagh later, how she'd refused to let him in, and he'd been reduced to shouting through the letterbox, no doubt leaving him feeling, not for the first time, like a bit of a chump.

Then came the old stir of guilt in her veins. Joshua Vaughan wasn't the enemy, but simply their messenger, as he had quite rightly pointed out, only doing his job. She resolved to be a bit nicer to him next time. Knowing there would definitely be a next time.

Lilly sat down at the kitchen table with the intention of resuming her breakfast. But with matters more pressing than her stomach's growl of hunger, she opened up her rather worn, red leather address book, running her finger down the page until she found the number for Denzel Bashington. She had known Denzel for decades, one of Bertie's crowd, and even though he was long retired, and now lived in a lovely garden apartment in Hampstead with his husband, Juan, he was still the only person she turned to for legal advice.

'Denzel.'

'Dah-ling!'

She smiled at the way he had always greeted her, greeted everyone! Lilly explained the dire situation and listened as her old friend gave it some thought.

'The trouble is that these large developers have more money, time and resources than you. They could tie you up in legal knots that would be costly, and you could end up with nothing. They are quite powerful. It's a David and Goliath battle that I'm afraid, in this instance, David nearly always loses. Even if I was still in practice, I would advise you to take the money, take as much money as you can, and run. They won't budge for you, darling Bob. I'm sure that's not what you wanted to hear.'

It was in fact the very worst news. She felt her stomach drop to her boots, now entirely without appetite. How could she possibly run from here? This place that meant more to her than she could say, her *home* . . .

'Not really, but I appreciate your honesty, Denzel.'

'Always. See you soon, dahling.'

'Yep, see you soon.'

This was how they always ended a call, even though they rarely saw each other. It felt nice, the promise; a reminder that there was still some of the old crowd in the city.

The survivors.

1972 – aged 16

The man had a brother, Christopher, who played the euphonium in the same orchestra as her dad. This was how the introduction had come about. Lilly was unsure about the whole idea. I mean, yes, she wanted a job, needed a job, but this sounded a little highbrow and not at all what she had envisaged. Plus it came with its own pressure – the fact that he was connected to her dad, even loosely; she'd never want to let him down, embarrass him.

She had been hoping to maybe work at *HMV* on Oxford Street, thinking that might be cool, and any discount on records was not to be sniffed at, or even a boutique in Carnaby Street, somewhere like *Lady Jane*. Her dad, however, seemed keen for her to take advantage of his connection.

'Some of those places in the West End attract all sorts. You can't be too careful.' She had no idea what 'all sorts' meant, and chose not to confess that she was eager to find out. 'Bertie is a legend and a gent. If he takes you on, and there's no guarantee he will' – her dad extended his index finger – 'it might just be the making of you.'

This in turn invited another question: was he saying she was unmade now, and what the heck did *that* mean?

Lilly went along for the interview, half hoping she didn't get it, half hoping she did. And having stopped en route at *Moody's* – the café on the corner – now stood before her potential employer with a hot, bitter espresso sloshing in her veins, which had made her feel a bit fizzy. In a good way.

'So, Chris said you live on the banks of the river, you lucky old thing!'

'Yes, in Vauxhall.'

'Oh, you poor love!' The man shook his head, fingers splayed on his chest.

Lilly didn't know if he was being funny, and so continued, 'Yes, it's a small block.'

Bertie Barnes, the gallery owner, gasped and now clutched his chest as if mortally wounded. 'No! No! NO! Do not ever call it a block! Not ever! That word is enough to bring me out in hives, and I'm far too pretty for that. You live in a small development, darling, a small, *bijou* development.'

'What's the difference?' She was confused.

'The fact you need to ask tells me there is much work to be done with you!'

She laughed to hide her nerves.

'And you like art, Bob?' the man asked as she looked around the walls at the carefully curated exhibition of monochrome minimalism that put her in mind of zebras and Everton Mints. Wisely, she chose not to share this astute observation. Her love of art stemmed from all she saw from the riverbank outside the small, *bijou* development where she lived. What had started as a means to appease and please her dad had quickly turned into her favourite obsession.

If Lilly had her way, she would quite like to spend each and every day sitting on the towpath with her easel, capturing her view from the south side of the river. It was her happy place, and there was something quite hypnotic about staring at the water, always starting with a small wave across to the other side, of course.

Seconds became minutes that slipped into hours and she, blissfully unaware of time, felt nothing but peace, as if this were the spot where she belonged, doing the thing that brought her joy. Becoming an artist had also piqued her interest in art. Her dad had been right: in this city there was an abundance of galleries for her to indulge her passion.

'I do, yes, and it's—' She tried to interject, to explain her name was actually Lilly-Bob, but he wasn't listening.

'Good! Good!' The man clapped, his turquoise chiffon scarf floating up from his neck and settling again on the shoulder of his pale safari jacket as he turned quickly on his built-up heel, almost twirling. He clasped his hands under his chin, his large garnet signet ring looking way too heavy for his pinky. This observation, too, she kept to herself. He was a handsome man, putting her in mind of David Cassidy. 'So, who's your favourite? *What's* your favourite? Tell me all!' he asked with an enthusiasm that was infectious.

'Oh!' It felt very much like being put on the spot. 'My favourite is my dad, I guess. He's great, kind and funny, an artist too' – she nodded as if this might give her some pedigree – 'and he loves music. We always have music playing. And what' – she tapped her teeth with her index finger – '*what* is my favourite? I guess reading followed by napping, I'm big into naps, but what I love most is sitting by the river, and I paint too. But I'm not as good as my dad.'

Bertie Barnes stopped and stared at her. 'You sweet, sweet thing. I meant who is your favourite artist, what is your favourite painting or medium?'

'Oh, oh!' She felt her cheeks flush red and was glad no one else was around to witness her humiliation. 'I'm a bit nervous. And I had a coffee at *Moody's,*' she offered by way of explanation. 'Sorry.'

'Never apologise, Bob. You're quite delightful, is what you are!'

His lovely manner helped put her at ease, erasing some of her embarrassment.

'My favourite artist changes, but at the moment I am fascinated by the work of Emma Amos. Her paintings have life, movement, colour; I feel like I know her through them. Some art feels anonymous, don't you think? People claim it, sign it, and it might be wonderful, thought-provoking, beautiful, detailed, but it doesn't necessarily allow you to get to know the artist. Doesn't make you *feel* . . . But Amos's work is like looking at her family album, her diary, her soul . . .' Aware she'd gone into a mini monologue, she took a breath and stared at Bertie. 'Do you know what I mean?'

'I do indeed, my dear, and so will my clients here at *B'Art*. Always trust that voice of instinct when it comes to what you like and don't like. A piece only has to appeal to you – you can't give a hoot what anyone else thinks, remember that. I think you'll do splendidly! Welcome aboard!'

'Thank you!' She felt the explosion of joy in her chest: she had only gone and got the job! Her dad would be over the moon.

'So what kind of painter are you? Is it a labour of love, or are you a tortured artiste? Is it a hobby, or do you feel the need to improve?'

'I'm not sure. I want to get better. I'm still figuring it out. I can paint, but I'm not proud of my work, not yet,' she admitted.

'You need to relax into it, let the brush move, let the paint create what your eyes see, don't overthink it. Allow the picture to form in a way that is natural, capturing the way it makes you feel, so much so that it's almost a surprise to you when you see the finished article. Does that make sense?'

'Yes.' She nodded, even though it didn't, not at all.

'Now, first things first, what are you like at making tea?'

'Good, I think.' She beamed, knowing no one had ever complained about the strength of her brew.

'I think I'll be the judge of that. Now, go and put the kettle on. I want to hear more about your hobbies. Napping sounds fascinating!'

She laughed loudly at his sarcasm, falling more than a little bit in love with the handsome gallery owner. It was after they had sunk three large mugs of tea that Bertie produced a packet of Garibaldis, which they unashamedly dunked while sitting in the back room cum kitchenette.

'You gotta boyfriend?' he asked casually. How she loved their chat! Like they hadn't just met, like they were friends.

'No!' She snorted, insinuating that she was not exactly girlfriend material.

'Well, that will all change when you get to art college. I can sense it, you are ready to bloom!'

'Maybe.' She shrugged, unwilling to admit, knowing how crackers it sounded, that she shied away from romance. Because to have a special someone would feel cruel, knowing her dad was alone while her mum cavorted in a flat above a shop on the Tottenham Court Road. She figured that if she, too, were to have a great love, it would mean he was the only one without it, and she hated the thought of making him feel that way. It wasn't a topic that reared its head at home, knowing her dad still thought she was a baby in some ways. A baby with a job! The thought thrilled her.

'I have!' Bertie danced his feet on the blue linoleum floor.

'You have what?' She bit her Garibaldi, having lost the thread.

'A boyfriend!'

'Oh!' It wasn't his homosexuality that was a surprise, but rather his comfort in expressing it. She felt it was both a privilege and a tie that would bind them closer, in the way that sharing secrets often did. It made her feel like a grown-up.

'His name is Jack. He's beautiful – I mean, stunningly beautiful! He works in fashion and is entirely unsuitable; from

Croydon, of all places.' He pulled a face. She nodded but was unsure why being a Croydon resident made Jack unsuitable. 'I mean, it's so provincial! Net curtains, knitted loo-roll holders, pampas grass and Viennese Whirls resting on a saucer! Can you imagine?'

'I really can't.' She spoke the truth, without the first clue as to what he was talking about.

'I like you, Bob.'

'Thank you. I like you too.'

'I do worry, though, that we sound like an old music-hall act. Bertie and Bob!'

She laughed out loud. 'What would our act be?'

'Oh, it would have to be a song-and-dance number – I'm seeing a top hat, fishnets, hot pants, high heels . . . and God only knows what you'd wear!'

This time she laughed until her eyes watered.

'Another cup of tea, Bob?'

'Why not!' She lifted her mug.

'Well, you know where the kettle is – what am I, the waitress?' Bertie scoffed, and already she knew that she loved her job and was very glad her dad had made her apply.

Her walk home from Pimlico had been a joy, filled as she was with the lingering delight of success in her veins, and far more caffeine than she was used to consuming.

'I'm home!' she yelled as she kicked off her clog sandals and hung her suede fringed bag on the coat peg.

'In the kitchen!' her dad called out. 'Just making a quick bite to eat before I head out. We're playing at the Guildhall tonight!'

'How fancy!' She beamed.

'Well, don't keep me in suspense, how did it go?' He looked up at her, pausing mid sandwich-making, the butter knife in his hand.

'I got the job!' She jumped up and down on the spot.

'Hey! Congratulations! That's marvellous news! This calls for a celebration! How about we go for a walk tomorrow evening and get gelato?'

'I'd love that, Dad.' It was a treat, to wander the riverbank up towards Westminster Bridge, where there was a late-night Italian deli that served the most glorious gelato. Her dad always had the Sicilian lemon, while she couldn't get enough of the pistachio. Again she thought of Bertie's question about her non-existent love life, wondering what it might be like to walk the riverbank with a boyfriend, to show him the Italian deli and to judge him if he chose a flavour she disliked, like tutti-frutti.

'What will your duties entail?' He was all ears.

'I'm not entirely sure, but making tea for definite, chatting to Bertie and I think sitting at the little desk, helping answer any questions. I'm making it up, Dad! We didn't really talk about it in great detail!'

'So what did you talk about?'

Bertie's boyfriend . . . Viennese Whirls . . . Our music-hall act . . .

'Just general chit-chat. The gallery is lovely!'

'It's a big day, Lilly-Bob. Your first job! Are you going to give your mum a ring and let her know?'

There was a telephone box right outside the back of their building. Whether still emboldened from her caffeine-fuelled time spent with Bertie while speaking so freely on matters of a most adult nature, or whether still feeling the wrath towards her mother, having recalled how she was living her lovey-dovey life with Derek Manners while her dad did his best here, was neither here nor there. The words tumbled from her mouth just the same, without consideration.

'Why would I call her? The bitch!'

It wasn't even a word she used! The atmosphere changed in a second. Her dad's face was thunderous. And to her horror she saw his hand flatten, rise and head towards her face. She gasped, her tears coming instantly, and her face crumpled. He stopped short of contact, curling his shaking fingers into his palm, his face flushed, his own eyes misting. It was a terrible, terrible moment. A life-altering thing that she was sure her dad would remember for ever, as would she.

'Don't you ever, *ever* refer to your mother in that way, not ever! Do you hear me?' His voice hoarse, his throat tight, spit flying from his mouth, emotions running high, sandwich abandoned.

Lilly nodded, watching, quite afraid as he walked towards the sink and leaned on it, visibly shaken.

'I'm sorry.' Her words were whispered from a mouth contorted with shame and regret.

He looked up at her then, his eyebrows knitted in confusion and his lips quivering with all they tried to contain.

'She's your mum.' He spoke quietly now, calmly, and she was glad of it, watching as he wiped his mouth with the back of his shaking hand. 'She is the only mum you have. She gave birth to you. She made you.'

'I know.'

'You don't get to choose, Lilly. None of us do. We don't get to choose our parents. Sometimes we get lucky, sometimes not so much, but there's not a whole lot we can do about that.'

'I got lucky, Dad. I got you.' Her tears fell steadily now. It was both asking for forgiveness and giving it too.

'That word.' He sighed and rubbed his eyes with his thumb and forefinger. 'The B word – there is no male equivalent. A terrible word, I think, and not one I would ever want to hear directed at you or your mum. The two women I love.'

'Do you miss her, Dad?' It felt like the time to ask, to break the rule that no one had set, to touch on the subject they steadily avoided and had done for years.

'Do I miss her?' He gave a rueful smile. 'With every breath I take, every minute of every day.'

'Did you ever think about trying to get her back?' She had often thought about this, whether he had given up on her too easily, as easily as she had given up on them.

He took his time forming a response, as if even the recollection was almost too painful.

'I tried very hard.' He swallowed. 'I wrote to her, I begged her, I visited, I sat in a chair while your mum made tea in a strange kitchen, and I could see her bed jacket hanging on the back of the open bathroom door. I could see lamb chops defrosting on the sink drainer, that she would cook for his tea. I saw the ring on her finger, the wedding band I'd given her replaced by a big old sparkly number. Yes, I tried. But as she explained to me, it was like someone had shown her this other lovely life, a bright life, a shiny life, and it was a life she wanted. And that was that.'

'I thought we had a lovely, bright, shiny life when she was here.' The words left her mouth like a sigh, coasting out on a breath of relief as she opened up Pandora's box.

'Me too.' His voice broke and he took his time, speaking slowly, meaningfully. 'Your mum is not a bad woman and not a bad mother. We don't have to understand her choices, but we do have to respect them, and her.'

'I'm sorry, Dad,' she apologised again, speaking with clarity now.

'I'm sorry too.' His expression was pained, as if recalling, as was she, the flat of his hand travelling towards her face. 'One thing I've learned, Lilly, is that sometimes the kindest thing to do for those we love is to let them go.'

She knew that she'd remember this day for always or, more specifically, three things from this day. One: how great it felt to be offered a job. Two: that her dad had almost hit her. And three: that it made her dislike her mother even more, knowing that her dad had loved his wife enough to let her go, no matter if his heart was broken and he missed her with every breath he took . . .

Present day

'I don't want to move.' Apollo picked up a thin stick and pointed it like a sabre as they walked along the pavement on the way to school. It had obviously been on his mind, as they had returned to the topic. Lilly's heart flexed for him, knowing how unnerved she was by the whole fiasco, and she had a grown-up brain, better able, allegedly, to make sense of it all.

'I know, but very often the things we don't want to happen or don't look forward to turn out to be for the best!' she added with false enthusiasm, hoping it might be infectious, or at least reassuring. Careful, too, not to negate or invalidate his fears. Trying to think of a suitable example. And failing.

'I don't know how to get back to our old house. The house where my dad used to live with us. My mum says we can't go and see him, but I left some of my cars there in the cupboard. Two of them were my favourites.'

'I see.' Lilly didn't know how to respond, not without it seeming like she might be prying, something she would never do.

'He doesn't know where I am now.' Apollo spoke with a wobble to his bottom lip that tore at her heart.

'I remember my dad telling me that I would always be able to find my house because all I had to do was find *Big Ben* or walk towards the river and follow it. He told me that Old Mother

Thames would always lead me back, all the way home! And so even if you have to move, you can always find your way back to me.' She hoped it helped in some small way, to know that not everyone was disappearing from his life.

Apollo looked up at her. 'But what if they've knocked your building down? How would I find you then?'

It was both heart-warming and emotionally galling, how aware he was for a little one; her sadness bloomed again at the possibility of disruption to the family unit that meant the world to her.

'Well, that's the thing. You know I'm outside on most days, painting the river! So you'll always be able to find me in my usual spot.' She tried to envisage a situation where she might paint on the towpath with a stack of Polo mint apartments rising up behind her, an image almost too awful to conjure.

'Will you look after my stick for me?'

'I will. I promise.' Lilly took it from his little hand, as was customary, happy to place it in the corner of her hallway with the growing collection, each one representative of a precious journey taken with this child.

'Bye, Lilly-Robot!' He giggled as he made his way through the school gates, the funny little thing.

'Bye, Apollo!'

She relished the walk home, lifting her hand in a wave at the owner of the cat who liked to survey his kingdom from the lid of the wheelie bin. It happened in these pockets of the big city: streets became villages, and neighbours smudged the boundary between acquaintance and friend; it helped everyone feel as if they belonged. This thought only helped muster her enthusiasm in the fight for Waide House. She would not roll over and fling her flat keys in the direction of Portland and bloody Montague, she would not!

◆ ◆ ◆

'Bit of a chilly wind!' Glenda joined her on the towpath and pulled her soft cotton scarf closed at her neck.

'Yes, but that's why I wanted to paint today. Look at the way the water's moving. It's like a giant is blowing on the surface with a straw!' She chuckled as the ripples moved quickly in a uniform way. 'Plus, I'm used to it, Glend. I've got my layers on. This ain't my first rodeo!' She wiggled her fingers inside the fingerless gloves. It felt easier to joke, to laugh, instead of giving in to the heave of distress in her chest at the thought that her days here were numbered, that she might just be helpless, entirely without power when it came to the future of her home and whatever might come next.

'Or you could just paint on a warmer day.'

'I could! But I don't let anything put me off, not weather or fear!'

'Fear?' Glenda stared at her with her mouth downturned.

'Yep, often when I was sitting here, particularly when I was younger, I got the feeling someone was staring at me.'

'They were probably thinking, there's that nutjob again, sitting in the same bloody spot, painting in all weathers!'

'Possibly, dearest.' Lilly smiled, knowing the ease of their ribbing came from a place of companionable closeness. 'But it was odd. You know that sensation when you're aware of someone's eyes on you – it was a lot like that. I figured it might have been someone in the flats opposite who studied the water as I did – it made sense. I remember telling my dad, and he agreed it was that. Which is odd, because I'd always waved at the other side of the river, still do sometimes.'

'Who are you waving at, you dozy mare?' Her friend chuckled too.

'No one in particular, just saying hi to whoever might be looking back.' She didn't want to explain further, not when Glenda considered her actions those of a dozy mare.

'Well, you're braver than me. The thought that someone was watching me' – Glenda shuddered – 'that would have scared the shite out of me, put me off for life. I'd have definitely found a different place to paint!'

Lilly huffed at the thought; her friend had kind of missed the point. 'But that's the thing, I don't want to paint anywhere else. It's all here for me: the variation in light, weather and conditions that feed my compulsion. Different every day. And it *is* a compulsion, no doubt, like collecting something. People get obsessed, don't they? They want them all, worrying they might be missing out on part of their collection, needing to fill the gaps! This is no different. I want to capture as many facets of this river as I can from this point right here. That said, in heavy rain I give it a miss, and on the very rare occasion we have snow, but other than that? I set up my old easel and my camping stool and away I go.'

'You must have thousands of these pictures, Lil.'

'No. I only keep some. A few of the better ones go to the gallery. They sell quite well. Most canvasses I reuse over and over, and some I dispose of or gift to charity shops.'

'What will you do, love, when you have to move away? Come back and set up in front of the building site?' This, too, was something she loved and hated about her friend, her directness. It meant topics others might consider too sharp or painful to voice were flung from her mouth without too much care or attention. On the positive side, Lilly never had to wonder what her friend was thinking or feeling and always knew where she stood. It was also a topic that she and Apollo had raised earlier in the day. Not only did Lilly hate the thought of it; she also feared that putting this acceptance, this proposed solution, out into the universe might help it come to fruition, which was the last thing she wanted.

'Truthfully? I can't think about it too much.' She took a slow breath. 'I know that might sound cowardly or like I'm putting my head in the sand, but I don't let myself dwell on it. I'm trying to remain confident that I won't be going anywhere.'

'Norm says that once these decisions have been made and palms have been crossed with silver, the powers that be rarely change their minds or go back on it.'

'Did he now?' She widened her eyes at yet more wisdom from Norman. 'Well, I'm not going to go without a fight.'

'I told Norm, if you leave Waide House, it'll be like the ravens leaving the Tower, the whole bloody place would fall down, and he said it'd save the builders a few bob in demolition costs!'

'That's funny.' She spoke without the faintest whiff of humour, glancing back at the building and trying to imagine it as just bricks and rubble. She felt sick at the prospect. The topic of demolition was not one she could find amusing, not at all. It made no sense to her that this place, its history, her history, could be gone in a blink! A concept that she felt diminished her very existence.

'He did have one good idea though.'

'Let's hear it.' Lilly dipped the brush into the murky khaki she'd mixed in her porcelain pot and dabbed it on to the canvas, trying to recreate the dappled surface of the muddy water.

'He said you should paint placards, put them in your big window. Make a fuss. There's always plenty of people walking past or on the river.'

Lilly turned to look at her friend, feeling the glow of enthusiasm at this rather great idea. Maybe Norman wasn't short on good advice after all. She pictured him then, way back when, reaching out to lay his hand on her arm, his voice steady . . . *Life goes on, Lil.* A good man.

Make a fuss . . .

'That's actually a really good idea!'

'He does have them occasionally.' Glenda winked at her.

'Come on, let's get packed up. No time like the present. I've got black paint, and we can have them dried and up in the window by this afternoon!'

Lilly knew they must have looked quite comical, the two of them, grabbing the paraphernalia that ensured a comfortable session by the river and hurrying along the path, back to the entrance of Waide House with easels, paints, collapsible camping stools, her large Thermos, a jar of water, and her box of brushes under their arms.

'Slow down! Bloody hell!' Glenda called, lagging behind.

But Lilly did not slow down; she was on full throttle and raring to go. This idea was the fuel that the fire in her belly needed! Placards! It was genius!

With everything dumped in her flat, and layers removed, Lilly called to her friend, 'What are we going to write?' She pulled a large canvas from the cupboard in what was now her art studio, formerly her bedroom, and placed it on the kitchen table.

Glenda clicked her fingers. 'How about *Local homes for local people?*'

'Oh no, no, no.' She shook her head. 'That sounds horrifically close to the racist sentiments I hear on the radio. Soundbites offered by morons who don't understand how this melting pot of a city works, how it's always worked. No, I think we direct it at the developers, something like . . .' She exhaled, trying to think. 'Something like *Portland and Montague – dismantling our history, destroying our architecture, selling out the poor, putting profit before people,* and, erm—'

'If you don't mind me saying, Lil,' her friend cut her off, 'you're either going to need a much bigger canvas or a much shorter slogan. And besides, you're not poor.'

Lilly laughed out loud; there it was again, one of Glenda's favourite topics. 'No, but a lot of the people I care about in this development are. You're probably right about the slogan. What would you go for?'

'Hmm . . .' Her friend took a seat at the table. 'I'd keep it short and say something like *Don't knock down my home. I like it here.*'

Lilly smiled. 'Do you know, that's not half bad.' She liked the simplicity of it, with its twist of drama. It might make people think. If they, too, liked their home, would they want it knocked down? 'Let's give it a go!' She prised the lid from the black paint pot and gave it a stir.

'You should call the papers too. They're good at making a fuss.'

Lilly clapped. 'You're right, Glend, they are!'

Her enthusiasm helped partially erase the sense of doom that had dogged her since Mr Vaughan's last visit. It felt good to be doing something – anything! Other than sitting and waiting for the axe to fall.

'No time like the present!' Abandoning the tin of paint, she rushed to the desk in the lounge, opened her computer and searched for the number for the *Gazette* . . .

◆ ◆ ◆

'Call me Jake.' The journalist walked straight towards the window. She liked his Che Guevara T-shirt. He reminded her of the long-haired philosophical wannabe boys of her youth. 'Wow!'

'Yep.' She smiled.

'Wowsers!'

'Yes.' She understood.

'Flippin' marvellous! That's some view!'

'It really is. One of a kind, a bit like Waide House.' She extended her hand, encouraging the young man to take a seat on the sofa as she sat in the chair opposite, hoping to keep him on track and to get this interview over and done with. It had felt like a great thing to call the paper when she was high on the adrenaline of a good idea and with sugar fizzing in her blood. She and Glenda had, between them, eaten almost an entire packet of custard creams. Now, however, as she sat opposite the journalist, who took out a laptop and flipped up the screen, she wasn't quite so sure.

'Do you mind if I take notes as we chat?'

'I don't mind at all.' She folded her hands into the folds of her voluminous green linen skirt, which she had paired with a thin, cotton, mustard-coloured jersey over a green and gold striped T-shirt.

'So . . .' Face set, back straight, he tip-tapped on the keys as if trying to injure them, each stroke loud, severe and, in her view, entirely unnecessary. His art, the opposite of gently waving a brush over canvas, and she was thankful that it wasn't hers, knowing she'd find this frenzied bashing quite stressful as an occupation. 'I'm thinking the angle is *Original resident booted from home to make way for luxury development by big-money investors* – kind of thing?' He looked up at her.

'Erm . . .' Not for the first time, Lilly doubted her decision to involve the press, concerned by the man's lack of subtlety. 'It's not so much about the big-money investors. I mean, please, yes! Big-money investors, *do* come and invest in our postcode! We need an improved library, we need breakfast clubs and after-school clubs for little ones, we need sporting facilities for our teens, literacy classes for adults, training and job opportunities, you name it! There's much we could do with a great big whack of investment!' She sat back in the chair, watching as Jake stared at the ceiling, his fingers mid-air as if wanting to bash away on the keys but unsure of where to strike.

He tried again. 'But your gripe is that you're being booted out?'

'*Gripe* puts me in mind of something mealy-mouthed and possibly sounds a little bit woe-is-me, and *booted* is a curiously violent word that I don't really feel applies here.' She smiled at him.

'What would you suggest?' He folded his arms across his chest.

She couldn't quite tell if he was genuinely asking for her assistance or being sarcastic.

'I might go for something like *coerced* – it feels a lot like coercion. And possibly *railroaded*. I might not like them, but the developers have been very fair, really. Offering me the market value of my home and giving me notice, which I ignored, but that's not really their fault, the letters fell down the back of my cupboard. I don't really like admin.' She paused. 'And Mr Vaughan, who they send to talk to me, is only doing his job, a nice enough young man, I'm sure. And I do rather rile him, made him talk to me through the letterbox, despite him having a bad back on account of his cricketing debacle.'

Jake looked at her through narrowed eyes, and she didn't like his scrutiny. It felt unfavourable, and that was never nice, especially in her own home. 'So, just to clarify' – this time there was no mistaking his sarcasm – 'you say you don't have a gripe, are not being booted anywhere, the developers have been very fair, and you get on with the chap they send to deliver the bad news. So what are you, Mrs Cooper, slightly miffed?' He made the suggestion with a downturn to his mouth.

'It's Miss.' She held his eyeline. 'And I'm slightly more than miffed. *Miffed* rather suggests mild irritation and not the level of distress I feel about the whole thing. I can, for example, tell that you, Jake, are slightly *miffed* by my dislike of your original angle, which makes you seem inflexible, precious and oversensitive, but that can't be helped. Far better we get it right, don't you think?'

'Yes, Miss Cooper.' He sounded like a child who had been suitably admonished.

'What I feel about this whole upheaval is a lot closer to grief. I think anyone who has experienced such a thing will tell you that it's a rather grinding state of affairs, a slow drip of desolation that colours even the brightest day with sadness and taints the taste of good food.' She pictured her mum at the countertop, before Jeannie had taken a hammer to their family, dishing up supper with the radio playing, and her dad, sitting at the kitchen table, reading the very newspaper for which Jake worked, and felt a lump forming in her throat. 'It wraps your whole world and fills you with a sorrow that feels permanent. A sorrow that *is* permanent, no matter that it might dilute a little over time. This feels a lot like that. This is where I live, where I have always lived. The rooms in which I have celebrated every birthday, each Christmas and even a funeral. I've laughed here, cried here, eaten nearly all of my meals here, dreamed here, slept here, watched TV, done my homework, read books, fallen in love, and vaulted the line from child to teen to very old woman. All of it within these walls. And it happened in a blink.' She clicked her fingers and he stared at her, his shoulders dropped a little, his arms unfolded, his stance not quite so rigid. 'I am bereft at the thought that not only do I lose my home, my memories, my history, but this city loses this wonderful, untouched example of 1950s architecture and the community loses nine flats in which eight families, other than my own, can live at an almost affordable rate. I think it would be a great loss in so many ways. So, yes, I'm more than miffed, Jake.'

He tip-tapped a little more gently now, and she was glad of it.

'I suppose' – he looked up at the ceiling again – 'that those in favour of the development would point out that the hike in property prices once the new apartments start selling is good for those who own around here. A rising tide raises all ships, and all that.'

'I suppose they would. But it's not those who own property I fear for, Jake.' She looked him in the eye. 'Indeed, I own this property, and as you say will undoubtedly gain financially, but things can't only be about money, can they? Surely there has to be greater consideration of the wider context? It's about those who just about manage, those without housing security, those who in a rising tide fear drowning!' Her emotions rose at the thought of Clodagh and Apollo living away from her, upsetting this lovely little routine and the circle of support that they had formed. She wondered how many more sticks might clutter up the hallway yet, knowing she would treasure and appreciate each and every one.

'I guess the counterargument might also be that the money the authorities get could be spent on social housing and other projects?'

Lilly gave a soft laugh. 'It *could*, Jake, and I might win the Turner Prize.'

'Have you a piece under consideration for the prize?' This seemed to have caught his interest. A bigger story, no doubt.

'No. And I guess that kind of sums up my point.'

'Can I take some photographs of your sign in the window?' He pointed over his shoulder. 'I can do it from the walkway.'

'I'm not sure.' She was, in that minute, mistrustful of how Jake might represent her and her story and decided she'd rather not have her placard, her window, her address and her business splashed all over the *Gazette,* or worse, the internet. With only herself to blame for getting caught up in the moment, she regretted the enthusiasm with which she'd made the call, aware she might have wasted his time and her own.

The journalist closed the lid of his laptop and reached for his rucksack, from which he'd magicked it earlier.

'If I'm being honest, I'm not sure there's going to be enough meat on the bones here, Miss Cooper.'

'Maybe not.' She exhaled with something that felt a lot like relief.

'And if you want my advice, I'd take the money and run! These big development companies have pockets stuffed with cash. I'd take them for every penny, fill my bank account and get out of the city. It's a filthy shithole, really, sinking fast. I've been here for four years, and I've seen the decline.'

'Four years, eh?' She surreptitiously mocked the young pup.

'Yep, the Tube and buses are disgusting, crowded cesspits, the air quality is rotten, there's people everywhere, all crammed in, and don't start me on the cost of everything.' He tutted, reminding her of Glenda. 'Yep.' He zipped up his bag and slung it over his shoulder. 'A nice little cottage away from the masses, a smallholding in the countryside, a dog, a real fire, a vegetable patch and a decent village pub, that'd do me!'

It made her smile, his lack of populist sentiment, very un-Che.

'That's very kind of you, Jake, but I don't.' She walked into the hallway, knowing he would follow.

'You don't what?' The man seemed to have lost the thread as she opened the front door wide and stood back to allow him to pass.

'I don't want your advice. But if I might give *you* some in return, it would be this: be nicer about this city, this postcode, this area about which you write and from where your readers come. This area, in which I have seen so much change and upheaval, watching her go from an almost forgotten industrial heartland with the gasworks slap bang in the middle of it to a place full of life and possibilities! A place about which those of us who are born and bred here really care. Some of us love it here, absolutely love it, because it's all we've ever known, and every inch of pavement, every tree, every corner, each pigeon, every crowded corner and grubby bus, even the bloody traffic, we love it, because it's our village, our home.'

'Actually' – he raised his hand – 'that might be the angle.'

'Goodbye, Jake.' Lilly closed the door before he had the chance to expand. 'Tea, that's what I need, a lovely cup of tea!'

It was as the kettle boiled that she cursed herself for having listened to Glenda, who had listened to Norman. 'Bloody Norman!' She laughed, surprised that her laughter quickly turned to tears that slipped down the back of her throat and tasted a lot like defeat. It had felt easy to be bold in front of the stranger, but now, alone in her home, her gut folded with the agonising thought of having to leave.

'I don't want to go!' she whispered into the ether. 'I don't want to go anywhere!' she managed, her mouth contorted with sadness.

'Lilly!' This time it was a different and far more endearing voice that called through the letterbox.

Quickly she sniffed away her distress, wiped her eyes on the hem of her skirt and rushed to the door to find Apollo and Clodagh.

'Mum said we could come and see you!' He raced in and ran around the hall, his very presence a tonic that could lift the most melancholic of moments.

'I should warn you, we are full of beans tonight!' Clodagh, who already looked a little tired, pulled a face. 'He wanted to come and see you, but if you're busy . . .'

'Never too busy, darling.' She ushered the young woman in. 'Just making tea!'

'I think I sensed it, heard the kettle boiling from the road.' Clodagh took off her coat and laid it on the floor, placing her bag on it. 'Are you okay, Lilly?'

Lilly knew her face no doubt carried evidence of her tears.

'I am fine! Nothing a good strong cuppa can't cure!'

Clodagh seemed to take her cue and smiled tightly. 'How was your day?'

'Oh, a bit of a dud. I didn't get much painting done, Glenda distracted me with a bonkers scheme that fell flat on its face, and it's all passed in a flash!'

'Can I watch TV?' Apollo jumped up and down on the spot.

'Is that okay?' Clodagh asked.

'Of course! But I only have the regular channels, nothing fancy or extra.'

'That's all we have,' Clodagh reminded her. 'I think the more there is to watch, the more he'd want to watch, and I try and keep him away from it if I can help it.'

'Quite right too.' Lilly popped the TV on and watched Apollo kick off his shoes with the Velcro fastening, revealing his odd socks, one stripey, one with spots, before sinking back into her velvet beaded cushions and popping his finger into his mouth. Clodagh was in the kitchen and had already fetched the mugs. She liked the ease of the woman in her home, actions that went beyond friendship and spoke of a closeness that verged on family. Those darned tears threatened again; she was aware that losing Waide House meant she would lose all of this too. 'Apollo asked me this morning how he would find his way back here if he needed to once you've moved. He also said' – she kept her voice low and leaned in – 'that he'd like to go back to the house his dad lived in as he's left some of his favourite cars there.'

'Oh.' Clodagh laid her arms and head on the countertop as if weakened by the topic. 'The reason I don't talk about it, Lilly, is because I'm embarrassed. No, worse than that, I'm ashamed.'

'Shame is a hard one to wash off the skin.' This much she did know. 'It's your life, your history, and is no one's business but your own. I didn't raise the subject to pry or to get you to open up. You don't have to share your past with me or anyone else, Clodagh, not ever. But know that if you do need someone to talk to, this is a no-judgement zone. We all have our secrets to bear.'

I'm sorry . . . I am so sorry . . . We were not meant to be, you and I . . .

And then the lights faded, and the voice echoed,

That's a good girl, count backwards from ten for me . . .

And then . . . nothing.

'I was kind of, kind of, lied to. And I fell for it, hook, line and sinker.'

'You won't be the first or the last.' This, too, she knew to be true.

'I worked with him, Apollo's dad.'

'At the sports shop?'

'Yep.' Clodagh straightened. 'He was my section manager, nice-looking, nice to me, nice to everyone, really. He was my first proper boyfriend, and I was just' – she blew out through bloated cheeks – 'I was like obsessed! Completely obsessed, convinced there'd never been a love like it. He lived with his parents and so we'd go to mine or go out and he was with me all of the time, like *all* of the time. I loved it. When I got pregnant it was just a lovely thing. A lovely, unplanned thing, but I was happy, we were happy.'

'And what a joy he is!' They listened to the sound of Apollo roaring his laughter from the sofa at something on TV. Lilly, even at her age, felt the twinge of loss in her breast – a child's laughter, something that was never going to fill this flat after she moved out, this flat that Portland and Montague wanted to reduce to rubble.

'He is, he's everything. Sab moved in with us – that's his name. And I've never been happier. We were in this bubble, the three of us. I'd wake up in the middle of the night and feel this kind of panic, because it was too perfect. I had it all – this man I adored, our beautiful baby asleep in the crib next to us, and a little flat that felt like home because we were in it, a proper family. Truth is, I felt a bit smug, knowing I was already doing better than my mum ever did. There was no chance of me going clubbing or on holiday with a stranger – nothing like that. I just wanted to be at home, with Sab and our baby. I remember feeling so content. It was perfect.'

Lilly smiled; it sounded lovely, idyllic, and she remembered waking up in a bed in Chelsea with a similar glow of contentment, wanting nothing more, not ever . . .

'Then one day' – Clodagh paused; her mouth had gone a little dry – 'Sab was at work and there was a knock on the door and this woman was standing there, his fiancée, and she was beautiful and smart and—' She caught her breath as if even the memory of it was shocking. 'She told me their wedding was booked, planned, a big affair, and that she'd followed him to the flat, had her suspicions, apparently.'

'Oh, Clodagh.' Lilly's heart squeezed for the young woman, understanding what it felt like to have happiness ripped from under you.

'She didn't know about Apollo, and I didn't tell her. What would have been the point, other than destroy her, destroy them?'

'That took some strength.'

Clodagh nodded.

'I packed up all his stuff, and when he came back from work I handed him his bags and I didn't say a word, not one. He just took the bags and started crying, and I got the feeling he had been expecting it, waiting for the hammer to fall. He told me he was trapped and all kinds of rubbish, but he lied to me, Lilly, and he was lying to her, lying to his family, lying to Apollo. She had showed me pictures of their engagement party, and it was bigger than any wedding I've ever been to. He was dressed up to the nines and beaming into the camera with his arm around her.' Her voice broke. 'He left. It wasn't the same in the flat. I could see him in every chair, lying in our bed, making promises to me the day we brought Apollo home. It was like torture, so I moved out, went to a shared house that was really grim and then we came here, and that's that.' The young girl wiped her nose. It was the day, it seemed, for tears.

'You have no contact with him?'

'None.' Clodagh shook her head. 'It's better that way, cleaner. Easier for Apollo too. The idea that Sab could dip in and out of his life would only be confusing. I just want things to be steady.' Lilly remembered Glenda saying something similar a long time ago now. 'I guess that's why I'm thinking we should probably take that flat in Kennington. Apollo can stay at school, and we'll only be twenty minutes or so walk from here. That's nothing in the scheme of things.'

'That sounds like a good idea.' Lilly smiled to hide her desire to sob, daft as it was. Her tears were for the inevitable separation that was looming, but also for Clodagh's broken heart, Sab's broken promises and all that she, too, had endured. It really was monstrously unfair, all of it.

'I'm okay though, Lilly. I don't need him, don't need anyone. I'd rather be on my own than be with someone who is not going to show up for me, pick me.'

Lilly poured the tea and considered Clodagh's words: *obsessed! Completely obsessed, convinced there'd never been a love like it . . .*

'I understand, my love, I really do.'

1973 – aged 17

Lilly was happy. Her course at art college filled her with joy! It was a dream come true to spend her days studying beautiful paintings, learning the techniques of sculpture and collage, her two chosen modules for this year, and listening to experts debate the hidden meaning behind classic works of art. And she'd made a friend, a best friend, no less. Glenda Brooks was a Londoner, like her, who lived with her mum and dad in Enfield and commuted in and out each day. Feminism and the push for equality hadn't quite reached Glenda's street, and while Lilly had joyfully attended the protests against the Miss World competition, Glenda had declined the invitation to come with; her sole ambition, it seemed, was to get married and have kids. She spoke about it often, stating how she couldn't wait to bag a husband, leave home and get a house of her own where she could start her Pyrex collection. This would give her the freedom her strict parents denied her.

Glenda had explained the hoops she'd had to jump through just for them to give her permission to attend art college. Her parents were persuaded, finally, by a conversation with the local priest, who extolled the virtue in honing a God-given talent, and how Michelangelo himself had only grown closer to God as he painted the Sistine Chapel. And by the ace up his cassock sleeve, the fact that Luke himself, one of the four evangelists, was indeed an artist, ta-dah! Glenda was a skilful ceramicist and Lilly hoped that marriage, whenever it came, wouldn't curtail the successful career that beckoned, firmly believing that in this new day and age it was far easier for women to have it all. Her plan was to carry on working for Bertie, curate her own exhibitions, maybe get her own work to a standard that meant it might sell and, like Glenda, she too wanted to get married and have babies. I mean, who didn't? But all in good time.

'So, do you go to church and stuff?' One of the first questions Lilly had asked her new friend, after hearing how the priest had swayed her parents.

'Do I heck as like!' Glenda's eloquent response kind of told her all she needed to know. 'My parents practically live in front of the altar. My mum has her nose so far up Father Shaun's arse I'm sure she'd know he had haemorrhoids before he did.'

Lilly had laughed out loud at her friend's crude and confident humour.

She and Glenda were quite unlike most of the girls on their course, who lived in shared flats, delighting in the new and unexplored playground of London that, for girls like Tilly who had grown up in Shropshire, Liz who was from Harrogate, and Julia from Bath, was nothing short of one adventure after another. These girls hung out in coffee shops in the West End and went out with boys who had very long hair, boys who wore suede and fancied themselves as poets. Boys who smoked grass and liked to hypothesise about utter bollocks while confusing the reading of Kafka and Sartre with actually being Kafka or Sartre. These girls were pleasant enough; it was just that their lived experience and hers was so very different it was hard to find common ground. The main difference, she quickly came to understand, was money. Tilly, Liz, Julia and others like them had grown up with it, and she had not. A shared love of art could only take them so far, but when they had, on a whim, decided to go to Paris, booking flights as casually as she'd buy a bus ticket, Lilly knew she was not in their league.

Her job at the *B'Art* gallery in Pimlico did, however, buy her a brief whiff of popularity, as Bertie Barnes was momentarily famous, or infamous, depending on who you asked. This was after his *alleged* affair with a senior-ranking Tory was splashed all over *the News of The World*. The person who looked the least impressed in the rather grainy paparazzi shots being said Tory minister's wife.

'Have you seen this?' She had rushed into the gallery with a copy of the paper in her hand, brandishing it in the air like a flag.

'Oh, don't! Yes, I have.' Bertie had covered his face with his hands. 'My nose looks big, don't you think? It's a most unfortunate angle. Do you think my nose looks big?' This apparently was his most pressing concern. That, and how upset Beautiful Jack had been by the indiscretion.

Bertie continued to be a friend and a huge influence in her life. He was a fount of knowledge! His expertise was broad, covering a variety of subjects from how to style her hair and the right choice of accessory to pep up any outfit to where to find the best cappuccino this side of Watford. She worked in the gallery on weekends, the odd evening and during her holidays and, frankly, would have done so for nothing; the fact that Bertie paid her handsomely was just a wonderful bonus. He was, she came to realise, terrible with money. It was quite typical when he sold some artwork for a hundred pounds and immediately treated himself to a Murano glass chandelier that set him back nearly two hundred.

'Can we afford it?' she'd asked tentatively, as he admired the stunning twisted loops of glass in greens and blues.

'Don't be so vulgar! We never talk about affordability!' He had thrown the *Tatler* at her in protest.

'Is talking about affordability more or less vulgar than knitted loo-roll holders, pampas grass and Viennese Whirls?'

'Oh, Bob! You have the best memory! How I love that boy, Beautiful Jack!' He closed his eyes and clasped his hands. 'Do you think he'll forgive me?'

'I'm sure he will.' She hoped it sounded convincing.

'Maybe I should give him a call . . .' he'd murmured as he wandered off.

◆ ◆ ◆

This was her favourite kind of day, warm and breezy. With her easel set up on the towpath and the sun casting nets of diamonds out over the surface, Old Mother Thames sparkled! The only fly in the ointment was the dust and noise created by the plethora of workmen who toiled in their donkey jackets to widen Vauxhall Bridge. A mammoth undertaking that upset the rhythm of life on this side of the river.

She lifted her hand in a wave to the other side of the bank.

It was as she pondered her palette, trying to imagine the colour combination that would perfectly capture the way the light seemed to be coming from beneath the water, that not for the first time she got the uneasy feeling she was being watched. Quickly turning her head to the left and right, she held her breath, more than a little unnerved. Finally she narrowed her eyes across the water, figuring her dad was right, that it was most probably someone in one of the flats or offices opposite, just as in love with their stretch of the river as she was. Maybe they, too, were drawn to the tiny cresting jewels being pushed up to the surface, no doubt by a river nymph, or maybe that leviathan whose head they'd once spotted, trying to show the world that he was in fact a nice guy.

'What are you painting?' A man's voice made her jump, so lost was she in her imaginings.

This was not an unusual question. There seemed to be a certain fascination for anyone passing the moment they spied her, brush in hand.

'Oh.' Lilly looked up at him, shielding her eyes from the midday sun with her hand.

With his back to the light his face was in shadow, but his shoulder-length hair, curls – dark curls – were part hat, part halo. This made her smile, thinking that if you swapped the shadow for an apple, he was a walking Magritte. She didn't like anyone looking at her work when it was underway, not really, didn't like *talking* to anyone about her art mid-progress. Especially strangers, who typically didn't really want to know about her style, materials, inspiration or perspective but rather wanted to use her work as a vehicle to talk about their own technique; what they liked or didn't like, how they hadn't painted since school, or once went to an exhibition, yada . . . yada . . . yada . . . Everyone was a critic.

'Just the river, the water.'

She kept it vague, doing her best to sound polite, responsive but with just the right amount of dismissal to her tone that might encourage him to shut up and go away. There was something about sitting at an easel that was akin to opening her diary and inviting the world to come and take a look. Trouble was, she hadn't yet figured out how to paint in this, her favoured spot on the towpath, without such interruptions.

'Mind if I sit?'

Yes! Yes, I do! I mind very much! Please just leave me alone! was her mental response; 'erm' the rather pointless word that actually left her mouth.

The man seemed to take her lack of decisiveness as consent and perched on the wall by her side, but said nothing. It was a silence that was odd. The kind of quiet that might occur when you were well acquainted with someone but not when you were total strangers. It made the whole encounter most peculiar, if a little energised. Not that she was a stranger to peculiar or odd, having been called both, and recognising both within herself.

Bertie had said not to think of herself as odd, but rather unique! This was the mantra she repeated when her confidence was flagging, and it helped, a little. Glenda had roared her laughter when she'd shared this trick with her.

'Unique? Sweet Jesus, we're all unique, Lil, but that doesn't mean it's a good thing. Some of us are unique and bat-shit crazy, some of us unique and absolutely miserable! I'd settle for being bloody average. Not too many highs, very few lows, but bloody average, that'd do me.'

It struck her as the oddest of ambitions, that and wanting to get married quickly so she could start collecting Pyrex.

'How long have you been an artist?' His question was most endearing, suggesting she was an actual artist, recognising her as such, in contrast with the feeble, almost apologetic explanation she would offer when asked if she painted: *Oh, I kind of dabble, you know, and work in a gallery and other stuff, but yeah, I paint a bit . . .* as if she had no right to such a lofty ambition or an artsy leaning. Not a girl like her from the banks of the river, who, despite winning a place at art college, had practically grown up motherless and couldn't afford a ticket to Paris.

His words were empowering and lovely.

'I guess the corny answer is that I was born an artist!' She spoke the last three words with faux pomposity, which made him laugh. Not a raucous giggle but rather a slow, considered body laugh where his shoulders came in, his head shook and his face bore a wide grin. A handsome face, she now noticed. His eyes were so dark she couldn't see his pupils. His beard was thick and his fringe long over his forehead, which gave him the habit of having to shake it out of his eyes. He was wearing a Pink Floyd T-shirt with the triangle and prism of *The Dark Side of the Moon* on it.

'Lucky you. I was born a mathematician.'

It was her turn to laugh.

'I guess, in the career stakes, your skills might rate a little higher, so . . .'

He seemed to study her, as if taking in all the details, which was thrilling and terrifying all at once.

'I think Picasso died very rich,' he pointed out, the artist having shuffled off his mortal coil only a few months previously.

'Yet Van Gogh died poor,' she countered.

'Hmmm . . . true. I think a mathematician is more likely to die contentedly, as life, like anything else, is just a mathematical puzzle, and death kind of solves it, doesn't it? The final piece of the jigsaw, whereas artists, phew' – he exhaled, arms splayed – 'do they ever figure it out?'

'Figure what out?' She was curious, conscious she had stopped painting and that the light was changing.

'Life! Love! Loss! The greatest mysteries of them all!'

'This is a most extraordinary conversation. I have known you for all of five minutes and we are already on the meaning of life. I don't even know your name,' she fished, quite obviously taking the risk in the way that Bertie had tried to coach her.

No one remembers the meek, Bob! Be bold! Be open!

'Do you want to know my name?' he teased her.

'Oh God, last time I played this it turned out his name was Rumpelstiltskin and he got so mad that I guessed it, he tore himself in half!'

There it was again, that confident laugh of his that spoke of much more than frivolity, as if they were building a connection. Yes, exactly like that.

'What's your name?' He held her eyeline, inviting her to go first.

'Lilly.' She gave the simplified version, wanting this to be simple, uncomplicated and lovely, in the way she had hoped flirting might be.

Confident, if this was what was happening here. The feeling sprang from no more than the particular way he looked at her.

'I'm Wilkie Jones.'

'That's an unusual name.' A fact she was glad of, knowing that even if she never saw him again, his name, like this unusual exchange, would live on in her mind. *Unique . . .*

'You think so? Where I come from Wilkies are ten a penny.'

'Really?'

'No! Of course not!'

This time they both laughed.

'It was my grandfather's name, and I got stuck with it. An honour, so I'm told, within my family, and yet if it's such an honour, why are my brothers so relieved to have been called David and Arthur?' He tutted.

'That's a very good question.'

'So, Lilly?'

'Yep.'

'Are you named after anyone?' He twisted on the wall so his body was facing her, his legs slightly splayed, creating a V that she pictured getting up from her stool and nestling between, standing as close as she could to him, putting her hands on the thighs of his flared jeans, pushing her body against his.

'Umm . . .' She coughed to clear the embarrassment from her throat, worried he might be able to read her lascivious thoughts. 'Yes, actually, my full name is Elizabeth-Roberta. My dad is Robert, so . . .'

'I can see why you go with Lilly, much quicker.'

'Yep, and with all the seconds I get to save by not having to say Elizabeth-Roberta, I do fun things.' She smiled at him.

'Like what?' He leaned forward, elbows on his legs, his head closer to hers. She felt the breath catch in her throat.

'Like chatting to random strangers on the towpath.'

'So you do this a lot?' He tilted his head to one side.

'Well, no, I've only saved so many seconds, so this is the first time.' She lifted her hand and rubbed the back of her neck, wanting to reach out and touch him so badly that it felt necessary to occupy her fingers. She saw his eyes dart to her breasts, the outline visible beneath the thin fabric of her cheesecloth shirt, then back to her face, this one simple gesture enough to light a flame of desire inside her.

'So a . . . a mathematician?'

'Yes. I'm a teacher, actually, visiting the big smoke.'

'Oh, right.' Older than her then, which was obvious, and not that it mattered. 'And you're visiting alone?'

It was the closest she could get to enquiring as to whether he was married, single or attached, knowing it was nothing to do with her, a nosy stranger, and yet wanting desperately to know!

He looked from his left to his right and all around, as if comically trying to locate someone. 'It would appear so!'

'Where do you teach?'

'St Ethelred's, a school in York.'

'You're from Yorkshire?' He didn't sound like he was from Yorkshire.

'No, from Basingstoke, but that's where the job took me. And I love it up there. Beautiful countryside.' He closed his eyes as if recalling it.

'I've never been.'

'You should go.' He smiled at her.

'I don't like to leave London.' Her admission came easily, without consideration.

'Oh my God! Really? You don't leave London?' He stared at her wide-eyed in disbelief.

'I said I don't *like* to, not that I don't.' She shrugged.

'So you do?'

'Not very often, no.' She smiled at him.

'But there's a whole wide world outside of this city, lovely as it is, a whole wide world!'

'So I believe. I once saw one of those round things with countries and oceans on it. Like a map but a ball!' she mocked.

'Sorry, you're right, it's absolutely nothing to do with me!' He held his palms up in defence.

'Truth is, I don't like to leave my dad. It's just me and him.' She was grateful he didn't ask for further details of their set-up. 'Plus, I have this crazy compulsion to paint every day. To sit right here, in fact, and paint this same stretch of river. And if I don't, I get kind of . . . agitated, as if I might be missing something.' It was as close as she could come to describing what was almost a compulsion.

'Every day?' He screwed his face up as if doubting her.

'Well, nearly every day. I mean, not if I'm working or studying or the weather is really bad. No point trying to paint in thick fog and rain if you can't see the water and the damp makes your colours run.'

'I guess not.' Wilkie hopped off the wall and dusted his palms on his jeans. 'So this means you'll be here tomorrow, about the same time?'

'Probably.' They shared a lingering look, as if both aware that this was no casual enquiry but was in fact an arrangement. Her heart jumped in her chest at the prospect. She sucked in her stomach and pushed out her chest, trying to look coy, sexy, demure, alluring and all the things she had never seen herself as. Trying to look like anyone other than the girl who had never quite fitted in, like someone else entirely.

'See you tomorrow then, probably.' He gave her a slow smile, as if very aware of the effect he was having on her.

'Yep, see you tomorrow,' she managed, almost breathless at the prospect of seeing him again. *Wilkie . . . Wilkie . . . Wilkie . . .*

Present day

'What are you painting?' The man was a Londoner like her, his interruption an irritation. She did her best to find a positive tone, aware that he was only being curious, friendly, and had not deliberately set out to spoil her day. At least she hoped not.

'The water, the . . . the river.' Using her paintbrush, she pointed in the general direction.

'It's a nice spot.'

'Yes, that's why I'm here again!' She clicked her tongue against her teeth.

'Again?'

'Yes. I paint here often, more than often, and have painted this scene more times than I care to admit.'

'Really, how extraordinary! How many times have you—'

'Hundreds and hundreds. And hundreds.' She cut him short.

'The same picture, same stretch of the river, every time?' he asked with a rise of disbelief.

'Every time.'

'Why?'

'Why?' she asked with her face screwed up, nose wrinkled, an expression that said more than her words ever could, as if he were an idiot for asking, not her the idiot for repeating her composition over and over.

'Yes, why? I mean, there's so much to see along here.' He pointed to the right, where the Houses of Parliament, Big Ben and Westminster Bridge sat beyond Lambeth Bridge.

'You're right, there is lots to see. Maybe I'll switch it up when I've captured this correctly.' Again using her slender brush as a pointer, she tapped the canvas, hoping her comment might be enough to satisfy him, to send him on his way.

'What is it you're trying to capture, exactly, that means you need to keep repeating the process? If you don't mind me asking. I find it fascinating!' It seemed the man had a lot of questions that rather forced her engagement.

She looked at him now. He was older, tall, stocky, with an air of confidence that she suspected came with the wearing of his sharp-cut suit that reeked of Savile Row. His brogues were shiny, his hair expensively trimmed, his shave thorough and his watch a weighty bauble beyond the edge of his pale-pink double cuff, as if it were important to let it be seen. The barrow-boy-made-good-in-the-City look.

How to explain, where to begin? Phrases and words she knew she'd never share formed in her mind. She tucked her lips inward to stop any of them from escaping.

I started painting to try and please my dad, I guess. Then I wanted to capture my life here with my mum, because even if she was gone, the river was just the same, then it was life with my dad. Then it was him . . . him, Wilkie. The day he sat on the wall, the way the light fell on the water, casting sea diamonds over the surface that were so beautiful I thought about diving in and scooping them into my hands and keeping them in my pocket for ever. The way the sun held him in shadow yet sent tiny flickers of gold to rest on his curls, the colours of his T-shirt, the buckle of his satchel. The one or two boats that ambled, part of our story, as if they, too, were caught up in the slow and heady delight of happiness and possibility that filled the air with its sweet summer scent. The misty smudge of joy all around us as if we were the only things distinct – as if the day, the scene, the moment, was ours and ours alone and we were oblivious to everything and everyone and they to us. Trying to capture the magic. The magic of having him close to me and looking at me and knowing that it was our beginning and that we were going to matter to each other. Those seconds as he sat and I stared at him under the guise of taking in the background, preparing my sketch, aware our lives would change, that I would be changed, the very shape of me, the very fabric of me and all that I believed was possible . . .

'Just trying to get it right.' She shrugged. This felt safer, easier.

'Each to their own, I guess.' He sniffed.

'Urgh! I hate that phrase so much!' Her tone was reflective of the rise in her heartbeat at the thought of that day, of him . . .

'So it would seem. Sorry if I've offended you!' He laughed then, suggesting he wasn't sorry at all.

'I can't help it! But – *each to their own* . . . It's purporting to be supportive, liberal, open-minded, accepting, but it's anything but! It's actually saying, *I don't get why! I'm judging you, even though I make out I'm not! It's not for me, but you go ahead, even if, in my humble opinion, you're wrong!*'

'Goodness, you got all of that from *each to their own?*' He laughed again, a nice laugh, his blue eyes crinkling as he did so.

'Yes. Yes, I did. It's not so much what they say but *how* they say it!'

He stared at her now, seeming to take her in. She didn't look away, holding her own, as irritated by the man as she was attracted to him. Drawn by his handsome face, confident air and his obvious interest in her.

'Are there any other phrases that make you similarly angry?' He was toying with her, no doubt, and she let him. It was playful, flattering, nice.

'There are, actually.'

'Well, let's hear them!'

Lilly drew breath. '*Cheer up, it might never happen!* That pisses me off more than I can say. How dare someone, usually a man, often in a hard hat, demand a different reaction from me that might suit him better! And how does he or anyone else know what I'm going through, or what might warrant such a sober face or sad expression. As if I have to be pretty or pleasing for him!'

'Yep, I get that.' He nodded.

'Oh, and . . . and *I knew that was going to happen!* When something goes wrong, gets broken, or worse. When what you really need in that moment is support, kindness, help. That self-gratifying reflection drives me crackers! And it's a lie, because they didn't! They categorically did not know it was going to happen – they might have suspected it, predicted it, wished for it even, but they did not *know* it was going to happen! They should just shut up!'

'I see.' He swallowed.

'And—'

'There's more?' he asked with a wide-mouthed look of horror.

'Yes, a couple. You did ask.' It felt good, letting the frustration of all she was going through over Waide House flow from her mouth.

'True, I did. Carry on!' He folded his arms across his wide chest as if settling in.

'*It'll all turn out okay in the end!* Just grrrr!' She actually growled. 'Isn't that the biggest pile of rubbish ever? It might *not* turn out okay in the end! It might turn out horribly, painfully, disappointingly, people might die, in fact people *will* die, everyone does! It will *not* all turn out okay in the end! And why does anyone think I might need to hear that? What am I, six?'

'I can see I've touched a nerve.'

'Again, you did ask.' She took deep breaths to regulate her heart, which was racing.

'To be honest, I'm kind of wishing I hadn't.' He, too, took a deep breath. 'Would you like to go for a drink?'

'What?' She had heard but, as a seventy-year-old woman who had shown him her less-than-smiley side, was sure she must have heard incorrectly.

'I said would you like to go for a drink?'

'What, as in . . .'

'A drink, with me. Hot or cold, coffee or wine, I'm open to both.' He unfolded his arms and put his hands in his pockets, suggesting the vaguest hint of nerves, which was endearing.

No one remembers the meek, Bob! Be bold! Be open!

This was certainly a novelty, and a lovely distraction from her battle over the flat, worrying about Clodagh, and the other tiny pigeon pecks of irritation and concern that had left their mark.

'Are you married?' She was direct. At seventy she'd figured out the value in it and could not cope with anything that wasn't entirely straightforward.

'Not any more. Divorced for a while now. Two daughters, both married. Five grandchildren. Oh, about to be six, actually! My youngest is pregnant and due in a few months – all girls so far! They will be the death of me.' He tried to pull a face of disdain, but his eyes beamed with something that looked a lot like love. 'A Londoner, born and raised in East Ham, made my fortune, moved out to Essex, where I have a farm. Virgo, pescatarian, likes sea air, country walks, swimming, reading the papers on a Sunday, and music – can't imagine my life without music. Hate food waste, airs and graces, rudeness, inconsiderate drivers and the tiny little strips of plastic with a tiny arrow thing on the end they put under the lid of milk bottles and orange juice, which I can't grip because of my inept fingers and cause me no end of frustration. I have an unfounded fear of quicksand, which I thought was going to feature far more in my adult life than it actually has, and littering. Drives me crackers.'

'What music do you like?' This was the thing that had caught her attention.

He exhaled and looked into the middle distance. 'Everything from The Rolling Stones to Beethoven. When you've lived a good, long life, you collect music, don't you think? I love songs that remind me of certain days, particular people, life-changing moments both good and bad. You reach a certain age and understand that you've curated your own soundtrack.'

She smiled then, so powerfully reminded of her dad and the soundtrack of his life that played regularly in her head.

'Cold.' She nodded.

'I'm sorry?'

'You said hot or cold. I'd prefer cold, the drink.'

'Well, that's great!' He clapped his palms together, his face smiling.

'I'm Lilly, by the way.'

'And I'm Alfred. Alfie.'

'When would you like to go for our cold drink, Alfie?' She tested his name out loud. It sounded nice. He seemed nice.

'I say no time like the present, unless that's a phrase that bothers you?' he asked with mock caution.

'No, I rather like that one. It's go-getting and purposeful, both things I greatly admire.'

'In that case, I think we are going to get on splendidly.'

She began to pack away her easel and painting paraphernalia, wondering what Glenda would make of her rather rash decision to go and have a drink with a complete stranger!

. . . women can't afford to be so forward, not without being seen in the wrong light . . .

This memory she scrubbed from her thoughts, and she smiled at Alfie, a pescatarian who had made a fortune and lived on a farm.

Apparently.

1973 – aged 17

Lilly hadn't slept much. Partly because every dream, every minute, when her mind threatened to slip into the world of slumber and imaginings, left her in a state of high agitation that saw her toss and turn on her narrow mattress as she pictured Wilkie. His thighs held a particular fascination for her, trying to imagine what it might feel like to place her hands on them or to feel them pressed against her. The slight curve to his full bottom lip that she wanted so badly to kiss. And his conversation: easy, smart and curious, seeming to match her word for word, thought for thought.

You from Yorkshire?

No . . . Basingstoke . . .

I've never been.

You should go.

I don't like to leave London.

. . . you don't leave London?

I said I don't like to . . .

This was how she spent much of the early hours, replaying their conversation in her mind. It threw up as many questions as it answered. Why was he in London? How long was he staying? Did he want to kiss her, too, by any chance? It was at this latter thought that Lilly lay on her front, pushed her face into the pillow and beat her feet on the mattress until her excitement settled and she was able to breathe a little easier . . . All of this over a boy! She couldn't wait to tell Bertie. Glenda, too. Glenda who now had a boyfriend, Norman Glaser, and they were officially courting. Norman seemed nice enough. He had a car, a navy-blue Ford Cortina with a wide chrome grille. This was evidently enough to impress Glenda, who seemed to ignore the fact that Norman rarely spoke and spent much of the time staring at the pale suede Hush Puppies on his feet.

'He's a bit quiet!' Lilly had pointed out after he'd joined them in the Prince of Wales in Pimlico for a snifter after work.

'That's a blessing, Lil. You don't want a chatterbox in your ear morning, noon and night, do you? It'd drive you mad! Kindness counts for a lot in my book, and even better if it comes from a quiet man, someone who's calm, allows you to think.'

Lilly wasn't so sure. But it wasn't her who had to climb into Norman's Cortina three times a week for him to drive her back to Enfield. Not her who excitedly sat in the passenger seat while they took a detour to Pymmes Park to neck under the moonlight. Not her who made sure she fixed her hair and smoothed her clothes before she walked into the house she shared with her parents, lest they see she had been acting inappropriately in the eyes of God. No, it was Glenda who had to do all that. Lilly was sure it was only a matter of time before Norman popped the question and Glenda could start picking out material for her bridesmaids' dresses, choosing her white, white frock and selecting Pyrex from the shelves of Woolworths with which to start her collection.

Lilly had chosen her outfit carefully today: suede miniskirt, red knee-high leather boots, and her beaded smock top with the buttons undone to reveal the lacy lilac edge of her Cross Your Heart bra. She sat down, waved to the other side of the river and tried to settle, but it was hard to paint, difficult to concentrate when her actions were no more than a ruse, her paintbrush a prop. Even if the day had presented thick fog and rain, making it impossible to see the water, and the damp had made her colours run, she'd still have been there, perched on her stool, with Aqua Manda scent dabbed on to her wrists and neck, just on the off chance that he might stop by, *Wilkie* . . .

'So, here we are again.'

His voice behind her, deliciously evocative and a thrill like no other – he was here! He was actually here! His tone slightly sarcastic and assumptive, as if they were mid-conversation, as if he, like her, might have been carrying on yesterday's chat throughout the night, when alone, and conjuring images that she wouldn't share with anyone, ever. Her gut bunched with pure delight! He was here! He was actually here!

'So it would appear,' she said over her shoulder, trying to sound cool while her stomach did somersaults.

'How was your day?' He sat on the wall as if they were better acquainted, neighbours, colleagues, friends even.

'My day was' – she paused – 'great, actually.'

'You sound surprised.'

'I am. I love my job, which makes me very lucky, I know, but there are some days when I really love my job!'

'And today was one of them,' he chimed.

'Yes, and today was one of them.' She focused on her canvas, in case he saw in her eyes that part of the reason for such a splendid day was the prospect of seeing him.

'What do you do for a living, if it's okay to ask?'

'It's okay to ask. I'm not with MI5.' She smiled at him.

'Hmmm . . . that's the kind of thing someone who was with MI5 might say, just to throw me off the scent.'

She laughed out loud because the sun was on her skin, she'd had a brilliant day at work and now she was chatting to this man, who seemed . . . interested. Interested in her, in everything.

'And has it thrown you off the scent?' She looked comically to the left and right, as if checking the coast was clear.

'No. I'm on to you.' He held her stare, which ordinarily would have been awkward or intimidating, but was neither. 'So what's your cover story, what "job"' – he painted inverted commas in the air with two fingers of each hand – 'do you tell people you have?'

'I tell people I work in an art gallery, and that I get to sit among fabulous pictures all day and then I sit here and paint, just to make it look as convincing as possible.'

'Well, I'm entirely convinced.' He removed his leather satchel and placed it on the pavement, sitting back on the wall that edged the river, a sheer drop below of some twenty-odd feet, down to the foreshore, where she had spent her childhood mudlarking; she still had some of the treasures she'd found secreted away. 'So what made today great, actually?'

She liked the sideways slant to his mouth; it was endearing, imperfect and unique. 'We have a new exhibition, officially opening on Saturday, a very talented up-and-coming artist whose work is just lovely, layers of fabric and clay – textural and tonal, beautiful. Each piece changes with the light and, as you can tell, I'm rather taken with it, anyway,' she breathed. 'A couple came in earlier, just passing, and bought everything, every single piece! The artist is dizzy with delight, and my boss, the gallery owner – well, he's probably already spent the very handsome sum, but that's another story! Plus I get commission on everything I sell, so . . .' She bit her lip as excitement threatened to explode from her.

'So will you still have an official opening? Is there any point if there's nothing left to sell?'

'Oh, gosh! It's the absolute dream! When art lovers and collectors find out there's nothing to buy they almost froth at the mouth, wanting what they can't have! The artist can take commissions and the value goes up – it's remarkable!'

'Ha! That is' – he shook his head – 'really exciting!'

'It's like discovering a new Lucie Rie!' she gushed.

'Well, that's . . . that's great.'

'You have no idea who she is, have you?' Her laughter burbled from her.

'None whatsoever!'

'So, what are you doing in London? Working?' She looked at his leather bag.

'Kind of, I'm teaching at an international school for foreign students, subbing, if you like, for the holidays. Feel more than a bit guilty; lots of my mates are on a three-day week and there's me getting paid ridiculous sums of money to teach maths to hopeless young men who have about as much chance of becoming mathematicians as I do of winning the Grand National. And I've never been on a horse.'

'Oh dear. Poor, hopeless things.'

'Yep, but good for me. A lovely boost to the coffers, given to me by these parents with more money than sense.' He pulled a flat Golden Virginia tin from his pocket and began to roll a smoke.

'You don't think it's deceiving them, taking money under false pretences?' she teased.

'Nope.' He pinched the loose tobacco and laid it in a scattered, wispy sausage across the width of the Rizla paper which rested on his leg. 'I figured the ninnies are going to give their pound notes away anyway, and so why not to me? And besides – their truth is that they are doing the best for their sons, throwing money at a problem and hoping cash can fix it. They don't feel like it's a waste of time, they think they're solving an issue.'

'Their truth . . .'

'Exactly.' He grinned at her.

'You should come along to the . . . the erm . . . the exhibition opening. Only if . . . if you . . .' The words had taken courage, the painful and awkward aftermath as she awaited his response almost unbearable. I mean, who was she? Some girl he'd met on the towpath – what was she thinking!

'Yeah, I'd like that. I'll come along.'

'Great!' She tried and failed to sound a little aloof, a little indifferent, knowing she was neither when it came to spending time and conversing with this man. 'You should probably do your research first though, try and learn as much as you can about Lucie Rie.'

'Really?' he asked, sounding more than a little concerned.

'No, of course not! Just come and look at the art, meet Bertie Barnes, my boss, and drink champagne. That's it!'

'I can do that. Probably.'

'Probably . . .' She smiled, sensing a connection already, a shared thing, and how lovely it was! 'How long are you in town?' she enquired as casually as she was able. It felt prudent to ask.

'Few weeks, maybe more. I mean, if I'm having a good time, I might be tempted to stay longer.'

'And what might possibly tempt you?' She threw her hair over one shoulder to expose her decolletage and positioned her legs just so to show off her skin, wanting him to want her in the way she wanted him, and knowing that if Glenda were to witness such shenanigans, even she might just pray for her. It was playing a part, adopting this persona, and she liked it very much. She felt sexy, grown-up and invincible all at once!

'You are quite lovely, Elizabeth-Roberta.' His tone was sincere now as he stared at her, and she felt the pulse of want in the base of her throat. His words had the biggest effect – swooning, almost, she feared she might fall off her perch.

'Am I?' Her voice was a whisper.

'Yes. You really are.' He stood and came close to her. 'I was thinking about you all the way here, trying to figure out, if you were a season, which season you would be.' He narrowed his eyes as if still undecided.

'I hope summer.' She liked the idea of it, all that warmth and light.

Wilkie shook his head. 'Summer is too predictable. I think you'd be spring.'

'Spring?' She bit her lip, trying to work out if this was a good or bad thing.

'Yep, spring. Secretly, quietly powerful, having to fight to break through hardened soil to bloom, to be noticed, but once you do, you dazzle, absolutely dazzle! Delivering colour, fragrance and hope that has been missing for the longest time!' Reaching out, he ran the pad of his index finger over her cheek and her whole body shuddered, tightening and aching for more of it. 'And hope is surely the greatest gift, is it not?'

'I'll take it. Spring,' she managed, almost breathless.

'And beauty . . . beauty, too, let's not forget that. The intoxicating flush of pure beauty after a bleak and dull winter.'

'I'm not and never have been considered beautiful.' She shook her hair over her face once more, feeling suddenly self-conscious, wanting to hide.

'What a ridiculous statement.' He withdrew his hand. 'How could you possibly know how you've been perceived by everyone who has ever encountered you?'

He was right. The simple truth was, she had never considered herself beautiful and therefore assumed everyone else must feel the same.

'I suppose . . .'

'I think you're beautiful, Lilly.' He spoke with a confidence that was irresistible.

'You don't have to say that.' She wanted to be clear that while she wanted him to be as enamoured with her as she was with him, he didn't need to resort to corny flattery or predictable clichés.

'You're right, I don't have to say anything, don't have to *do* anything. I choose to say it because it is my truth. And I'm here because there is nowhere else on the earth I'd rather be right now.'

'And your truth doesn't have to be *the* truth?'

'It can only be my truth, can't it? My thoughts, my voice, my feelings right now, in this moment . . .'

'I guess so,' she said.

Lilly felt her heart jump in her chest. Despite having only ever thought of those long-haired fakes who flattered girls like Tilly, Liz and Julia with their pseudo-philosophy as charlatans with ulterior motives, suddenly she understood the power in these words of seduction. Not that she placed Wilkie in the same category, but she certainly recognised she wore the same dreamy expression as those girls, doe-eyed and compliant, addicted almost.

'So' – Wilkie ran the tip of his tongue over the gluey strip of his roll-up and folded it over with a deftness to his fingers – 'the day after tomorrow, then. Time?'

'Seven thirty.'

'Place?' He put it into his mouth and lit it with a silver lighter that thunked shut as he flicked it.

'*B'Art* Gallery, Eccleston Street.'

'I'll see you there.'

'Yes, see you there, probably.' She beamed at him, feeling a shiver of want along her limbs as he placed his bag over his shoulder and walked along the towpath without looking back, not once. Yet he moved with an awareness, as if confident that she watched his progression, taking in his particular walk, the way his hair lay on his shoulders and the shape of his arse in his jeans.

The moment he was out of sight Lilly packed away her paints and easel, left the towpath and stashed them in the flat. She was excited, busy, motivated, jumpy, on high alert, and felt the need to share what had just happened with someone – anyone! Her dad was out for the evening; orchestra rehearsal night. Not that she would have been able to discuss it with him, not really, aware that he still saw her as a child, but also never wanting to make him feel less than, to be like her mum, with a fancy new man while he was still very much single.

On no more than a whim she grabbed the loose change from the little wooden bowl on the shelf by the front door and ran to the phone box at the back of the building. It would have been hard to explain why, but she felt the need to call her mum. She supposed at some level she wanted Jeannie to know she wasn't the only one who was desirable, who could trap a man – not that Wilkie was anything at all like dull-as-ditchwater Derek Manners. It also felt good to be wanted, to be asked, to be flirted with, and this she wanted Jeannie to know. The woman herself might have walked out, chosen a different life, but Wilkie was choosing her! Her preference would have been to call Glenda if she'd been home, but Lilly knew that right about now she was in Norman's blue Cortina, no doubt necking somewhere while she dreamed of wedding bells and Norman probably dreamed of more than necking . . .

To share this bloom of joy and excitement felt vital, as if putting it out into the world made it real somehow. At the end of the day, Jeannie was her mum, and Lilly was going through something, and it felt kind of important to share this thing. With her heart beating fast and a breathless energy to her excitement, she dialled the number that she knew by heart, having learned it just in case.

'Double five, three one four, double six.'

Her mum stated the telephone number clearly and with confidence, further erasing her early history, as if she had never lived in the flat without a phone. Without a phone – but with a daughter, a marvellous husband and an unrivalled view of the river. Lilly, by choice, hadn't seen her for nearly eight months. The last time was at Tottenham Court Road, where her mum had laid out a buffet that Lilly, her stomach squeezed with anxiety and nestling somewhere under her throat, had been loath to pick at.

'I did your favourite, pineapple and cheese on sticks!' Her mum had shoved a large foil-covered potato in her direction, covered with toothpicks, on the ends of which sat sweating cubes of orange cheese and chunks of pineapple.

'I don't . . .' Lilly didn't know what to say, aware her mum had gone to some considerable trouble, but the thought of eating the odd combination off a little wooden stick made her feel nauseous. 'I don't really like them . . .' She'd kept her voice small.

'Well, you used to like them – you did! You'd say, *Mummy, make me a hedgehog!*' There was no mistaking the crack of emotion to her mum's voice, and Lilly, unsure of what to say or what to do, stared at the woman, wondering when this might have been.

That was the thing when your mum left home, left you: she took all the small and yet significant stories of your childhood with her.

Lilly had made her exit shortly after, inventing a sudden, pressing chore that she had to get home for. It was only when she stood in the street outside her mother's claustrophobic hideaway that she breathed, taking great, gulping lungfuls of air that helped clear the distress of yet another failed visit.

'Mum, it's me.' Lilly shot the two-pence piece into the slot. The beeps stopped, and they were connected.

'Lilly! Is everything okay?' Her mother sounded more than a little panicked.

A question that perfectly demonstrated how infrequently they talked, her mum clearly worried that something must be amiss.

'Everything's fine.'

'Oh good, good!' Jeannie breathed out with obvious relief.

'What are you doing?' Lilly closed her eyes, cringing, pushing the cigarette-scented Bakelite mouthpiece towards her face, wondering when it had become so hard to talk to the woman who had given birth to her. Not that she had to wonder at all, knowing the exact day, the exact minute.

How long has she gone for?

. . . I think that if we assume it's for ever then we won't be disappointed. And if it turns out not to be the case, then we'll be extra happy if she comes home.

'We're just about to have our tea, then watch *M*A*S*H* – Derek loves it!'

She didn't want to talk about Derek Manners or his fancy TV set, wishing she hadn't asked.

'What are you having for your tea?' This, too, she didn't really want to know; it was like prodding a rotten tooth with the tip of her tongue, a painful habit.

'Cold meat, chips and beans. We always have that on a Thursday . . .'

Lilly felt the stir of hunger in her stomach and knew she could have devoured a plate like that. Her mum had always made really good chips. Golden on the outside, fluffy in the middle and always served piping hot. She and her dad had used the same blackened chip pan, the fat cooled and heated with regularity, but they never tasted quite the same.

'You sure everything's all right, love? I mean, don't get me wrong, it's lovely to hear from you, *so* lovely!'

She could tell her mum was crying, and this was, as ever, conflicting. So much emotion from the woman who had chosen to pack a bag and leave.

'I met someone. I met a boy,' she blurted, cringing again at the inadequacy of those four words, unable to convey the excitement, the anticipation, the joy! And laughing a little at calling Wilkie a boy. He was no boy.

'Lilly-Bob! Goodness me, that *is* news! Well, what's his name, what does he do, how old is he? I want to know everything! Tell me, tell me!' Jeannie giggled.

'His name is Wilkie.' She smiled as her mouth formed the words.

'Wilkie? Well, that's not one you hear every day. How did you meet?' Jeannie sounded enthusiastic, excited, sniffing up her tears, banishing them, no doubt, in light of this big news. It encouraged Lilly to let the information drop from her tongue, and sharing it tasted delicious.

'We met on the towpath. I was painting—'

'Of course you were!' Jeannie interrupted, in the way that mums did when you were in their lives and they were in yours and you knew each other so well that you could predict the other's response and thoughts, habits. It was at once familiar, insightful, comfortable and a lie. But it was also comforting and addictive, just the idea that they were close, and that Jeannie wanted to know all about this boy who had turned her daughter's world golden. *Pretending* . . . Pretending Jeannie had not run off, pretending she had not chosen a life of mediocrity with the cardigan-wearing Derek Manners, pretending she hadn't left Lilly and her husband alone . . . This thought left Lilly feeling a little winded – what was she thinking, confiding in this phoney mum when her dad was in the dark? Her lovely dad, who never had to pretend, because he'd been there through it all, the real deal.

'So, what does your dad have to say about it?' With these words it was indeed as if her mother had insight into her thoughts.

'I haven't told him yet.'

'I see,' Jeannie whispered, and in the pause she knew that her mum, like her, was letting this fact land. Lilly had told her first, chosen her, confided in her. It was as this properly registered that Lilly felt the trickle of disloyalty in her veins, wishing she hadn't called at all.

'I . . . I should go, Mum.'

'Oh! I . . . Lilly, please! I wasn't prying, I just wanted to . . . to . . . I'm pleased for you, so pleased!'

'No . . . it's . . . I just . . .'

It was as Lilly wondered how best to extricate herself from the call that the beeps went, and she was saved, carefully replacing the receiver and allowing her mum to think she had run out of money.

Much easier that way.

She left the phone box, kicking the nest of cigarette butts, the empty, flattened can of Double Diamond and the toffee wrappers that had gathered on the floor as she did so.

Making her way back to the flat, she felt a little deflated, a little embarrassed, wondering why she had thought it a good idea to share the news with her mother.

The coins made a pleasing sound as she dropped them back into the little wooden pot in the hallway. Standing now in front of the open fridge that buzzed, she stared at the shelves that had rusted on the edges where the plastic had worn off and turned her nose up at the saucer of sausages that looked a little grey, the three carrots that were slightly shrivelled, and the half-bottle of milk that sat in the door. A paltry offering by anyone's standards. And despite the pure joy of knowing she would get to see Wilkie the day after tomorrow, her tears gathered, falling like glass rods down her face, as she pictured her mum and Derek Manners sitting down to a plate of cold meat, chips and beans.

Present day

Alfie produced two wrapped sweets from his jacket pocket and handed her one, which she accepted gratefully, of that age when a little sweetie was treat enough of an evening to cure any desire for a sugary dessert.

'I think there are two sorts of people in the world, Lilly.' He spoke in the easy manner that had been most attractive as she'd stared at him across the tabletop on the deck of the *Tamesis*, the beautiful old Dutch barge on the Albert Embankment, a fabulous place to have a drink and take in the view. 'Those who bite a mint humbug the moment it enters their mouth, and those who suck it until it's no more than a tiny sliver of sugar glass sitting on your tongue that eventually melts away to nothing.'

'Which are you?' She liked his irreverent sense of humour and the fact that they hadn't stopped talking. Not for a second.

'Oh, I'm a cruncher, and proud! And, frankly, I feel sorry for those without the moral fibre or daring sense of adventure to delight in the fracturing of the outer shell, allowing the thick sticky interior to clamp to your teeth!'

'Sorry to say, I'm actually one of those lacking in moral fibre and a daring sense of adventure.'

'Never!' Alfie shook his head in obvious disappointment.

''Fraid so.' She sucked air through her teeth. 'I think I used to be a cruncher, but nowadays I'm more worried about fracturing the outer shell of my weakened molars. Age has made me cautious,' she admitted.

'In some ways, yet you still let an old fart like me take you out for a drink.'

'I did. Call it a moment of madness.' She fell into step alongside him as they walked by the riverside.

'Days like this remind me what I love most about this city.' He breathed in slowly through his nose as if taking in the essence of the place. 'There's something about being near the river . . .'

'As you know, I am rather fond of it myself.'

'Do you ever take to the water, go boating?'

'Err, no.' She laughed at the prospect. 'I did get a water taxi once back in the nineties, just to try it out, and it was odd. Having spent so much of my life looking at it, to be on it was strange, but it was a quick trip, over in a flash.'

'That's a shame. I feel excited when I walk along it, get close to it.' He stared across the river.

'Every day is like that for me. There's nowhere else I'd rather be,' she confessed.

'Really? You never want to run for the hills, go to the sea or follow the sun?'

'Nope. I like the odd day out, but' – she shook her head – 'not really. People talk about going abroad, keen to tell you all about the sights and sounds that they found awe-inspiring – the crystal-clear waters of the Maldives, the cobbled streets of Paris, the canals of Venice, the skyscrapers of New York, the deserts of the Sudan . . . All unique, beautiful and shaping the human experience, and I get all of that. But that's exactly how I feel about my little corner of London. That same feeling that I'm experiencing something beautiful, something fleeting. I find it awe-inspiring just looking at this old river.'

'I think I fell out of love with her a bit, this city of mine. I like to come back, and I do, weekly, but I also like to walk my fields and listen to the birdsong.'

'That sounds nice.' She finished her sweet. 'I find there's a huge difference between Londoners and those that visit. Tourists and day-trippers talk about the sights and the lights, the theatre, the crowds, but those of us who *know* the old girl understand that it's moments that make this city great.'

'What do you mean by moments?' Alfie stopped walking and turned to face her. It was both pleasing and encouraging, to seemingly hold his attention in this way.

'I mean the little glimmers of pure joy and life-affirming wonder that can fill you right up, like—' She wanted to eloquently raise the points that rattled in her head. 'Like being on the top deck of a bus that goes over one of the bridges at sunset when you get that unique, fleeting view of the buildings on the river, back-lit with the red and gold of the setting sun. Or, seeing the face of a tourist the first time *they* see St Paul's or Trafalgar Square. Their excitement, it's infectious! And flags – we are very good at big old rows of flags, any excuse, all along The Mall, and St James's; jubilees, royal weddings, state visits, whoosh! Up they go! They fill me with pride. Popping into a shop or café and the person behind the counter recognising you and chatting to you, letting you know that of all the millions of people jostling for space and connection in this big city, they *know* you because you are a part of it. Or that feeling of lying on the grass with your eyes closed in one of our parks, on fresh-cut grass with roses blooming in the flower beds and ducks quacking, quite bucolic, yet still with the hum of traffic out of sight but not earshot.'

He laughed and nodded, as if he, too, had those moments.

'And is there anything more glorious than a cold breeze through the open doors of a crowded bus on a hot day, or when the Tube doors open right where you are standing on the platform as if it's your own personal transport! Knowing a shortcut, the best bakery, where to get great coffee, and chatting to other Londoners who share your childhood and education because it's the same as theirs. Lying in bed at night, knowing that however lonely you might feel, you're never alone. And that London hum; the collective noise of the capital, interspersed with horn toots and shouts! This city is twenty-four-seven, and you only have to holler out of the window or into the hallway and someone will come if you need them to.' She felt her face blush, having shared her enthusiasm and possibly too much with this man, a stranger.

'You feel lonely?'

'Sometimes . . .' She was not about to admit that her biggest fear was the bone-deep loneliness of isolation, that particular silence that had noise . . . and it felt stupid to say she still half expected her dad to call out his welcome when she arrived home. 'But doesn't everyone sometimes?'

'I guess so.' He swallowed. 'Yes, I suppose we do.'

'When are you loneliest?' It felt a little like prying, but as they were sharing . . .

'First thing in the morning and last thing at night,' he answered without hesitation. 'When the only sound in the house is me. It's one extreme or the other, really, either the girls and grandchildren are there creating mayhem, or it's deathly quiet. No London hum in the countryside.'

Lilly appreciated his openness, matching her with his vulnerability. 'It might just be me, of course, and my blinkered love of London that colours the way I see it. In the same way a mother will look at an ugly baby with a look of such pride as if no one has ever created a human so beautiful or perfect or unique.'

'Like being eighteen, wearing beer goggles and finding every girl beautiful because you're three sheets to the wind!' he chimed.

'Yes, exactly like that. And I don't want to sound cruel. I've never been a mother, so who knows how I'd have viewed my own offspring!' This she did with intention, letting him know she was childless, and she did so with a small laugh, hoping it smothered the knife of loss that went right through her breast at no more than the mention of it.

'Well, if you were anything like me, I was definitely that kind of parent who looked at my *very* ugly kids and could say with certainty they were the most beautiful creatures ever born, the cleverest, too, and the funniest. I think that's why it took so long for us to accept it, my ex and I, to admit our marriage was over, because it was like' – he paused – 'it was like, how can we not still love each other when we have made these incredible humans together? And I joke, but they are beautiful inside and out. Take after their mother, obviously.' These last words he offered without humour. It was gracious, kind, intelligent.

'Obviously.' She smiled at him. 'I understand that, not wanting to give up because something good came out of it.' Lilly coughed, now feeling slightly uncomfortable as her emotions surged, wishing they could go back to discussing mint humbugs and sunsets spied from the top deck of the bus. 'I mean, I've never been married. That all . . . all passed me by.'

'How did it pass you by? If that's not being too . . .'

'No, no, it's a good question. How did it all pass me by?' It struck her then as the saddest of statements, that marriage, children, a shared life, things that seemed to fall into the laps of just about anyone who wanted them with varying degrees of success, had not come to her. She took a beat. 'I always thought it would be easy, just what happened. You grew up, got married, had babies, worked hard, died. That was kind of the blueprint for life.'

'Sounds bloody miserable!' he added.

'With obvious pockets of pure joy, if you knew where to look! Fulfilment in your career or whatever, a love of music, yada . . . yada . . .' she added to appease him. 'It honestly didn't occur to me that I might not do those things. My mum and dad's marriage didn't work out, and I think that was the first time I was aware of this feeling of otherness, that my life wasn't the same as other people's because my mum walked out. I was an oddity back then.'

'Yep.' He nodded, of the same generation as her, when couples stuck together no matter how miserable or due to economic necessity, societal pressure or lack of choice. Everyone seemed to have a mum and a dad and at least one sibling under their roof, and if you didn't, well, what was wrong with you?

'That otherness seemed to stay with me, I don't know why really, but my life wasn't like other people's. I look at my friend Glenda, and it's been very simple for her. She's followed the blueprint without trying, really. It all just fell into place for her.'

'Do you resent that?'

'No, no!' She was emphatic. 'Not at all. It's more that I didn't realise I wasn't in the race until it was too late and everyone else had crossed the finishing line, if that makes any sense. I kind of had my head down and then had my head turned and then had my head messed up a little bit, and by the time I came up for air I was in my early forties, and everyone around me was paired up.'

'Forty? No age at all!'

'Not now it isn't, but at the time . . .' She smiled at him, knowing he'd get it, how every decade helped you realise how very young you were only ten years ago. There it was again, that darn bulge in her throat of sorrow at just how quickly the decades had indeed passed. 'My nan once said to me, and I remember this even though I can only have been maybe six or seven, that you might be like the last sock at the back of the drawer, one of those odd socks that lingers until another odd sock comes along and, just for the sake of neatness, someone brings you together and you become a pair. I wonder if maybe that affected my perception of myself, my view of having a relationship with another person. Maybe it was that lingering, almost subconscious view that I was the oddest of socks?'

'You never met another odd sock?'

It made her think about Rex, who for a while had so very nearly fallen into place for her. Lovely Rex, a fling . . . She hadn't thought about him for the longest time . . . One thing Lilly did know was that pondering what might have been didn't get you anywhere; another lesson Bertie had taught her.

'Not really.' She coughed to budge that lump. 'I did have a dear, dear friend; love of a different kind, someone who you could definitely describe as an odd, vibrant, wonderful sock!' She smiled now to think of the glorious Bertie Barnes. 'And romantically, I have had a couple of . . .' She ran out of words, unsure how to phrase what she had experienced without that, too, sounding bloody miserable. 'I did meet someone, but there was nothing odd about him, not at first. I was curiously drawn to him, as if fate had put him there.' Lilly was aware that she had been more open than was comfortable. 'Anyway, don't know how we've veered on to that stuff and nonsense! I guess, in short, I was never really drawn to the idea of a summer wedding, a floaty frock, pastel flowers and all the shenanigans that go with it. I never felt like it was for me.'

'You don't believe in fate?'

'No, I don't, not at all. But I believed in him.' She drew a sharp breath; it was not only painful to make such an admission but also a shock that she had felt comfortable enough to do so.

'Hmmm.' Alfie started walking, at a slower pace this time, and she matched him.

'I don't regret the way my life has turned out, not now. I've been freer than a lot of my friends, unencumbered by the day-to-day running of a kitchen, looking after a family, kids and all of that.' The words sounded a little hollow, even though there was some truth in it.

'Do you think your obsession with the river, if I may call it that, is because you have been freer, not distracted by the routine of caring for a family, cooking meals, and all the stuff that goes with it? I'm not sure if that's okay to ask. I am having to remind myself that we have only just met and this has taken a very deep dive!'

'Yes, it has.' She chuckled as he echoed her thoughts. 'So, are you suggesting I am married to this river, and that it holds my attention in the way my children might, or a devoted husband? And that the hours I would spend defrosting fish fingers or darning socks, odd or otherwise, packing lunches, or whatever it is parents do – are you saying the time I would spend on all of those tasks, I instead lavish on this body of water?' she asked, half in jest.

'Well, I suppose I might be!' He smiled at her then, a warm, connecting smile that promised another day just like this one.

'And I suppose you might be right.' She held his eyeline.

'Not that it's anything to do with me, of course. I mean, each to their own.'

He raised his hands over his face as if she might strike him; instead, she laughed. He was funny and smart, and she knew this was the kind of moment that made life in this city wonderful. *Exactly* this.

1973 – aged 17

'Is your dad coming? We do like Robert!' Bertie Barnes clasped his hands under his chin.

'We do like Robert, but sadly, no, his orchestra is playing in Weston-super-Mare.'

'Oh, of course! Yes, Chris said he'd be away this weekend.'

Such was the lovely closeness of Lilly's friendship with Bertie, it was often easy to forget that their introduction had come about via their orchestra connection.

'In that case, I'm thinking of coming across as a concerned parent and asking this Wilkie chap outright what his intentions might be!'

Lilly regretted calling her mum, letting her in. It felt disloyal. Bertie was of course neutral, her friend, and she had then confided in him, happy to have someone with whom she could examine the detail and rehash conversations between her and Wilkie. It was a glorious new preoccupation.

'No! Bertie, you mustn't! Please don't!' Her face flushed with embarrassment at the thought.

'I'm teasing you! Fret not, Bob, I will be charming!'

'That's equally as worrying,' she admitted, unsure how Wilkie might receive Bertie's charm.

He turned to her, his expression suddenly serious. 'I know you're a grown-up, almost.'

She rolled her eyes.

'But I need to tell you to be careful, to take care of yourself and not to dive into anything that might not feel quite so inviting once you are fully immersed. Remember, the water always looks lovely from up above. It's only when you're paddling in it that you find you're ankle deep in mud and shopping trolleys.'

'I am not immersed in anything!' She laughed, unwilling to admit that she wanted to be fully immersed. Wanted to jump into Wilkie's arms, wanted to devour his body, to feel his skin against hers, wanted to sleep in his arms and to hear his heart beat beneath her cheek. She wanted it all. Whether this was normal or not was a whole other thing.

Glenda was, she knew, saving herself for marriage, although she and Norman had 'fumbled', as she put it, on the back seat of his Cortina. Anything, however, that involved going inside underwear, actual flesh-to-flesh contact, was strictly forbidden, even for a girl like Glenda, who while not exactly nun material, was still awash with Catholic guilt that even the temptation of a stud like Norm couldn't sway her from. Lilly smiled, although it was a mean thought. Norman didn't deserve her derision, he was just quiet, but seemed kind and committed and did drive her friend all the way back to Enfield three nights a week. She figured the stop at Pymmes Park and associated fumbling must make it worth it.

Lilly shared no such religious concerns and was ready to go all out. She had read about sex, studied art, where it was in every stroke of the brush. She liked the eroticism of work like Manet's *Olympia* and was drawn to the gloriously pendulous Greek sculptures that graced many a museum. Her literature choices, too, had grown a little risqué as she'd matured, and there was currently a battered copy of *Lady*

Chatterley's Lover secreted under her mattress. She was not shy when it came to trying to understand sex, and yet her physical experience was zero, but since making Wilkie's acquaintance she thought about little else. And try as she might, it was almost impossible not to confuse the physical sexual act with thoughts of love – *love!* Finding herself staring at couples who walked hand in hand along the towpath, imagining her and Wilkie doing similar. A fine, fashionable couple with all the answers, he a mathematician, she an artist; they had all bases covered. And what adorable children they would make! Yes, her mind went there – picturing curly-haired, plump-cheeked kids who would create glorious mayhem, happy chaos, grandchildren whom her dad would adore! Children for whom she would cook hot, golden chips! Now, how many kids would she like . . .

'Bob!'

'Three!' she shouted in response, confused from her daydream.

'Three? *What?*' Bertie stared at her, as her face blushed again. 'Where were you?' He clicked his fingers. 'You were bloody miles away! I was saying that people are gathering on the pavement, a fabulously eccentric crowd! Are we ready to dazzle, you wonderful creature?' He took her head in his hands and kissed her forehead; she felt the cool metal of his large garnet ring against her temple.

'I'm ready!' She nodded and went to open the double doors.

Bertie had taken care of every little detail, reminding her that all the night required to be successful was 'good lighting, great music, cold drinks, delicious canapés, the right guest list and plenty of pzazz!' He then made out to sprinkle invisible magic dust in an arc around his head. It seemed he had sprinkled just the right amount, as the place was buzzing!

Invited guests flowed through the door like one of Mother Thames's tributaries. Like fish swimming upstream, or the clutch of little ducks she liked to watch from the flat as they sat behind their mum and let the tide take them up and down, carried along at the will of the current, tiny wings tucked in, feet paddling, stopping only to peck at the murky surface of the water with their new beaks, gobbling insects and bits of goodness-knows-what that looked appealing enough to swallow. These guests were brightly dressed in striped suits of candy pink and green. Gold lurex shirts, tight, tight jeans, silky short shorts with knee-high socks and roller boots, feather boas, the odd fedora, even an elaborate silk turban with a feather on the front. White suits, chiffon scarves, ornate caftans, stacked heels, platform-soled clogs, and enough blue eye shadow to paint a wide stripe right around the room. They smoked cigarillos, sported chunky gold chains, and instead of quacking, like those tiny ducklings she so admired, their call was a single word, offered in so many variants:

'Darling!'

'Dahling!'

'Daarling!'

'Dah-ling!'

'Da'ling!'

She couldn't help but laugh, because this was one of those moments she'd remember, because it was exciting to be among it, and because Wilkie was on the pavement, looking past the ensemble right at her, as if it was her he had come to see, her who was the draw, and because she was seventeen and falling in love!

She spied Beautiful Jack in the crowd and waved at him.

'Darling!' was his reply.

The exhibition opening was loud and dramatic! A mini scuffle ensued when a flailing arm knocked a large tumbler of red wine over Denzel Bashington's mohair *Kilgour, French & Stanbury* blazer. Denzel, one of the louder members of the crowd, a trainee barrister, no less. Bertie had been in the thick of it, of course, doing his loud and level best to break it up, while his eyes sparkled with delight, as if happy to be part of the theatrics. Two women had raised their voices when one had inadvertently, apparently, called the other by the name of her husband's mistress. All very exciting!

As the liquor ran out and the last of the guests were ushered from the premises, a gaggle of them left en masse to go dancing in Soho, with Bertie and Beautiful Jack leading the charge. Lilly locked the doors and turned on the pavement to look at Wilkie.

'Is it always like this?' he asked, his expression a little shell-shocked.

'No! It's usually just a regular shift: Bertie and I, Radio Luxembourg and a few mugs of tea, while we natter and put the world right. We have been known to break out the biscuits on occasion.'

Wilkie exhaled. 'And there was me thinking the world of algebra and improper fractions was exhilarating!'

'You survived?' She put the keys in her suede fringed shoulder bag.

'Only just! So where to, Cinderella? It's not yet midnight so can I assume we have time before your carriage turns into a pumpkin?'

'You can assume that.' She fell into step beside him as they walked towards the river.

'I'm following you. This is your neck of the woods. I'm just a poor teacher visiting from the country! No idea where we're heading.' He doffed his invisible cap.

'When I was little, my dad explained that I could never get lost in this city, not really, as all I had to do was find a landmark near the river and follow the water all the way home.' She felt the smallest flare of guilt; here she was, building a relationship, no doubt like her mum had with Derek Manners, both behind her dad's back.

'I like that. It's important, isn't it, giving kids the tools and not just the cliché? Showing them *how* rather than just telling them that everything will be all right in the end.'

'He's always been good at that, helping me figure out how.'

'He sounds like a good dad.'

'He is.' She smiled, looking forward to introducing the two men, knowing in advance they would get on.

'And your mum?' His enquiry was casual and not unusual. Yet still she felt the cool wind of shame ripple over her skin. *She left us . . . left me . . .*

'Not around.' Felt easiest. And she was thankful he didn't press the topic.

'So where are we headed, Elizabeth-Roberta?'

She liked it when he said her name.

'I want to show you something.'

'In that case, lead on, Macduff!' He pointed over her head.

'You like Shakespeare?' She turned to him, grinning because they were together, and she had a plan.

'Oh, is that Shakespeare?'

'You are a lost cause!' She ran, and he ran after her, catching up as they neared the end of Vauxhall Bridge, her heart beating too fast and her breath stuttering in her throat. Wilkie took her hand and spun her towards him, as if they were shaking, rattling and rolling in a jive. It happened quickly, her body landing against his and his mouth coming down on to hers as he kissed her long and hard. It was the kiss she had imagined, the kiss she had longed for! Right there on the end of the bridge where the lights of Pimlico pooled in juddering shadows on the water and the moon looked particularly large and beautiful. This contact, this desire, proof that the attraction was a mutual thing, the relief of which was extraordinary. Her body responded by lifting clear off the ground and allowing her to float overhead, watching from above as she spiralled among the stars. This was the very moment she transitioned from girl to woman, or at least that was what it felt like.

'I'm thirty-three,' he whispered when finally she landed.

'You're very old,' she replied in jest, running her hand over his lower back, feeling beneath his shirt to touch his skin, to scratch him with her nails, to indicate that she was no child and was aware of where this contact was headed.

They held hands as they meandered their way back to Waide House. Stopping to lean against the wall that edged the river, to kiss and gasp and murmur their pleasure, all the more intense because of what it promised.

'Is your dad at home?' he asked nervously as she fished in her bag for her door key.

'I'm alone tonight.'

Stumbling through the front door, Lilly wasted no time in taking his hand and leading him to her bedroom, where all of her dreams and imaginings were made real. Wilkie wrenched off his clothes and stood in his pants before shedding those, too, and reaching for her once again.

'Is this . . .' he breathed into her hair between kisses as he helped her out of her shirt and bra. 'Have you . . .'

'No. But I want this, Wilkie, I want you. I do.'

Quickly now, he kissed her with an urgency as they tumbled back on to her rather narrow bed.

◆ ◆ ◆

It was the next morning that Wilkie asked, 'What was it you wanted to show me?' She handed him a mug of tea, laughing as he pulled the silk edge of the blanket, which he'd fashioned into a kind of toga and now wore at the kitchen table. A strange moment where she understood that, in the space of hours, his presence in her family home, his nudity, his body, his most intimate secrets, his moments of release and vulnerability were all familiar to her in a way that only yesterday would have been unthinkable. At seventeen, she had come to understand it was this way with life – those seconds when the world flipped upside down and what was beyond comprehension and imagination one minute was the norm in the next.

Mum has moved out . . .

Is this . . . have you . . .

No, but it's what I want . . .

'Ah yes, follow me for the big reveal!' Reaching for his hand, the novelty of which she knew might never wear off, she pulled him up and guided him into the lounge, watching as he, like everyone else who had spent time in the room, walked straight to the wide window with the exceptional view.

'Wow!'

'Yep, wow!' It was delightful to see he was as impressed as she'd hoped he might be. It was important to her.

'It's incredible! Like you're almost in the water, over the water – not sure how to describe it!'

Wilkie stared at the river and sipped his hot tea. Lilly blinked as if her eyes were the shutters of a lens so she could capture this moment for always. His hair resting on his shoulders, his unshaven chin, his eyes still a little puffy from lack of sleep. His pale skin, covered in dark curls that tufted on his chest, his lower back, his shoulders and shins.

'This is some place.'

'I never take it for granted. I think that's why I paint it a lot, or try to. I want to capture it, but it's never the same one minute to the next.'

'An impossible task, then.' He turned to smile at her, tea in hand, wrapped in the peach-coloured blanket that had been next to her skin since she was a small girl. She liked the fact that when he wasn't here she would be able to put it against her body, knowing it carried the imprint, the scent and essence of him.

'I guess so, and yet, oddly, that doesn't put me off. In fact it makes me more determined.'

'Tenacious, undaunted and beautiful. You really are the whole package, Elizabeth-Roberta.'

She didn't feel the need to correct him, giggle or play dumb, because this morning she felt beautiful! Felt alive! And knew for a fact she was tenacious, which meant she would keep painting until she got the picture just right.

'I wanted to ask you, what season would you be, if I'm spring?' She sat in the chair and folded her legs beneath her.

'Ah, I'd be winter, no doubt.' He spoke without hesitation, suggesting he'd given it some thought.

'Winter?' she laughed.

'You seem to disagree!'

'Yes, I disagree! Surely not winter.'

'You don't know me.' He turned to face her then, his tone cool, wintry.

'I know enough.' This the truth, *her* truth: that after the physical union they had shared, the way he had looked her in the eye as his face hovered mere inches from hers, the intensity with which he had held her tightly, breathed against her, found a mutual rhythm that was as hypnotic as it was binding, she knew him enough. Her first . . .

'And that's another adorable thing about you.' He smiled. 'Your transparency, your trust. It's all still there, intact, because experience hasn't yet taught you to think differently.'

'That sounds ominous!' She pulled a face.

'It's the truth. You have that guileless exuberance of youth that is a magic elixir!'

'I see.'

'You don't. You can't possibly,' he countered, as if reading her mind, 'but don't think of it as a negative thing. It's wonderful.'

His words and tone verged on the patronising, and she didn't like it, folding her arms around her body and looking out towards the water, wanting him gone in that second, punishment almost for making her feel like a child.

'I am almost double your age, Lilly. Double!'

'And?' she fired back, facing him now.

'Not so disastrous, maybe, with you at seventeen, but if you were fifty . . .'

'You'd be a hundred!'

'And if you were seventy . . .'

'A hundred and forty – now that *is* old.' She widened her eyes.

'A lot of people would have a lot to say about the age gap.' He shook his head, as if she just didn't get it. 'You're a bud, beautiful, tightly packed, about to burst forth, and I am already wilting at the edges . . .'

'Wilkie, you're thirty-three, not eighty-three!'

'Physically maybe, but my mind is old, my ways set, my route planned, my life on track.'

'You and I are not set, not planned! This is spontaneous and glorious!' She beamed.

'Indeed.' His face broke into a smaller smile. 'It's both of these things, and the realisation of that makes me feel old, understanding how rare it is for me to feel this way. Others would see me as old, in comparison to you, young Elizabeth-Roberta, too old. They'd question my right to take this exuberance, this moment of youth, from you.'

'My dad says you can only truly find contentment when you worry less about what other people think.'

'Oh, sweet one.' He came close to her now and ran his fingers over her cheek. 'It is in these lovely words, repeated so faithfully from such a trusted source, where my point is entirely made.'

Lilly didn't fully understand what he meant but felt her resolve and petty frustration melt away under the heat of his touch and the prospect of what lay ahead.

'Why winter?' It had bothered her; she asked with her eyes closed.

'A cold, bleak blanket of darkness that covers all things bright and colourful . . .' He spoke in a low voice of doom that made her laugh. He was not and never could be winter, not to her.

'What would you like to do today? Is there anywhere you need to be? Do you have plans?' Doing her best to sound indifferent, not wanting to appear too keen or overbearing, her heart lifted as he reached out and took her hand into his fingers.

'Yes, I plan on taking you back to bed. Lovely as the view is . . .'

Lilly laughed out loud again, delighted, excited and eager to get back to the task of learning every inch of his body.

◆ ◆ ◆

The weekend passed too quickly, and when her dad arrived home on Sunday afternoon, the first thing he did was put a record on and let the joyful hopping notes of Vivaldi's '*Spring*', part of *the Four Seasons* suite, fill their space. The connection wasn't lost on her, a sign from the universe, no doubt, it had to be a sign!

It took all of her concentration to remember not to blurt out, *I am so happy, because I've spent the most glorious hours in my bed with a man called Wilkie Jones who thinks that if I were a season, I would be spring!*

'The place looks nice. Did you have to clear up after a party?' he asked affectionately as he filled the kettle and reached for a mug. His humour telling, confident that she would never have a party, never disrespect their home, and to his knowledge did not have enough friends to invite to a party.

'Hardly!' She smiled at him from the table, where she was attempting to write part of her essay on the importance of texture and contrast in collage. 'How was your concert?'

'Good, good! Yes, we got a lovely reception, and it was nice to get some sea air. Not that there was much sea to see. The tide goes out for miles at Weston, more mud than water, but still lovely. And we had a decent fry-up at the boarding house this morning, full works: bacon, sausage, egg, beans, fried bread, the lot.'

'And you do love a good breakfast!'

'I do indeed.' Her dad stared at her, and she looked away, wondering if he could tell, just by looking, that she was quite altered since he saw her last.

'You seem . . . happy?' he asked with the crease of confusion at the top of his nose, and she understood that since his wife had gone, happy was for him always a little out of reach. Yet how she wished it for him! It was hard not to let his lack of it bleed into her veins, which were bursting with the stuff.

'I am.' She blinked and bit her bottom lip; it was impossible not to think about Wilkie kissing her mouth until it felt a little bruised, a little pulled about. Her whole body, in fact, ached in a glorious and exhausted way that she knew she would never tire of.

'How was the exhibition opening? Was Bertie pleased?' he asked as he took the lid off the biscuit barrel with his thumbs and delved inside, pulling out three flaky Lemon Puffs that were his treat.

'He was. A great success, actually.' She did this, sanitised some aspects of Bertie's life that she felt might be a little too hard for her dad to fathom. He was of a different generation, from a different era. A man who had fought a world war so that she could enjoy all of her freedoms. He didn't need to know that Bertie had been at the centre of a scuffle, something and nothing really, over a mohair suit that got splashed with red wine, but had left at the end of the night beaming, as he and Beautiful Jack had traipsed off with their eclectic crowd to go dancing in an underground Soho club.

'Good. We have a proper treat for supper later; I stopped by Brodin's on the way home.' The Brodin brothers ran a fish stall on the banks of the river, near Westminster Bridge, famed for its seafood fetched fresh daily from the trawlers of West Mersea. Her mouth watered in anticipation. 'Skate wings and a large pot of whelks!'

'Oh, lovely!' Her stomach rumbled, ravenous at the thought of supper.

She remembered then her call to her mum and felt the shawl of disloyalty about her shoulders. The inescapable fact was, in a perfect world, her mum would be sat on the other side of the table with her own cup of tea and a biscuit, and they'd no doubt be sharing surreptitious looks. The two, like sisters, conspiratorial and friendly, sharing this huge life-changing thing that had thrown a rock into her world, the ripples of which Lilly hoped she would feel for ever. It was a whole new way in which to miss her mum, and it hurt.

'I love you, Dad.'

He paused and beamed at her, as if lit from within. 'And how very lucky that makes me!' He smiled, licking off the syrup that the Lemon Puffs were coated with, leaving fingers sticky with their residue.

Present day

'So give me the details again.' Glenda sipped her tea. 'He just walks past, asks you about your picture and you end up spending the afternoon with him?'

'Yes, that's about the sum of it.' Lilly put the milk back in the fridge.

'Well, I'm not sure what I think about that.' Her friend pulled the face of disapproval she'd been pulling for the last fifty years or more.

'You don't have to think anything about it, Glen. I'm a grown-up. I made a decision and went for it, trusted my gut, and it was only a drink – we didn't elope!'

'Yes, but you don't know the first thing about him! He could be an axe murderer!'

'Why is that always the first place people go? Why don't they think he could be a scammer or a strangler or a con artist or a knife-wielding maniac? Why do we always go for axe murderer?'

'I don't know, Lil.' Her friend took another gulp of tea.

'I mean, how many murders are actually committed by axe? I'm guessing not many.'

'I know you're being funny, so I'm just going to ignore you.' It made Lilly smile. 'So was it a date?' Glenda asked as she reached for a Hobnob, snapped it and placed one half in her mouth so the pointy angles stuck out in her cheek.

'I feel daft saying *date* – I'm seventy!' Lilly then giggled in a way that was girlish and giddy and all the things she most definitely was not.

'But if pressed, would you say it was?' Glenda persisted.

'I suppose, if pressed.' She smiled.

'And you're seeing him again tonight?' her friend asked with the unmistakeable undertone of disapproval.

'Yes.'

'Bit keen, isn't it?' Glenda crunched her biscuit.

'I suppose it is.' She sighed, secretly thrilled at the idea of his keenness. 'We've arranged to go out for supper, the Gordon Ramsay place in Battersea.'

'Ooh, very nice. Hardly sharing a bag of chips, is it? That'll cost a few bob.'

'Yep.' It was then she decided not to share the words 'fortune' and 'farm', knowing how Glenda could be about money.

'You should have a look at the menu online and see what you fancy before you go.'

'That's a good idea!'

'Norm always does it, in case a place is only vegan or vegetarian and he can pop a sausage roll in the glovebox for on the way home. Makes the kids laugh. Our Bradley's vegan now.'

'Oh, I didn't know. Alfie is a pescatarian, so just fish.'

'Pescatarian? What's that all about!' Glenda scoffed. 'I mean, is it any less cruel to eat something that's had a hook through its arse than it is to eat something that's had a bolt through its head?'

'Hmmm, that's a very good question, Glen, and one I shall be sure to raise with him.'

There was a knock at the front door, and Lilly went to open it.

'Clodagh! Hello, love. Glenda and I were just having a cuppa. Would you like one?'

'Yes, please.'

Lilly noted the way the young woman avoided eye contact and had clearly been crying. She placed her hand on her narrow back the moment she walked inside.

'Apollo not with you?' It was strange to see her alone outside of school hours.

Clodagh shook her head.

'Are you all right, darling?'

'Not really, no.' This was enough for a fresh batch of tears to fall down her face.

'Come through, come on.'

Lilly guided her to the kitchen, where Glenda thankfully budged up at the table.

'Oh no. What's the matter, love?' Her friend was as moved as Lilly to see her young neighbour in such distress.

The two women watched as Clodagh placed her arms in a cradle on the tabletop and put her head on them, crying heartily now as her shoulders shook and she sniffed and snuffled.

Glenda pulled a wad of tissues from her handbag and placed them on the young woman's arm.

'There, there, my love. Nothing is as bad as it seems at first.'

Lilly was thankful for her friend's wisdom and kindness. Glenda might be a funny old soul at times, but this was at her core.

Clodagh's fingers snaked out and pulled the tissues inside the dark confines of her table cave, and she blew her nose and wiped her eyes before sitting up. Her skin was blotchy, her eyes were red and her mouth was quivering.

'Apollo's . . .' She paused. Lilly felt the stutter of her heartbeat, waiting to see what came out of Clodagh's mouth next. Apollo was what? Hurt, ill, lost? All the terrible possibilities ran through her mind. 'He's with his dad, Sab.'

Lilly exhaled, unaware she'd been holding her breath. This relief was instantly replaced with new concerns: *why* did Sab have him, *how* had he got him?

'Well, if he's anything like my Norman, they'll be having a lovely time. Nothing to cry about, love.'

She knew Glenda meant well, taping clichés over the direst of wounds in the hope that it might make things feel better.

'He's not seen him for a long time, and he just turned up at school.' Clodagh gave Glenda the potted version.

'How did he know where you were?' Lilly, of course, knew the backstory.

'Apparently, Milar's mum works with his sister and mentioned that she knew me from nursery, she told her about Apollo, and I guess they put two and two together.'

'Oh God.' She could only imagine the consequences of this coincidence.

'I was so shocked, I didn't do anything, didn't say anything, I just stared at him. He's got a flash car now, and of course Apollo went nuts when he saw him. He ran into his arms, and Sab was crying, and it was like this wonderful reunion for everyone, apart from me. I felt like I'd been shot. I was rooted to the spot, and Sab asked if he could take Apollo to the park and I didn't know what to say. What I wanted to say was no, no way, but I wasn't sure if I could or should. Then Apollo starts jumping up and down, so excited to be going in his dad's car, and so I just nodded and told him to be back in an hour and a half and gave him our address. He's going to drop him off here, and that means I have to see him again, and it means he now knows where we are, and I think, legally, he might be able to see Apollo, even if I don't want him to. I don't know what's happening!' She cried again.

'Okay, okay.' Lilly spoke as softly and calmly as she was able, feeling an anxious soup of concern slosh in her stomach. 'We are going to take this one step at a time. The first thing is to sit tight until Apollo is home safely.'

'You think he won't come home safely?' Clodagh asked with a rising note of hysteria.

'No! No, of course he will!' Lilly hoped she sounded more confident than she felt. 'Then after a good night's sleep we will look at all the options. You have rights.'

'But he does too!'

'Yes, but he hasn't seen the boy for a long time, and he lied to you, and there are other things at play. I'm no lawyer, but we can get advice, Clodagh. You are not to worry yourself over things that might not happen. Okay? No worrying until you absolutely have to.'

'Lilly's right,' Glenda chimed.

'Good Lord, did you hear that?' Lilly elbowed Clodagh, softly. 'Glenda just said I was right. That's a first!'

'Cheeky mare! She's only being cocky because she's got a date tonight!' Glenda's eyes lit up, thrilled to share such gossip.

'A date? Who with?' Clodagh sniffed and wiped her eyes, this the perfect diversion, something for the three of them to get their teeth into.

'Well, his name is Alfred – Alfie.'

'He's a pescatarian and can't be short of a bob or two, he's taking her to that Gordon Ramsay place in Battersea.' Glenda filled in the gaps.

'Wow! You dark horse, Lilly! I'm just glad one of us is getting some action in the romance department.'

'Speak for yourself!' Glenda tutted. 'My Norm is quite the romantic. He always saves the end of the bread for me because he knows I like a knob, and he lies on my side of the bed on a cold night so that when I get in my bit of the mattress is warm.'

Clodagh covered her face as her shoulders shook.

'Oh, don't cry, love! Please don't cry!' Lilly wondered what had set the girl off. It was only when Clodagh removed her hands that it became apparent she was in fact laughing, not a tear in sight.

'I'm sorry!' It seemed once Clodagh had started, it was almost impossible to stop.

'What's so funny?' Glenda asked Lilly, as if she'd missed the joke.

'You said . . .' Clodagh wheezed as she banged the tabletop, trying to get a grip, 'you said that Norm knows you like a knob and I wondered where you were going with that!'

'For the love of God!' Glenda tried to sound stern, but pretty soon all three were chuckling away until they were breathless and more than a little giddy.

Their laughter was brought to a halt by a knock on the door.

'It's like Piccadilly bloody Circus in here today!' Glenda shouted as Lilly went to open it, and the three laughed again, as you did when you got the giggles.

Lilly's smile faded as she came face to face with Joshua Vaughan.

'Mr Vaughan! To what do I owe the pleasure?'

'Can I come in?' He pointed over her shoulder.

'Oh, why not!' She sighed. 'Come through! It's not as if anything you may or may not have to say won't reach the ears of these two anyway. Cup of tea?'

'Yes, please!' He looked more than a little delighted to have been asked.

'Who's this, then?' Glenda eyed the young man suspiciously.

'This is Mr Vaughan, from the company who want to knock down my home.'

'And you let him in?' Her friend narrowed her eyes at him.

'Hello!' He lifted his hand to give Glenda a nervous wave, before turning his attentions to Clodagh. 'Hi, Miss Newman.'

'Hi.' Clodagh wiped her face and sat up straight, finding a small smile as her cheeks bloomed.

There was something about the way he looked at the young woman that made Lilly do a double take. A certain linger in his eye contact, a reluctance to look away, the slight flush to his neck, and the way he swallowed as if trying to contain words and feelings that might want to leap from his throat. And for the first time she felt a rush of kindness towards the young man, who was clearly a very good judge of character, as Clodagh was entirely wonderful.

'I just wanted to let you know that things have moved on a little, and we have a date.'

'It seems everyone has dates on their mind around here!' Glenda laughed at her own joke. Lilly and Clodagh practically ignored her, understanding better that this might be important news.

'Portland and Montague have worked with the relevant agencies, and you will have thirty days to accept the offer on your flat or they will proceed with compulsory purchase and things could happen quite quickly after that.'

'Can they do that?' Lilly asked Mr Vaughan, in a way that suggested he might be on her side.

'They can, and they have.' He gave a wan smile, as if he might indeed, even just a little bit, be on her side. Her instinct was to shout, to wail! Thirty days – a blink! She felt the bloom of panic and did her best to keep it from her face, not wanting to alarm Clodagh or Glenda and wondering who she should write to next to plead her case.

'Thirty days. That's not long, Lil!'

She looked at her friend. 'No, it isn't, is it?'

'And what about me? What's my timeline?' Clodagh picked at the skin around her fingernail, nervously.

'As . . . as per the terms of your last letter.' He blushed, and Lilly saw it then, the widening of his pupils, the dry mouth, the red scalp and the almost painful inability to hold the young woman's eyeline, lest she look into his soul and see his feelings. 'We will endeavour to have you settled in the new apartment within the next eight to ten weeks.'

Eight to ten weeks! It would pass in a flash. Lilly felt the echo of loneliness that was her greatest fear, the very thought of losing this place and moments like this in the kitchen when the kettle boiled and she and the girls laughed around the table – all of it about to be lost, and it felt like there was very little she could do about it. Quite out of ideas as to what might be her next move, how she might be able to effect a different outcome.

There was a knock at the door.

'Lord above!' Glenda shouted for no particular reason, but it certainly added to the drama.

Lilly went to the door.

'Hi, is Clodagh here?' The young man was handsome, well dressed and smiling as he gripped Apollo's hand. 'She said to try here first, so . . .'

'I've been to the park!' Apollo yelled as he slipped his hand from his dad's and ran into the apartment. *Mayhem . . . glorious mayhem . . .*

'Yes, let me go and get her for you. One sec.' She decided against asking Sab in; this was, after all, a safe space for Clodagh, a refuge, and the last thing she wanted to do was put memories of Sab in it. She knew how those images and thoughts could linger and taint a place, picturing her dad at the kitchen table crying, not long after her mum had packed up and shipped out.

Although if what Joshua had said was true it seemed almost inevitable that they were both on the move. The date made it seem very real, imminent, and she recalled Denzel's advice, that the wealthy developers had more money, time and resources than her. *They could tie you up in legal knots that would be costly, and you could end up with nothing. They are quite powerful . . . I would advise you to take the money, take as much money as you can, and run.*

'We're right here,' she whispered to Clodagh. As she passed in the hallway, Lilly gave her an intense stare which she hoped conveyed that she was only a few feet away, should the young woman need anything.

Lilly hovered out of sight by the bedroom door, not to eavesdrop but to be on hand should the need arise.

'All right, Clo?' she heard Sab ask.

'Yep.'

'I think he had a nice time.'

'Yes, he loves the park.' It was heartbreaking to hear Clodagh's voice sound so shaky.

'He's grown so much!'

'Yep. Look, Sab, I don't want to argue with you, but you can't just turn up like that and take him. I was put on the spot. That can't happen again.'

Lilly recognised the tremor of fear in her voice, and it took all her strength not to rush forward and scoop her up.

'And you can't kick me out of the flat and do a runner, but that's what happened!' He raised his voice.

'I didn't kick you out, I sent you back to your fiancée. The fiancée who is probably now your wife. You strung us both along – we had a child!'

'I'm aware – a child you took away from me!'

There was a beat of quiet and Lilly held her breath.

'As I said, Sab, I don't want to argue with you, not here, not anywhere, but especially not here. This is my friend's flat.' Clodagh's voice had calmed a little.

'Well, we need to sort it out. I'm not going to let you disappear for eighteen months and not let me see my son! You won't be doing that again!'

'Okay, okay.' Clodagh was doing her best to keep the situation civil. 'I hear you. I think we should let things settle and make a plan, calmly and sensibly, like adults. You have my number now, so call any time; tonight, next week, whenever you're ready. As I say, let's talk calmly and make a plan and—'

'You are not going to shut me out again, Clodagh. He's my son!' Sab yelled then, igniting the atmosphere in an instant.

It was as Lilly was deciding whether or not to intervene that Joshua Vaughan ran from the kitchen and came to a stop in the doorway.

'She said you can call her any time to make a plan. She *literally* just said that, and yet you're still shouting!'

'And who are you?' Sab, jaw tense, stance rigid, pointed at Mr Vaughan.

'I'm a friend.'

His presence seemed to do the trick. Sab shoved his hands into his jeans pockets and looked directly at Clodagh. 'Next week, then.' These parting words sounded curiously threatening as he made his way down the stairs.

Lilly came out into the hallway.

'Thanks.' Clodagh smiled up at Joshua as she closed the front door.

'S'okay.'

Joshua Vaughan's face broke into a smile that quite changed him.

'Do you . . . do you like dinosaurs?' Apollo asked, standing by the man's leg. His little voice speaking quickly, his breathing loud, the only clues to suggest that seeing his parents shout at each other had upset him.

'I do.' He nodded.

'Do you like sticks?' was the little boy's next question, a little calmer now.

'Some sticks, not all of them.'

'Do you like playing cars?'

'Yes.'

'What is your favourite kind of pasta?' Apollo asked with his usual wide-eyed smile of interest, which was most endearing.

'Erm . . .' Joshua looked skyward, as if considering this. 'I quite like the swirly corkscrew stuff. What about you?'

'Pasketti.' Apollo spoke as if *this* was the definitive answer before running off.

'I see, pasketti!' Joshua nodded.

Clodagh laughed, looking up at the man and smiling, as if seeing him for the first time; this young man who had very obviously shown up for her.

It was as ironic as it was conflicting that the one good thing that might come out of the harrowing possibility of losing her home was that the bearer of all the bad news might just be the person who brought joy to Clodagh and Apollo. Lilly honestly didn't know whether to laugh or cry.

1973 – aged 17

Lilly looked up, letting the sun glance on her face as she sat on the bench outside the Tate Gallery on Millbank.

'How was your weekend?' Glenda asked, as she pulled the lid from the shallow Tupperware box and sniffed the contents, before pulling out a decidedly limp white bread triangle from its confines, pasted together with Heinz Sandwich Spread. 'Want one?' She pushed the box towards Lilly.

'No, thanks.' Glenda's food tastes were a little different to hers. The glorious memory of that deep-fried skate wing, slathered with butter, still lingered on her tongue. A culinary triumph for her dad. Or maybe in the light of her awakening with Wilkie, food just tasted better, in the way that colours seemed brighter, music more meaningful and the world a generally rosier place to be. 'Yeah, weekend was great. What about yours?'

It was tricky; Glenda was undoubtedly her friend, her best friend, and yet Lilly wasn't sure how she'd react to the fact that Lilly had spent the weekend frolicking beneath the covers with her older lover. She smiled at the secret that filled her with joy and felt the golden glow of excitement, counting down the hours, minutes and seconds until she got to see him again and strip his clothes off. Her dad had no plans to go away again any time soon, so she had agreed this weekend to go to Wilkie's digs in Royal Avenue, where, against the strict rules of the Chelsea boarding house run by the magnificently named Mrs Helen Horn-Haverington, Wilkie planned to sneak her in under the cover of darkness! It was illicit, daring, and all the more thrilling because of it. Her face broke into a smile at the thought as her skin tingled at the memory of his touch.

'Norm and I drove to Southend. Took the Cortina for a run.'

It made Lilly smile, the way she made the Cortina sound like a pet.

'That sounds nice.'

'Well, it would have been, but his mum decided to come, too, and she insisted on sitting in the front. Not much I could say about that, was there?' Glenda bit into her sandwich, her demeanour decidedly downcast.

'I suppose not.'

'I was stuck in the back for what felt like hours, and his mother, Mrs Glaser, didn't shut up, not for a second, going on and on about their neighbours, Norm's school days, his wayward brother, Barry, the time he got lost on a trip to Canvey Island. God, Lil, it was incessant. I imagined wrapping the seatbelt around her neck and strangling her.'

'Probably not the best way to endear yourself to the future in-laws.'

'True, but I was still tempted. It was bloody awful.'

'Sounds it.' Lilly felt sorry for Glenda, who had had her weekend hijacked by Mrs Glaser, the chatterbox. It explained to her why Norman was so quiet; he'd probably spent his life trying to get a word in edgeways.

'Norm kept looking at me in the rear-view mirror when he could take his eyes off the road, and it was nice, the way I knew what he was thinking, that he wished it was just the two of us.'

'I can imagine. I mean, you could hardly stop off at Pymmes Park for a snog with his mother in the car!'

'Honestly, Lil, I wish I'd never told you about that! We have a connection that runs deep. There's more to us than snogging in the car!' Glenda shoved the remainder of her sandwich into her mouth.

'I didn't say there wasn't, but it's important, isn't it? Kissing and the like.' It was the closest she could come to admitting her new and absolute carnal fascination with Wilkie.

'I suppose so.' Glenda stared straight ahead, as if only just considering it.

'You want to rip his clothes off and go further though, don't you? When the time is right, of course!' Lilly laughed at the caveat.

'I've not really thought about it.' Glenda turned to face her.

'You haven't?' It was hard to keep the shock from her voice.

'Well, I know that, once we're married, that will be part of it, but as my mum has always said, we need do no more than our duty and then, when the kids have arrived, it can all be done and dusted with. Like tarmacking the drive or building a shed: do it right first time and it will last a lifetime.'

'I . . . I guess . . .' Lilly stared at her friend and felt an inexplicable sadness that this was how Glenda thought about this most life-affirming of things. Only in her infancy on this sexual journey, she already knew it was something she was keen to explore further, something she liked very much. Was that not normal? Was there something *wrong* with her? Was it odd to think about it as much as she did, to be so keen to feel Wilkie's skin against hers? Lilly was now clear on what Glenda's mum thought about it all, but wished she could speak to her own mum about it, wished her mum wasn't the abandoning kind, wished her dad had not had his heart broken by her, wished a lot of things . . .

'My mum says it's important to give men what they want, but that it all wears off eventually. The fuss dies down and then you can live a simple life, an easier life.'

'Jeez!' Lilly felt aghast at the prospect of all the fuss dying down and did not, if no sex was the result, want to live a *simple, easier* life like that!

'Maybe that's just how your mum feels. Maybe once you and Norm get underneath your candlewick bedspread, you might feel differently?' Lilly spoke softly, kindly, trying to open her friend's eyes without indicating that she might have actual experience or a view to the contrary.

'Maybe.' Glenda dug her fingers beneath the remaining sandwich, produced a McVitie's Taxi and peeled off the wrapper. 'Want a bite?' Glenda was the consummate sharer.

'No, thanks.'

'I think we're probably going to be like our mums though, don't you? I mean, we learn from them, we're half of them. So I think I'll probably feel the same as she does.'

This thought made the breath catch in Lilly's throat. Was there something wrong with her own mum too? Was it Jeannie's dark and desperate sexual desire that had driven her out of the arms of Lilly's dad and into the arms of Derek Manners? Did Lilly herself have the same damaging, destructive streak marbling her veins, meaning she, too, had the capacity to break the heart of someone lovely, someone worthy, someone like Wilkie? And all for what, a taste of the addictive elixir that was good sex?

She shook her head, trying to rid herself of the image of her mum in bed with the cardigan-wearing TV repair man in their flat above the shop. And then a thought that was worse: what if her dad shared the same desire, the *same* want for his wife, and now felt only the loss of it, of her? No wonder he missed her with every breath he took, every minute of every day.

'I want it to be lovely and passionate and for ever.' She spoke the words softly, putting her thoughts out into the world and ridiculously hoping they might float across the city and land in Wilkie's ear.

'I'm more of a realist than you.' Glenda snapped the lid back on the Tupperware box. 'I think more practically about life. I want it to be steady, and Norman is steady; hard-working, doesn't drink or gamble, he's neat, clean and would never raise a hand to me.' Lilly opened her mouth as if to say that should be a given, but chose to stay quiet, not wanting to throw any more tension into the conversation. 'He has also said that one day we will have a lovely little house with a garden and that I can fill it with nice things.'

'And that's enough for you, Glenda?' She knew her friend was a talented ceramicist with a passion for cups and mugs. The thought of her giving it all up to be a housewife, to stay at home and collect the kind of china she was more than capable of making herself, was a sobering one. Lilly wanted marriage, kids, all of it, eventually. But she also wanted to marry the kind of man who would encourage her work, inspire her to paint, and not hem her in or limit her. Even though it was very early days, she felt that someone smart and open like Wilkie might be just what she was looking for. It was a thought that caused her stomach to bunch with excitement! This, too, she was not about to share with Glenda.

'More than enough.' Glenda held her gaze. 'I also think the old phrase is true: no one is going to want to buy the cow if you give the milk for free.'

Her friend stared at her as if she was not quite as in the dark about Lilly and Wilkie's fumblings as she suspected.

'Well, what a terrible phrase that is!' Lilly knew it was one that would make Bertie laugh in the retelling.

'It's true though, Lil. Women can't afford to be so forward, not without being seen in the wrong light. You might not like it, but it's very true. You sure you don't want something to eat?' Glenda held out her lunchbox.

With her friend's words echoing in her thoughts, she had never had less of an appetite.

'Positive, thanks.'

◆ ◆ ◆

Lilly bent over laughing, resting her hands on her knees as she wheezed and tried to catch her breath. 'I can't do it! I can't!' She leaned on the railings outside a house as Wilkie held out his coat.

'You can! Come on! It's an excellent plan. You hide under here and I'll carry you over my shoulder like a rolled-up carpet and lug you up the stairs.'

'What if Mrs Horn-Haverington sees me? She'll think you've committed murder! What with my skinny legs dangling down your back.'

'You might be right.' He rubbed his chin. 'Okay, I've got it.' He clapped his hands together as a thought occurred, a ludicrous idea, fuelled no doubt by the pints he'd consumed in the Prince of Wales pub, while she had sipped shandy. 'What if you shimmy up the drainpipe, I'll go ahead and open the window on the landing, and you clamber in? Are you afraid of heights?'

'No, I'm afraid of falling! There's no way I'm doing that! What if the drainpipe came away from the wall, or what if the window didn't open? I'd be stuck, and you'd have to call the fire brigade!'

'You're putting the kybosh on all my brilliant plans. So, what do you suggest?' He pulled her to him and kissed her on the mouth, a hard and deliberate kiss that was full of promise. Her stomach folded with want.

'I suggest you open the door, I'll quickly run up to the landing, while you loiter and make a noise and chat to the landlady, and then you come up and find me and we slip into your room and lock the door!'

'That might work.' He kissed her again. 'I mean, it's not as funny or as adventurous as the drainpipe suggestion, but it might work.'

Doing her best not to laugh out loud, Lilly stood with her hand clamped over her mouth, as Wilkie, as quietly as he was able, unlocked the front door. True to her word, she sprinted across the hallway, up to the first landing, and stood in a doorway, listening, as Wilkie coughed loudly and rattled the doorknob. As Lilly had suspected she would, the landlady appeared from the parlour.

'Good evening, Mr Jones. Thought I heard the door. Trust you've had a lovely night?'

'I have, thank you.'

'Smashing. My husband and I are watching Parky, and you're more than welcome to join us for a nightcap if you'd like?'

'That is very kind, but it's been a long week. I'm exhausted. My bed's calling.'

'I quite understand. Well, breakfast is in the dining room as usual from seven thirty to nine thirty.'

'Thank you. See you in the morning.'

'Yes, see you in the morning, Mr Jones.'

Lilly heard the parlour door close and watched as her lover tiptoed theatrically up the stairs. He reached for her hand, and with a feeling of triumph in her veins, she let him lead her across the square landing and into his room.

With the door locked behind them, she paid no attention to the detail, could not have told you anything about the burgundy flock wallpaper, scarcely noticed the old, wide, walnut wardrobe, nor the sink on the wall with a tooth mug and a glass shelf on which sat a rolled flannel and a bar of Imperial Leather in a small green tray of marbled plastic. Couldn't have accurately described the dark velvet drapes or the armchair in the corner on which Wilkie had piled his clothes – none of it.

Only able to focus on him, his mouth on hers, his hands tearing almost at her jeans and T-shirt in a desperate hurry to remove them, as the two stumbled, entwined, a jumble of arms and legs, on to the green, puffy, silky eiderdown that sat on top of the double bed. Compared to the narrow single bed of her childhood, this was a luxury!

Their union was this time without the tenderness or initial hesitancy that had wrapped their first encounter, but was instead mutually urgent, hurried, more mechanical certainly, but no less lovely for that. It was only as they slowed, and dawn threatened and birds sang to welcome the coming light, that Lilly found herself physically weary yet mentally wired as she lay back on the downy pillows and stared out of the sash window. It was a rare and lovely thing, to see this little corner of London on the other side of the river. Here there wasn't the abundance of concrete, high rise and the smoke of industry that blighted the Vauxhall skyline. The Victorian lamppost right outside of the lodgings on this modest street in Chelsea reminded her of *Mary Poppins*, a film she had been to see with her mum when she was nine and it had hit the big screen. Not that she wanted to think about her mum right now.

Lilly knew she had never felt so happy, so content, as she did in that moment. Lying in a double bed with Wilkie's naked, sleepy form by her side. Her body spent, warm and cosy beneath the sheets, and a feeling of pure contentment on her skin, aware that if she could stay like this for ever it would not be long enough. It was everything she had dreamed of and more.

'I love you.'

Her voice was a whispery croak; her words had left her mouth without planning. It was a second or two before he said anything, seconds that felt like hours as each tick of the hand on the bedside clock moved slower and louder. Her heart rate increased and what had been a moment of pure peace turned into a fraught period of fear. She silently willed him to respond, her naked body *begging* him to respond!

Turning on to his side, Wilkie propped his head on his hand, his elbow firmly planted on the mattress.

His words were calmly yet resolutely delivered as he toyed with the end of her hair. 'You don't, my lovely young thing. You don't love me.'

There it was again, that slightly patronising undertone that wasn't present during sex, when there was parity in their connection, only in the aftermath. A voice of reason that she imagined he might reserve for his pupils.

'But I do.' She held her position, speaking plainly and willing him with every fibre of her being to admit to feeling the same.

'No.' He shook his head and sat up, propped against the headboard with his pillow cushioning his pale skin against the dark wood. His denial was a dagger that lodged in her breast, the pain just as real. Lilly closed her eyes, unable to look at the man who was negating her, confusing her, hurting her. 'Look at me.' He reached out and touched her cheek.

She opened her eyes, hating the tears that gathered, feeling that this emotional outburst only confirmed in his view that she was indeed a lovely *young* thing.

'You don't love me, Elizabeth-Roberta.'

'You don't get to tell me how I feel, and you certainly don't *know* how I feel!' she insisted.

'I do know that what is coursing through your body is a confusion of hormones and lust and infatuation and novelty and all that wonderful, wonderful stuff, but not love.'

'How could you possibly know that, Wilkie?' Her throat was hoarse with all it tried to contain.

'Because I'm old, remember, thirty-three. Nearly double the life you've had.'

She might have only been seventeen but understood enough to know that his words, no matter how phrased, meant he did not love her in return. It shouldn't have been a surprise, but was however still disappointing, just as it had been the first time, when her own mother had walked away, and no amount of sugar had helped that medicine go down.

She thought of Glenda, wondering if her friend was right; was she the cow who had given her milk away for free? She hated the phrase even more now that it cloaked her in something very close to shame.

'I think I should . . . I should go.' Looking around the floor, she sought out her jeans, T-shirt, pants and bra, feeling, despite the intimacy they had shared, suddenly awkward at the prospect of having to get dressed in front of him, the man who did not love her. It was with a sense of desperation that left her feeling hollow.

'I don't want you to go.' He reached out and pulled her towards him. She fell against him, letting her cheek rest on his chest, listening to his heart beat as her tears gathered, clogging her nose and mouth. His fingers tracing her spine again lit the fire of want, which felt mistimed and was for the first time conflicting, as even in this moment of sad reconciliation, her body yearned for him.

'You're amazing.'

'You don't need to say that.' It was the last thing she wanted to hear, his words of consolation that sounded a lot like pity.

'I wish . . .' he began, taking a deep slow breath in and out that hinted at more.

'What do you wish?'

She looked up at the underside of his throat, his Adam's apple rising and falling and the sprout of whiskers where he shaved the base of his beard, the delicate white skin, frail and enticing and where she wanted to plant her lips for reasons she was still yet to fathom.

'I wish I had the verbal and emotional freedom to speak as you do, to state with such certainty something that is no more than a seed of an idea. I truly envy you that.' He bent his head and kissed hers.

'Are you saying that what you feel for me is hard to express?' It was light at the end of a bleak emotional tunnel, it was hope to cling to while she was all at sea.

'I am saying that, exactly that.'

It was incredible how quickly his words could change her mood, dry her tears, as if he were steering her with a suggestion, a phrase. And in this heightened emotional state, her tears only made her love him more, long for him more! It was part of their journey, their story! Her joy once again threatened to bubble from her as she twisted on the mattress to straddle him. Holding on to her with his hands either side of her face, he spoke softly, slowly, using words that were magical, pure and full of intention.

'All in good time. How could anyone not love you, Elizabeth-Roberta . . .'

◆ ◆ ◆

It was late on Sunday morning, with breakfast missed, when Wilkie watched Mrs Horn-Haverington wander along the street with her trusty hound on a leash. This was Lilly's cue to leave. The two dashed to the front door, which he held wide for her.

'When will I see you?' She stood on her tiptoes and kissed him.

'Tomorrow.'

'Tomorrow?' She had expected to have to wait a couple of days, as was his MO.

'Yes. Will you be on the towpath, the usual time?' He kissed her mouth, her neck, her cheek, running his hand over her hip and thigh as he did so, clearly as reluctant as her to part.

'Probably . . .' She laughed as she trotted down the stairs and out on to the street, looking back at the fabulous man who she loved – *loved!* And who, if he had the verbal and emotional freedom to speak as she did, would say he loved her too. It was enough, it would have to be, until he found a way to set his words free.

He lifted his hand in a wave, and she blinked, taking another picture with her mind's lens, capturing his casual stance as he leaned on the doorframe, dark hair about his shoulders, glorious thighs inside his jeans.

She couldn't wait for tomorrow, bewitched as she was by this old, old man.

'Hel-lo!' she called out as she let herself into the flat at Waide House, still, after all these years, half expecting her mum to call out her reply of 'Yoo-hoo!' like she used to. The sound of her dad practising in the window filled her ears, the beautiful light legato style of an accomplished violinist. It never failed to impress her. And in the emotion of his music, she felt the swell of guilt and the taste of deceit on her tongue, lying to the man she loved the most, and who had lost his great love, something that she, in the throes of this new and glorious affair, felt even more keenly.

'In the lounge!' was her dad's hearty response as he stopped playing.

'Hi!' She popped her head through the door, keen to have a bath and change, to check her appearance and relive the night just spent in her mind before she chewed the fat with her dad.

'How is Glenda's mother doing? You are a good friend, going to sit with her while her mum's poorly.' He lifted his cigarette that sat smouldering in the ashtray, and she felt the flush of discomfort over her skin. It didn't come easy to her, lying to her wonderful, trusting dad, but it had felt entirely necessary to secure a night with Wilkie.

'On the mend.' She nodded.

'Well, that's good news. Kettle's just boiled if you fancy a cuppa?'

'Just going to jump in the bath, Dad, then I'll make us both a fresh one.'

'Smashing.' He winked and resettled his violin beneath his chin, eyes closed, bow drawn.

She wanted desperately to share with him the words Wilkie had said, how she was impossible not to love! Wanted to share it with the world, but knew now was not the moment, that he wouldn't understand, not at all. What was it Wilkie had said?

All in good time . . .

◆ ◆ ◆

'Well, this is a lovely surprise!' Bertie clapped his hands as she walked through the door of the gallery. It was his greatest gift, the way he made people – *all* people – feel as if he'd been waiting for them and that their presence was the most wonderful thing imaginable. No arrival was ever an inconvenience; he always made time. She watched the eyes of those he greeted light up at his warm welcome, and was not immune to it herself, for the simple fact that it was not a performance but was due to his gorgeous, genuine, kind nature.

'I thought I'd pop in on my way home.'

'How was college?' He was, as ever, interested in her and her life. The very best compliment.

'Yeah, fine. My head's not really in it today.' She smiled at him.

'Hmmm, would that be because your head is full of a certain maths teacher from Yorkshire?' He pulled a face.

'He's from Basingstoke, actually, but teaches in York.'

'Well, pardon me! Either way, whether he's from Basingstoke or Timbuktu, I can see you've got it bad.'

It was lovely to be able to talk about Wilkie openly, a relief.

'I have got it bad. I think I love him, Bertie.' She kept her voice small.

'Love! *Love?* Oh, well now we're in trouble. And I thought I was a fast worker!' He sat behind the small desk and put his elbows on the table, hands under his chin. 'And he feels the same?'

'Kind of.' She kicked at the wooden floor with her clog.

'What do you mean, kind of? There is no *kind of* when it comes to love and devotion. You're either in or you're out!' He raised his voice.

'Maybe it's not that straightforward.' She felt the need to defend Wilkie's corner, regretting being so open with her boss, friend and mentor.

'No! Uh-uh! No! No! No!' He waggled his finger. 'There are always complications, timing clashes, geographical challenges, whatever!' He flung his arms in the air. 'But when it comes to love there is no *kind of*, no *maybe*, no *possibly*, no *let me see* . . . there is only a big fat resounding yes, as in Yes, yes, I love you! I love you madly! I love you deeply! I love you with every fibre of my being and every breath in my body and every thought in my head, I love you!' he shouted.

'Do you love Beautiful Jack?'

'Yes.' He held her eyeline, unflinching. 'I do love Beautiful Jack. And he loves me, there's no doubt. But it's complicated, we're not exclusive, but love him? Yes, I do. When I finally plucked up the courage to say the three fateful words, he cried and held me close and told me he felt the same, and it was like . . . like a weight was lifted, a prize received! The loveliest thing in the world is to love and be loved, to know that my search was over, his too. We'd found our people!' he gushed.

‘So you know what it feels like.’ She rubbed her hand over the base of her throat, where excitement and confusion liked to gather.

‘I do, Bob, but I also know that it’s often a gradual thing; it certainly was for us. I mean, the lust was instant, but that’s a different thing entirely. You’ve only known Basingstoke boy for five minutes! And you’re a mere baby!’

‘I’m eighteen next month, and besides, you said you liked him!’ She reminded him of his words, spoken with enthusiasm after the gallery opening.

‘I do like him, what I’ve seen, I like him very much, but I’m also a little wary, a little more worldly wise.’

‘Oh, don’t you start with that! Wilkie was saying the same thing, about how I’m only seventeen and have a whole lot of life left to live and stuff to figure out . . .’ She rolled her eyes and let this trail.

‘Well, now I like him even more, as he’s echoing my thoughts. I just don’t want you to get hurt, Bob. I don’t want you to leap and find that the safety net you were banking on isn’t in place.’

‘Why can’t everyone just be happy and excited and think the best of it! I’ve never felt like this before. It’s the most intense, unshakeable, joyous way to be! And I want it to last for ever.’

‘Oh, sweet one.’ Bertie stood from behind the desk and wrapped her in his arms. As ever, he smelled divine, doused heavily as he was in Paco Rabanne Pour Homme. ‘If that’s your wish, then I wish it too, but he’s right: you do have a lot of life to live and a lot of stuff to figure out.’

‘Do you think when it comes to love and sex and choosing who you end up with, we’re like our mothers?’ It was still on her mind, what Glenda had said. Lilly didn’t want to abandon her man, walk out on her family, make a mess of things, break someone’s heart, she didn’t want any of that. It was vital she got it right.

Bertie let go of her. 'Well, I can only speak for my own mother, and I can categorically say without hesitation that yes, I am *definitely* like her in that regard.'

'Really?' She had hoped for a different answer, desperately hoping she had avoided the curse and was not going to be the kind of woman who was no good; morally slack, of all things!

'Absolutely.' He flicked his scarf over his shoulder. 'My mother and I both have a thing for Burt Reynolds.'

Lilly laughed out loud. Bertie was, as ever, just the tonic she needed.

'I'd better go. I'm meeting Wilkie.' She beamed and pulled her shoulders up to her chin as excitement rippled through her limbs.

'Don't do anything I wouldn't.' He issued the stern warning.

'Might be a bit late for that,' Lilly whispered as she reached for the door handle, giving him an insight into this love, this beginning, this heady joy!

'Good Lord, Bob! That's what I'm worried about.'

The two shared a lingering, knowing look, before she blew him a kiss and made her way home.

Having set up her easel on the towpath, Lilly arranged her hair over one shoulder and opened the top button of her blouse, before twisting her large silver and topaz ring on her index finger. She wanted to look her most alluring when Wilkie saw her, and she'd do as she always did, make out she hadn't seen him immediately and give him a moment to privately admire her! Her stomach bunched in anticipation. Already she was thinking of where they might be able to go for sex, somewhere quiet, possibly back to his boarding house on Royal Avenue. The thought of having to sneak in again was thrilling, not that she'd be able to stay all night, still feeling bad about having lied to her dad about Glenda's mum being ill. But a couple of hours would be wonderful . . . Who was she kidding? A couple of *minutes* would be wonderful!

Removing her brush from the old jam jar, she ran the bristles over the canvas, before taking on some blue paint and dipping that back into the murky water, creating a shade with which to coat the surface entirely. It was how she worked, building layers, removing the light, erasing the nothingness, the space, until all that was left was the detail: the water, the riverbank, the outline of the buildings opposite and the reflection on the surface of Old Mother Thames.

'What are you painting?' The question was asked over her shoulder, familiar, predictable, and yet still she struggled a little with how to accurately respond. She turned, smiling at the girl, who looked to be about ten, wearing canary-yellow dungarees, roller skates and a *Peanuts* T-shirt.

'Just the river, the water.'

The girl wrinkled her nose at the damp canvas.

'You should put a boat on it.'

'A boat? That's a very good idea.' She laughed to herself as the girl rolled off along the path. She couldn't wait to tell Wilkie, knowing he'd find the humour in it.

The sun dropped and the sky took on the bruised hue of dusk and with it the warmth of the day was replaced by a breeze that was a little cool. Lilly felt the shiver along her limbs as her skin prickled into goosebumps.

'Hurry up!' She spoke aloud to the wind, waiting for her lover to arrive. Her heart jumping, her mood lifting as every new person, dog, bike or tumbling leaf drew her eye, thinking it might be him.

It was as night began to fall that she understood he was not coming. The disappointment sat like a physical thing at the base of her throat. A million reasons why ran through her thoughts, ranging from he'd been kept late at work, there'd been an emergency on the Tube, to the fact that he might have come down with a terrible disease or been hit over the back of the head and left for dead in an alleyway . . . Either way, he was not with her, and her heart flexed with frustration.

◆ ◆ ◆

'Can I make you a sandwich, love?' her dad called from the kitchen after she'd returned to the flat, the strains of Tchaikovsky's *Romeo and Juliet* coming from the lounge and filling her room. The melancholic pull of the oboe was enough to reduce her sorrow to a thick syrup that slowed her heart and made her breathing a little laboured.

'No, thanks. Not hungry,' she managed, turning her face into the pillow to catch her tears.

'You'll waste away!' he laughed, and she thought she just might, if she didn't see Wilkie soon.

Wilkie didn't come the next night.

Wilkie didn't come the night after that.

Wilkie didn't come the night after that.

Nor the night after that.

Nor the night after that.

And Lilly carried her heartache like a heavy stone in her arms, unable to sleep, rest, work, eat or think straight, entirely preoccupied with the space next to her where she wanted him to be.

Present day

Lilly took her time choosing what to wear. Her love of colour meant that whatever she selected from her wardrobe wasn't going to be bland. She settled on a turquoise tunic with an embroidered, beaded yoke, and white linen trousers, with endless strings of multicoloured beads looped around her neck, and two very large, eye-catching gold rings, one on the middle finger of each hand, and her favourite tan Menorcan leather sandals.

Her conversation with Alfie had been on repeat in her thoughts and it was no coincidence that she chose Etta James's '*At Last*' as the music to listen to as she got ready, curating her own playlist. Understanding it was kitsch, predictable and even tempting the fate she didn't believe in, but the beauty of it was, no one would ever know!

This might just be a simple date for some, a casual get-together for dinner, but for Lilly it was significant, not only because of the rarity of such a thing but also because she was the owner of a fractured, mistrusting heart and so to take a leap like this was a big deal. There he was again, without invitation, the image of Wilkie in the front of her mind, even after all these years – *poof!* He continued to pop up and taunt her from afar. But Alfie had kind of got under her skin, why, she wasn't sure, but she certainly wasn't getting any younger and figured that if she was going to keep that silent loneliness from her door, maybe the better question was, why not? The fact that her world was shifting on its axis – leaving the flat, losing the daily closeness with Clodagh and Apollo – was encouraging her to broaden her thoughts, to take the risk. There was another thought, however, that whizzed and prodded her from sleep with the excitement of a teenager, not so much why not, but *what if* . . . Not that she chose to share this with anyone, knowing how ridiculous it sounded, such daydreaming from a woman who was old enough to know better.

She laughed, this, too, a phrase that irked her – she must remember to tell Alfie. Wondering at what point she might be old enough to know better? Wondering if she ever would! Even now she felt the shiver of unease at how she had called her mum, way back when she was a kid, full of excited anticipation – *I met a boy!* The humiliation at having to admit it had come to nothing was still quite excruciating.

She had decided against Glenda's advice and chose not to look at the menu before she arrived at the restaurant, wanting the evening to be spontaneous and unexpected! With her hand on her stomach, she recognised the feeling as butterflies of excitement that swirled in there. Her fingers pressed against the unsightly line of scar tissue that went from her belly to her pubis.

That's a good girl, count backwards . . .

A reminder every single day of what meeting that boy had led to.

'Get a grip, Elizabeth-Roberta. Butterflies? You're seventy, not seventeen!'

Yet it was a fact that, had she closed her eyes and not looked in a mirror, the way she felt was exactly the same now as she had then, as if the thief of time had not come along and erased those years when no one was looking.

Three squirts of her favoured perfume, one on her neck, one at her wrist and one a cloud through which she strutted, snapping her fingers and flicking her head, just as Bertie had shown her so many years ago. And she was set.

The plan was to meet on the path where they'd first met and walk along the river to Battersea, where the redeveloped power station was the place to be seen. Very different from the out-of-the-way, run-down shell it was in her younger days, where she'd once gone to see an art installation. She could recall very clearly stumbling in the dimly lit space over loose bricks and dumped builders' waste that littered the floor, before having to run all the way home in the dark when the police raided it. No one had told her the event was the brainchild of an artists' collective that specialised in raves and art, the two supported by the liberal application of hallucinogenics and speed.

It made her smile, all those experiences that she catalogued; more London moments.

There was a familiar knock on the door. She posed as she pulled it wide and stood, waiting to be admired.

'Wowsers! Lilly! You look lovely! Really lovely! Thought I'd come and say good luck.'

'Bless you.'

It warmed her heart to see Clodagh standing there in her pyjamas. It spoke of their closeness and mutual affection, their trust, and there it was again, the stab of sadness that it all might be coming to an end. Not that she was going to think of that tonight, didn't want it to spoil her mood.

'Not sure about the hair.' She ran her fingers through her curly grey mop and squeezed the curls to help shape them into ringlets, as if her hair did not have a life and will of its own.

'Leave it down, it's fabulous.'

'You're sweet. Apollo asleep?'

'Yes, soundo. After three readings of *Stick Man*. I know it by heart.' Clodagh groaned.

'How are you feeling after your run-in with Sab?'

'Worried,' was her instant reply. 'Really quite worried. It's been a nice way to live, not having to look over my shoulder. He puts me on high alert, ties my stomach in knots that makes it impossible for me to eat.'

Lilly was already aware of Clodagh's very slender, pale frame, and this insight bothered her, remembering that time in her own life when, riven with sorrow, the prospect of food had been the most awful thing.

'He hasn't called yet?'

'Not yet. Every time the phone rings, I jump. Something that would delight him, I'm sure.'

'Maybe he won't call?' Lilly suggested, unsure if this was a good or bad thing.

'Oh, he'll call, but because it was me who suggested he call tonight or this week, he'll leave it till the very end of the week, so it's almost the week after, trying to make it on his terms.'

Clodagh rolled her eyes. If that was the man's level of pettiness, Lilly could only hope they worked it out and reached an amicable solution, for Apollo's sake.

'I thought it was nice of Mr Vaughan to speak up.'

'I don't know how I feel about it. It was nice, yes, and he's nice, no doubt, but also it's none of his business. We're strangers, really, and it was kind of chivalrous, but it's a chivalry I don't need. I mean, he doesn't know me. I don't need a man to do that for me. I've been fine on my own for the last eighteen months, and for a long time before that. I know it came from a place of kindness, but it felt a bit too bold. Is that possible?'

'Hmm, yes, it is, and I hadn't thought of it like that. I get it.'

There's a good girl . . .

'Anyway, he's coming over for a coffee, to talk about the move and everything, so . . .' Clodagh blushed.

'I see. So none of his business, chivalry you don't need, but you're meeting for a coffee?'

'Doesn't mean I don't like him. I do, or at least I think I do.' She flashed a smile. 'I just need him to not . . .'

'Not what?'

'Interfere.'

'Ah, I think you'll find that's what he does.' Lilly pictured him bent low and calling through the letterbox.

'How are you feeling about the move?'

She hated how the topic could put a rock even in the most excited stomach full of butterflies.

'I think I'm in denial, love,' Lilly admitted. 'And until I figure out what to do next, it's a place I'll stay.'

'I understand. It's hard for me too, and compared to you, we've only been here five minutes.' Clodagh squeezed her hand, and Lilly patted her arm in return; she didn't want to feel this level of emotion, not tonight, when she had so much to look forward to.

'Right, you can't be late. Also, Lilly, I wanted to say before you left that I'll keep my phone on, and if there's anything that bothers you, or if he tries anything on, call me and I'll see the missed call and we'll come and rescue you, Apollo and I.'

'Isn't he in bed?'

'Yes, but that's not the point! He has an enviable stick collection that can be used for whacking the keenest of suitors!'

They both laughed.

'I don't think Alfie's going to try anything; we're a little over the hill for that.' Lilly laughed, thinking that actually, with those smile-crinkled blue eyes, him trying something, when the time was right, might be quite agreeable. Not that she was about to share this with Clodagh, or anyone else, for that matter. 'Besides' – she lifted and splayed her fingers – 'I've got these knuckledusters on, should he try any funny business!'

'Knuckledusters!' Clodagh laughed, another reminder for Lilly that some of the phrases she had inherited from her dad were quite alien to the young woman.

Having locked her front door, Lilly trod the stairs with the tiniest feeling of trepidation. Supposing he didn't show? The concern melted away instantly as she stepped down on to the riverwalk and there he was, early and waiting. Lilly stopped for a minute and blinked softly, as if taking a photograph to store in her mind, one for the album. The sun was setting behind him, the sky had taken on a dusky mauve hue. He was wearing jeans, a navy linen blazer, a white shirt with the top button open, double cuffs, and that watch on display again. He looked just as neat and well put together as he had the first time they'd met. Her heart squeezed at the sight of him, a novel and welcome flutter of attraction that she hadn't felt for the longest time.

It was curious, the lack of awkwardness, no weighted silence, which she had half expected. Instead, he lifted his crooked arm and she slipped hers through it, as if they were simply picking up where they had left off and had done this a thousand times before and would probably do it a thousand times more. Strolling in the direction of Battersea from Vauxhall, they ambled along the riverwalk like they had all the time in the world. She liked his lack of urgency, suggesting it mattered not if they arrived or didn't, happy to roam, as if this was what mattered most, this time together, beginning.

'It's very nice to see you again, Lilly.'

'It's very nice to see you again too. Before we get too far into the evening, I have a couple of questions from my friend, Glenda. I've known her for donkey's years.'

'Oh, you should have brought her along!'

'Really?'

'No!' He shook his head. It was nice to be reminded that he was funny. 'What is it Glenda wants to know?'

'First, why you're okay eating fish but not meat? She figures the suffering is about the same for both species, so . . .'

'Glenda is a very wise woman, no doubt.' He locked eyes with her briefly. 'The answer is simple. I love meat, love a big fat juicy steak, roast chicken, pork chops, a decent banger, the lot! Stick me in front of a BBQ and I'm one happy man. But the old cholesterol was getting high.' He patted his heart. 'I wanted to eat healthier. My youngest daughter has been nagging me for years about changing to a vegetarian diet, and I agreed. I did that for about a month and was so tempted to go back to meat. I missed all the things I loved, so I decided to treat myself to fish and chips, also one of my great loves, just once a month, and that's what I do. Just once a month!' He held up a finger. 'I say I'm a pescatarian so I don't get it in the neck from those who want to shout that they thought I was a vegetarian when they see me eating my chish and fips! But better for my health, better for the planet, better all round, but please, Glenda, let me have my chippy tea just once every four weeks.'

'I shall pass that on.'

'Thank you. What was the second thing?'

'She was worried that you might be an axe murderer.'

'Ah, yes, well, you can tell Glenda that I'm not. Although I'm aware that if I was, I'd likely not admit to it, so not sure of the value in my denial. And isn't it strange the way people always plump for axe murderer and not just a regular murderer? I mean, how many people are actually murdered by axe?'

'That's exactly what I said!' The ease of their chatter was as promising as it was reassuring, reminding her powerfully of another time in her life when easy conversation, physical attraction and a willing spirit had led her down a dark and life-changing road. At no more than this thought she felt a bolt of caution fire through her gut and her arm now sat a little awkwardly through his. 'Can't remember the last time I went out to dinner.'

'I eat out more than I eat in. I tend to have most of my meetings in restaurants, convenient when in London, and certainly saves me having to cook. I never really look forward to it – all those meetings merge into one in my mind – but I've been looking forward to this all day, very much.'

She liked his confidence, his openness. 'Me too.' And just like that her arm once again softened against his.

'So what has your day held so far?' he asked, like they were far more familiar and used to catching up.

It was a nice way to phrase things, indicating that the best part of the day was yet to come. She thought he might be right.

'Not much is the truthful answer. I own an art gallery in Pimlico, and even though I'm not involved in the day-to-day running, I like to keep an eye on the books and plans for the year. Truth is, I find the administration of it a bit of a chore, don't want to be worrying about business rates and security cameras, but I guess it comes with the territory. Anyway, this morning I spent looking over the portfolios of two promising artists who would like to exhibit, both incredibly talented, both so young and clearly going to make their mark, so that was exciting. Sometimes, the gallery will send me work, and my heart sinks. I wonder if I just don't get it or if it truly isn't up to scratch or maybe my expectations are too high, but it's stood me in good stead all these years, trusting my instinct. My friend taught me that. So today was a joy in that regard, two fabulous new artists to display!'

'I think you're very fortunate when your work is also your passion.' He spoke as if this was something he understood.

'Is your work your passion too?'

'Yes!' His reply was emphatic. 'Yes, absolutely.'

'What is it you do?'

Please don't say gangster, career criminal, mobster, hitman . . . She figured she could cope with anything other than these, although it would explain his rather dapper suits and suave air.

'I'm a very dull businessman.' He gave an awkward laugh. 'Can't make it sound any more glamorous than that. I am in business to make money, and I have a knack for it. Which is lucky, as I have no education to speak of, no degree scrolls framed on the walls and no trust fund to fall back on. My dad worked at Billingsgate Market, man and boy. Mum was a tea lady at the Trebor factory in Forest Gate, kept hundreds of workers topped up with tea.'

'A happy childhood?' She guessed the answer by the warmth with which he spoke about his parents.

'Very, a close family. I have three – *had* three – sisters; one has passed on now' – he swallowed – 'and a whole raft of nieces, nephews. Growing up, there were countless aunties, uncles and cousins, all round my nan's of a Sunday to listen to the gossip, eat cake and play the old Joanna!'

'It sounds lovely.' She felt the ache of loss that her family had been so reduced, her mum cutting it to pieces on the day she left for a life with Derek Manners. Just her and her dad at the kitchen table, eating quietly with Vivaldi in the background.

'It was. No matter how tough things got, and there were times' – he paused and changed tack – 'walking through my nan's front door was like stepping into a warm hug. I still miss it, even now, and I'm an old bloke. But it was the only place I spent time and felt like everything was going to be all right. Those few hours were like a shot in the arm that could get you through the week.'

She liked the picture he painted, liked the fact he was comfortable sharing it with her even more.

'Mine was quiet, really. Just me and my dad for most of the time. I adored him. He was always patient with me. He loved music, art, books, and had a sense of adventure – he'd go walking for miles! I thought it was because he wanted to travel, but I think, now I'm older, he was probably trying to clear his head.'

'I can understand that.' He gripped her arm with his. It felt nice.

'Oh, I know what else happened today. I've had it confirmed that two young people who I feel have the power to make each other very happy might just be building a bridge to each other. Isn't that lovely?'

'That is lovely. We do love love, right?'

'We do,' she echoed. 'One of them is in the wrong job, but that's a whole other story.' She pictured Joshua Vaughan and Clodagh, hoping it might develop. They rounded the bend on Nine Elms Lane and saw the power station lit up and in all its glory, slowing to take in the view.

'You haven't captured that river yet, then?' he teased.

'No, not yet.'

'It must be a daunting prospect.' He faced her then.

'What?'

'Knowing that, one day, you'll look up at your canvas and realise that you've done it, got the painting just right. Finished your mission.'

'Daunting, why?'

'Because it's what you do! It motivates you, keeps you busy. What would you do with all that time you got back?'

'Are you suggesting I'm *afraid* to get it right, to pack away my brushes, easel and my rather comfy camping stool that I fear might give way every time I sit on it?' This time, she squeezed his arm against hers.

'No, I am not suggesting that, I'm stating it, very firmly and decisively. I think you must be scared about what comes next.'

'Wow!' She took a beat, and was put in mind of something Clodagh had said earlier: *he doesn't know me . . . it felt a bit too bold . . .* 'I wouldn't say *scared*.'

‘What would you say?’ He held her eyeline, clearly curious. A chance for her to take in his rather lovely features and those blue, blue eyes.

‘I’d say I paint to try and recapture the past. Everyone says, don’t they, that we need to look forward, always looking forward, running towards the horizon! But I don’t really understand that. The past is a place I like to visit often and spend time. In fact it was the best place I’ve ever been, ever seen! And I *like* to think about it, remember it, remind myself what it felt like, that happiness, the joy! Memories of being young, those times when I took my body for granted, the absence of all the aches and pains.’

‘Tell me about it,’ he laughed.

‘I don’t have the big extended family that you enjoyed, and so there’s no one to share the memories of playing canasta with my dad of a Saturday night while he smoked his infernal cigarettes and we made cheese on toast under the grill. He and my mum, dancing on the parquet flooring of the lounge, all of it. No one else remembers it or knows about it, and so I like to sit by the water and paint the view, the same view. Trying to capture it, as if, while I’m doing that, the past that I miss is still going on in the flat behind me. It’s the only place I’ve ever lived, my home. And I loved that feeling back then, when it felt like everything was possible and everything was going to be okay. Because my dad was around and I was young and I was in the greatest city on the planet, and there was a whole life stretched out ahead of me and I had someone to rely on – him. I could always rely on him. It’s just me now, been just me for the longest time. So yes, I guess I like spending time in the past.’

‘I feel like that about Norfolk.’

‘Norfolk?’ It was her turn to laugh at his unexpected admission.

‘Yes.’ He glanced at her without a whiff of irony. ‘When we go on holiday, invariably to Norfolk, the girls, all the kids, a whole bunch of us – for that week, my life feels different. I feel different. I laugh more. Drink more. Eat more. Sleep deeper. I have this kind of peace that settles over me, and it resets me for whatever the next fifty-odd weeks might throw at me until I can go back.'

'Have you ever thought of moving there? It sounds like a nice way to live.'

He shook his head and let his eyebrows rise and fall. 'No. I think it feels that way because it's temporary, not real. An escape. The thought of living there and it becoming normal, average, losing the magic, well, that would be the worst thing. Not having it to think about, a place to mentally dwell, when life is swirling all round me before it hits the fan. Yes, that would be the worst thing.'

'You don't have that kind of peace on your farm? I can only picture it as a green country haven.'

'Oh, it's peaceful, no doubt, but not the same. Plus, I get up most days and make my way into the city, so hardly a life of rest and relaxation.'

'Is that the life you want, Alfie? To slow down, rest more?'

'I don't think so.' He considered this. 'I believe being busy keeps me young. I'm not one to sit in the sun or spend my days on a golf course. I like working.'

'Me too.' She knew her life was richer because she kept busy.

'But I think if I had someone to slow down with, I'd work less, probably, and do more that was fun.'

'So, it's a daunting prospect, the idea of having all that free time, working less?'

'Daunting, why?' He screwed his nose up.

'Because it motivates you, keeping busy. Having meetings in restaurants that you don't really want to go to. I mean, what would you do with all that time you got back?'

'Touché, Lilly. Touché.'

He gripped her hand and they walked on, as if holding hands was normal and she didn't feel the spark of joy travel all the way up her arm and along her chest at the feel of his palm against hers, so lovely it made the breath catch in her throat. It had been a long, long time since she had felt this, not since . . . it took a while to remember, not since Rex, lovely Rex, decades ago now.

'Do you *feel* older?' he asked as they walked under the festoon lights that lined the walkway; it was pretty.

'You mean do I feel seventy?'

'I didn't want to ask your age!'

'I'm seventy, Alfie—'

'Seventy-two,' he interrupted, as if keen to share.

'I feel my age a lot of the time. Recent weeks have been quite stressful for a number of reasons, and I've certainly felt it then.' She was not about to give him the details of her living situation and the fact that someone wanted to raze her home to the ground, not tonight, when everything was pretty perfect. 'But when I'm laughing out loud or dancing alone or walking my little friend Apollo to school or even getting dressed up tonight to come and meet you, then I feel the same as I did when I was young and it's great.'

'No one tells you that, do they, that your body might clock up the years, but your mind stays the same.'

'No, they don't.' She wondered what age her brain thought she was. Late twenties, probably. 'I think ageing is such a privilege. Not that it's been easy. I always think if the universe had given me a list of all that was going to happen in my life when I was young – all I would encounter, have to give up, all that would hurt me – I would have told you categorically that I would never, ever get through it. It'd be too much, the prospect of it, worse than anything I could imagine. The strength it would require, the energy, the mental dexterity, the character. All of it far more than I possess. And yet I have, I've survived it all.

I live to tell the tale. I'm often amazed by myself!' She laughed. 'But I'm damaged, Alfie. Make no mistake that survival comes at a cost. If you live long enough, you pay a price. We all do. It changes you, don't you think?'

'Changes you how?' He evaded her question with a question.

'Erm, subtly, really. Nothing overt to anyone who has always known me. I have the same temperament, the same sensibilities, intolerances, desires, beliefs, but inside . . .' She paused, unsure how much she wanted to confess to this charming man who had wheedled between the cracks of her armour, disarming her with his honesty, his openness, encouraging her to respond in kind. She decided then that the detail could wait. This was, after all, only their second meeting, far too soon to be shedding skin. 'I guess I'm of less substance than I used to be, a little hollowed out.' She bit her lip to stop it trembling, knowing this was not a night for tears. 'I present as super-confident, but actually, I am in some ways quite fragile.'

It was the closest she could get to admitting to her fear of loneliness, and the feeling of utter despair, of defeat, that dogged her in the early hours, as Denzel's words jumped in her thoughts . . . *these large developers have more money, time and resources than you. They could tie you up in legal knots that would be costly, and you could end up with nothing.* It was horrible to feel so vulnerable. It made her feel old.

'So fragile you feel the need to live with one foot in the past, painting the same scene on the riverbank and imagining those you have loved and lost all around you?'

'Yes, Alfie, exactly like that.' She sniffed, cursing the pull of tears that she managed to contain, just.

'I understand, Lilly, more than you think.'

'Why, are you fragile too?'

He took a second to respond. 'I have a failed marriage that didn't just fail, it imploded! According to my ex-wife, I put my business first, prioritised making money over spending time with her and the kids and, on reflection, I can see she was right. And I can never get those years back. Never make up for my absence. I live in a big old farmhouse all alone, and I've already told you I get lonely. And with work, I can't see the end game any more, and that's an odd one for me. My goals always had yardsticks, metrics which meant I knew when I'd won, or the thing was finished, X amount of pounds made, or the dotting of the Is on a contract, but not any more. It's grown so much, it's like being on an endless travellator with one thing merging into the next, and it's less rewarding because of it. So yes, a little fragile and tired, quite tired.'

'Sounds like you might need that trip to Norfolk.' She smiled at the man.

'I think you might be right. Are you hungry?'

'Ravenous! You?' Her stomach gave its customary rumble, as it did around dinnertime.

'Always.'

They quickened their pace.

1973 – aged 18

July slipped into August. Her birthday came and went without too much fanfare – her dad made her a delicious coconut cake, her mum sent a padded card with a kitten in a champagne glass on the front, and signed it *Love Mum and Derek.* Lilly put it straight in the bin, but first retrieved the book token that was secreted inside. She didn't want a card signed from her mum and Derek – just the sight of his name was enough to fire her irritation. *Love Mum and Derek.* It was hard to see the name of the couple who had taken the leap, committed to each other no matter the consequences, when all she longed for was to see Wilkie's face. *Mum and Derek.* It would never get easier not seeing *Mum and Dad*, not for her. Lilly felt angry with herself all over again for calling her mum that night when excitement had threatened to explode from her! Angry that she and Jeannie shared a secret, knowing it smacked of duplicity. The fact that her mum knew of her love while her dad was still in the dark had been a rotten thing to do, disloyal.

And she hated disloyalty.

London grew hotter, the nights almost insufferable in the heat as tourists flocked to the streets to eat ice cream, stare at the buildings, walk in slow, irritating gaggles along the river and marvel at the fountains and lions of Trafalgar Square. They bothered her, the clusters of grinning, happy strangers. She wanted them gone so she could fret in peace without having to sidestep on the pavements as they ambled at their leisure, taking in the beautiful city that was her home. Their happiness only seemed to magnify her sadness, her longing to see the man who had gone quiet. She spotted him everywhere. The back of a head, the colour of a jacket, a dark beard . . . Of course it never was him, but that didn't stop him popping up in her imagination as she rode the bus or stared out of the gallery window, scrutinising every passer-by, willing one of them to be Wilkie.

'What am I going to do, Bertie?'

'Eat something?' was his practical suggestion, looking her up and down as if taking in her rather weakened state. She had no appetite, none at all, and a lack of sleep made her look as if she was suffering from something. This she already knew, heartsick as she was over the lack of contact.

'I mean, what am I going to do about Wilkie? I still haven't seen him.'

'For how long?'

'Ten days, now.'

'Might he have been taken ill?' There was something distinct in his tone that told her he didn't believe this for a second and was just trying to be nice. It irritated her. She needed practical solutions, not a sticking plaster for her pain.

'Maybe.' She shrugged.

'You know where he's staying?'

Lilly nodded, thinking about the way the light from the Victorian lamppost had fallen through the sash window, striping the green eiderdown and their naked flesh as they lay gloriously entwined. That beautiful street that had put her in mind of *Mary Poppins*.

'Well, that seems like a good place to start. Do you want me to come with you?' It was a sweet offer and she felt bad for how much he'd irritated her only seconds before.

'No. I'll go, but thanks.' She stared at her friend. 'What should I say to him?' She was in equal parts excited and terrified at the prospect of pitching up at the house in Royal Avenue.

Bertie drew breath. 'I'd let him speak first, allow him to explain his absence for the last ten days, and then, based on what he says, use your judgement to decide whether you believe him or not. And then, when you've decided, state what it is you want.'

To be with him every single night, for ever, and for him to never let me go . . .

'Okay.' She grabbed her bag, knowing there was no time like the present and to spend another torturous night longing for him was not going to serve her well.

'I'd also say keep calm, keep your chin up and do not beg, not ever. Don't give him the upper hand. If he wants you, Bob, and has a good reason for going AWOL, then be cool and confirm he's made a good choice, because you are magnificent! And if he's had a change of heart, then keep calm, be cool and walk away, allowing him, in time, to understand that he has made the biggest mistake of his life, *because* you are magnificent!'

'I do love you, Bertie Barnes.' She smiled at the man who was himself most magnificent.

'The feeling, my dear, is entirely mutual. Go get 'em, tiger!'

Lilly laughed as she left the gallery, feeling more mouse than tiger, hoping she didn't see Wilkie and squeak. Thankful for the walk, she tried to figure out what she was going to say to him. It was conflicting, wanting nothing more than to fall into his arms, sickness or not. Yet she was also mad that he had not shown up, written her a note, tried to make contact. She understood her mum didn't want her, had chosen Derek Manners, but Wilkie . . . he had made the running! He had flirted right back! And no matter how poorly, he could have called the gallery, knowing Bertie would take a message. She smiled, however, knowing that whatever the reason, her joy at seeing him again would elbow out any lingering resentment. It was Wilkie she was talking about – *Wilkie!*

Royal Avenue was a little busier than it had been in the late evening when she'd snuck in and the early morning when she'd snuck out. Unsure of exactly how she was going to introduce herself, she blew the fringe from her forehead, removed her Wrigley's Spearmint and shoved it in a tissue that she popped into her handbag, and lifting the lion's head knocker, banged on the door.

'Can I help you?' The woman who now faced her on the top step was the very one who had offered the kind invitation for Wilkie to join her and her husband to watch Parky. Her manner was decidedly frosty, which for Lilly was odd. She understood the woman's wariness of a stranger at her door, but at the same time had expected something a little warmer from the woman who was not a stranger to her, Lilly having slept in her sheets, gripped her headboard, cried into her pillows, peed in her bathroom, crept down her stairs . . .

'Yes, sorry to bother you. I am here to see Mr Jones, Wilkie, who is staying with you?'

'Oh!' Helen Horn-Havering agitated her pearls with her pink-painted nails and bit her lip. '*Was* staying with us.'

'Was?' Lilly understood the word, of course, but was having difficulty in making sense of it with regard to Wilkie, who would not have left without saying goodbye, without leaving a note, without getting in touch with her. They had had sex, multiple times. He had held her while she slept. They had drunk too much in the pub and laughed until they cried.

'Yes, he *was* staying with us, but not any longer. Sorry I can't be of more help.' The woman made as if to close the door, and Lilly burst into tears, as ten days of pent-up fear, longing and frustration burst from her. 'Oh, no! Oh dear! Don't cry!'

It was a pointless instruction that Lilly could not heed as her tears filled her nose and throat and turned her skin blotchy.

'I need to speak to him, urgently! Where . . . where is he?' She hiccupped.

'I'm not in the habit of giving out private information about my residents. This is a reputable establishment. I am sorry.' She spoke softly, as if her regret were genuine, a small act of kindness that only made Lilly cry harder, great, gulping tears, not least because she had the image captured in her mind of Wilkie standing in the doorway, the last time she had seen him after that glorious night, when she had made her confession of love.

'Oh my goodness! Please don't cry!' Helen Horn-Havering looked along the street, as if a little embarrassed by her display.

'Where is he?' Lilly squeaked from a mouth riven with distress.

She watched the woman sigh and look skyward as if making a judgement call.

'He's gone back to York, packed up and left a few days ago. Paid in full. That's it. That's all I know, and I probably shouldn't be sharing that,' the landlady whispered.

'Gone?' Again, it was a word she understood, of course, and yet it made no sense. None at all! Why would he just go without saying a word, without saying goodbye to her! Without making a plan!

'Yes, gone, and if you want my advice, young lady, I would say dry your eyes, dust yourself off and get on with life.'

'I don't.' Lilly spoke as she wiped her face on the sleeve of her suede jacket. 'I don't want your advice. And I don't want Bertie's advice! I don't want to dust myself off and I don't want to be cool. I just want him, I want Wilkie!' she sobbed.

'I'm sorry. I really can't help you.' Helen Horn-Havering shut the front door.

Lilly walked the pavement of Royal Avenue, feeling like her heavy heart might fall right through her body and out on to the floor; not that she needed it any more, broken as it was.

◆ ◆ ◆

Lilly, quite bereft, had taken to her bed. It was where she liked to spend her time, eyes closed, sleeping when able, running her hand over the pillow that had felt the weight of Wilkie's head. Patting the peachy-coloured silk-edged blanket to her cheek, remembering him wearing it like a toga as she tried to make sense of what had happened. It was hard for her to accept that she had been duped, used by the handsome charmer, preferring to think of all the plausible, more palatable reasons that he had been unable to say goodbye, to write, or make contact.

She had trusted him with her emotions and her body, handed him her virginity as if it were no more than a vol au vent at a party – something to grab and consume without discussion or care. One of the hardest aspects of his disappearance was that there was no one she could really discuss it with, apart from Bertie, who was busy with the gallery and spending time with Beautiful Jack, who he loved and who loved him back, lucky things.

Glenda was no doubt looking forward to seeing her at the start of the college term, but Lilly knew she couldn't confess to her friend just how far she'd taken things with Wilkie, especially now he had left her high and dry. *Given it away for free . . .* These words were enough for her to feel nauseous.

Her dad was clearly worried, tempting her with home-made leek and potato soup, despite the warm weather, and hot toast spread thickly with butter and lemon curd, courtesy of Mrs Devlin, who played percussion in the orchestra. And tea, lashings and lashings of tea. It was lovely of him to be so attentive, but she half wished he would leave her alone to stew. He kept his music low, as if the sound might be an intrusion, given whatever ailed her. Still the mellow sounds of Dave Brubeck filtered under her door.

'What's up, little love?' he'd asked tentatively from the doorway only a couple of nights ago. 'I'm concerned about you.'

She hated that she was causing him a second of worry. This abandonment by her love felt like just punishment for lying to her dad, for thinking a relationship with someone as wonderful as Wilkie might be possible for someone like her. Was this how her dad had felt when Jeannie up and left? Her heart twisted for him, not least because, despite her feelings of regret and confusion, there was a small part, actually a medium-sized part of her, that longed to feel her mum's arms around her, telling her all men were pigs and that it was all going to be okay, believing that only another woman of the world could possibly understand what she was going through.

'Just women's troubles, Dad.'

It was cruel in a way, knowing the catch-all, the mumbled umbrella term used to suggest menstrual cycles, womb activity and bleeding was enough for him not to ask again.

'I see.' He'd swallowed, taking a drag on his cigarette. 'Would you like me to call your mum?'

It broke her heart that he, too, thought her mum might have the answers, might be able to succeed where he was failing. It made her want to rage at the woman she had stupidly shared her news with, letting her in, choosing her, telling her how she'd met a boy.

'No, Dad. I'll be okay, just want to rest.'

'Rightio, love. Well, if you need anything . . .' He backed out of the room, letting his words trail, as if he, like her, really didn't have the first clue how to make things better, especially when it came to women's troubles.

It was an hour or so later when he called from the hallway. 'You have a visitor, Lilly!'

She sat up in bed, her first thought that it was Wilkie, returned and about to beg for forgiveness, which she would of course give, before instantly falling into his arms and holding him tight as they made a plan for their future. But it was not Wilkie, the disappointment enough to send a fresh batch of tears to douse her pale cheeks.

'It's Bertie! Shall I send him in?' her dad called again.

'Yes.' She did her best to keep the quaver of distress from her voice.

The two men now stood in her doorway, her dad looking worried. Bertie scanning her room, no doubt taking in the rather bland decor, peach-painted woodchip wallpaper, an old pink tasselled lamp and the white Formica bedside cabinet. Not a Murano glass chandelier in sight.

'Would you like a cup of tea, Bertie?'

'Oh, bless you, Robert, tea would be lovely.'

Her dad made his way to the kitchen.

It was lovely to see Bertie, looking handsome in his pink paisley shirt and white flared jeans, always so hip. The moment her dad left the room he swooped forward and threw the curtains open.

'What are you doing?' She shielded her eyes from the sudden bright light, having been cocooned in her dimmed hideaway for days now, like a mole rat being forced above ground.

'What I'm doing is taking my life in my hands and travelling to Vauxhall, of all places, to kick you up the arse.' He picked her jeans up off the floor and folded them. 'I usually only come over to this side of the river under the cover of darkness to visit the Royal Vauxhall Tavern, so consider this an honour!' He stared at her now. 'This will never do, never! You can't let the bastard win! You just can't! That's the rule!'

'I don't care about the rule! He left me, Bertie, he just left, he never even said goodbye!' She thought he might need the reminder.

'You think I haven't had my heart broken a thousand times? The key to surviving is to get straight back up and keep going; otherwise life stops, Bob! It just stops, and that cannot be the case. You will look back at this time of your life and be so grateful for it! You will never again be as young as you are now, never have so much life stretching ahead of you. You're a goddess! And you can't waste a day of it sitting here looking at those dreadful curtains. They are enough to make anyone depressed!' His humour was usually enough for her to snap out of any mood, but not tonight.

'But I love him!' She felt her bottom lip tremble.

'Love!' He flapped his hand in front of his face. 'It's a small thing, it comes and goes, and it holds you in its thrall, like being caught in a wave, but never doubt that you are at its mercy and therefore there's nothing you can do to control it, even if you think you can.'

'It wasn't a small thing to me.'

'It will be.' He perched on the side of her narrow bed. 'It will be one day, when you have lived a long and happy life and you look back. You'll realise that this *Wilkie*' – he almost spat the name, and she loved the solidarity of it – 'you will realise that he was only a page in your life story, not even a chapter, or more likely a paragraph. Yes, just a bloody paragraph! No more!'

Lilly nodded, tears falling down her face, so wanting to believe what her good friend was telling her, and yet still feeling struck at the mere mention of her lover's name.

'I have this' – she placed her hand on her chest where it hurt the most – 'this pain!'

'He's hurt you, sweet thing, and it's the first time. I remember what it feels like. We all do. It leaves an indelible mark that you think is a scar, but I promise you, I absolutely promise you, that you will reach a point in your life when it's just a smudge where the ink of that paragraph has spoiled over time, no more.'

'I want to believe you,' she levelled.

'Two things.' Bertie wiped the tears from her face with his silk handkerchief. 'First, I have never and will never lie to you.'

She nodded and smiled, knowing this to be true.

'What's the second thing?' she sniffed.

'I think we should forfeit the tea and go and find some champagne. What do you say?'

'Maybe.' She smiled at the brilliant Bertie Barnes, who was everything.

'Well, it seems to me you have choices. You can either put on your glad rags, if you have anything clean' – again he scanned the bedroom floor, where her clothes lay in heaps – 'or you can go and phone Mr Wilkie Jones and tell him how you feel, see if there is any way forward, although I am sincerely hoping you do not do that. I want you to dance on and forget all about the rogue!'

'Oh my God, Bertie, I *can* do that! I can call him!' She sat bolt upright in the bed, energy flowing though her veins, just the thought enough to halt her tears, completely ignoring her friend's preference.

'You know where he is?'

'Yes, yes, I do! I've just remembered, he told me he teaches at a school in York, St Ethelred's!'

'Well, there we go. Boy am I glad I mentioned it.' He exhaled his sarcasm. 'I guess it's better you do something. Anything is preferable to lying here letting the world pass you by.'

'You're a genius!' Lilly flung back the covers as her dad arrived with two cups of tea.

'Oh! You're up!' Her dad beamed, delighted with this sudden change of events.

'I am, Dad, up and raring to go!'

'Women!' Her dad shook his head and rolled his eyes at Bertie as he handed him a cup and saucer.

'Tell me about it!' Bertie took the tea from her dad and winked at her. Her dear, dear friend.

◆ ◆ ◆

By the next day, with Bertie's words ringing in her ears, Lilly knew he was right: she had to do something. Short of jumping on a train at great expense and taking time off work, lying to her dad, again, and trawling all the way up to Yorkshire, making the call seemed like the next best option. With the scrap of paper in her hand, she studied the number that she'd got from directory enquiries.

'Oh my God!' She breathed deeply, bent double in the phone box, riven with nerves. 'Come on, Lilly!' She raised her voice, straightened and put her finger in the little circle to dial the number. It was answered almost immediately and at the sound of the beeps she plied the slot with coins.

'York two eight six four four, St Ethelred's, how may I help you?'

Lilly had hoped that Wilkie would answer, while simultaneously praying he would not. She was unsure what she would say, at the same time having an entire monologue cued up on her tongue. And now she stood with the complex combination of relief and disappointment forming a stopper in her throat. Holding her breath, she almost forgot to speak.

'Hello?' the woman asked again.

'Yes, hello,' she managed. 'I was wondering if it might be possible to speak to Mr Jones, Wilkie Jones.'

'I'm afraid he is currently teaching.' The woman sounded friendly, welcoming, sweet, exactly the kind of voice you would want answering your phone if you were a school. 'I'm the headmaster's secretary. Can I take a message?'

A message? What to say?

Tell him he broke my heart. Tell him I can't sleep. Tell him I miss him day and night. Tell him my body yearns for him. Tell him it was love, at least it was for me. Tell him that if there is the slightest chance that we might grow from this, I will pack up my life on the riverbank, abandon Old Mother Thames and head north. I would do anything for one more night with him by my side . . . the spring that follows his winter . . .

Of course she said none of these things. Instead she found a smile and did her best to keep her tone as even and unflustered as possible.

'Erm, no, that's okay. When is it best to call back?'

'Well, that's a tricky one, I'm afraid. He's teaching most of the time, and then there's playground duty and clubs after school. As I've said, I'm more than happy to take a message, or would you like to leave a number so he can return your call?'

Lilly let her eyes rove the grubby interior of the phone box.

'No, that's okay.' It seemed hopeless, and she felt the stutter of tears at the thought that her lover was so very far away.

'Is it anything I can help you with, or another member of staff?' the woman asked most helpfully.

'Not really, no.' She drew breath. 'It's just that he left something in London, and I was wondering how to return it to him.' It was a ridiculous fabrication, the first thing that popped into her head. Lilly pinched the bridge of her nose with her thumb and forefinger, as if this might help relieve the unseen pressure.

'Oh, right. Are you calling from Mrs Horn-Havering's boarding house? I know we haven't spoken before, but Wilkie has spoken very fondly about his time with you in Chelsea.'

'Yes, I am,' Lilly lied, eyes closed, heart racing, unsure of how things were getting so muddled, even more muddled! But it wasn't entirely untrue, he had left something in London: her. He had left her. He had left them, abandoning the beautiful beginning to their story, left it all behind.

'Ah, well, it's wonderful to be in contact. I'm Georgina Jones, Wilkie's wife.'

Wilkie's . . .

Lilly felt her body slide against the wall of the phone box as the strength left her legs and she thought she might faint. Her preference would have been to sink to the floor, were it not covered in a nasty pile of compacted dirt, newspapers soaked in fish and chip grease, empty cans of Tennent's Extra, cigarette butts and a mammoth stack of peanut shells.

'I would suggest,' Georgina Jones carried on in her sing-song voice – a happy voice! – 'that anything he's left can be popped in a box and sent to the school. I know you have the address. We live on site. He'll be more than happy to pay for the postage.'

We . . . we . . . we . . .

'I will,' she whispered. 'I will do that, Mrs Jones.' To say the words felt surreal, disgusting and jarring all at once.

'Right, better let you get on, and thank you so much for calling. I know Wilkie really appreciated your hospitality. I've joked that I might come down myself for a holiday; with two little ones under five, I think I could do with a rest!'

Two little ones under five . . . children . . . children! The words were knives that cut her skin and pierced her heart and hurt her in the way that she deserved.

'Anyway, must dash, the bell is about to go for end of school, but thanks again!'

She heard Georgina replace the receiver and stood with the phone in her hand, thinking of her dad, who had gone after his wife, had written to her, begged her, visited her, sitting in a chair while his wife made tea in a strange kitchen and he could see her bed jacket hanging on the back of the open bathroom door. Her dad who had fought and lost, and still Georgina's words echoed in her mind, *two little ones under five . . .* Georgina Jones, who, whether she was aware of it or not, had fought and won.

A banging on the side of the telephone box made her jump.

'Get a move on, love, I haven't got all day!' an older woman in a headsquare growled, her voice muted through the little panes of glass etched with graffiti, the word *repent* scrawled in large uneven letters.

'Give me a minute!' Lilly mouthed through the glass as she pulled the coins from her purse and made a second call, this time to Mr and Mrs Brooks' house, hoping, praying, Glenda was home. Reluctantly, with shame dripping from her mouth, she'd finally told her friend about Wilkie when he hadn't shown up.

It was a sweet relief when Glenda answered the call.

'Lil? Are you okay?'

She could hardly speak, as shock and distress almost rendered her mute.

'Glen . . . Glenda.'

'Oh my God, what's happened? What's wrong?'

'He's . . . he's married.' She hid her mouth with her other hand from the old woman, who sneered at her through the window.

'No!' Her friend's gasp of air confirmed her thoughts, that this really was the very worst thing a girl could experience. 'Oh, Lil, no!'

'I don't know what to do.'

'Let's meet at college tomorrow, let's go and find somewhere to sit and talk it out. It will all be okay. Just hang in there, we can talk about it all then.'

'Thank you, Glen.' Relieved that her friend offered no judgement, she wiped her face as the call ended, knowing she would hang on until she could see Glenda, a girl of her age who understood. Not that quiet, reliable Norm was anything like

Wilkie, and Lilly was glad, never wanting her friend to feel how she did now.

As Lilly stumbled from the dirty space, the impatient woman pushed past her.

Lilly stood for a while, facing the stream of traffic, the headlamps of buses blurring under her tears as she attempted to walk on legs made of lead, trying to make sense of the newly presented facts. Wilkie was married with children, married to Georgina, the headmaster's secretary. *Georgina* . . . who had a lovely voice and kindly demeanour. Lilly realised in that moment that she was "that woman". He had made her *that* woman, one just like her mother, who had no regard for the vows of marriage, one who messed up the lives of kids, one who was selfish, brazen and morally slack, a terrible, terrible person.

Wilkie had done this to her, and she had let him. She made a silent vow to never call her mum again like that, never to endorse the woman's shitty behaviour – the shittiest! Knowing that with the same damaging, destructive streak marbling her veins, she too quite obviously had the capacity to break the heart of someone lovely, someone worthy, someone like Georgina Jones, who sounded sweet and was a mum to two little ones, and it was best she kept her distance from everyone.

Love, she decided, just wasn't for her; how could it be?

Present day

The Bread Street Kitchen & Bar had a cool New York loft aesthetic that Lilly really liked, with industrial exposed features in keeping with the redeveloped power station. The bar was long, sleek and well stocked, and the butter-coloured leather banquette seating looked inviting. A waiter waltzed past with a tray on which sat two flutes of wine that bubbled temptingly. Alfie turned, raised his eyebrows and smiled at her as if reading her mind, suggesting they might just be ordering a similar glass or two.

'Good evening, sir, madam, lovely to see you. Do you have a reservation with us this evening?'

She felt the rise of excitement in her gut. The woman had addressed them as if they were a couple, and it felt nice, no matter how new, no matter how uncertain. Did they look like a couple? Did they look good together? Lilly was unsure what was happening to her but knew there had been a shift. Maybe it was the prospect of losing Waide House, maybe it was understanding that she was seventy, not seventeen, and that time was ticking by. Whatever it was, Alfie was disarming her bit by bit, removing the shield of defence she had erected with every word of connection, each moment of laughter, every glance at her with those blue, blue eyes . . .

'We do indeed.' Alfie stepped forward and took control in a way that suggested it was the norm for him.

'And the name, sir?'

'It's Portland. Mr A. Portland.'

It took her a moment.

A second or two while the name that sounded familiar travelled from his mouth to her ear and registered in her brain. He spoke casually, as if caught up in the excitement, clearly forgetting just what coming clean would detonate. The smile slipped from her face, as an expression of something a lot like horror rose on his.

Who are they?

Ah, yes, sorry. She pictured Joshua as he explained. *Mr A. Portland and Mr P. Montague, the developers who are taking over the block . . .*

'I . . . I need to—' The room suddenly seemed airless as Lilly staggered back towards the door.

'Lilly!' He followed her as she turned and walked as quickly as she was able towards the exit, knowing there would be no glass of bubbly for them tonight or any other night, pausing only long enough to swallow and take a breath, fearing she might vomit.

Alfie caught her up and reached for the top of her arm. She pulled free.

'Don't you dare touch me!'

He raised his palms, suggesting he came in peace, which she knew was a lie, the whole thing a lie, pretend. *God, I'm such an idiot!*

'I'm sorry!'

'Don't insult me with *sorry.* Don't you dare!' She pointed her ringed finger at him, her hand shaking, her whole body, in fact, trembling with a potent combination of sorrow and rage! Knowing if she had less self-control, she might well have been tempted to use her ring as a knuckleduster. It took her a while to visually locate the exit, but once she'd got her bearings she marched towards it.

'Lilly!' he called as he followed her. 'Please, just slow down and talk to me.'

Ignoring him, she carried on walking until she found herself outside, the cool air offering some relief. She took deep breaths and turned her head skyward, eyes closed. Trying to focus on her breathing, anything other than the fact that, not for the first time in her life, she had been duped, taken in. Her anger was directed equally at him, Alfie the great pretender, and at herself for thinking for a moment that he might have been interested in a quirky old soul like her.

The key to surviving is to get straight back up and keep going; otherwise life stops, Bob! It just stops . . .

'I wanted to tell you. I was going to tell you tonight.'

'Of course you were! I don't want to hear it.' She looked directly at him now. He was good, she'd give him that, quite convincing, even now, his downcast mouth, eyes misting. He was very good. 'Leave me alone.'

'I won't leave you alone. We need to talk, need to—'

'I don't *need* to do anything where you're concerned. Just piss off!'

Without any thought of continuing the evening and not a morsel of food in her stomach, she looked towards the river, then the landmark where she stood, in front of the mighty chimneys of Battersea. With her eyes closed, she took a deep breath. All she had to do was follow the winding silver ribbon, all the way home. Her home that this man and his associates wanted to pull down and replace with something new and shiny. Erasing her history, erasing her.

Now at a brisk pace, no more of the leisurely amble that had taken her there, Lilly began to walk, irritated and uncomfortable at the fact that Alfie walked by her side.

'I'll walk you home.'

'I neither want nor need you to walk me home. These are *my* streets, remember? Not that I need to remind you of that. You already know all about me.' This thought was enough to enrage her further. 'There's me giving you snippets about my life, telling you about my dad, my childhood, opening up . . . What kind of kick did you get from it? And what a horrible, horrible thing to do to someone, to do to me!' Her voice broke now, and she had to slow her pace a little; rushing was making her feel a little dizzy.

'It's not like that.'

'I don't want to hear it!' She turned to him briefly as she shouted, 'You and your lackey, Joshua Vaughan, you must have both been having such a giggle! I can imagine it, *I've got the silly old fool on a hook!* Like one of those fish you eat once a month! Just a daft single woman who responded to a bit of flattery! I'm so mad at myself!' She clenched her fists.

'I'll admit I came to the river because Joshy said you might be there.' *Joshy . . . Joshy . . .* It was a nickname that smacked of affection and familiarity, both of which made her want to scream! Was his supposed interest in Clodagh just another ruse to smooth their plans? 'I thought I might be able to talk to you, help you see sense.'

'Help me *see sense?*' She felt the tension in her jaw. 'That, Mr Portland, is one of those phrases. Suggesting I cannot think straight or form an opinion without the guidance of someone like you, as if I have not fully grasped the situation and need someone, a man, to explain it to me!'

'That's not what I—' He looked down.

'I think you'll find that if that was all it took, good old *Joshy* would have come back to you some weeks ago now with a positive report and a contract signed and sealed, as he has *explained* it all to me several times over!'

'That's not what I—'

'You seem intent on telling me what you have *not*, but allow me to clarify what you *have*.' She took a beat, feeling the squeeze to her heart as her truth, *the* truth, fell from her lips. 'You personally have upset me. You have unsettled me, and you have made me feel stupid, which is the very worst feeling. You have lied to me by omission, something I absolutely detest! And your company, the developers, for that's what you are, Mr Portland, a builder, a developer, not merely a businessman – your company has placed me under the most extraordinary pressure, threatening to dismantle all I hold dear. Every brick, every panel, every wire, every particle of dust that makes up my home – it's where I belong, where I have always belonged. It's my Norfolk.' Again she cursed the crack to her voice as her tears gathered and there was very little she could do to stop them.

'Lilly, please! Give me a chance to explain.' He reached out as if to take her hand, something she had welcomed not half an hour since. But Lilly knew that life could turn on a penny like that. One minute you could hold all your dreams in your palm and the next they were covered in warm, sticky blood.

She took a step backwards out of reach.

'Don't touch me! And don't talk to me. Don't you dare talk to me! And if you think I will leave my home no matter what underhand ghastly tactics you might try, you can think again.' She turned in the direction of home. 'I don't want you to walk me home. I don't want you anywhere near me!'

Thankful he didn't try and follow her, she made her way cautiously along the riverwalk as dusk gave way to darkness. Concentrating on every stride, she worried that with the uncertainty of every step, she just might stumble.

Her phone pinged with a text. Sweary words of rebuttal itched her fingertips in anticipation of it being from Alfie, knowing she could not stand to read his pithy words of apology.

The liar.

But no, it was from darling Clodagh.

Swallowing the tears that threatened, she replied with a kiss. It would have to do. Riven with disappointment, cloaked with anger and embarrassment, she was entirely without the energy to offer anything more. It made her feel foolish, the thought that she could outrun the horrible legacy of being Jeannie's daughter, that she might find someone to spend time with and had, in a private moment, even flirted with the idea that it wouldn't be the worst thing to love and be loved by a man like Alfie. The trouble was, she had no idea who Alfie was, only having been drawn into the charade, the lie, all part of a carefully orchestrated plot to make her hand over her keys and go quietly. Why in the world had she thought that time might make a difference, turn her into someone else entirely? Tonight was a reminder that she was, despite the passing of decades, still the woman Wilkie had run from, the woman who had failed with Rex, who had tried so hard, and now this . . .

'God, I feel so stupid!' she whispered, biting her bottom lip until she felt the pinch of it, angry yet again to have been so duped. Duped at her age, seventy; *old enough to know better* . . .

It was ironic, really; she had wanted the evening to be spontaneous and unexpected! And in that regard, she had not been disappointed.

◆ ◆ ◆

Lilly hadn't slept well for the last few nights, and as ever that lack of restorative sleep had taken its toll. Feeling worn and a little world-weary, she sat on the sofa and closed her eyes, hoping her thoughts might still for long enough for rest. The moment Alfie had let slip his name in the restaurant replayed in her thoughts. His face, that look of horror, had matched her own, she was sure. She couldn't help but wonder what might have happened if he hadn't let his guard down, slipped up, and she had, in blissful ignorance, enjoyed a glass of bubbles and some lovely grub, laughing at his jokes, tapping their feet under the booth to the blues that tooted in the air, sharing their histories and thoughts of retirement. Or worse, what if she had invited him back to the very flat he was intent on destroying? What if she'd taken him to her bed and let him see her scar, what if he'd asked, what if she'd told him . . . *what if . . . what if . . . what if . . .*

Jumping up, again disturbed by overthinking, she rummaged through her dad's very impressive vinyl collection, immaculately cared for by him, then her. Having found what she was looking for, she gently lowered the needle on to the LP at just the right spot. And there it was, instantly soothing, distracting in the way good music could be, a balm to her busy head, as the sound of Gordon Lightfoot's '*If You Could Read My Mind*' filled the room. A stunning poem set to music that had the power to move her. Sitting back on the sofa with her favourite view of the river, she breathed deeply, able, almost, to detect the scent of her dad's tobacco.

'What do I do now, Dad? What the hell do I do?' She spoke into the ether, felled with sadness at the lack of response.

The sound of the letterbox closing alerted her to the post. Since ignoring so many letters from the dastardly underhand Portland and Montague had landed her in such hot water, she had started to pay greater attention to everything that plopped on to her welcome mat, still remembering to booo at the brown envelopes. Today it was a letter, singular, that had arrived and carried a fancy gated crest on it. Lilly whipped it from the envelope.

'*Dear Mrs Cooper.*' She paused reading and looked skyward. 'I give up!' she shouted before turning her attention back to the printed letter. '*Thank you for your most recent letter regarding the proposed development of Waide House as part of the regeneration . . .*'

She skipped the detail, didn't need to be told of the wonderful plans of Messrs Portland and Montague. '*It is, we believe, in the wider interest of the community that this development goes ahead. The social, economic and cultural benefits of such a build cannot be ignored, and having carefully considered all arguments, it is still our belief that to allow The Fortescue Tower to be built is the very best thing . . .*' She stopped reading and balled the letter in her palm, throwing it on the floor with as much energy as she could muster. She felt more than a little beaten, a little low, a little sick and tired of her life being upended and rerouted at the whim of someone else.

Mum has moved out . . .

I'm Mrs Jones, Wilkie's wife . . .

. . . subject to a compulsory purchase order . . .

There was a knock on the door.

'Morning, Glen.'

'Morning, love. How you doing?' Her friend walked past without waiting for an invitation, such was their ease with each other. 'Heard from him?'

There was no need to expand on who the him in question was; she had filled her friend in on the whole debacle over the phone. Lilly had been comforted by Glenda's tuts and sharp draws of breath that validated her mournful story of betrayal.

'No, I won't hear from him, and I don't want to hear from him.'

'Well, I did say that it was all a bit quick.'

'Did you? I remember you saying that he might be an axe murderer and you were worried about the moral dilemma of his dietary choices, but I don't remember you saying it was a bit quick.' She filled the kettle.

'Well, if I didn't, smart arse, I certainly meant to.' Glenda sat at the table. 'Norm says you can probably sue him.'

'Sue him? What for?'

'For wooing you under false pretences.'

Lilly welcomed the laughter that burst from her, a much-needed hiatus for her furrowed brow and tight mouth; it made her feel a bit better. 'Is that a thing, wooing under false pretences?'

'It should be!' Glenda tutted. 'What was his plan? Seduce you, get you sloshed and make you sign over the flat?'

'I have no idea.' She rubbed her face, feeling the loose skin move under her fingertips. 'I think more than likely he thought he could butter me up and get me to agree that flattening my home was a good idea.'

'He doesn't know you then, does he, love?'

'No, he bloody doesn't! I wish Bertie was still around; he knew a lot of shady characters who would break a finger or a leg for a fee.'

Glenda seemed to consider this. 'Do you think it was more expensive to get a leg done over a finger?'

'I suppose so, Glen. There's probably a sliding scale for the size of the limb or appendage.'

'Probably. Reckon it would be cheap to get Norm chopped or broken. He's pretty small all over.'

Lilly again roared her laughter. 'Poor Norm!'

'We can joke, Lil, but I know how these things can set you back, make you feel rotten.'

She sat at the little table opposite her friend. 'I do feel a bit rotten, a bit out of sorts. It's thrown me.'

''Course it has.' Glenda reached out and gently placed her hand over Lilly's. 'You and I both know that you are made of sterner stuff. You have weathered far worse than this, love, and you will be right as rain in no time. You can't let him have the satisfaction of hijacking your thoughts.'

'Bit late for that. I've barely slept. I feel so stupid.' It took all her courage to admit it.

'You, stupid?' Glenda sighed. 'You've run your own business for all these years, and your own home, looked after your dad, been the best friend to me. You're an incredible artist. You're stylish, funny and smart. Ain't nothing stupid about you, Elizabeth-Roberta.'

Lilly felt the rush of emotion up the back of her nose. To be called that . . . It reminded her so powerfully of Wilkie, who, even after all these years, still had the power to reduce her to tears. It had hit her hard, no doubt, because she was low. Alfie's duplicity had floored her, bringing back some dark memories, igniting the flame of rejection that had burned brightly since she'd found her mum to be no more than a fragrant shadow that lurked in the corner of the room.

'Thank you, Glen. Don't know why I'm so upset. It just all feels like a lot.'

'Because it is a lot.'

'Truth is, I just can't see how I hang on to the flat. I don't know who to talk to about it, or what to do!' She laid her hand on the tabletop, taking a moment to think of all the meals, card games, cups of tea, the jigsaw puzzles, all of it having taken place right here on this little table. 'I got another letter from Mr Passmore, the MP, who only confirmed what he'd already said: that it's a wonderful opportunity and is all going ahead. I'm just a gnat in the ointment for him. I don't count, not in the grand scheme of things, and that's one of the hardest aspects of it for me, the fact that this is my home, and the loss of it . . .' She swallowed. 'I spoke to Denzel a while back and he said it was almost pointless trying to fight it, told me that these companies have so much money and sway that the flag-waving of one old lady who would rather not shift cuts very little ice. It's made me feel insignificant, and no one wants to feel like that. I'm disappointed. It feels so unfair. I haven't let myself think that I might actually have to move, not really, until now. But it feels likely, and I am utterly bereft at the prospect, but I'm also tired, Glen' – she rubbed her eyes – 'and a bit beaten.'

'Where do you think you might like to go?'

'Where I'd like to go is nowhere, I want to stay right here, but where I will go, I have absolutely no idea.' The thought of having to search felt more than a little overwhelming.

'The good news is Norm and I can help you pack up. Bradley and Andrew, too, they'll pitch in.'

'Thank you.'

'And we've got a spare room in New Cross so you can always come and stay with us.'

'Glen, that is a very kind offer.' Lilly wiped her nose and face on a sheet of kitchen roll. 'But honestly? I couldn't live with you. You'd drive me crazy! I'd kill you!'

'With an axe?' her friend asked as she went to fetch the mugs to make tea.

'More than likely.' She smiled at her. 'More than bloody likely.'

1973 – aged 18

The bus pulled up and Lilly jumped off the back, staring at the dirty London brick exterior of the hospital where fumes and grime had licked the surface for centuries. Not half an hour since, she'd left her dad at the kitchen table with The Teddy Bears' '*To Know Him Is to Love Him*' playing loudly.

'This is such a beautiful song, Lilly! A classic!' He had tapped his fingers in time to the music.

''Tis,' she'd managed, strangling the sob in her throat. Her dad was right, the words and melody were so very beautiful.

'And you're off on your field trip! That's exciting!' He'd taken a drag on his cigarette.

'Yep, I'm meeting Glenda at Victoria and we're going to travel together.'

How easily these words had slipped from her mouth and how hard it was to reconcile them in her mind. Every lie she threw in his direction was weighted with guilt and remorse, aware as she was of the disservice she did him every time she believed him naïve enough to swallow it, which he did. Her lovely dad. A couple of days at the seaside with her friend, what could be nicer . . .

He'd then sat back in the chair and closed his eyes, moving his head in time with the music. She wondered when it reminded him of, and who. Her mum was the most likely candidate. It was that melody that went round and round in her head now. She wished it would stop, not needing her emotions to run any higher today.

The foyer was busy, people coming and going, some coughing into white cotton handkerchiefs, others crying. A woman winced as she hobbled on an obviously damaged ankle. And a small child with a cut head and a splat of dried blood on his little forehead cried with gusto as his mother cooed, 'There, there,' and dabbed at the injury with a damp paper towel.

Trolleys and wheelchairs pushed by brown-coated porters moving the old or infirm formed a two-lane highway, while those of a less than tolerant nature leapfrogged between them, trying to beat them to the lifts.

Lilly hung back and looked at the confusion of signs before spotting the department she needed and making her way slowly along the wall, her fingers trailing it as she walked. This was for two reasons. First, because nothing felt real, and this wall, this solid thing beneath her fingertips, reminded her that it was no dream. And second, if the pain rose again, hitting the peak it had yesterday, there was a risk she might fall down or crumple, and this wall would be what saved her, enabling her to slither down it rather than tumble forward.

The lift was a little crowded, and she felt faint, wishing the juddering metal cage would hurry. Two women with distended stomachs, empire-line smocks and wide smiles stood in the corners, both with their husbands in close proximity. One of the women took a long drag on her cigarette before treading it underfoot on the lift floor. Each man carried the jumpy air of one who was two parts excited and one part petrified. The one with a droopy moustache and stacked heels gave her a wide-eyed look of acknowledgement, as if they were in the same club. She looked away. They were not in the same club, not even close.

The lift doors opened. The two couples and Lilly got out. The waiting room of the maternity ward was a thick fog of cigarette smoke, as men, mainly, and other relatives paced, smoked and chuckled nervously in the room with the incredible view over the London rooftops. A stunning vista, no doubt, but hers, from their lounge window of Waide House, was better. She wished she were there right now, just a little way along the river, wished she wasn't in this situation, wished she could wind back the clock to the day Wilkie had wandered along the towpath.

What are you painting?

Oh, I'm painting 'Piss off back to your wife and two small children . . .'

Yes, this was how she wished she had responded on that day when it all started and her life began to unravel.

She queued at the reception desk until a ward sister in a starched white pinny and hat greeted her with a stern tone that suggested efficiency and instilled confidence.

'How can I help you?'

'My name is Elizabeth-Roberta Cooper and I called yesterday because I was bleeding. The nurse said if I was no better to' – she paused as the breath caught in her throat, the pain sharp and unexpected, requiring all of her attention – 'to . . . to come in. It's . . . it's got worse, and so—'

The sister stood and walked quickly around to the front of the desk. 'Nurse Maddox?' she called out.

A younger nurse came quickly.

'Wheelchair, please. Take Mrs Cooper to room twelve.'

Lilly concentrated on breathing, beyond relieved that she was here and that someone was taking control, because for the last few weeks she had been in freefall.

At first it had been hard to accept she was pregnant, and she'd spent the time in an altered state of disbelief. This had been quickly followed by the white-hot, paralysing fear of indecision. How was she to navigate this disaster without coming clean to her dad, without admitting that she had messed up spectacularly, the lying to him almost as soul-destroying as getting pregnant by a married man, words that still sounded as surreal as they did implausible. How could this be her life?

She told no one, not wanting to be judged, not wanting her friends to see how far she had fallen, not wanting to admit it to anyone, which would make it real, not knowing how to phrase it, not willing to face the fact that her future, however she tried to picture it, looked entirely bleak.

Harder still were the moments in the wee small hours when her palm lay on her stomach and she felt the ripple of wonder at the fact that this was a life she and Wilkie had created. Wilkie, the man she was trying so very hard not to love because he belonged to someone else. But this seed that had taken root, this baby – was it not a sign, a gift? Lying on her narrow bed, she allowed excitement to fuse with daydream and pictured Wilkie holding their newborn, beaming at her, *his girl* . . . Daylight peeking through the curtains shed light on the reality that it was not a gift, but was in fact a fearful situation, with only two outcomes – to raise the baby alone, to give the baby away – and right now, as she waited at the reception desk, it seemed that the probable outcome was entirely beyond her control. This realisation brought her both immeasurable sadness and immeasurable relief, a most confusing combination. There was no doubt that to lose this baby would mean the problem had disappeared, but oh, to hold her baby, to meet her baby . . .

Be still, I've got you, whatever comes next, I've got you. She spoke the words of comfort in her mind, hoping they would travel down to her womb.

She closed her eyes and leaned on the arm the sister offered. Almost immediately, Nurse Maddox returned with the wheelchair, and carefully they lowered her into it.

Room twelve was small and nondescript. The walls were half covered in cream tiles that curved over the sill of a frosted tilting metal window. A large chrome light was positioned over a bed, where a white sheet and pale blue blanket were pulled taut.

'Can you hop up?' the younger nurse asked kindly.

'I can, but' – she felt the swell of embarrassment in this strange, grown-up environment – 'but I'm bleeding.' Her eyes darted to the pristine bedlinen, aware of the warm, damp feeling that spoke of nothing good.

'Oh, don't you worry about that.' Nurse Maddox's eyes crinkled in understanding as she helped Lilly up on to the bed, where she immediately drew her knees up towards her chest, which offered some relief.

The sister removed a clipboard from the end of the bed and began asking questions.

'Name?'

'Elizabeth-Roberta Cooper.'

'Your date of birth, Mrs Cooper?'

She blinked at the assumption and wondered how to handle the delicate situation, as the sister jotted down her answers with a ballpoint pen.

'Twelfth of August 1955.'

'Weight?'

'Nine stone two.'

'Place of birth?'

'Here, St Thomas's.'

'Ah, one of ours!' The woman paused in her writing and smiled at her broadly.

Lilly felt the rush of tears, trying to imagine her mum in this very building, her dad no doubt smoking in the waiting room, as her life had begun by the side of the river. It made her incredibly sad to be here alone, opposite *Grand Benjamin*, the landmark she only had to find so that she could follow the river along its path, knowing it would take her all the way home . . .

'Now, now. Let's not cry. We shan't have tears!' The sister nodded, her voice stern, as Lilly did her best to comply. 'They don't help in any way at all. How far along are you, Mrs Cooper?'

There it was again.

'Erm, ten weeks, twelve weeks.'

'You haven't had an antenatal check?'

She shook her head. Hadn't seen a doctor, hadn't told a soul, hadn't wanted it to be true while simultaneously fighting secret feelings of ridiculous excitement at the prospect.

Oh, if only, if only we could both hang on a little longer, how long? A day . . . a month . . . a year . . . a decade . . . it's rotten timing is what it is. How I would have loved you! And how I will always love the idea of you . . .

'Now, I'm sure the last thing you want to do is disturb your husband at his place of work, my dear, but it really is advisable that we contact him. Do you have a telephone number for him?'

Nurse Maddox lifted Lilly's limp wrist and with her other hand held the little upside-down watch that dangled from the apron of her starched blue uniform, taking Lilly's pulse.

She knew it was time to come clean, to admit the thing that she had been dreading.

'I don't have one, actually.'

'Don't have a telephone number?' the sister asked softly. 'That's okay, we can find it, I'm sure—'

'No.' Lilly cut her short and took a breath. 'I don't . . . don't have a husband. I'm . . . I'm not married.'

'No husband?' The woman's lips were now quite thin.

'No.' Her voice was a whisper. The shame – oh, the shame! Her skin prickled with the cold sweat of discomfort.

'I see.' The sister breathed through pursed lips and, just like that, Lilly no longer felt like one of theirs.

Nurse Maddox let go of her wrist mid-air and her arm fell back on to the bed. It felt a lot like being discarded, something she was not unused to in recent times.

'Well, I'm assuming you do *not* want us to contact your mother?' the sister asked with a slight sneer of disapproval, suggesting that if Lilly were her daughter, she would not want this brought to her door.

She more than understood, thanking her lucky stars that this woman was not her mother. But then again, her actual mother was not that much better. Her tears threatened once more, as they tended to do in recent times because, in spite of it all, she wanted her mum here! She wanted Jeannie to smile at her and smooth the damp hair from her forehead and to tell her that it was all going to be all right. And she hated herself that she wanted this from the woman who had left them, the woman whose destructive tendencies and need of sex she just might have inherited, the very tendencies that had landed her here in the first place.

'No, I don't want you to contact my mother.'

The sister wrote with purpose. Lilly could hear the nib of the pen digging the surface of the paper as the woman, seemingly angry, scrawled something wordy on the top sheet of her chart and replaced it at the foot of the bed. The two women left, whispering under their breath as they did so. Lilly lay all alone, staring at the overhead light, the rubber swing doors that led to the corridor and the frosted-glass window that was tilted open and through which came the sounds of the real world outside. The London hum. She placed her joined hands between her legs, trying to stem their tremble and, when she looked at them, they were covered in the warm, red blood she had been so concerned about.

Well, this is a rotten mess, is it not, my darling? Try not to worry . . . It will be okay. I'm here . . . I'm right here . . .

Unsure how long she lay there, it was a surprise and a relief when a portly, balding doctor walked briskly through the swing doors, stethoscope dangling around his wide neck, white coat open and flapping. He reached for her chart. So preoccupied was he she genuinely wondered if he had seen her. Eventually, he looked up.

'Right, let's have a look at you,' were his first words as he pulled on some rubber gloves, stretching them over his porky fingers before letting them snap on his wrists. He stared at her blood-soaked jeans. 'We need to get these off. Nurse?' he yelled over his shoulder. A different nurse, younger than Nurse Maddox, came into the room.

'Yes, Dr Rudd?'

'I can hardly examine the patient if she is fully dressed, can I?'

'No, Dr Rudd.' The young woman, quite flustered, rushed forward, and Lilly assisted as far as she was able, by unbuttoning her Levi's and doing her best to ease her jeans and pants over her narrow hips. It was uncomfortable, embarrassing and awkward, lifting her bottom, resting on her elbows, as the nurse gripped the soggy, clinging denim and pulled.

Lilly's thighs and bottom were sticky. She shivered with cold, watching as the nurse folded her jeans and placed them in a clear plastic bag that she set on a chair. The doctor produced spectacles from the top pocket of his white coat and placed them on the end of his nose. He pulled the metal stirrups that had been folded by the sides of the bed frame wide.

'Lie back, please,' he instructed with a certain detachment. Lilly did as she was told, and her embarrassment switched up a gear to complete mortification as he manhandled her feet and placed them into the stirrups. With her legs wide, naked from the waist down, his head disappeared out of view, and she felt the cold touch of something metal against her most delicate skin.

'Deep breath,' he instructed in a most matter-of-fact way. She did as he said before the sharp discomfort of something metal inside her. 'Yes, as I thought.' He withdrew the object, peeled the gloves from his hands and dropped them into the plastic wastebin before restoring his glasses to his pocket. 'You are miscarrying. Do you know what that means?'

'Yes.' Lilly nodded, keeping her voice small. She had known what it meant when she started bleeding heavily the day before.

'We will perform a D&C. Do you know what *that* is?' He spoke to her as if she were stupid, which figured. How smart was she to have ended up here in this most dire of situations?

'I don't.'

'Dilation and curettage, a procedure where we remove any tissue from the uterus. We'll get you prepped.'

A procedure? Did he mean surgery? It was as questions formed on her tongue, and she gathered the courage to ask, that Dr Rudd left the room and the young nurse handed her a paper-type gown.

'Slip out of your bra and top and put this on. They'll wheel you down to theatre in a bit.'

'Can I . . .' Lilly tried to sit up and pointed at her feet.

'Oh, yes! Yes, of course!' The young nurse eased her feet from the stirrups and Lilly coiled into a ball, trying to order her thoughts. She felt sad, scared, but also strangely hollow, empty, which was ironic, as she was far from empty. If she had been empty, there would be no need for the procedure that the doctor had made sound most ordinary. Lilly wondered when she might be able to go home, knowing her dad would only worry. Her dad who thought she was at the seaside, having a lovely time. It was almost more than she could comprehend, the deceit, the procedure, the fact that Wilkie had left her, *married* Wilkie.

After the nurse had left, Lilly sobbed into the thin pillow, realising the sister was wrong on at least one count, her assumption that tears did not help at all, as Lilly found them most cathartic.

It was a couple of hours later that two porters came and transferred her to a trolley before wheeling her along the corridors at what felt like speed. Pulling the blue blanket they had placed on her up to her chin, she stared up at the bright strip lights overhead. The occasional bump in the linoleum jolted her. All the while she was diverted by the whistling porters. She liked it, the whistling. It reminded her of her dad, who, if he wasn't playing music, was whistling something.

The operating theatre smelled of bleach and chemicals, causing the instant rise of nausea in her throat.

'Age?'

The question was asked over her head by a man in a blue mask that covered his mouth and nose and who wore a hat made out of J Cloth. A woman – a nurse, she assumed – gave the answers.

'Eighteen.'

'Weight?'

'Nine stone two.'

'Splendid!' the man shouted, and this, too, made her jolt. 'Here we are, Mrs Cooper . . .'

Miss. It's Miss. She looked up at him.

'Dr Rudd is ready for you now. You will feel a sharp scratch on the back of your hand and, before you know it, you'll be waking up in recovery. Right.' He clapped, and she jolted for the third time. 'Let's get this show on the road!' His jollity gave the whole experience a nightmarish quality.

I'm sorry . . . I am so sorry . . . We were not meant to be, you and I . . .

And then the lights faded, and the voice echoed, 'That's a good girl. Count backwards from ten for me . . .'

'Ten . . . nine . . . eight . . .'

Then nothing.

Nothing.

Present day

Alfie's betrayal had cut her deep. As disappointed as she was angry, it took all of her strength to paint on a smile and walk Apollo to school. It was alarming, the thought that this routine might well be on a countdown, coming to an end, and the thought of the quiet mornings that would follow, wherever it was she might be waking up. She shivered. Where the hell was she supposed to go if they took her home? It wasn't a case of money – she was in a most fortunate position, as Glenda liked to remind her; she had means – but what did that matter when there was absolutely nowhere else she wanted to be? It was beginning to feel like the most likely outcome, having to move, and the thought terrified her. Maybe she should get back in contact with Jake the journalist and let him write his aggressive copy, maybe she should stage a protest, or . . . or write to the prime minister! Maybe all three.

Stopping on the pavement, she bent down to Apollo's level as he handed her the stick of the day, which now required no instruction when he entrusted it to her for safekeeping. There was a healthy pile of them, all shapes and sizes, in her hallway; Clodagh had apologised for the accumulating clutter. Lilly had felt it important to point out that it wasn't clutter, but treasure.

Big difference.

There was a brass-hinged wooden box in the cupboard, along with her dad's precious things. His violin, annotated sheet music in a battered leather case, his medals, wedding ring, birth certificate, death certificate, a couple of old photographs of him as a child and one of him and her mum on their wedding day. Jeannie had looked lovely in a sharp-cut, pale-grey suit with a pencil skirt and a pillbox hat, and her dad looked skinny and tanned inside his uniform, fresh back from fighting in Italy. From her mum's hand dangled a silver horseshoe on a white ribbon, and her bouquet was a small posy of spring flowers, pretty. Lilly hated to look at the picture, not only saddened by the reminder of how young they had been and how quickly they'd got old, but also by the look of hope and excitement on their faces as they took vows that for her mother, at least, were no more than lies. It felt cruel almost, and uncomfortable, to see the image with the knowledge of how things had unfolded making a mockery of the whole event.

Inside the wooden box was her very own treasure, a brittle tissue folded with a smudge of red, red lipstick in the middle of it, and objects she and her dad had scavenged from the soft silt of the riverbank at low tide while mudlarking. Each item they had found and washed gave them both the biggest thrill! Three old clay pipes, various horse teeth, buttons, buckles, shards of pottery and their very best find – an old coin.

'When was it proper money?' she'd asked her dad's friend, Malcolm Tenterdon of the local historical society, never forgetting the way his eyes had shone!

'It's not one of the rarer ones, but it's old, Lilly-Bob, and this symbol' – he pointed at the wreath – 'in my opinion, makes it Roman.'

'What does it mean?' she'd asked, a little confused by the absolute delight displayed by the men, who drew breath and chuckled their delight.

'It means everything,' Malcolm had whispered.

'You have the history of London, of this river, right there in the palm of your hand . . .' Her dad had looked close to tears.

Yes, it was important to know the difference between clutter and treasure.

'Have a great day, Apollo. Make good choices, eat all your lunch, have fun!'

'Do you think my dad might come and pick me up from school?' he asked with a hopeful anticipation that was galling to hear.

'I don't know, little one! But someone will be here, like always. Just concentrate on having a lovely time. See you later.'

Keen to change the subject, she waved until he was safely inside the building and in the hands of his teacher, who waved back. She doubted very much that Sab would be picking him up from school any time soon. Clodagh still hadn't heard from him, not that she was surprised. It was his MO apparently, overtly and publicly tearful over what he couldn't have, like a foot-stamping toddler, but entirely unreliable when making a commitment of any kind. A man-child. Sabre-rattling at its best, but to see how much it had unnerved the young woman, a fantastic, hard-working mum who deserved so much more, was hard.

It was a beautiful blue-sky day and Lilly, having written her letter to the prime minister and left a message for Call Me Jake the journalist, decided to set up her easel when she got home, in the mood to paint the river. It was almost impossible to imagine that her days and nights at Waide House, too, were on a timer. Far easier not to think of it, not to let the dagger of loss pierce her breast every minute of every day. She would pack up, when she had to, make a final plan, when she had to, but today, she would paint!

Having waved, as was customary, to the other side, Lilly now sat on her camping stool, closed her eyes and took a deep breath, feeling the rush of feel-good thoughts swirling in her head at the prospect of her morning by the river as she made broad brushstrokes on the canvas. Countless were the days she had sat here in the exact same spot doing the exact same thing, and yet now she knew it was coming to an end the whole exercise took on a new poignancy. As with anything that was diminishing, it felt important to take it all in, appreciate every fine detail, commit it to memory. The last cup of tea with her dad, the last time she saw Wilkie, the last meal her mum cooked them when they were a family, Bertie's last day in the gallery . . . all of these and much more, catalogued and captured in perfect detail, giving them the importance they deserved.

She had meant it when she said to the charlatan Mr Portland that she liked to visit the past.

A breeze lifted her hair and her spirits as she let the morning sun warm her face. It was as she turned her head, looking up towards *Grand Benjamin,* that she spied him on the path before he came into full view, his height and auburn hair a giveaway. Her stomach folded in advance of the inevitable interaction. What she wanted to do was stand up and rage at the man, throw her jar of water over him, but of course she wouldn't because he was young, only doing a job, and she wasn't that kind of person. It was beyond irritating, however, how his mere presence could put a nail in the wheel of her lovely morning.

'Miss Cooper.' He spoke as he approached. His manner was slow, hesitant and wary, as it should be.

'Go away, Mr Vaughan,' she groaned, denying him the courtesy of eye contact.

'I . . . I wanted to come and see you and explain.'

'What is it with you people?' She turned to face him, allowing him to gauge the full weight of her disappointment. 'You and your snake of a boss, do you not understand that I don't want to hear your explanations? I want nothing to do with you, either of you, and I deeply regret allowing you to step over my threshold and making you tea. There is no explaining to be done. The situation is quite clear to me, and I want no part of it, and I will still, even if the tide is against me, cling on until the last! I'm not beaten yet, not quite. Now if you would be so kind, please leave me alone to enjoy my morning.'

Much to her irritation, and knowing there was very little she could do, as it was, technically, a public thoroughfare, Joshua Vaughan sat on the small wall behind her. She sighed as loudly as she could without it being overly theatrical.

'I don't know what to say.' His words were accompanied by his sigh.

'Then do as my dad always said: *If in doubt, say nothing*. That would suit me just fine.'

He ignored her.

'It's all my fault. I told Alfie he could find you on the towpath that day. He said he wanted to talk to you face to face.'

'Yes, to help me *see sense* – how lucky we women are to have men around to put us right on so many issues.' Her sarcasm wasn't lost on him, as a brief glance at his face that flushed red confirmed.

'The next thing I know you're out on a date.'

'It was not a date.' She felt the urgent need to clarify, to regain a little of her dignity in the face of her humiliation. 'It was categorically not a date! It was a nasty and calculated ambush.'

'He's not a bad person.'

'Just a dishonest one,' she countered. 'Lying through omission is the worst.'

'He's my mum's brother.'

'What?' She screwed her face up at him.

'I know what you mean about lying through omission, and so I thought I should say: Alfie is my uncle. My mum used to be Rita Portland, then she married my dad and became Rita Vaughan. I'm the youngest.'

'Oh, well, that figures! A family affair, how delightful.' There it was again, that sarcasm.

'Everything is messed up.' Joshua ran his fingers through his hair.

'Oh, don't worry. I am quite confident, even though it causes me great pain to admit it, that despite my plans to resist, you will still get your grubby mitts on my property and all that lovely profit. I'm coming to realise that I am just an old woman with no voice. It's a terrible feeling to be so ignored. Galling that people think I can be appeased with the odd letter and suggestions of how I might go forward, even the mention of money, as if I am no more than a problem to be solved, a bill to be settled, an irritation, and not a person with a whole life!' She hadn't meant to rant, but there we go.

'I didn't mean that. I meant Clodagh, Miss Newman. We were getting on really well. And now . . .'

Lilly laughed then. Joshua looked crestfallen, and it was funny, kind of; she was losing her home, potentially losing her fight, and he was more concerned that his uncle's subterfuge might have put a spanner in the works of his dating plans.

'She's far too good for you.' She spoke half in jest. 'She's honest, for one thing!'

'Do you think she might still come for a coffee with me if I ask her?'

Lilly turned to face the young man, who was, despite her anger at the whole situation and her wariness of his uncle, an open book. It irritated her how much she liked him in spite of his part in this whole fiasco. The gentle putt-putt of a boat reversing into the dock filled the air.

'I don't know. Maybe. You'll have to ask her yourself.'

'Thank you.'

'What are you thanking me for?'

'For not telling me to stay away from her and for not chasing me off the towpath.'

'I'm sorely tempted to do both.' It was her turn to come clean.

'I need to say something, but I don't want you to shout at me.' He squinted.

It was strange to hear the quaver of fear in his voice, as if she were *that* person, someone whose wrath he ought to fear, which could not be further from the truth.

'Say what you need to and I will not shout at you. I rarely shout!' She shouted the last bit, remembering how she had first met Clodagh on that glorious day that was to be their beginning, right here on the riverbank.

I don't think I barked. The thing is, he threw rubbish into the river – plastic! He threw plastic!

'Alfie told me to give you a message. He said that he would be here around eleven to pick you up.'

'Urgh, that man! I don't want a message, and kindly tell him not to waste his time as I will not be going anywhere with him any time soon.' Her blood raced at the sheer audacity of it.

'I . . .'

She watched Joshua's mouth flap, as if it were trying to find the words.

'What is it, Mr Vaughan? Spit it out.'

She figured the sooner he had said his piece, the sooner he could leave and let her get on with her picture.

'He's already here.' He pointed along the path towards the dock, and there was Alfie, walking towards her, open-necked shirt, no jacket, less formal than she'd seen him before, in deck shoes, chinos and with his sunglasses on his head. It was infuriating the way her heart was yet to catch up with what her brain understood and gave a squeeze of delight at the sight of him. Turning to her paint palette, she mixed a little blue with grey and a splash of water, trying to get the tone just right.

'I know I'm one of the last people you want to see.'

'That's not true.' She answered without looking up.

'Oh?' he answered with a note of optimism.

'Not *one* of the last, *the* absolute last, the *very* last!' she emphasised.

'Literally?' Alfie stared at her.

'Literally!' she confirmed.

'So if Attila the Hun were here, you'd prefer that or . . . or an axe murderer?' He tried a smile, which she didn't reciprocate, knowing this time it would take a lot more than his smooth-talking, easy humour and handsome face to win her over.

'Precisely that.' She stared at him.

'I think I'll . . .' Joshua held his small leather attaché case aloft as if he had somewhere he needed to be urgently, which she guessed was anywhere other than here, as he stood to leave.

'Speak later, Joshy.' Alfie waved before turning towards her. 'Lilly,' Alfie began.

'Why are you ambushing me like this, tag-teaming me with your nephew!' she fired. 'Why can't you just leave me alone! Who knows how many days I have left to sit in the sunshine and enjoy my work in peace, but it seems it's not enough that you're taking that from me, you want to pitch up to harass me as well, spoil what limited time here I may have. It's awful! You are awful!'

'I was thinking about what you said.'

'Clearly not about the bit where I said I don't want you anywhere near me.' She offered the reminder.

'No, the bit where you said you'd only been on the river once before, on a water taxi back in the nineties, and so I thought it would be nice for you to see your home from the river. I brought my boat.'

Her eyes followed his extended arm towards the breathtaking wooden slipper launch that had only recently moored. A stunning craft, beautifully proportioned, its wood shiny. She knew her dad would have greatly admired it.

'Thank you, but I'm quite content not to go for a ride on your very expensive boat.' She returned her attention to the canvas. It bothered her that he thought she might be the kind of woman who would roll over at the sight of his fancy boat or the gift of a bauble, or a nice dinner in Battersea, come to think of it. He didn't know her at all, and never would.

'Lilly!' His tone was close to exasperation, which made her stop what she was doing and look up. 'If I was the villain you paint me as I would not be here, trying to talk to you. I'm asking for an hour of your time. That's all, just one hour. This building you are so fond of, it's a chance to see it from all angles, to really take it in.'

Before it's gone for ever . . . She filled in the blanks.

'After that' – he raised his palms – 'if you still insist, you won't see me again, I promise. And contrary to what you might think, I am a man of my word.'

It was conflicting; she felt relief that he might keep his word and a little distressed at the prospect too. It was such a shame he was a liar and an arsehole because she had really liked him. He was right, however, about the chance to see Waide House from the river, to take a snapshot in her mind. It would be lovely.

'I hate how everything feels like it's in turmoil.' She put her brush down and, weary from the fight, spoke freely. 'I was so happy, content, before your letters started arriving and your nephew was sent to knock on my door.' The sadness that flared in her breast was raw and uncomfortable.

'Please, Lilly, come out with me on the boat, just for an hour.'

'So you can what? Twist my arm, give me all the reasons why it might be to my benefit to move on? I've heard it all and my heart is still broken.'

'No, no arm-twisting. Come out with me because it's a nice way to spend time.'

It was a once-in-a-lifetime offer and one she knew she might live to regret not taking. Folding away her easel, she packed her brushes and, in a well-practised manner, took her painting paraphernalia into Waide House and popped it inside the wide hallway; she'd take it up to the flat later, after one last glimpse of this place she so loved. With her hair tucked inside a peacock-blue silk scarf, she walked towards him.

'One hour.' The reminder as she made her way out on to the dock.

Alfie lifted his hand to help her down into the launch and she had no choice but to take it. There it was again, that darned frisson of excitement. What was it about men like Wilkie and Alfie that had the power to make her feel this way? Why was she attracted to the liars, the cads, the cheats? Rex had been different, she remembered. Sweet Rex, kind Rex, who had not, despite his best efforts, had the same effect on her. What she had felt for him was a pale imitation of the passion, the desire, the need, she'd had for Wilkie.

Stepping down into the interior, she was fascinated. The design and craftsmanship were impeccable; the hand-stitched leather of the two wide sofa-like seats at the rear and front, the highly polished dashboard with a leather-covered steering wheel that looked fresh out of an expensive vintage car.

'She's beautiful.' Her fingers trailed the butter-soft upholstery as the boat gently rocked in the swell.

'*Lady Margery*, named after my mother.'

Lilly kept her eyes on the river ahead, not wanting any more of his history, the personal details that had helped lash him to her with confidence; she wanted no more of that. Alfie sat next to her and switched on the engine, which purred as, with incredible skill, he pulled away from the dock and out into the river.

'I'll take her upstream slowly so you can see Waide House properly – then we'll turn her about, and you can do the same from the other direction. There's nothing like seeing your city from the water. A different perspective altogether, like the difference between travelling on the top deck of a bus or underground on the Tube. When you're on the river you get to see the lines at the top of the buildings, understand their placement along the water's edge and take in the whole expanse.'

It was thrilling, no mistake, being on the stretch of river she knew so well. A sensation quite unlike any other; and he was right, so much detail she had been unaware of! The proximity of the towering apartment blocks to her building, the small spaces between the plots filled with tiny squares of garden where people shoehorned in snippets of nature. And how tiny Waide House looked, a stocky little anomaly among the shiny skyscrapers.

'Look at her.' She wasn't sure if she'd said it aloud. It was an almost visceral reaction, the sight of her home, the building in its entirety sitting there like a dusty little thing among the shiny giants, a relic among the new. Her tears fell in a steady stream, distressed at the utter abhorrence of the fact that the block was to be razed to the ground, not a brick left. Alfie was strangely quiet. 'If I look at the flat, I can see me standing in the window when I was little, looking out at the wonder of it all.'

'Yet I see potential homes for hundreds of people.'

'Oh, please! Let's not pretend you are doing this for altruistic reasons. You're doing it for profit!' She cut him short.

'It doesn't have to be either or, Lilly. Yes, it's a great business proposition for me, a legacy—'

'And why do you need that?' Again she interrupted, turning to look at him now, her breath stuttering as she wiped her eyes on the back of her hand.

'Why do I need that?' His expression told her he was not unmoved by her tears.

'Yes, why is it so important for men to build something big, to build anything at all?'

'It's what I do, what I've always done.'

'So I guess some would say surely you've built enough?' She toyed with him.

'Nothing like this.' He studied the skyline. 'This is my opus, my swansong. It's a building that will shape the London skyline – what an opportunity.'

'Huh.' She managed to steady her breathing. 'Why can't your legacy be like my dad's: that he never knowingly harmed anyone, showed everyone kindness, gave me a love of music, never laid a brick, as far as I know, but what a wonderful way to remember a person.'

'I want to do something that matters.'

'My dad mattered! I matter! My home matters! Things don't have to be on a grand or exuberant scale to matter! Are you so keen to show how far from that crowded house in East Ham you've come that you have to do this?'

'Yes, probably, and if it's amateur psychology you want, why is it you're so afraid of landing that you can't fly? You don't even leave the city!'

I'm afraid to fly because there is no one, absolutely no one, to catch me if I fall . . . This was her first and most distressing thought. 'You know so little about me, even if you think you do. I want to fly, Alfie! I want to!'

'So what's stopping you?' The boat slowed, and the engine ticked, as if both vessel and man waited for her response.

'I've always been too afraid of . . . of . . .'

'Of what?' His tone was softer now.

'Of this not being here when I got back.' She gave a wry smile at the irony of it all.

'This what, Lilly?'

'This home, this view, this river, this feeling like I belong! This place, this history, these memories.'

'That wouldn't change just because you weren't here any more.'

'Wouldn't it?' she snapped.

'No! People change, things change, you just have to figure out how to change with it! Give life a chance!'

'You don't know, Alfie! You don't know anything!'

'So tell me. Tell me right now!' He put the boat into gear, and they headed up the river, the breeze in their faces, the spray hitting the side of the boat as *Lady Margery* motored gently through the very heart of her neighbourhood, carried along on Old Mother Thames.

'Tell you what? That I ate my toast, packed my bag, walked to school, had mint sponge with chocolate icing with custard for lunch, which made it a very good day.' The details of this last day, too, were etched in her mind, as all her hurt and the impending sense of loss bubbled up into her throat, making it feel easier to let it all out, to rid her mouth of the poison. 'I played netball, and then wandered home, put my key in the door and stepped into a different place, a different world, where everything was changed because my mum had packed her vanity case and left. She left me, and she' – Lilly hiccupped on her tears – 'she didn't even wait for me to come home to say goodbye. She just . . . just went. She left me for Derek Manners, who was dull! So dull, and so if that life with him was preferable, what did that say about us? My mum wasn't like *Lady Margery*, there were no Sunday gatherings with our extended family, my mum wasn't my safe place, the flat was. Waide

House was. Even after Dad, it was my place, my haven. It's always been that, until now.'

'I think you're incredibly strong. You've weathered your fair share of storms.' He spoke with compassion that made her huff; he only knew the half of it . . . 'You deserve to be happy, not tethered. And you carry your dad with you – it's not about a room or a view. Even if it wasn't my company, Lilly, I would still, as your friend, tell you that it's a chance to start over. It could be very exciting if you let it!'

'Could it, Alfie? Could it be very exciting if I let it? And you are most definitely *not* my friend! You're not!' Her voice was hoarse as memories came thick and fast. 'Why do men like you think it's okay to take things away without asking, why do you do that?'

'I'm not trying to take anything away, it's an opportunity . . .'

'Not for me. It's a loss, a huge loss, all because you've made the decision to take it from me, from all of us, so that you can sit back and say it's your legacy, as if that's all the justification you need. No matter what it costs me, and people like me. We are the rightful owners of the space – it's *our* legacy!'

'I . . . I don't know what to say.' He took a long, slow breath and blinked as if tired. 'But I can see that nothing I am going to say is going to convince you.'

'Nothing at all.' She jutted her chin in confirmation.

Alfie clicked his tongue against the roof of his mouth and shook his head as this seemed to register, and with regret.

'Where would you like to go next, up towards London Bridge or back towards Battersea?'

Lilly took one last long look at her flat from the river, and there she was on the towpath, young and smiling in her suede miniskirt, red knee-high leather boots, and her beaded smock top with buttons undone . . . It was true what she had said earlier: why did men like him think it was okay to take things away without asking, why did they do that?

That's a good girl . . . count backwards from ten for me . . .

'Just take me back.' She didn't want to be distressed in front of him, didn't want to be in front of him at all. 'Take me to the dock. I want to get off your boat. I want to go home now.'

'But we still have forty minutes left.' He sounded almost panicked.

'I don't want to spend one more minute here. Please, just . . . just take me home.'

1973 – aged 18

When Lilly fully came round it took her a beat to understand that she was in a ward with ten beds along one side and ten more on the other. Women were sitting up, tucked beneath pristine white sheets like dolls. Her stomach pulsed with the dull ache of loss and the lower half of her body was very sore. The level of discomfort was unexpected. She had, in her naivety, thought it would all be over once the procedure was complete, that she'd be able to pop her jeans back on and walk slowly home, letting her thoughts settle and the sight of the river calm her. The sadness that rippled through her, however, was entirely expected as tears trickled over her temple, a visceral reaction as her distress leaked from her.

Her baby was gone.

Her link to Wilkie gone.

His lingering presence, the last connection that would have kept them bound for life, had been severed.

The sound of mewling was the first clue that she was in a ward for new mothers and their babies. Looking to the bed next to her, Lilly smiled weakly at the new mum in her twenties who was feeding her baby, feeling a flare of envy laced with distress. The woman opposite applied mascara while her newborn slept in a plastic crib on wheels next to the bed. It was almost more than she could stand, seeing these new mothers, hearing a child's cry. The silence around her bed, the absence of a bassinet, were physical reminders that it was all over for her.

It was a silence that she had always hated, feared even, one that carried weight.

The voice of reason told her she needed to do her best to put it behind her and get on with her life, but her heart wasn't listening. Placing her hand on her stomach, she was surprised to find a wad of bandage, gauze and medical tape, as if she had been injured. This, too, was most unexpected, as was the pulse of pain that came from the contact.

It was some while before Dr Rudd strode through the ward and pulled the yellow, orange and pink curtain open around her bed, the thin floral cotton offering only a modicum of privacy.

'Mrs Cooper, how are we feeling?'

'Sore.' She spoke from a mouth that was dry, voice croaky, her lips stuck together.

'That's to be expected. We can get you some tea.' He took a step closer and put his hands behind his back. 'I'm afraid I have some rather bad news.' His tone, contrary to what his words suggested, was buoyant, indifferent almost, overly loud, practised but seemingly not adjusted for good news, bad or the worst. The very worst.

Lilly stared at him, wondering briefly if something had happened to her dad, this the worst news she could imagine! And just the thought of him at home along the river, no doubt smiling as he imagined her on her field trip, was enough to encourage more tears. She watched as Dr Rudd rocked on his heels and spoke as he looked over her shoulder towards the glossy magnolia-painted wall behind her bed. 'As can happen on the odd occasion, we experienced some difficulties in what should have been a rather routine procedure. There was a severe uterine perforation that resulted in us taking the decision to perform a hysterectomy. Do you know what that is?'

'I'm not sure,' she whispered, thinking she might know but figuring she must be mistaken, as the consequences of such a thing . . .

'It means we had to make an incision in your tummy and remove your womb, cervix and uterus. It was entirely necessary, and I'm delighted to say was a *great* success – no bleeding, no more issues – but it does also mean that there will no more babies, not for you, but there we are.' He nodded and took a breath. 'I will say to you what I say to all women who find themselves in a similar situation: you are young, you and your husband will learn to adapt and will find joy and satisfaction in other areas of your lives, like hobbies and travel. It could be very exciting! There is also always adoption, of course. Plenty of babies looking for nice Christian homes.'

Lilly stared at him; there was so much to take in, to unpick, she found herself struck dumb. His words were a cryptic jumble in her mind, a code it would take her a little while to decipher.

'Right.' Dr Rudd opened the thin curtain, the closing of which had done nothing to prevent all in close proximity hearing his dire news. The woman in the bed opposite gave her a slow smile of kindness. 'A nurse will be along in a short while to bring you some tea and you will be able to go home in about a week to ten days.'

'Ten days?' she said, her voice quite hoarse.

'All being well.' And just like that he was gone.

She sat for a while, a little numb, a little confused, trying to make sense of it all while a nurse did indeed bring her a cup of tea.

No more babies . . . What did he mean exactly, no more babies? It was a most bizarre concept that failed to register in her mind. *No more babies* . . . Surely he didn't mean not ever? That couldn't be right.

'Can I get you anything else? Would you like a cheese sandwich?' the young nurse asked, softly. Lilly was glad of her kindness, relieved the obnoxious sister was absent.

'No. No, thank you, but I think I might need to make a telephone call.'

'I can bring the payphone on wheels to your bed. Do you want it now?'

'In a little bit, if that's okay?' She wanted to get things straight in her thoughts and figure out exactly what she was going to say.

''Course it is.' The nurse winked at her. 'I'll bring it over.'

Lilly knew she had to call someone, tell someone; the question was, who? Certainly not her dad. And not for the first time in her life, she wished she had the kind of mum who she could call. This alone was enough to cause her to sink down under the sheets and close her eyes. *No more babies . . .* She was eighteen! How was that even possible?

Gathering herself, unable to move with ease, Lilly did her best to twist towards the phone and held the coins in the palm of her hand.

Glenda's mum answered almost immediately.

'Oh hello, Lilly love, how's you?' The warm sing-song question sounded motherly and interested and was a chop to her throat; how come other people got mothers like this while she got Jeannie the cheat?

'I'm fine, Mrs Brooks.' The last thing she wanted to do was make small talk, fearful of being overcome by emotion and blurting the whole terrible truth out about where she was and what she had been through, knowing that the God-fearing Mrs Brooks would not let Glenda associate with her then. This was a thought that struck fear into her. Almost as much as the words of Dr Rudd, *no more babies . . .* She figured there must have been some kind of mistake, surely that couldn't be true! 'Is Glenda there?' She spoke with her eyes closed, shutting out the other women, their husbands, the babies and the general hubbub of the maternity ward that echoed around her, emphasising her solitude and holding up a mirror to a life that wasn't hers.

'Yep, one sec. *Glenda! Phone! It's Lilly!*' Mrs Brooks called loudly. 'She's coming, Lilly. See you soon, love.'

More pips sounded, and Lilly topped up the coins, waiting for her friend and wishing she'd get a move on.

'Hello, mate!' Glenda sounded pleased to hear from her.

Lilly tried to speak, tried to form the words she knew she needed to say, but at no more than the sound of her friend's voice her sadness broke its banks and she could only sob wordlessly.

'Oh my God, Lil! What's wrong? What's happened?'

'Can you come and see me, please. Please, please, Glen, please!' It was the first time she had begged for anything in her whole life.

'Of course I can. I'll come tomorrow. Where shall we meet? College?'

'No.' She sniffed, doing her best to control her breathing and halt her tears. 'I'm . . . I'm in St Thomas's, in . . . in the maternity ward.'

'What you doing there?' Glenda laughed, and Lilly understood; it really was as preposterous as it sounded.

'I've been admitted.'

'I don't—' Her friend swallowed. 'I don't know what to say.'

'Promise me you'll come, Glen! Please!' she pleaded again.

'I'll be there. I'll be there, I promise. Just hold on, Lil. Sleep, rest and I'll see you tomorrow. Everything's going to be okay.'

Lilly replaced the receiver and slunk down on to the mattress as the incision on her stomach throbbed with pain.

No more babies . . . This the phrase that still rang around her head. *No more babies* . . . And as much as she trusted her friend, she wasn't so sure that everything was going to be okay, not ever again.

◆ ◆ ◆

Ten days later, Lilly managed to take a bath, and had even washed her hair before Glenda arrived to collect her, doing her best to look like she had spent the time at the seaside living it up with her friend, studying art, taking in the sea air, and not like she'd been cooped up in a ward feeling as if the world around her was being dismantled piece by piece. And not just any hospital ward, but the maternity ward, where women with shiny gold bands on the third fingers of their left hands left with blanket-wrapped newborns tucked into their arms like hot, fresh loaves, smiling with a satisfaction and love that she would never feel.

She did her very best to put it out of her mind. The word, the meaning, the consequences of a thing like a hysterectomy, all of it. To be considered when she felt a little more stable and the risk of her falling apart had faded. God, how she hoped it would fade.

Glenda had proved to be the most wonderful friend, there in her time of need, which Lilly knew she would never forget. Not ever. She felt awful about embroiling her in the lie, but it had seemed like the lesser of two evils, in that Glenda might be quietly disapproving, but Lilly having to tell her own dad, she was sure, might just kill him.

'You want me to say *what*?' Her friend had needed it explaining again.

'That you and I are at the seaside on our field trip, and we're staying for ten days, and you are calling him at work as I am in a lecture that I couldn't get out of and I didn't want him to worry.'

'And he'll go for that?'

'He will.'

This Lilly knew because she trusted her dad, and trust was trust. Just like she had trusted Wilkie, the man who was in York with his wife and two young children, the kind she would never get to have. In those moments of connection, their bodies in sync, fingers entwined, she had let herself think of love and marriage and kids and a life together, all of it snatched away so suddenly. Not that she could think about that now. It was like the word 'hysterectomy', only to be considered further down the line, when the facts would not break her, fragile as she was.

Her jeans had been washed, and for this she was thankful as she sat on the edge of the bed, waiting for her friend to come. It was a shock to see Norman walking in with his girl on his arm. The sight of him made her feel vulnerable, exposed, concerned – he would without doubt know why they were there and exactly what had happened to her. She could barely meet his eye.

'Norm said he'd give us a lift back to yours,' Glenda explained, with a slight nod and a small smile of understanding, no doubt hoping to assuage Lilly's fears, letting her know Norman was a man to be trusted.

'Th— thank you, Norm.' Nerves stole her poise.

The man of few words, never a chatterbox, lifted his chin in response.

'How are you feeling?' Glenda almost whispered, still a little ill at ease when it came to navigating the topic and circumstances.

'Bit better. I think I'll be fine after a night in my own bed. It's hard to sleep soundly here, so noisy.' It was the expected response and the one she gave with regularity to anyone who asked. *Bit better . . .* It was true, to a degree: she was physically less sore, slightly more mobile, could sit on the loo if she went slowly, take a bath if she took her time, even sleep a bit if she stayed in one position and swallowed paracetamol before nodding off. What she couldn't yet do was come to terms with what had happened, accept that she had indeed had . . . that *H* word that she was not yet considering.

'Good. Come on, then, let's get you home.' Glenda tried for joviality, as if her positivity might be infectious. 'And one good thing is that, unlike everyone else in this ward, you're not going to be up at all hours tending to a crying baby. I bet they envy you that!'

Lilly stood on wobbly legs and took her friend's arm, knowing Glenda meant well as the words hit her squarely in the face and landed hard. The three made their way to the lift, Lilly walking with hesitancy. As she passed the reception desk, she remembered arriving and the warm welcome turning to a sneer on the sister's face, exemplary of the treatment she had received during her time here, like she was one of *those* women; no good, morally slack. Just like her mother. Not that she could really deny it now. It was another layer of shame to wear on her skin, to coat her thoughts and damage her self-esteem. Wilkie hadn't wanted her, and now no one else would either. Could it be punishment for liking all of that sex? Her body shivered at the terrible thought.

'Lil? I said are you warm enough?' Glenda pulled at the front of her cardigan, suggesting she'd give it up. Lilly, having been miles away, shook her head, knowing the cold kernel of regret that lurked in the base of her stomach was nothing the addition of a woolly cardigan could fix.

Norman had parked his Cortina at the front of the hospital, among the black cabs and the odd ambulance, mere feet from the entrance, and she was grateful. Movement after such a long time immobile was a challenge, and she felt quite unable to walk long distances, was glad she didn't have to hop on the bus. Not only weary, but with the nasty pulling feeling inside where cuts were healing, and her scar, criss-crossed with thick metal staples, stretched as she righted herself. He opened the back door, and she clambered in. Glenda sat next to her and quietly reached for her hand. Lilly was glad of it and, on the short journey back to the flat, she held on tight, thankful for the reassurance Glenda offered.

She stared out of the window, taking in the view of the river, her river, just as she had left it, just as all who had gone before her had left it, going right back to the Romans who had built that first bridge, and whoever lived here before that. So many lives, so many people, all with stories of love and loss and change and upheaval, and yet that river just carried on flowing, a reminder of the insignificance of those who clung to its shoreline and stared upon it.

'Thank you for this, for everything,' she said to her friend with a jolt of apprehension as Waide House came into view.

'What are friends for?' Glenda responded with a squeeze to her fingers. 'I'll come in with you.'

'No! No, that's fine.' She spoke with urgency, knowing it would be far harder to lie, to smile and pretend to her dad, if her friend and Norman were present, adding another layer to the deceit, becoming an even bigger part of the whole charade. 'Just drop me at the back. It's only a couple of flights of stairs; I can manage that if I take it slow.'

'You sure? I don't like leaving you.' Her friend looked concerned.

'Yep, positive.' She was far from positive but would figure it out.

Norman pulled the car into the rear yard, where the big bins were located, and jumped out to open the door and help her out of the back seat. He reached in and she held his arm, manoeuvring her legs from the space and standing as best she could, straightening bit by bit, holding her breath until she was fully upright.

'Thanks, Norm. I really appreciate you driving me home and for bringing Glenda in and everything.'

'I wanted to say' – Norm spoke, coughing once to clear his throat, his cheeks flaming red with the effort, but softly and calmly – 'I wanted to say that life never does quite turn out how we think it will, and that's okay.' His voice and empathy saw her tears bloom; Glenda was right, that kindness counted for a lot. 'Things for you might be changed from now on, and that's okay too. Because life goes on, Lil. It has to.'

Lilly hadn't meant to fall into his arms, but she did. Awkward, quiet Norman held her tightly, while Glenda rubbed her back. She closed her eyes, trying to imagine what her life might be like if Wilkie had been more like Norman and how differently things would look for her now. This, however, was a not a road she could mentally travel, knowing the futility of it and the sadness it would bring.

'Come on, my lovely mate, let's get you inside.' Glenda spoke with obvious emotion. It was as Lilly pulled away and caught the look between Glenda and her Norm that she felt a different kind of pull in her gut. It was a twinge of envy, recognising the kind of love that would endure, the kind of connection that meant Norman was not going to hotfoot it up the motorway to York or lie to the woman he truly loved. She was happy for them, no doubt, yet also felled by the sight of it.

She heard the car leave and, even though it was scary and unnerving to be alone in the stairwell without an arm to reach for, a hand to hold, a voice of gentle encouragement in her ear, it was also strangely galvanising. She had to do this, to present as normally as she could to her dad.

With her key in her hand, she hesitated, taking deep breaths and finding a smile.

'Hel-loo!' she called, doing her best to stem the tremor to her voice and smother the emotion that threatened. She was home, finally home, and she had been through a lot. The sound of Bread's '*It Don't Matter to Me*' floated on the air. It was easier to close her ears, block it out, knowing she had to dig deep, act fine, pretend, and could not let her emotions rise in time with the tempo and the mournful, beautiful, haunting lyrics.

'Here she is!' Her dad's delighted response was enough to put a shard of glass through her lying heart, and to focus her. 'Hello, my love!' Clearly over the moon to see her, his enthusiasm dripped from every syllable. 'Did you have a good time?' He came at her quickly, in comparison to her movements and thoughts, both of which were slower than normal. She lifted her arms, as was customary, and he wrapped her in a brief, agonising hug that seemed to make her whole body twist in a way that was painful.

Thankfully, post hug, he turned away and made his way to the kitchen. 'Let's get the kettle on and you can tell me all about it. The weather's been a bit ropey for you, I know, but I said to Mrs Devlin at rehearsal the other night, all the better for moody landscapes and rolling waves! I wouldn't mind having a go myself, trying to capture a dark, brooding sky over the big sea – fantastic! What was your boarding house like? Glenda said on the phone you were having a nice time. I bet it's done you good, all that fresh air and big breakfasts! It's the secret to a good ramble, you know, a hearty breakfast – just the right fuel to keep you going!'

He spoke cheerfully and without pause, glad no doubt to have someone to talk to, not a man who always liked the quiet of his own company.

'Talking of breakfast, can I get you something to eat? I've got new bread and some fresh eggs in; I could rustle you up egg on toast?' He turned to face her and stopped talking. 'Are you okay? You look proper pale.'

She leaned on the wood-panelled wall and took a moment. 'Do you know, Dad, I think I'm just exhausted. It's been a long journey.'

'Ah, 'course it has, and no doubt you've been burning the candle at both ends! Do you want to forfeit tea and have a nap? We can catch up when you're ready.'

'Do you mind?' Her body sang with relief at the prospect of lying on her mattress.

''Course I don't mind! You go make yourself comfy. If you need anything, just holler! I'll be right here.'

'I will, Dad.' It was hard to meet his gaze; his words, concern and kindness only made her feel worse. She walked as normally as she was able across the square hallway.

'You all right, Lilly? I'm a bit worried about you. You don't seem yourself.' His worry was etched at the top of his nose.

'Women's trouble, Dad.'

'Ah, I see.' He looked away.

It tasted foul on her tongue, the lies, all of it.

It was odd to find her room just as she had left it when everything about her was so changed. Gingerly she lowered herself down on to the bed and bunched the pillow under her cheek, waiting for sleep. She lay in her warm bed, knowing there was nowhere else she would rather be right now, with her daddy right there across the hallway, in case she needed anything.

The sound of the album *Bread* floated under her door.

She pictured Glenda and Norman, no doubt chit-chatting as they made their way to Enfield in his Cortina, and wondered what their future held: marriage, no doubt; kids, probably. And here she was, listening to her dad whistling in the kitchen, lying on her childhood bed, knowing there would be no kids for her, not now, not ever. Her tears came then, snaking their way over her nose and running across her lips as her hand sought out the padded gauze that covered the incision on her stomach, beginning to understand that this cut, this blood-crusted, roughly stapled line, would in part define her, setting her on a path that she had never thought she would walk.

No more babies, not for you . . .

Present day

Lilly delved into the drawer in the kitchen and placed her hand towards the back. 'Aha! I knew I had one.'

Pulling out the black marker pen, she handed it to Clodagh.

'Thanks, Lilly, you're a lifesaver. I've started putting a few things in boxes, toys Apollo doesn't play with much, some winter clothes and things.'

'Probably wise. I haven't considered packing yet, still hoping my letter to the prime minister might make a difference.' Lilly winked, trying to smother her rising sadness with a joviality she didn't feel. A mask, no doubt.

'How do you know it arrived safely?'

'I don't, but I have imagined it being delivered on a silver platter for them to read while they eat their scrambled eggs for breakfast, as if my letter describing my plight might take precedence over any other business they might be having to contend with.'

'I'm sure you're right. You will absolutely be a priority!' Her lovely neighbour smiled with a twitch of concern in her eyes, suggesting she didn't believe writing would make the slightest bit of difference.

Lilly chose not to share that this was actually how she had pictured it, the call to arms over breakfast, trying to manifest the moment while doing her best not to admit defeat. Jake the journalist had not responded to her recent messages. She wished she hadn't given him such short shrift and hated how she was now having to rely on people who didn't know her and who would, as she had hinted to Clodagh, no doubt have other more pressing things on their minds.

She could hardly stand to think about it, Clodagh packing up to leave, as no doubt would Mr Chaplin and the rest of her neighbours in the coming weeks. It was happening, the thing she had dreaded, the thing she had half believed she could outrun, prevent; it was happening, and the feeling of impotence as her life shifted on its axis was almost paralysing. She had no idea which avenue to turn down. Denzel had always been a fighter, there for the underdog, and loved nothing more than a good legal tussle, yet even he had suggested she admit defeat before the starting pistol had fired, urging her to take the money and run. The truth was she felt old; old, tired and out of ideas.

She hadn't heard from Alfie since the day he'd taken her out on *Lady Margery*. Joshua Vaughan, too, was conspicuous by his absence, probably because there was very little to be done or discussed at this point. It was all down to lawyers and paperwork, no longer any need for the devious strong-arm tactics that required human-to-human interaction, nor the manipulation at which they had been so masterful. Alfie's words of explanation, his desire for a legacy, had sickened her a little; this need for a shiny tower at any cost meant he was not anyone she wanted to engage with. No matter how good he had looked in his open-necked shirt, driving his fancy slipper launch up and down the river. Wilkie popped into her thoughts. He, too, had looked good, a wolf in sheep's clothing, and just about as dangerous.

'How are you feeling about it all, Lilly?'

'I think I've shifted from denial and am now edging towards resigned, but I am still far from happy and I've not given up just yet, I have a few irons in a few fires.'

'I wish there was something I could do.' Clodagh removed the scrunchie from her wrist and secured her trademark pineapple on the top of her head.

'Me too.'

'I got my assignment back from college. I got eighty-four per cent, which would be a first if it were being marked for my degree.'

'Clodagh! That's brilliant!' It was wonderful to see the young woman succeeding.

'My tutor has put me in touch with a sports clinic in Victoria and they're going to offer me a placement, work experience kind of thing, and if they like me' – she crossed her fingers – 'it might lead to a job.'

'It feels like everything is falling into place for you. Nothing short of what you deserve.'

'I've never had anyone like you, Lilly.'

'What do you mean?' She gave the woman her full attention.

'I mean, I've never had anyone look out for me or give a shit about me like you do.' Lilly knew enough about Clodagh's mum for this to make sense, and was truly touched. 'It's had a huge impact on me and Apollo, more than you'll ever know. I was thinking about it this morning, and it's the simple things that make a difference.'

'Like having someone to call on if you need a marker pen?' Lilly smiled, feeling she needed to downplay the compliment to keep her own emotions in check, anxious as she was about fully lowering her emotional drawbridge. It was easy to remember what it had felt like when she was small and, on the odd occasion when her mum had popped up, she had felt unable to touch her, in case Jeannie flinched or turned and walked away again, knowing that to feel physical rejection for the second time would be almost unbearable. It was a fear that had put an impenetrable shield between them, one they never found a way to break through. It would forever be a sadness, that lack of closeness, as Lilly did her best to navigate her mother's rejection, right up until Jeannie had passed away. Clodagh's words, however, were also a balm of sorts, confirmation that Lilly might not have had a loving mum, but it seemed she was getting it right; instinctively offering this young girl help, a haven, love, in the way a mother might.

'Yes, exactly like that.' Clodagh smiled at her. 'Because it's not just about this pen' – she waved the marker in the air – 'it's about the fact that whether I need a marker pen, advice or a shoulder to cry on, I'm comfortable enough to ask. It's about trust. It's that feeling that Apollo and I are part of your life. Like it's more than just the two of us. I didn't know what it felt like having someone watching out for you, someone with nothing to gain, who doesn't want anything in return, who loves you just because . . .'

'I do.' Lilly managed to speak through a throat narrowed with emotion. 'I do love you just because . . . Reckon that little Apollo has come along and stolen a big old chunk of my heart. You both have.' There, she had done it, admitted to the way she felt, wary still after all these years on the planet of telling someone she loved them and then watching as they ran away, *her mum, Wilkie . . .*

'Kennington's not that far, not really, we'll make it work, right?'

'We will indeed!' Lilly added with false brightness, hoping they could make it work and petrified that it may not. Who knew where she was going to end up?

'I think about the day we met, when you told Apollo off and I nearly grabbed his arm and ran, I'm so glad we stayed and chatted. So grateful for you. We're lucky really, aren't we, Lilly?' the young woman asked as she made her way along the hallway, no doubt to go and continue her packing.

'We are' – Lilly could only nod – 'very, very lucky.'

With the front door closed on Clodagh it made Lilly wonder if maybe she should start the process of boxing up her possessions, torn between seeing it as an admission of defeat and yet feeling slightly panicked at how much there was to do in order to facilitate a move, should the worst happen. She had already decided to store some of her favourite paintings in the basement of the gallery, where she knew they would be safe, only until she knew exactly where she would be hanging them next. There had been one or two rental properties that she thought might do while she decided on something more permanent, and of course she could always go and stay with Norman and Glenda in New Cross – if Lilly promised not to kill her friend with an axe. The key, she felt, was not to make a rash decision that she might live to regret, still ridiculously hoping beyond hope that she wouldn't have to move at all.

With a sturdy cardboard box set on the floor, the large cupboard in her old bedroom, now her art studio, felt as good a place as any to start. The right-hand door was already permanently ajar as it tried to contain the various items deemed too important to throw away. Her gran's old Singer sewing machine, probably a collector's item now. Board games in battered boxes that hadn't seen the light of day since the 1980s, and amusingly, a stack of video tapes, mainly her dad's old Westerns; she no longer had a machine on which to play them. It was as she pulled the stack of tapes from the cupboard and placed them in the box, destined for a charity shop, that she saw the edge of white paper nestling against the back panel. On her knees now, Lilly bent low and stuck her head into the dusty, musty confines. Reaching in, she grabbed the paper, part of a bundle, and brought it out into the light.

She found it wasn't in fact a sheet but rather an envelope, one of several all bound in the rough twine that her dad had used for everything from securing plants to wrapping presents. It was a shallow bundle, one of maybe six letters, all addressed to her dad and in a script she recognised as her mother's. She let her fingers linger on the twine, knowing her dad was the person to have tied it, and that alone made it precious. And to see her mother's handwriting had a curious effect on her. It was profoundly moving, this unique marker of the woman who had written her numerous Christmas and birthday cards. And in the early years had scribbled shopping lists, the provisions from which she used to cook tea for Lilly and her dad, *eggs, ham, butter, bread, milk, sugar*... normal mum stuff that had made Lilly feel like she had a normal mum.

It was curious, jarring, these things in her home that she hadn't seen before, hidden almost, for how long she wasn't sure. It was with apprehension and interest that she studied the stamps, which all bore the Queen's head and were postmarked Camden. The first letter she pulled from the envelope was only two sides in length. It had yellowed where it had been folded and was dated September 1967. She did the quick maths: she would have been twelve. Her heart raced as her eyes scanned the script.

Dear Robert,

Thank you for your letter.

Lilly looked up, wondering what her dad might have written to her mum, and how often he wrote. It was an odd concept – she couldn't imagine her dad sitting down and writing to Jeannie at the address she shared with another man – yet it was also strangely reassuring. She had always assumed there was zero communication between her parents, as she hadn't witnessed any. She could only hope that any contact made him feel less lonely, gave him some kind of closure.

I can only agree with you that to leave my family, my home, is unfathomable and yet that is what I have done.

Your mother called me selfish, criminal and some other less than savoury things, which I won't write here, and maybe she's right, maybe I am selfish, criminal even, but if I'd stayed I would have disappeared. I know it. I would have disappeared.

I don't blame you, Robert, I've never blamed you, but I have been angry for the longest time at how you seem content not to address the demons that have lived with us in our marriage. I tried, I tried so hard, for you, for Lilly-Bob, for us, but I can't try any more. I am exhausted, beaten by the battle.

You're not a bad man, Robert, but neither are you the only one to have had the most terrible war, seeing things no man should see, hearing things no man should hear and then back in Blighty, expected to put it all behind you, to buckle up and carry on, having to live a smiling, normal life as if horror does not lurk behind your eyelids as you sleep.

Lilly paused as the breath caught in her throat, winded by the words, so raw and open. She looked out of the window, seeking the comfort of blue sky and breathing slowly as her heart lurched for all her lovely dad had quietly endured. All her mum had quietly endured; it occurred to her then that her mother might have hinted at such things years back, at her dad's funeral, but Lilly had been too distracted to give it proper credence, thinking her mum was speaking of her irritation, as if trying to justify her leaving, but to see the words written down in the cold light of day . . . How she wished they had opened up to her, both of them.

She read on, one hand clamped over her mouth.

Your nightmares, insomnia and the fortress you have built around your emotions have kept me locked out. I've never felt such loneliness, such despair, to see the man I love suffer and yet not let me in, not let me get close to you.

I know it's different with Lilly-Bob. I can see how at ease you are with her and it's beautiful. But I'm withering, Robert. I'm growing smaller and quieter and sometimes I fear I may look in the mirror and find I've disappeared altogether.

I have taken nothing. It's important that Lilly's home is intact, important she has the stability of a life with you. But I don't know where I fit into that little life, and I want more. No, I need more, for my sanity, for my health. And I think I deserve more, and one day, I hope for happiness. I am not sure true happiness is possible without seeing Lilly-Bob every day. She is my heart, my whole heart, and the pain I feel at not seeing her is indescribable. I can be sick just thinking about it. I love her. I love her so, so much.

But I know to take her might finish you off altogether. I understand that bond you share. She adores you and I couldn't do it to either of you, knowing neither of you would ever forgive me. This feels simpler, although there's nothing simple about it.

But I must insist that I have access, I must see her often – anything less would kill ME, finish me off! I must see her, Robert. She can have a room here, spend some time with me, talk to me. I need that – she is my daughter, my only child, and she will need that too.

I hope in time you will understand, nearly as much as I hope you find a way to stop whistling, to stop hiding behind a smile and a tune, because you deserve more too.

with love, Robert,

sincerely with love,

Jeannie.

Lilly felt her body slump against the wall, as if winded; the words had punched her squarely in the stomach.

'I did need that! To spend time with you, to talk to you, I did need that, Mum!'

Instantly her mind fled to that first visit to the flat her mum had shared with Derek Manners on the Tottenham Court Road, could see her mum crying while smiling behind her tears.

'I'm not hungry.'

'What would you like, love?'

'Err . . . to go back to my dad?'

'I'm sorry, Mum!' she wailed now into the ether. 'I am so sorry!'

She'd had no idea that her mum wanted to see her! No idea that the thought of not seeing her was something Jeannie feared might kill her! Lilly felt the tightly packed shame of rejection leach from her bones, felt the fractures of abandonment start to knit back together at no more than the fact that her mother had wanted her – she had *wanted* her!

Quickly she opened the next letter, handling the paper with less reverence than the first, devouring the words, wanting to better her understanding, desperate to know more, no matter how much it hurt.

Dear Robert . . .

. . . you are right. You are right. It wasn't what I hoped it would be. She didn't want to be here. But don't think I will give up, I won't! There are times in your life when you instinctively know that something has run its course and it's time to walk away, because that is the best thing to do for a million reasons, it's how we progress, but that will never be the case with Lilly-Bob. Never! I will keep trying . . .

'She loved me.' The words were whispered from a mouth that trembled. 'She loved me!'

Her whole body folded at the most longed-for sentiment so simply expressed by her mum. It was a lot to process, but certainly it threw light on the desperate loneliness Jeannie must have felt and the sacrifice she had made for her husband. Lilly knew her mum's assumption was correct, to have taken Lilly might just have finished him off. The reasons why her dad had kept them apart, hadn't encouraged her to see her mum or shared with her just how Jeannie felt about leaving Lilly behind, was something she would have to try and pick apart, unsure in this moment if his motivation was protection or revenge. She would never know for sure, *could* never know for sure. And did it really matter why? It hurt just the same.

PTSD, that was the trauma response her dad had done his best to hide from her, a trauma that had caused his marriage to implode. It was like solving a puzzle, as small fragments of memory dropped into place to help form a complete picture.

'*Robert . . . Robert! . . . ROBERT!*' Her mum banging a saucepan with a spoon to get his attention, after calling and calling and calling, and him practically jumping in the chair as if he had been miles and miles away . . . His bad dreams that caused him to shout out in the night and the lingering tension on the days that followed . . . His constant need to whistle or play music, as if afraid to be left alone with his thoughts, and a million other small indicators that now, in light of her realisation, made so much sense.

'What a bloody mess!' She rubbed her hand over her face.

Flicking through the other letters revealed much of the same. Her mum making pleas for Robert to get help, and then a line that caused her to put the paper close to her face so that she could read and re-read it.

> *She only told you she THOUGHT she was being watched while she was painting, not that she actually saw me. I promise I'm very discreet. I stand between the flats opposite, in the shadow. There's an alleyway. No one knows I'm there. The last thing I want to do is alarm her, but please, please, I am begging you, do not stop me from coming to watch her. The idea of not seeing her . . . I can't do it! I won't!*

Lilly brought the paper to her face and rested it against her cheek.

'I felt you there. I *knew* someone was watching me, Mum! I always knew it. I just wish I'd known it was you.'

◆ ◆ ◆

Lilly stood on the pavement, staring at the uninspiring 1970s building with a wood-cladding front, once pale green, but the paint had peeled and now hung in thin strips to reveal bare dark timber. The windows were wide, white and plastic with locks on them, and the roof was flat. The front door, housing two large panes of safety glass, was reached via a shallow, ugly concrete ramp with two sturdy rails on either side. The kind of thing that was built for practicality without any consideration of aesthetics. Lilly understood why. She let out a long, slow breath, trying to calm her pulse before pressing the button on the entry system, and waited until a tinny, slightly harassed voice came over the intercom.

'Can I help you?'

'Yes, please, my name is Lilly Cooper. I called yesterday, about coming to visit . . .'

Without any further interaction, a buzzer sounded. This was it; too late to back out. She pushed on the metal door plate that revealed a thousand smudged fingerprints, and it opened. The place carried the potent and unappetising odour of urine and cabbage, putting her in mind of every horrid municipal facility she had ever imagined.

It was a surprise to find the curved reception desk unattended, where dusty plastic daffodils sat in a vase, unattended. She stood, feeling a little awkward, her tasselled poncho hanging down over her jeans, wondering if coming here was such a good idea and looking for the door release button, in case she wanted to make a hasty exit. An old woman using a walker, being chaperoned by a young carer in a pale lilac tunic, walked past. Slowly.

'I'm seventy-six!' the woman shouted, as if delighted by the achievement.

Lilly offered a benign smile while feeling the grip of horror in her stomach when she realised this lady was only six years older than her, yet Lilly was young, so young! The borrowed phrase that Bertie had always favoured stuck in her mind, one that had stood her in good stead: *It's not how old you are that matters, darling, but how you are old!* It had never felt more true than in that moment.

'Be with you in a sec!' The young woman raised a finger towards Lilly and patiently wandered along with her charge.

It was some minutes before she returned, giving Lilly a chance to study the noticeboard that was haphazardly covered with notices and postcards. Apparently there was a sing-along in the TV lounge on Tuesdays and Thursdays with Wendy on the piano. Armchair yoga on Wednesday morning. And anyone wanting to go on the coach trip to St Leonards-on-Sea had to pay the deposit to Linda by next Friday. It was heartening, to see so many activities, the sense of community, despite the slightly depressing exterior.

'Sorry to keep you waiting. We've only just had lunch so always a lot of rejigging and getting residents to and from the dining room and cleaned up after lunch.'

'Of course.' She felt guilty for having interrupted the busy schedule, knowing she should have enquired as to when was the best time to visit.

'Who are you here to see, my love?' The young nurse had a wonderful way with her that she was sure must be most reassuring if this was your home.

'Erm . . .' It felt odd to be saying the name in anything other than a derisory way. 'Derek Manners.'

'Oh, yes. Lovely. Is he expecting you?'

'No. No, he's not.' Lilly shook her head and laughed nervously, knowing she'd be the last person he'd be expecting. 'He's my, erm . . .' *What was he?* She had never let him get close enough to be a stepdad. But as someone once reminded her, a lot of water had flowed under a lot of bridges. 'He was my mum's husband.'

'Right. Well, just sign in and I'll take you to his room.'

Lilly filled in the time and date and signed before following the young woman up a flight of stairs and turning right along the wide corridor.

'This is him.' The carer smiled and rapped her knuckles on the door as she opened it. 'Derek, love?' Her voice was loud. 'You have a visitor!' She pointed at Lilly, who waved awkwardly from the doorway.

'Good Lord!' Derek looked like he might have been about to doze, and she felt bad for interrupting, watching as he shuffled into a more upright position in his recliner chair and pushed his glasses up on to his nose. He was very old, frail and pale. Lilly could only reflect on how similarly she had aged since she had seen him last, on the day they buried her mother. A quiet, poorly attended affair that had felt as awkward as it had sad.

'I'll leave you two to it.' The young woman left them alone and Lilly wondered if this was such a good idea, was almost tempted to ask her to stay.

'Pull up a chair.' He pointed to a dining chair that was in a corner with a tapestry cushion on it. 'Well . . .' He took his time, speaking slowly, yet clearly, robustly really, for his age. 'This is a turn-up for the books.'

'Yes.' She sat on the chair she'd pulled closer to him. He looked neat, hair brushed, whiskers trimmed, and wearing a camel-coloured cardigan that was buttoned up with a clean, pressed shirt underneath.

'I got the fright of my life when I looked up.' He paused. 'For a minute I thought you were Jeannie! Thought she'd come to get me. Not that I'd mind. I tell her that every day. "*When you're ready, love!*" I say.'

'Oh.' She hadn't expected to get on to the topic of death or her mother quite so quickly. 'I wasn't sure you'd recognise me.'

'I'm ninety-seven, the old legs have given up the ghost, my hearing's not too clever, but my memory is good. Some poor souls in here, they don't even remember who they are, let alone anyone else.'

'That's rotten.'

''Tis.' He nodded. 'Time is no one's friend in here, Lilly-Bob, so you might as well cut to the chase.' He folded his fingers, now with large, knobbly knuckles, over his stomach. He wasn't rude, exactly, but was certainly cutting her no slack. She understood that he had no need to watch his tongue or his tone, no Jeannie around to impress, no apple cart that might be upset, and he owed her nothing.

'How . . . how have you been?' She didn't know how to start.

'How have I *been*?' He laughed until he wheezed. 'What is it you want, Lilly?'

'I don't know really, Derek Ma—' She caught herself just in time. 'What do I want?' She thought about it, looking around the room, and her eyes landed on a shelf where, next to a thriving spider plant, sat a picture of him and her mum, laughing into a camera, decades younger. Her mum looked happy and in love; they both did.

'You still *hate* plants?' he asked with the smallest hint of irony to his question.

'No,' she conceded. 'I quite like them now.'

'Well, there we go. People change, right?'

'Yep, they do.' She took a deep breath, floored that he remembered that conversation too. 'I'm probably going to be moving from the flat.' It felt important to let him know.

'Where are you going?'

'Not sure yet.'

'I never thought you'd leave the place.'

'Neither did I. It's not by choice,' she explained. He shrugged, as if where she did or did not live would scarcely affect or concern him and, again, she understood.

'I'm clearing out cupboards, starting to pack up, and I found some letters that Mum wrote to my dad. And I guess I just wanted to come and see you, to ask you some things.' Her mouth was dry; this was a lot harder than she had anticipated.

'Because I'm the last one standing?'

'Yes, I guess so. It's always the way, isn't it? It's only when people have gone that you realise the many things you wish you'd asked them, all the curious small stuff that you ponder in the early hours.'

'Not me and Jeannie.' He smiled, as if the thought of her was enough to invoke joy. 'We left nothing unsaid: it was one of our rules – to always communicate honestly and openly. It stood us in good stead.'

'I bet.' She felt the pang of envy that they had known each other so well – *nothing* left unsaid – and yet her mum was to her, in so many ways, a stranger. 'I guess I've only just understood that she wanted to see me more, wanted me to come and stay, things like that.' Her words were coated with the embarrassment of her teenage self.

'Oh yes, that was what she wanted, but not what she got.' Derek nodded at her most matter-of-factly. 'What she got in fact was very little, and it hurt her. It hurt me, too, to see it. To love her and not be able to fix things, not able to give her what she *really* wanted.' He shook his head.

'I didn't know.' Lilly felt suitably admonished.

'Yes, well. Let's just say there were decisions made, boundaries put in place that your mum had no choice but to abide by.'

'By my dad?' Lilly pushed, sensing this to be the case but hoping for an explanation.

'I'm sure he had his reasons. He was a troubled man, Lilly, but not a cruel one, I don't believe. As with anything, hindsight is a wonderful thing, and I spent an age thinking how I might or should have done things differently. It was hard for me; I didn't really have a seat at the discussion table.'

'No.' This much she knew to be true. 'In one of the letters, Mum said that she used to come and watch me while I painted. Do you know anything about that?'

He leaned back in the chair and looked up at the swirl-patterned ceiling. 'Yes. It was your dad's suggestion, actually. Jeannie wanted to see you, but it was obvious you didn't want to see her. You were so angry, and your dad felt it was confusing for you.'

'I was angry. I found the whole thing confusing. I still do.'

'Kids aren't meant to get the detail. I guess your parents did what they thought was best to protect you.' The way he spoke suggested her mum and dad had further collaborated. This, too, was new information, and an odd concept, Lilly having always believed that her mum had simply left and hadn't looked back . . . 'But yes, she used to come and watch you paint. I tried to keep out of the whole thing, knowing I couldn't win, damned if I did, damned if I didn't, but I'd come with her sometimes. She just wanted to sit and look at you – your dad suggested you sit on the towpath one day so she could see you more easily from the other side of the bank. And then on the days he knew you were there, he'd call her, quietly tip her off.'

There's something quite lovely about sitting on the towpath, getting lost in the river, the sounds, the sights . . . Give it some thought. She remembered him suggesting it.

'It was a clever move from your dad.'

This hint of admiration coming from his rival was quite unexpected.

'Jeannie would sit and stare across the water, tears streaming down her face. And we'd get the bus home in silence, and she'd go straight to bed, no matter the time of day. Didn't eat, didn't talk, just lay on the bed with her arms wrapped around herself, like she was hurt, injured, and I can't say it made me very fond of you.'

Lilly felt the rise of tears and could only nod.

'The only time it was worse than that was on your birthday.' Derek paused and reached into his trouser pocket, from where he produced a white cotton handkerchief before wiping his eyes with it. 'She'd make a cake and put a candle in it, and we'd light it, and she'd make a wish. Same wish every year – that you might come and see her, let her in a little bit, not talk to her like she was the enemy. And not snap at me or disagree with everything I suggested. It was wearing.'

The sound of Lilly's sobbing filled the room, the messy, noisy, crying of regret, over which she had very little control.

'Do you remember that time you called her, to tell her you'd met a boy?'

'I do, I do.' She remembered everything about it, every tiny detail, the smell inside the phone box, the feeling of joy rising in her chest like she might explode with happiness! *Wilkie . . .*

'You should have seen her.' He shook his head. 'Cor blimey, she danced around the flat – she looked sixteen! So happy! She thought that might have been the start of something, of you being in touch with her, and just the thought was enough for her to . . .' He shook his head. 'She didn't want much, your mum. What she did want, she never got; time with you, forgiveness, a chance to explain.'

'Ex— explain what?' she stuttered.

'What it had been like for her.' Derek took his time. 'Your dad wasn't a bad man, not at all, but as I say, he was a troubled one. The war changed lots of men; they came back scared, broken. Your mum tried very hard to make it work, but he didn't want to talk about his problems, didn't want to face it, as was his right. And it was her right to go, to have a life, to rest, to be heard and loved.'

'I loved her.' Her words were a whisper, words she had rarely spoken in her mum's direction. 'I did, I loved her! I loved my mum, and I missed her every day! I still miss her every day!' The words poured from her on a wave of relief and love, love for her mum, who had made her bed, cooked her tea, sung along to Jimmy Ruffin, and danced with her dad when the mood was right. Her mum, who knew where to find things in jumbled drawers and the dark confines of cupboards, who knitted her jumpers by the electric fire on a winter's night, who brushed her hair when it was ratty, who ran her bath and warmed a towel for her by the fire. Her mum, who told her that she looked pretty when she put on a frock, who showed her how to put on two coats of lipstick and gave her a leaflet about menstruation on her eleventh birthday, 'just in case'. Her mum, who made her a birthday cake and covered the top with sprinkles and tiny pink, twisty candles bought from Woolworths that melted in drips quicker than everyone could sing or she could blow them out. Her mum, who'd made sure she had her mittens in the cold and her sun hat in the warm. Her mum, who made her soup when she was poorly, dabbed calamine lotion when she got chicken pox, read to her from *The Wind in the Willows* and let Lilly rest her head on her shoulder and fall asleep on the bus. Her mum, a *good* mum, a loving mum, whose leaving had left a giant hole in her life that Lilly had been trying to fill ever since.

'Well, I told her you did in your own way. Whether I believed it or not is another thing.'

'I did.' She pictured her mum in the kitchen, making tea in her pinny, hair set, Max Factor Ruby Red lipstick on her pretty mouth. 'I did.'

'I think the saddest thing is that it's all a matter of time, Lilly. The time we lived in. Women get divorced all the time nowadays; they don't feel the pressure to get married in the first place, they have choices. So many choices! They make decisions for themselves, and no one bats an eyelid, but Jeannie was demonised! She paid a heavy price for saving herself, for putting herself first. It shamed her, always. All she wanted was to stop being a passenger in her own life. She wanted to grab the wheel and steer herself in the direction of happiness!'

It was as hard to hear as it was to imagine, and yet she was strangely grateful for his candour.

'I'm sorry, Derek. Sorry for not . . .' She didn't know quite what she was apologising for, certainly the latent hostility with which she had always greeted him, the cool, indifferent way she had treated her mother, who had made her a cake on her birthday, every year. A thought that now shredded her heart and an image that she knew would stay with her for ever. 'Can I come and see you again, Derek?'

'If you like.' His words might have been verging on positive, but his expression was still impassive.

'I would like.'

'Well, there we go, then.' He gave a small, fleeting smile. So fleeting she might have imagined it.

There was a beat of awkward silence while they both stared at the walls.

'You heard about Lineker leaving *Match of the Day*?'

'Erm, yes, yes, I read about it.' Football wasn't and had never been her thing.

'Bloody fools. How can they have *Match of the Day* without Lineker?'

'I don't know, Derek. I guess life goes on, right?'

He took a deep breath and gave her a nod, and this time she saw it, for sure. It felt a lot like he was accepting her apology, and she was entirely grateful for it. 'I guess it does, Lilly-Bob. I guess it does.'

1983 – aged 28

Lilly had hardly slept.

She felt guilty, seeing Rex staring at her as she left him standing on the pavement. He'd taken a step forward, as if his body was still processing her words and he expected to come with her, planning no doubt to walk her back to the flat or persuade her to come back to his place, normal stuff after eighteen months of dating. He'd smiled at her, too, that crooked smile that she found irresistible, as if disbelieving her or expecting her to run back and shout, *Just kidding!*

She hadn't run or looked back and certainly wasn't kidding. It was only in her imagination that she saw him looking after her as she hailed a cab along the street and jumped in. His expression one she could easily conjure and which had kept her awake until the early hours.

There had, in the decade since Wilkie, been dates, sex, liaisons, thrills, moments, weekends away, and lovely, lovely Rex, who had lasted a whole eighteen months. Rex, who had broken through her barrier, smashed her shield and encouraged her to take a chance. The first since Wilkie who had managed such a thing, and he'd done so by disarming her with his honesty, his humour and his kindness. They'd met at a bus stop in Vauxhall, he trying to get back to the City, where he worked in finance, and she off to work at the gallery. In his suit, shirt and tie, he was struggling to make sense of the timetable.

'I've left my glasses at home!' he explained, and she liked his klutziness, the fact that he needed glasses to see and had forgotten them – who did that? It was endearing.

The bus was late.

They swapped numbers, and the rest, as they say, was history. Rex was funny, smart, kind – all the things that made for excellent boyfriend material, not that Lilly had been looking for a boyfriend, still a little broken and more than a little wary. A month after meeting and for their third date, he'd secured tickets for them to see *Japan* at the Hammersmith Odeon – they had sung along loudly to '*Life in Tokyo*', drunk warm lager and danced until their feet ached. She had felt the stirrings of deep, deep affection for the man. Not love, not that, something she felt almost incapable of, damaged as she was, but it had, nonetheless, been lovely, easy, predictable and a gorgeous diversion from her settled life.

Rex met her dad, who gave a wide-eyed nod of approval, and she had been invited to Sunday lunch at his parents' house in Oxshott. His father had carved a large slab of roast beef in the dining room of their faux-Tudor dwelling, and his mum had told her funny anecdotes about Rex's childhood that had made Lilly feel uneasy, knowing the story about her own mother doing a runner to shack up with her beau was the least funny story of all and yet the one that had shaped her the most. Not that she had shared the details with Rex, something that even now felt almost impossible to do, too personal, too hard.

But spending time with him had been lovely, all of it, each interaction edged with possibilities that she had flirted with, wondering if she might be ready to jump, to take the leap of faith, to trust again . . . until last night.

It was as they left Kensington Roof Gardens with the sound of Bowie in their ears and white-wine spritzer sloshing in her veins that he'd turned to her and uttered the words that ruined it all. A whip crack of a suggestion that had echoed in the air around them like gunshot and made her want to run.

'I'm just going to say it, Lilly! I want to make babies with you! I want to see a dozen little Lillys running all over the place! I want this for ever! I want to marry you! I want you, every day for all time, I want you!'

'Stop mucking about!' She had at first tried to defuse the situation with humour.

'I'm not mucking about. I mean it.' His expression, eyes glazed with emotion, confirmed this. 'I want you to marry me. Marry me, Lilly!' he almost shouted.

It had come out of nowhere, and left her cold, how quickly he had spoiled everything. Instantly sobering up, she gripped the lapels of his oversized blazer and looked him in the eye.

'I'm not the marrying kind . . .' *Damaged . . . I'm damaged . . . a little broken . . . hurt . . . rejected . . .* 'and no babies, not for me, not ever.'

'What do you mean, not the marrying kind?' He gave a wry laugh. 'No one is the marrying kind until they meet the person they want to marry! And you might say that now about babies, but . . .' Why wasn't he *listening* to her?

'No, Rex, not now, not ever.'

The flash of distress over his face told her that it was something he wanted; of course he did! He only knew what it was like to come from a family who drank wine with their Sunday dinner and where his mum's biggest concern was, had she remembered to put the hand towel in the guest bathroom? It was never going to work, she could see that now. They were cut from very different cloth, from different places, different worlds, and not only was she certain that she could never fully commit to anyone, never trust a man with her heart, even someone as lovely as Rex, but worse, she knew that to pull him into her world might just damage him in the process. She was a woman like her mum, no good, slack morals and all. She heard Georgina Jones's voice on the phone – '*. . . with two little ones under five, I think I could do with a rest!*' – and her limbs shuddered at the memory.

'I'm sorry, Rex.' She was sorry, truly sorry, knowing this was the kind of admission, revelation and moment that there was no coming back from.

He'd been lost for words, and she'd been lost for a reason to see him again. What was the point? She understood in that moment they were like tankers setting off on different courses and what might feel like a small difference at the start, something almost inconsequential at the beginning, would only widen the further they travelled.

Best to end it now.

And so she had.

'So what do you think, Lilly?' Her dad's voice pulled her from her thoughts of last night.

'What do I think about what?' She glanced at the clock above the cooker, knowing she didn't have time for a protracted conversation with her dad this morning. There was a delivery coming to the gallery and she needed to be there to open up. Bertie worked less and less now, letting her have free rein of the day-to-day running of *B'Art*, and she loved it! In fact she had hardly seen him for weeks and weeks – and was desperate to catch up, loving nothing more than hearing about his exploits and fabulous, colourful social life. Thank goodness one of them was out having a great time. She might live in the middle of this fantastic city, but in the last eighteen months, when not being wined and dined by Rex, she was far more likely to be found at home with her dad playing Risk or canasta, going to the cinema with Glenda, babysitting for her two little boys, Bradley and Andrew, or painting on the towpath, still trying to capture that river.

'My role in the Brink's-Mat robbery. Not sure what we should do with all that gold I've got stashed under the bed. I knew you weren't listening! I was talking about buying the flat!' He tutted, frustrated that she hadn't been listening. 'This *Right to Buy* malarkey, I got a letter about it, and it seems like a good deal.'

'I guess the two questions are can we afford it and why would you want to own it? I mean, right now, if something goes wrong or needs replacing, the council take care of it, and we pay rent. If we owned it that would all be down to us.'

'It's security, Lilly. I'm not getting any younger.'

'Oh, don't start with all that.' She smiled at her dad, teasing him in the way she did. 'You're only sixty! Plenty of life in the old dog yet.'

'You know what I mean – security for you. It's not like you have a husband and kids who will look after you in your old age. Although that Rex seems keen!'

'Well, actually, Dad, Rex and I broke up, so . . . And who says I need someone to look after me? I'm perfectly capable of looking after myself.' She shook her head as she sipped her tea, knowing she had to get going, doing her best to smother the memory of Rex's face. And the feeling of utter desolation that not only had she hurt this lovely man, but also that they had ended, finished, as up until the moment he had ambushed her with his surprise proposal, they had been having a really lovely time. No matter how much it hurt, she knew it was the right thing to do, freeing him to go and find a girl who wanted to waltz up the aisle and have babies. A girl without her shame, without her legacy, without her responsibilities. Her dad was her priority, had to be, as he was no one else's, and that was just the way it was.

'That's a shame. I thought he was nice.'

'He is nice, he's just not for me.' She clicked her tongue against the roof of her mouth, trying to remain a little cool, a little aloof, as screaming to the heavens about all that ailed her would help no one.

'I just worry, that's all.' Her dad lit a cigarette. 'I would like to see you settled before I go.'

'Go where? For the love of God, Dad, is there something you're not telling me?' She rolled her eyes.

'No, I just think we should go for it, buy the flat. It can be your pension, as I say, security.'

'Well, it's up to you, and I will support you whatever you decide.'

She grabbed her handbag and slung it over her shoulder; far easier to ride her bike when unencumbered. 'I'll see you later. Might be a bit late, but there's lasagne in the fridge.'

'Thanks, love, and who knows? I mean, it didn't work out with Rex, but you're still only a spring chicken, you might meet someone, fall in love . . . waltz up the aisle . . . I live in hope!'

'Can we please drop the subject!' With her emotions buried in the shallowest of emotional graves, she knew it wouldn't take much for her to sob, which would only invite more questions from her dad that she knew she couldn't answer. Not without coming clean about aspects of her life she had kept secret for the longest time.

It was some small consolation that contact with her mother was only sporadic, meaning there weren't two of them bombarding her with words of disappointment when it came to her new singledom. Jeannie had been delighted when they finally got a telephone installed.

'It's nice to be able to call whenever I want to hear your voice.' *Nice for you, maybe . . .* Lilly had kept this to herself. 'And are you keen on this Rex? The last time I thought you might have met the one was when you met that boy, the one you called me about? It felt like a big deal.' Her mother raised the topic out of the blue and it took Lilly right back to the desolation she had felt in the wake of Wilkie . . . She wondered if the pain would ever cease entirely. The comedown, the disappointment, the hurt and the raised bump of red vertical scar tissue that bisected her bikini line were constant reminders of what he had cost her.

'It wasn't a big deal,' was her succinct response, rather than explaining that Wilkie's truth and the actual truth were two very different things. 'Actually, I'm just rushing out,' she'd lied. 'Did you want to speak to Dad or . . .' Her tone of dismissal said far more than her words ever could.

'No, no, that's all right, I just . . .'

Her mother had floundered, and Lilly had done nothing to ease her agitation, letting the awkward moments of silence tick on. Listening to the irregular breathing, which smacked of discomfort, coming from the woman who had abandoned them. Thankfully, she called less and less now.

Lilly kissed her dad on the forehead and made her way down the stairs. It was a topic that made her uncomfortable, knowing she wasn't marriage material, something she had come to realise in the last decade, unable to trust fully, expecting everyone to run away eventually, just like her mother, just like Wilkie. This, coupled with the fact that she could not give Rex the babies he and no doubt his parents expected, was why she'd had to set him free.

Her Raleigh Caprice step-through bicycle with front basket she kept chained just inside the front door of Waide House. With her Walkman in her pocket, she slipped the headphones over her head and let the sound of Scritti Politti fill her ears. Her commute was a pleasant one, especially on cold, wintry days like this when the sun shone on the river and Vauxhall Bridge was quiet. Even the large, looming concrete structure of the Nine Elms Cold Store seemed to shine. A lovely start to what she was certain was going to be a lovely day. She was already looking forward to getting home and setting up her easel, knowing she'd find peace on the towpath.

The large khaki-coloured van was parked half on the pavement as she rounded the corner.

'Sorry!' she called as she came to a stop in front of the gallery and beamed her most apologetic smile at the driver, who looked only mildly irritated. 'I got held up.'

'It happens!'

She was grateful he was one of those drivers, a glass-half-full kinda guy who wasn't going to get ruffled by having to wait for a few minutes. It was a surprise to find the gallery door already unlocked.

'Hel-loo?' she called into the dimly lit space; all the main lights were off. Flicking on the switch, she was instantly aware of Bertie sitting at the desk. It was usually a delight to hear his greeting of '*Darling!*', to see his bright eyes, his tanned face, wide grin and his general air of mischievousness, but not today. He'd lost a lot of weight and, with his head in his hands, hair uncharacteristically flat without its usual bouffant style, and eyes closed, he cried noiselessly into his cupped palms. 'God, Bertie! What's the matter? Bertie?' Lilly flung her bag on to the floor and bent forward, wrapping her arms around him and holding him tight. Twisting his body in the chair, he leaned against her as he sobbed.

'Where do you want these, love?' the driver called from the doorway. She had quite forgotten about him. He stood with a cardboard-wrapped canvas in his widespread arms. Straightening, she looked at him, smiling broadly, trying to divert him with her faux jolliness, wanting to spare Bertie the scrutiny of a stranger.

'Just pop them in the corner and I'll sort it all out in a bit. Thanks so much.' She gave a brief nod and returned her attention to her friend. 'Bertie,' she said, 'what can I do right now? What do you need?' She rubbed circles on his back, feeling the knobbles of his spine beneath her fingers.

'Nothing,' he croaked, in a voice she had never heard before. 'Nothing.' Gone was his exuberance, his excitement, his joy! And in their place this growl of distress that made her heart race.

'Sorry, love, but can I get you to sign for them?' the man called, his eyes roving the walls, then looking back to his clipboard, which had a pen tied to the top with a piece of tatty string – anywhere other than at the man who sat sobbing behind the desk.

'Yes, of course!' She raced over, gripped the pen and signed.

The moment he left she pulled her bike in, laid it on the ground and bolted the door.

'Bertie, you're scaring me.' She breathed deeply and, returning to him, dropped to her knees on the floor by his chair and placed her hands on his jeans, understanding that contact might be good. It was some minutes before he garnered the strength to talk and, when he did, it was through a mouth contorted with sorrow, his eyes red and swollen, heartbreaking for her to witness.

'Jack died.' He shook his head as if even saying the words out loud could not help make sense of them.

'Jack?' She struggled for a second, trying to place Jack among Bertie's vast, varied, exotic and ever-changing crowd.

'Beautiful Jack.' He nodded, letting his head drop to his chest.

'No!' Beautiful Jack was a name she hadn't heard in a while, Bertie's ex, but she understood that he had always carried a candle for him, the beautiful, beautiful man. 'Oh no!' The two sat for a while, and she was sure that Bertie, like her, was picturing him in his denim shirt undone to the waist, and that face, that perfect, movie-star face. 'How old was he?' she asked softly, aware that to pick over detail might be difficult.

'Thirty-six.'

'No age.'

'Nope.' Bertie wiped his face and sniffed.

'How did he die?' She stared up into the face of her friend, boss and mentor, noting the dark shadows of fatigue beneath his eyes, the hollow cheekbones, his thinned hair, his grey pallor and the lesion on his scalp, a reddened crust. The seconds ticked by, and the weight of his pause pushed down on her bones.

'That's the thing,' he said, and just like that his face crumpled again.

And she knew.

Before he said another word, she knew. Her heart fell heavily and clumsily into her monkey boots, and the air left her lungs as surely as if she'd been punched in the stomach. Winded and shocked, she laid her head on his lap and sat for a while, letting the tornado of thoughts and realisation swirl around them. Too stunned to cry, too sad to speak, as she understood that Beautiful Jack had gone, and that Bertie most likely cried because he, too, was suffering from that same terrible disease, the word they had avoided for the longest while. A word that ate up beautiful young men. A word too fearful to voice in these turbulent times, when the stigma and fear of such a disease was rife.

'Bertie, no . . .'

''Fraid so, Bob old chap. I think we might have to cancel any future dates for our music-hall act. I'm packing away my fishnets and top hat.'

She had quite forgotten this, and her whole body rippled in horror at the thought of losing him. He placed the flat of his palm on her hair and she closed her eyes, taking comfort from the contact, feeling the warmth flow from his hand to her. It was maternal, it was kindness, it was love and it was the start of goodbye.

'What are we going to do?' She could barely stand to ask.

'I've found a place that offers some marvellous treatment and complementary therapies, in Cornwall, actually. So I'm going to head down there for a bit . . .'

'Cornwall?' She lifted her head, unable to imagine Bertie, the toast of London, in a place like Cornwall.

'Don't look like that! It's not the other side of the world!'

'Might as well be.' She reached out and ran her fingertips over the thin wrist of her lovely friend. 'Cornwall? I shall miss you.'

This was the mealy-mouthed phrase that popped from her mouth, when what she wanted to say was, *My heart is broken! I am utterly petrified! I can see now that you look ill! You've lost your verve! You look like you might die, and I can't bear the thought of it, Bertie Barnes! I absolutely cannot bear the thought of it! What in the world does my life look like without you in it!*

Sitting up straight, he stared at her now, as he placed his cupped palm over her fingers and held on tightly as his eyes misted. 'Tell you the truth, Bob, I'm going to miss me too. I'm going to miss all of it.'

'I . . .' Her lips moved, but still she struggled to find the eloquence that sadness had robbed her of. What could she possibly say to this man who had shown her another wonderful facet of the world, had given her a chance, and had always shown her love? And oh, how she loved him in return!

'I know, Bob. I know. The feeling, darling one, is entirely mutual.'

She let her head hang forward, doing her best not to give in to the tears that threatened.

'There is one thing I need to tell you—'

'Tell me when you get back.' She cut him short. Holding his eyeline. Her voice unwavering. 'Tell me all about it when you get back.'

Bertie nodded. 'Okay, I'll tell you all about it when I get back.' They shared a long, lingering look of pure love. 'I've never been to Cornwall.' He rallied as best as he could, his voice as bold as he could make it.

Lilly sniffed. 'I've heard it's all knitted loo-roll holders, pampas grass and Viennese Whirls.'

'Urgh!' He rolled his eyes and pulled a face. 'Shoot me now!' He laughed, but quickly this laughter turned to tears. 'Beautiful Jack!' he howled.

'I know,' she wept with him. 'Beautiful Beautiful Jack . . .'

Present day

'You all right, Lil? Haven't heard from you for a couple of days. I said to Norm, I'm worried she's fallen down the plughole!'

'I've started packing up, Glen, can't see a way to avoid it really, and it makes me sad and makes me think, but it's also galvanising me.'

'I bet, my love, a whole lifetime of memories. Did you take Apollo into school?'

'No, he's on half-term, so Clodagh's taken time off. I quite miss it!' It was nice to hear how Glenda's attitude to the young woman had changed.

'Oh yes, I think Bradley's boys are on holiday too. So what news?'

'I went to see Derek Manners.'

'You never did! Now there's a name I haven't heard in a while!' Glenda's shocked tone was a reminder of how she and everyone in her circle had always viewed him. Lilly knew that when it came to building a relationship with him, it was a case of too little too late, but she had been greatly touched by his words, knowing her guilt was something she would wrestle with. The fact was, he had loved her mum, made her happy, and Jeannie had chosen him for a reason. A reason Lilly was beginning to understand.

'I did. It wasn't easy. He told me a few home truths and I left feeling really weird. It's unnerved me. I feel like I've lived my life with only half the cards, Glenda, while she had the other half, and I just wish I could see her, talk to her.'

'Life doesn't work like that, mate, does it? We can't waste time regretting the things we can't change. It's futile and will only make us miserable.'

'True, and I don't regret much.' She toyed with the edge of the scarf that was wrapped around her head, trying to contain her curls.

'Can I ask you something?' Glenda lowered her voice.

''Course you can.' There was very little between them that was unsaid.

'Would you have kept it? Had you not started bleeding and all that came next, would you have kept it?' Glenda asked softly, as if making sure no one in the house could hear, her discretion, as ever, guaranteed.

'I don't know.' This was *her* truth and a thought Lilly avoided, finding it hard to picture a different life that had been just out of reach. She swallowed, knowing no good would come of such imaginings. 'I mean, if it was nowadays, I'd have kept it, no doubt, I'd have found a way, but back then? Different times. I was so scared. Every aspect of being pregnant was utterly petrifying. I didn't believe it was true and just as I was starting to accept it and wonder what on earth might happen next, I started bleeding. I can't imagine what it would have been like to do it alone.'

'Millions of women do!'

'They do indeed, and why not? But not so much then, Glen.' She again offered the reminder, all part of the cloak of shame and humiliation that Lilly had worn for the longest time, knowing that her words were true; different times . . . 'And then I think about how that was my one chance, my shot at motherhood. I just didn't know it. I sometimes wonder if it was a boy or a girl, not that it helps in any way at all to go down those rabbit holes. I might not talk about it much, but I think about it often,' she confessed. 'They'd be fifty-one now, my baby, nearly fifty-two, actually. A grown man or woman. Maybe with kids of their own . . .' She inhaled the smell of bleach, remembered the waiting room full of cigarette smoke and Dr Rudd addressing her as if she was insignificant, making her feel so small when she was at her most vulnerable. What a rotten thing to do.

'I know, my love.' Glenda sounded choked, as if she, too, might think about it often.

◆ ◆ ◆

With the help of the internet, a chat to her doctor and enough time having passed to enable the discussion, Lilly had researched, as far as she was able, what had happened to her in 1973, wanting to make sense of it. It had felt odd, yet wonderfully freeing, asking questions without it being something so poisonous on her tongue that to speak of it felt impossible.

'Different times, Lilly. Hysterectomies were very common. For reasons that nowadays seem hard to believe, sometimes heedlessly done, almost, I fear. I read a case once where a woman had presented to her doctor seeming *flustered* at the thought of another pregnancy and so they gave her a hysterectomy. She had one child and was twenty-five.' Marian, the GP, had shaken her head. 'I think partly it was because of a lack of availability of other procedures, and poor understanding of women's health. But also' – her doctor of three decades, a smart woman who of course knew her history, returned her gaze – 'it was a thing done to women by men. And I wonder if it was in part to stop those women coming back again and again, maybe because women who complained were seen as a little troublesome or *hysterical*?' she emphasised. 'That's my personal opinion. Hysteria was a common diagnosis right up until the 1980s, and some doctors believed hysterectomy cured a wide range of mental health symptoms, often non-specific in the detail, but it was even seen as a cure for promiscuity. And believe me, the definition of promiscuity was questionable – "*intercourse outside of wedlock*", if you can imagine that.' Lilly had felt her face flame and could indeed imagine that. 'I think possibly some of these older surgeons weren't so far removed from that thinking. It's very sad.'

'You think they, what, used it as . . . as punishment?' Lilly could barely get the words out.

'I think that's probably going too far. If we're being kinder' – Marian widened her eyes – 'I'd say that it's possible decisions were made with the wholly unacceptable weight of moral judgement behind them. Just part of the misogyny around at the time and the terrible inequity in women's healthcare provision. It got rid of the problem and was probably seen as the "right thing to do". There was much autonomy for these surgeons and very little by way of redress; they were seen as God-like, often.'

Lilly had stared at the doctor. Just the thought that she might have been punished for not being married . . . It was certainly what it had felt like, the way she was treated, ignored. 'Would I have been thought of as promiscuous, do you think?'

She remembered the way she had felt about Wilkie's body, the hunger for skin-to-skin contact, that weekend at Royal Avenue on that big old bed.

'We have no way of knowing.' Lilly liked her honesty. 'But what I do know was that your hysterectomy was because of uterine perforation, which means the wall of your womb was accidentally punctured and there was severe bleeding.'

'So he did something wrong, did something to me?' She pictured the condescending, overconfident Dr Rudd.

'These things can happen. Rarely, but they can.'

◆ ◆ ◆

'I thought you were remarkable, that day when Norm and I picked you up.' Glenda's words pulled her from her thoughts. 'You were calm and strong, and I was in awe of you, Lil. Still am a bit.' Glenda chuckled.

'I wasn't calm and strong, not really, I was in shock.' Lilly bit her lip. 'It was months – years – later that I fully understood what had happened to me. I don't think it fully registered until I met Rex.'

'Oh God! I'd forgotten about Rex, dressed like he was in *Miami Vice*! I liked him.'

'Mmm.' It had been a look. 'I liked him too, everyone did, but he mentioned kids, and it was like this cold creep of understanding that went through my veins when I realised what had been done to me and how.' It hurt even now to think of it. 'I can still picture the doctor, a pompous walrus of a man full of his own self-importance. I don't remember saying a single word to him. He was dismissive and made me feel as if I should be brushing it under the carpet and carrying on, like it was nothing. His error did it to me, caused me harm. It was negligent, but that wasn't even under consideration, I was just a silly girl who had brought it all on herself – or at least that was how I was made to feel. But it changed everything for me, everything.'

'I know, darling. But it's important to remember that it was done to you. You did nothing wrong. You didn't make the choice, didn't give permission, it was all done to you, Lil. You were just a little girl really.'

Her tears came quietly. Glenda was right: she had been just a little girl.

'Love you, Glen.'

'Love you too.'

Lilly ended the call. It was an odd thing to talk about, as they never did really, but it was true; she thought about it, often. And as for Dr Rudd . . . she knew she'd never forget a single detail about him or her time on his ward.

That's a good girl . . .

Ten . . . nine . . . eight . . .

Then nothing.

◆ ◆ ◆

It wasn't the bluest of days, but the light was good, bright, and it was warm enough. Despite the pressing need to pack and find somewhere to live, Lilly picked up her paintbrushes and made her way out to the towpath. Deliberately and calmly she placed her easel, adjusted her seat and pulled out her brushes and paints. Waving briefly to the other side as was her custom, feeling the pull of nostalgia and regret, knowing she might have inadvertently waved on occasion to her mum.

Sitting quietly before she began, Lilly closed her eyes and let the buzz of riverside life swirl around her, listening to the putt-putt of the boats, the laughter and chatter of those who walked the path, the toot of horns and the tick-tick of engines idling on Vauxhall Bridge, the wheeze of brakes, the caw of chip-seeking gulls overhead, even the toll of bells from steeples both north and south of the river. She let it all wrap her, the sounds of her city. The London hum. Her night song that she would miss, knowing that wherever she next laid her head, it would not be the same, not even close, how could it? Remembering what it had felt like to wake up on that bed in Royal Avenue, a different suburb with a different background song.

In truth, she longed for peace and stability, wishing things didn't have to change. The affection she felt for Clodagh and Apollo was the closest thing she had to family, and the thought of it changing in any way, this lovely gift that had given her life so much meaning, was almost more than she could bear. It felt more important than ever before to capture this time, this moment, this stretch of river, this view, because who knew where she would wake and what her view might look like in the future.

Tipping her head back, she cricked her neck and, when she was ready, dipped the paintbrush into the jar of water to wet the canvas.

The river took shape with ease, as it often did, the banks too, the brown, silty, treasure-laden beaches revealed only briefly at low tide, the broad hulls of the barge boats sitting low in the water, the white whip of a dinghy sail circling in the middle of the waters. The light, catching the wake, as ripples reached the shore and frothed in an urban wave against the wall of the towpath. It was as if she could see all of it, could feel all of it.

With her shoulders relaxed and her breathing even, Lilly felt awash with a sense of peace as she relaxed into the creative process, allowing the brush to move, letting the paint create the picture that took shape beneath her fingertips. She could almost close her eyes and still see what lay in front of her, so familiar was this stretch of river, as if she were part of it, in it, of it.

Entirely lost to the process, it was only as the light faded, her fingers cramped and the air grew chilly that she realised some hours had passed. Looking up for the first time, it was as if the painting had revealed itself without too much planning or forethought in a way that was so natural it was almost a surprise when she saw the finished article. Not only had she captured the river, but also, crucially, having raised her eyeline slightly, there was the outline of the buildings opposite, the bridge, the London plane trees sprouting where they had got a foothold on the pavement and now reached towards the light.

The breath caught in her throat and her eyes misted, but mostly it was with a sense of pride that she realised she had done it! Finally, she had done it! With her hand clamped over her mouth, Lilly stared at the perfectly captured view that had been her whole world for much of her life. She gasped then, a huge intake of breath that felt a lot like relief as she bent over her easel, weeping, her body spent. She had done it! This was the river that was her home, her view, this was the sight and feeling she wanted to capture. The light, just the way it had been when her dad had stared out from the wide window while her mum whipped up supper in the kitchen. The same sense of stillness as when Wilkie sat next to her on the towpath on that particular evening when love had first wrapped her in its glorious, suffocating hold. It was the background to her childhood, when Vauxhall had been the home of industry, a less than desirable place to live, but just look at her now! It was all of her memories, it was her whole life, right there on the canvas.

It was the words of her mother's letter that came to her now, letters that had unlocked so much of her past, letters that had given her insight into Jeannie and letters that now offered the direction she needed when it came to her future.

There are times in your life when you instinctively know that something has run its course and it's time to walk away, because that is the best thing to do for a million reasons . . . it's how we progress.

'Yes, Mum,' she whispered, knowing it was time to walk away from the flat where her mother had no longer been welcome, the flat where her dad had fought his demons and hid from his trauma, the flat in which she'd spent time, hiding with her head turned towards the past to avoid having to face a future riddled with guilt and bound by duty. Flat number six, Waide House, Vauxhall, London, her address for the longest time, but now it was time to go. It was time to progress. To let go.

Lilly sat back on her stool and closed her eyes, breathing deeply through her nose and out through her mouth. Her bones felt lighter, her thoughts edged with a new and welcome clarity, as if she were free . . . finally free . . .

It was then that she heard a voice behind her.

'Can I have a look at your picture? What is it?'

Sitting upright and steeling herself, she turned to face the teenage boy clad all in black, wearing unfeasibly wide jeans, a black beanie, an oversized T-shirt and with his skateboard tucked under his arm.

'What is it?' she repeated.

'Yeah.' He leaned in, his manner nothing but curious.

She did her best to swallow the next rush of tears that made speaking difficult.

'It's this little stretch of river where I've lived all my life, and here' – she took the end of her paintbrush and, using it as a pointer, tapped it close to the figure of a woman in a pale mackintosh, hands in her pockets, the merest slick of red, red lipstick – 'is my mum, and she's watching me. Watching me from the other side of the water. I could often feel her when I sat out here at different times throughout my life. And I can feel her now. It's actually a picture of my mum, and it's for my mum. My mum who loved me. She loved me very much.' She smiled, with the weight of rejection lifting from her shoulders, happy to know that she had been loved and that her mum had found the love she was looking for, too, in the arms of Derek Manners.

'Cool.' The boy skated off, and she was glad of his approval.

Carefully she carried the piece inside and removed the abstract oil painting that hung over the fireplace, replacing it with her picture. It felt fitting to have it hang there for however long she might have left in this flat. This flat where all her memories, good and bad, her entire life had been lived. It was lovely, to see her mum staring back at her, and she wondered how many times Jeannie had stood on the bank while her dad stared out through the wide old window looking right at her, the woman he never stopped loving, and Lilly, oblivious, sat caught between the two on the path, lost to her paint and easel.

'Welcome home, Mum.'

Sinking down on to the sofa, she closed her eyes, falling into a sleep that was deep and restful. Despite the upheaval, the uncertainty of where she might now move and a million other paper cuts of worry, Lilly was at peace, and she slept the kind of sleep that only comes with the security of knowing that your worries are few and that you are loved, so loved . . .

1986 – aged 31

Lilly hated funerals. The thought made her snort a brief, sarcastic laugh. I mean, did anyone like them? She pulled the black shift dress from the hanger and slipped it over her head. With thick black tights underneath and her long hair scooped into a loose knot at the base of her neck, fastened with a wide scrunchie, she figured she'd do.

'We'll see you there, Lilly-Bob.' Mr Chaplin and his wife, Alma, who lived on the first floor, waved as they passed her in the hallway. 'Our Judy is driving us.'

'Yep, see you there.'

It was interesting how these people, her neighbours, were a big part of her life and yet were strangers too, thrown together, connected by no more than the allocation of their flat by the council some years ago now. She was glad they were spruced up and coming along, knowing her dad would have appreciated it.

It was entirely ridiculous, comical even, the thought that he had died. Her dad. Dead! Nope, it made no sense and just wouldn't sink in, no matter how much she tried to make sense of it. Far easier to think he was at work, rehearsing with the orchestra, playing a concert, hiking somewhere green and muddy with his canvas knapsack on his back.

She'd had the radio playing since he died, nearly two weeks ago now. The most popular song, The Communards' '*Don't Leave Me This Way*'... it seemed to be on repeat on nearly every station, and the irony wasn't lost on her, even now as the lyrics rattled round and around in her head. It felt fitting. He loved music, had always loved music, his taste eclectic and fluid. He'd like this little tribute from Jimmy Somerville, she was sure. Again she fought the desire to giggle, waiting for him to appear, 'Ta-dah!', not dead at all, probably hiding or lost on a ramble, or asleep, or whistling somewhere, enjoying his packed lunch, having simply lost track of time. How they would laugh when she told him of the mayhem he had caused.

. . . and then the doctor said, 'He came in complaining of chest pains,' and the next thing I knew, we were in a lift, and they were taking me down to the bowels of the building to show me a body that looked very much like you. Can you believe it, Dad? Now, what are we having for tea?

The service was simple, fitting, with a lovely eulogy given by Mrs Devlin, who had played in the orchestra with her dad for decades and of whom he was very fond. As the velvet fringed curtains closed and the coffin was lowered to somewhere Lilly would rather not envisage, the sound of Albinoni's 'Adagio in G Minor' rang out around the crematorium, musical perfection for such a moment. Still, despite the sound of muffled sobbing all around her, Lilly was yet to shed a tear. Because it didn't feel real, any of it, and therefore her body couldn't cry, as her mind wouldn't let her.

The wake was busier than she had anticipated. 'A good turnout' seemed to be the appropriate phrase. The entire orchestra, his work friends from the music shop, members of the Ramblers' Association, neighbours, even the odd army friend or two. He would have been chuffed and embarrassed in equal measure to see such a gathering. There was an air of reverence in the Builder's Arms pub, where platters of cheese and pickle, and ham and tomato sandwiches, trays of Scotch eggs and bowls of ready-salted crisps had been placed on the bar, alongside a stack of paper napkins to aid with food residue on the fingers.

People she knew, and some she didn't, came to shake her hand, share a lovely anecdote, usually detailing something funny or kind her dad had said or done, and all with a genuine sadness about them that they wouldn't see him again.

Her mum came to the funeral; of course she did. What Lilly hadn't expected was that Derek Manners would be there too. It was obvious, really, that her mum wasn't going to pitch up without her husband of fifteen years, and in fairness to Derek Manners he had never done anything to directly hurt or injure Lilly, it was more what he represented. He was the man who had provided the open window through which her mother had climbed, keen to escape her unsatisfactory life in Waide House. More than that, he'd put up a rope ladder and placed a safety mat on the ground, promising to catch her if she fell. A neat exit from their flat, where not even that wide window and the view of the river was enough to tempt her to stay.

Lilly approached her mother with caution, still wary of rejection, still nervous to place her hand on her, to touch her in any way, never to tell her that she loved her, worried by not receiving the same in return. And even now, wanting to punish the woman who had promised so much with her regular dinners, laundering skills and bedtime stories, making the withdrawal of it all that much harder to bear.

'Thank you for coming.' She spoke with a certain formality, nodding at her mum, who looked older than she did in Lilly's mind, and sad, of course. It was a requirement for the occasion, even if it was a look that Lilly was struggling to achieve. Her mum narrowed her eyes at her. 'Of course. Of course we were going to come!'

We . . . We . . . We . . .

'It's surreal to me.' Jeannie drew breath. 'Robert was one of those people who was just always going to be around.' *Unlike you . . .* Lilly swallowed the thought. 'I can't imagine what you are going through, Lilly.'

'I'm fine!' She gave a brief, contained smile: proof. 'People keep telling me it's a blessing for him to have experienced such a swift and straightforward ending. I guess that's true.'

'I believe that. Derek's brother had cancer' – her mum shook her head and simultaneously exhaled – 'and there was nothing straightforward about that.'

'Right.' Lilly widened her eyes, in no humour to hear about the suffering of someone she had never met or heard of.

'How have you been?' Her mother toyed with the handle of her handbag, bitten nails nervously flicking the frayed edge of faux leather.

'Well, there's a question.' Lilly considered it. 'I've been . . . preoccupied, I suppose. Busy. No one tells you that, do they, about all the admin involved when someone dies. It's not actually the emotional stuff that gets you at the end of every day, not the longing for one more minute or the revisiting of moments and memories that reduce you to tears. At least it hasn't been for me.' She gave a small, awkward laugh. 'For me it's more about being physically exhausted, entirely unenamoured by the filling out of the forms in triplicate, the sending off of certificates, the numerous phone calls, arguing with the bank, cancelling policies and standing orders, closing accounts, all that rubbish.'

An image of her wonderful Bertie filled Lilly's mind, knowing his family had been exhausted by the long and laborious nature of his passing. The wasting away of the once vibrant man, watching him over a series of months reduce and reduce until he barely resembled the person they all adored. A living ghost. As if he had died long before he died. Applying lotions and potions and trying to find new and inventive ways to present the kaleidoscope of colossal pills that seemed both endless and pointless. The sleepless nights, understanding that at that stage, the end, the nasty disease paid no heed to the clock. And neither did her darling Bertie Barnes, who at the most irregular of times needed to use the bathroom, take morphine, or simply felt the need to make sure for the umpteenth time that she fully understood the workings of the safe in the gallery. The gallery he had left to her, this the one thing he had wanted to say before he died. It was hers because she was the closest to a daughter he would ever have, and he loved her so.

Lilly looked up and coughed, refocusing, as if remembering who she was talking to and what she was talking about. 'So yes, I've been preoccupied.'

'I guess it's one good thing, that he didn't suffer.'

'Oh yes,' she offered brightly, falsely. 'That *is* one good thing.'

'You sound' – her mum licked her lips, nervously – 'a bit bitter. Angry, actually. Angry with me.'

Lilly smacked her hand on her forehead. 'Now why on earth would I be angry with you?'

'I don't know, Lilly, because maybe you think if I hadn't left, your dad might still be alive, as if you think it was somehow my job to stay and look after him. Is that what you think?'

This time her mother didn't waste time agitating the handle of her handbag. Instead she placed her thumbnail directly between her teeth and ripped.

'I don't know what I think, Mum.' The sound of the word was still alien on her tongue. But that was a lie; Lilly did know. And what she thought was that, had her mother not abandoned her marriage, her husband, her life, then maybe, just maybe, her dad might not have kept his heart condition secret, might not have had a bad heart at all! As if one that wasn't broken had a better chance of survival than his, which his wife had taken and smashed into a million fragments.

I think that if we assume it's for ever then we won't be disappointed. And if it turns out not to be the case, then we'll be extra happy if she comes home . . .

It was a ludicrous notion, of course.

'Ignore me, I'm tired' – she rubbed her sore eyes – 'and my dad's just died and I'm trying to get my head straight.'

'That day, that day you called me to tell me about the boy you'd met' – her mum met her gaze and, just like that, Lilly felt the throb along her scar – 'I think about it a lot. It was like . . .'

'Like what?' Lilly's tone was clipped. This conversation, about all the things she kept boxed up and shut away, made her quite uncomfortable. The very last thing she wanted to do was open them up today, and especially not in front of her mother.

'It was like I always hoped it would be' – Jeannie's voice cracked – 'you phoning me, excited, sharing a little bit of your life, letting me in.'

Lilly had almost forgotten the thrill she had felt at relaying the news. Someone had picked her! Someone had wanted her! And he was, until she discovered otherwise, quite, quite marvellous! This memory was now edged with the embarrassment and sense of failure that she had grown accustomed to. How did this woman not understand that she had forfeited the right to all of those feelings the day she walked away, abandoned her!

'It came to nothing, obviously.' She spoke the words, knowing this was not what her mother was driving at.

'Oh, well, it seems like that might have been a great shame.' Her mum's voice was thin, as if finally understanding that Lilly was not willing to let her in, even now.

She could only nod, because yes, it was a great shame.

'He had a terrible war, you know.' Her mother swallowed and stared at her, her gaze intense. They didn't talk about this, none of it. Lilly felt her heart beat in an irregular dance and took a slow breath through her nose as Jeannie continued, giving information about her dad she had not asked for. 'A terrible war. It really affected him. Affected us. Me, it affected me.'

'Is that right?' Lilly fired, thinking that there must be very few people who'd had a *fantastic* war. The clue was in the name, right?

Her mum looked into the middle distance, her face contorted. 'Nightmares that I couldn't calm him from, no matter what I tried. That was rough. And the whistling, the constant whistling.' She spoke through gritted teeth and closed her eyes briefly, seemingly still irritated by the memory. 'And if he wasn't whistling, he practised his violin, or listened to music, any music. Creating a pleasant noise so he was never alone with his thoughts. Said it was the only way to blot out the things he'd seen, the sounds he'd heard. Whistling and singing and tapping and sawing that horsehair bow back and forth, back and forth . . . walking miles and miles and miles to the point of exhaustion, just to keep it all at bay. It used to drive me crackers.'

'Did it now?' Lilly was barely listening, choosing not to digest the facts, keeping her thoughts neutral and her distress under lock and key. Suddenly she felt very cold. Her dad's whistle, the background noise to her life, his music, a joy as well as an education, and his long, long rambles, these were his best hobbies! What did her mum know about it? What did her mum know about anything?

'Well, I can only hope that he knew how much *I* loved his whistles, his noise, his everything!' Keeping her voice as steady as she was able, she fired the verbal daggers at this woman who had jumped ship.

'Oh, he knew. You were his life, Lilly-Bob, his whole life.' Her mum spoke kindly, ignoring the jibe, as she pulled a paper tissue from the inside pocket of her grotty handbag and wiped under her nose and beneath her eyes. 'I think sometimes it might be good if you understood it all a bit better. If you understood me a little better.'

'Maybe.' Lilly felt the beginnings of a headache and knew that the very last thing she wanted to talk about today was her parents' marriage, particularly the ending of it.

'Do you still have all his old records?' her mum asked with a small smile twitching the corner of her mouth. Maybe she, too, was thinking about Bill Haley and jiving on that parquet flooring in her slippers.

'No, I don't,' Lilly lied, wanting again to admonish Jeannie, wanting her to think that she and her dad had packed away every remnant of that old life and thrown it out with the rubbish. They hadn't, of course, and if her mum were to visit and dig about a bit, she'd find a pot of Pond's face cream in the nightstand on the side of the bed where she used to sleep. Neither Lilly nor her dad was ever quite able to discard it. And a red, red kiss inside a folded tissue in Lilly's treasure box.

'I . . . I'd better get back to Derek. He doesn't like being left alone at these kinds of things.'

'I understand that. Being left alone really is quite shite.'

Her mum raised her hand as if wanting to touch her face, stroke her hair, or lay a hand on her shoulder. Lilly flinched while imagining all three, as her mother coiled her fingers, placing her shaking fist at the base of her throat as her tears spilled.

Derek Manners, it seemed, had had a similar thought, and approached looking sheepish, as was his way, his voice quiet, hesitant, nervous. 'I'm sorry, Lilly.'

She stared at him, wondering what he was sorry for – destroying her parents' marriage? Breaking her dad's heart? Taking her mum away from her? Or the fact that her beloved dad had died? She blinked, having rarely spoken to the man, seeing no reason to start now.

'We should probably get going.' Her mum spoke softly.

'Yep.' Lilly nodded.

'You heard about Lineker?'

'What? No.' It took her a second to understand Derek Manners was talking about the footballer.

'Barcelona have just paid over two million for him.'

'What?' Her confusion was genuine. This was his opener at her dad's funeral, the man he had cuckolded, ruining his life, stealing his wife, and any other Machiavellian cliché she wanted to throw in his direction? Derek Manners, the cardigan-wearing prick who lived in a flat above a TV repair shop on the Tottenham Court Road.

'Everton have sold him to Barcelona for over two million quid.' He shook his head. 'Can you believe it?'

Lilly pulled a face at her mum, her disdain evident.

'No, I really can't believe it!' She stared at the man until his face turned puce, and he blinked furiously, before she walked away.

◆ ◆ ◆

It had been a long day. Her body ached with fatigue, yet her mind was wired; she needed a hot bath and sleep.

Lilly put the key in the front door.

'Hel-loo!' she called out, waiting to hear his response.

In the kitchen!

On the sofa!

I've just put the kettle on!

Here she is . . .

Nor was there the sound of him practising his violin as he stood in the window. Drawing the bow across the mournful strings. The instrument, like him, now for ever quiet.

The sound of her breathing was loud in her ears amid the silence.

It hit her then, the ice pick of grief that landed sharply in her breastbone. She fell to the floor, lying in the doorway, half in, half out of the flat, sprawled on the polished concrete tiles. It was hard to breathe, hard to stay upright, longing for one more minute of him, wanting to go back to when he was here, home, waiting for her . . .

'Dad!' she called as loudly as she was able; her words, however, a whisper, as if all her fuel had been taken up in calling out at all. 'Daddy!' she tried again.

'Lilly-Bob!'

Mrs Chaplin stepped into the flat through the open front door. She bent low, touching Lilly's legs, as if trying to ascertain if the emergency was mental or physical.

'I want . . . I want my dad, I want him back!' She wept uncontrollably.

Mrs Chaplin shook her head, her tone warm and lovely. 'I know, my love, I know.'

'Help me!' Lilly called out to no one in particular as the woman manoeuvred her into a sitting position, with her back resting against the wood-panelled wall, where the smell of his cigarette smoke lingered. 'Please . . .' she managed, her breathing laboured. 'I don't know how to do it,' she whispered, this her truth and *the* truth, that she was without the first clue how to navigate a life without her dad, a man most extraordinary: Robert Cooper.

The absence of him made the flat seem a little colder, colours not quite so bright, even food didn't taste as flavourful, as if everything were subdued. No matter how she occupied her time, a small part of her was, and she knew always would be, on high alert, waiting for his safe return. He was, quite simply, a rainbow over her world, and she had adored him.

'Do you want me to call someone?' Mrs Chaplin's face was etched with concern mere inches from Lilly's.

She thought of Wilkie, who was a liar. She thought of Rex, who was, she had heard, now engaged to be married. Glenda would be at home, busy with the kids. She thought of her mum, who was no doubt in her flat with Derek Manners, and as it was a Thursday, probably eating cold meat, chips and beans. The thought of this horrible predictability was enough to make her smile a little and to halt her tears.

'No one that would want to hear from me, Mrs Chaplin, but thank you.'

'Well, you know where we are, love, just across the hallway.' The woman pointed, in case she might have forgotten.

'Yep, just across the hallway,' Lilly parroted, knowing she would never call on the Chaplins for help, embarrassed now that the woman had seen her in this raw state of grief. She wasn't that kind of person; she'd figure it out.

She always did.

◆ ◆ ◆

'Are you sure you want to be back at work?' Glenda asked as she ferreted in the petty-cash tin for a couple of pound notes.

'I'm positive. What else am I going to do, sit at home and fester? I need to be here, need to be busy.'

'Do you feel up to going to the cinema? I want to see that new film.'

'Who's in it?' Lilly asked, not one to be swayed by the hype of a hit movie, often preferring the indie offerings of the small cinemas in Soho and off the beaten track.

'Erm, no one I've heard of. Tom Cruise?'

'And it's about flying planes or learning to fly planes or something?' She'd read the blurb.

'Yes, but it's supposed to be good, fast, nice, romantic, good music!'

'All right, all right! Get tickets! Jeez!' It was nice to spend time with her friend, lovely that Glenda now worked a couple of days a week at the gallery.

They didn't speak about the six months without contact, both figuring that with so much history and a lifetime ahead of them, that hiatus didn't warrant close attention. Glenda had reached out in the wake of Lilly's dad's death, and she had welcomed her with open arms. The reason for the fallout would, she knew, live long in her mind, but her dad's passing had taught her some valuable lessons; that life was short, it could end quickly, and you could never have too many good friends in your corner to help see you through those rough times.

◆ ◆ ◆

Bertie had asked to see the gallery. The fact that it was for the last time was implicit and, as ever, she and his brother, Chris, had kept a jolly countenance, settled his fragile self into the wheelchair and brought him here. She had quite forgotten that she'd arranged for Glenda and the kids to pop by as Bertie ran his eye over the accounts, stopping to cough and sip from his glass of water via a straw. He'd even laughed as raucously as was possible, as they reminisced about a certain exhibition when a fight had almost broken out over a sloppily held glass of red and a spoiled mohair blazer!

'Oh!' Her friend's voice had come from the doorway, drawing their attention.

'Glen!' she'd called out, delighted to see Bradley and Andrew, her godsons, who both looked like little Norms. 'I'm such a dummy! I forgot I'd said we'd have lunch. Look who's here!' She had turned and pointed eagerly at Bertie, who had slunk down into the wheelchair, his bony physique offering little resistance against the plastic seating. He was like a little bird and about as frail, eyes sunken, mouth small, skin tight and with painful lesions on his forehead, devoid of his beautiful hair. A large woollen scarf was wound about his neck, as he felt the chill, even on the warmest of days.

Bertie had raised his bony fingers in greeting.

'Hey, kids!'

It was then, as the boys made as if to walk forward, that Glenda pulled them back, a split-second decision, anchoring them to her with her arms around their shoulders.

'We'll let you get on, Lil, I'll . . . I'll give you a ring.' Glenda spoke nervously, as she shepherded them out of the gallery.

'Okay, then!' She managed to wave them goodbye with enthusiasm. It was only as she turned back to Bertie that she saw he was crying. It had broken her, to see him so affected.

Lilly hadn't waited for her friend to ring and had dialled the number the moment she got back to the flat, relieved that it was Glenda who answered the phone, unable to imagine making small talk with Norm while her gut churned with all the fire it tried to contain.

'What on earth was that, earlier?' was her opener, as anger fizzed in her veins.

'What was what?' Glenda's confusion didn't fool her for a second.

'You know exactly what I'm talking about! The way you pulled the kids towards you as if you didn't want them infected! That!' She had raised her voice, picturing Bertie's tears, and unable to back down.

'I don't—'

'Don't deny it, Glen! I saw you, we all did, and you did that to our friend, our wonderful friend who is poorly, dying! He just wanted one last look at the gallery, and you did that to him!' She hated the crack to her voice.

'I wasn't going to deny it—'

'Are you for real?' she interrupted.

'I was going to say, I don't know how to make you understand.'

'Well, shame on you, Glenda! Shame on you! You're right, I will never understand!'

'That's right, you can't!'

'Jesus, how are you even trying to justify what you did!' Lilly yelled.

'I don't have to justify it, I just have to do what I think is best to keep my kids safe. And that's why you'll never understand because you don't know what it feels like!'

Lilly felt the sting of her friend's words slap her around the face. Glenda wasn't done.

'I wouldn't want to upset Bertie for the world!' Glenda cried openly now. 'But if there is a choice between offending him and putting my boys in danger, there's no choice, none at all!'

'Putting your boys in danger?' Lilly's voice was hoarse from a throat pulled thin with equal measures of anger and distress.

'You're not a mum, Lil! You don't have children!' The words had landed like a punch in her throat. 'I would throw myself in front of a speeding bus, I'd take a bullet, I'd do anything, anything to protect them, and we just don't know enough about it, and if there is the slightest risk . . .'

'Fuck you, Glenda. How could you? Fuck you!' She had slammed down the phone and they hadn't spoken for the longest time.

Six months, to be precise.

The call came, after her dad's funeral, as if time hadn't passed.

'Hey, Lil, I was so sorry to hear your news. How're you holding up?'

'Oh, you know . . .'

And that had been that; they had built a bridge back to each other.

◆ ◆ ◆

Glenda waved the pound notes in her hand. 'Right, so I'm nipping to the delicatessen on Lupus Street to check on the order for tomorrow. I'll grab us a couple of sandwiches for lunch. Back in a tick.'

'See you in a bit.' Lilly waved her off.

Placing the catalogues on the welcome desk, she pulled two dark petals from the outer edges of the full-bloom peonies that sat in an oversized glass vase and had started to discolour a little, reminding herself to give the stems a trim and change the water before she left for the evening.

With the exhibition opening tomorrow, Lilly wanted everything to be perfect, just as Bertie had taught her. He had always taken care of every little detail, reminding her that all a night required to be successful was '*good lighting, great music, cold drinks, delicious canapés, the right guest list and plenty of pzazz!*' She pictured him then, sprinkling invisible magic dust in an arc around his head.

How she missed him, especially at times like this when he would be enjoying the preparation, shouting joy into the space, oozing energy and enthusiasm with every breath. Her wonderful, wonderful friend. No matter how much time passed, she missed him like it was yesterday and suspected she always would.

The telephone on her small desk rang. Lilly removed her diamanté-and-drop pearl earring, holding it in her palm as she lifted the telephone, which had been ringing off the hook today; the *Standard* wanting to check the press release. The journalist from the *Guardian* going over the article about the young up-and-coming artist she was championing, whose charcoal studies of fish were making quite the splash. Then there had been the last-minute calls from the drinks supplier, and the harpist she had invited to pluck away in the middle of the floor, a talking point, if nothing else.

'B'Art Gallery, Pimlico, Lilly speaking.'

She would with hindsight claim that in the microsecond before he spoke, the small intake of breath, the way he paused, told her it was him before he uttered the single word, as if she could sense it. That might of course be pure poppycock, nothing more than a fanciful embellishment.

'Lilly.'

The sound fired a bolt right through her body. Two syllables that opened a portal that took her back in time to 1973.

It was him.

It was Wilkie, the sound of him on the end of the phone. She'd have known him anywhere.

'It's me, it's Wilkie.'

'Yes.' Her voice was a hushed, awkward whisper as her body shivered in response and she felt the horrific surge of longing that was a visceral response to hearing his voice. How she hated this reaction towards this man who was never hers, could never be hers. Her throat felt narrow, her legs too weak to support her frame as she fell into the leather chair. 'What do you want?' She kept her voice clipped, her tone level with just the right amount of dismissal. It bothered her that words like *my love . . . Wilkie . . . darling one . . . still* formed in her mind and floated around just enough to confuse her and threaten to throw off her cool demeanour. She pictured the two of them, rocking together on that big bed in Royal Avenue, her nails on his back, his breath against her face.

'It's been a while.' He dared to offer a small laugh, as if anything about the way he had treated her, his disappearance, his casual infidelity, was funny, not to mention the trauma he had left in the wake of his leaving.

'What is it you want?' It felt safest to repeat the question and not try to expand on any conversation he may or may not be intent on having.

'What I want is to hear your voice, to talk to you. I've thought about calling before, many times, but it never felt' – he paused – 'I saw an article in the Sundays about the gallery, and there you were, and I just thought . . .'

'What did you think, exactly?'

'That it might be the right time to call to . . . apologise, I guess.'

It was her turn to offer a small laugh.

'Bit late for that.' She gripped the receiver with both hands, yet still they shook.

'A lot of water has passed under a lot of bridges, Elizabeth-Roberta.'

She hated the bloom of tears now, his voice a reminder of what it had felt like to live in that addictive bubble of love and sex and how he had, in so many ways, spoiled her for good. It was also like stepping back through that portal to a time when she had indeed trusted him implicitly. Her faith restored, because despite her mother's best efforts, he had made her believe that love was possible, he had let her dream of a future . . . Guileless, riven with the exuberance of youth that was a magic elixir! And of course, at a time when her beloved dad was at home or playing in the orchestra, or working, but around, alive. There for her with his music playing and the scent of his tobacco surrounding him and his cups of tea and moments of quiet, the man who, according to her mum, had had a bad war. The man for whom she had a thousand questions that she had left too late to ask.

'You should have told me.'

'Told you what?'

Whether his words were grounded in ignorance or flippancy, it was hard to tell. Either way, his question made her teeth clamp together and her jaw flex.

'Oh, I don't know, that you preferred your tea weaker, that you can't swim, maybe given me a good book recommendation? What do you *think*? That you had a wife and children at home. *A wife and children!*' She raised her voice and all the toxic hurt she had tamped down over the years came bubbling to the top, leaving her throat feeling like it burned.

'I didn't know how.' His voice was now no more than a hoarse whisper.

'Yes, because that's the issue here, that you didn't know *how* to tell me, not the fact that you kept them secret at all! The absolute galling deceit that I unwittingly played a part in. You turned me into the kind of woman I have always despised. You've heard the names – *home-wrecker, slut, bit on the side* – none of them complimentary! You said I was naïve, and it irked me at the time, and it's done so ever since, unaware I was naïve to be trusting you, to be giving myself to you! You had the full set of rules, Wilkie, I didn't. I was playing a game without the first clue as to the consequences of losing.'

'It was wonderful. Don't forget that, how wonderful it was.'

'How dare you!' She wiped the tears that spilled on to her cheeks, in pain to be reminded of just how wonderful it had been and also how easily he could pull her in with that velvet voice of intent and his charm. It was as upsetting as it was infuriating.

'It might have been wonderful for those few weeks—'

'It was, wonderful, intense, beautiful,' he interrupted.

'But absolutely shit every day since!'

Good girl . . . count backwards from ten for me . . .

'How do you know I had a wife, and . . .' He swallowed, seemingly now, as then, unwilling to bring his children into this.

'I spoke to Georgina.' She spoke confidently and hoped he felt as winded as she had on that day so long ago.

'You . . . you did? When?' She picked up the underlying note of panic and was thrilled by it, knowing it was no less than he deserved.

'When I realised you'd run away.'

'I didn't run away!'

'Oh, forgive me – I didn't realise you called, left a note, sent a letter, went out of your way to explain the situation to me, came to say goodbye?'

She heard him exhale and there was a beat before he spoke.

'What did you tell her?'

'Nothing. I told her nothing because she sounded nice and she . . . she is a mum and I felt like the worst kind of person.'

'She is nice.' He sniffed – was he crying? It was hard to tell and harder still for her to picture. 'You'd like her.'

'I'd *like* her?' The words coasted on unnatural laughter; was he for real?

'Yes, everyone does.'

'Not you, apparently, Wilkie. At least, you can't like her enough, because liking someone, loving someone, means not treating them in that way, not lying to them, not hiding things from them, not sleeping with someone else.'

'You make it sound so straightforward.'

'Because it is! It really is! It's so basic, and a prerequisite I would hope, being honest, being open. How could you do that to her? To me?' She felt winded by the exchange as her adrenaline surged.

'We met at university, Georgina and I, a long, long time ago.'

'I don't know why you think I might be interested.' How she hated this version of herself, feeling the spark of petty jealousy, when she had no right, not at all.

'I don't know what to say that won't upset you.' He sighed.

'Which again begs the question why you called in the first place!'

'I just wanted to.'

'Well, if my whole sorry encounter with you taught me one thing, it's that what we want and what we get are rarely the same thing in life. You put my heart through a meat grinder and abandoned me.' She had chosen a long, long time ago not to confide in him about the baby, knowing it would serve no purpose other than to ladle more misery on to an already sorrowful tale. 'It was a horrible thing to do and there is nothing you can say or do that will excuse your shoddy behaviour. Nothing.' She felt a burst of pride to be standing up to him, to be saying all the things she had wanted to over the years, showing him she was no longer cowed or so easily swayed.

'Georgina and I had been together for so long, it was like we were friends, good friends, and I loved her, I love her, but then—'

'But then what, Wilkie?'

'I met you and I fell in love. Not the sedate, predictable, slow love that Georgina and I shared, but a fast, exciting, intoxicating, euphoria-inducing kind of love!'

It was conflicting.

Her heart flexed and her gut bunched. Here he was, confirming what she had longed to be true: the reciprocal nature of their entanglement. She had not been mad! She had not imagined it! Yet it sickened her, too, to hear that he could so easily pick up something shiny and new while his wife, Georgina, sat at home with their little children. Children Lilly would never get to have.

It was as exquisite as it was tragic.

'It was a funny way to show your love, by abandoning me in the way you did, making me think I was crazy.'

'I can picture it, you and I in the bedroom at Royal Avenue when you said it. You said *I love you* and I wanted so badly to say it back, to tell you how I felt, to tell you all about my life and to make a plan to abandon it. And it was the most wretched thing in the whole wide world. Knowing I was falling for you and that I had to choose, to hurt you or hurt Georgina and my kids. In the end it was a simple numbers game. Hurt one person or hurt three.'

'A numbers game?' She could barely get the words out. *Ten . . . nine . . . eight . . .* 'Well, as a mathematician, it must have been an easy equation for you. You were right when you said that I didn't know you. What I did know of you was a ruse, a mask, make-believe. And having had a lot of time to think about everything you did and said, I can confidently state that what I know, I do not like.'

'You loved me!' he pressed.

'But it wasn't real. You can't love someone if you don't know them, don't know all of them.'

'You knew enough.' He sniffed again. 'I told you my truth, as far as I was able.'

'Ah, yes, your *truth*, I remember those chats. And for years I struggled to make out the difference between the truth and your truth and it turns out the difference is that one is a lie. You're a liar. You lied to me in all you didn't say.'

'I honestly told you my thoughts, my voice, my feelings in the moment. That was all real . . .'

'Maybe.'

'I bought you a copy of *Grimms' Fairy Tales*, because I remembered that you'd told me about a previous boyfriend called Rumpelstiltskin.' She hated the flicker of joy in her chest at being reminded of that moment. 'I wanted to send it to you but didn't know what to write in it, wasn't sure how to—'

'I have to go,' she interjected, looking across the street to where Glenda waited to cross. It spurred her to end the call. 'You were right about one thing; you are winter, a cold, bleak blanket of darkness that covers all things bright and colourful. For the longest time I struggled under that blanket, could barely take a breath. But not any more. Don't call me again, Wilkie, not ever.'

She put the phone back in the cradle and found a smile as her friend walked through the door, two brown paper lunch bags in her hands.

'Well, all set for tomorrow. They'll deliver the canapés about five thirty and all we have to do is whip off the clingfilm at the last minute.' Glenda looked at her. 'You all right, Lil?'

'Yes. Just got off the phone with Wilkie.'

'Wilkie? You're kidding me!'

'Nope.' It was then she cried in earnest, great, gulping tears that tasted a lot like relief. It was done, it was done. No more loose ends, no more wondering.

'Do you want me to get Norm to beat him up?'

This made her tears turn to laughter, partly at the thought of Norm beating anyone up and that this was Glenda's first and best suggestion.

'I don't think that's necessary, not now. A lot of water has flowed under a lot of bridges.' She stole his phrase.

'Is he still a knob?' Glenda made her way to the kitchenette and filled the kettle, knowing it was time for a tea.

'Yep.' Lilly wiped her eyes, took a breath, and restored her earring. 'Still a knob.'

Present day

Lilly hoped that everyone had received the messages she'd sent and that they were going to arrive promptly. It felt easier to say it to the group rather than repeat her plans to individuals over and over, less galling, less emotionally draining. She glanced at her watch: plenty of time.

'Lilly?'

'Yes, Apollo?'

She braced herself; the questions he liked to throw at her on their morning walk to school were as random as they were varied. It could be anything from something dinosaur-related to how many frogs were there in the world, which she could only answer with: *a lot!*

'Are you my nan?'

'Oh!' It was one of those questions that had the power to floor her. Something that curiously hadn't properly occurred to her until middle age, that without becoming a mother, she was also denied a shot at being a granny. In some ways, this caused her more distress. She hadn't backed herself to be a mother, even if, mechanically, it had been possible, largely on account of the fact that she hadn't had her own mum around for long enough to learn from, but grannyhood? It seemed to come with more of the fun and less of the responsibility, and was something she felt she could have picked up quite easily!

'I am not, but maybe we should find out what it is that nans do, and I would quite happily do those things, if it's okay with Mummy for me to assume some of those responsibilities!' This she trotted out, ignoring the stab in her heart at the prospect of losing out when he and Clodagh moved away, another thought that almost floored her.

''Kay.' Apollo stared at her as if without the first clue what she was talking about. 'Can you take my—'

'Yes, of course.' She cut him short as he handed her the rather large and unwieldy branch of a tree that had been today's find, thinking that wherever she moved next, with a couple of apartments in Pimlico under consideration, they would need greater storage or space to accommodate what was turning into a small lumber yard in her hallway.

It made her smile all the way home, walking at an amble in her bright kimono and with an array of bangles on her wrist. She waved with enthusiasm to black-cat-on-wheelie-bin-lid owner, and he waved back. It was a curious thing that since she had read the letters her parents exchanged, finished her painting and hung it on the wall, and following her visit to Derek Manners, Lilly's thoughts had settled.

Her mind was no longer a jumble of frantic and intrusive thoughts, often dark memories, that left her riven with regret. Anguish over the loss of her dad, stoking the pain in her gut at the way her mum had walked out, and of course, Wilkie and the rather cruel legacy his actions had bestowed upon her.

What was it Alfie had said: . . . *people change, things change, you just have to figure out how to change with it! Give life a chance!*

'Maybe you're right, Mr Portland,' she spoke quietly to herself. 'Maybe you're right.'

It was as if she had found some kind of peace, understanding that her dad would have had his reasons for not doing more to allow her and Jeannie to form a deeper bond. And that her mum, Wilkie too, were only human. Flawed, imperfect, troubled, but human. It was a good lesson, understanding that it was possible to love these people in spite of their flaws, important to forgive them too, and most important of all, to let them go . . .

The gallery was ticking over and she considered for the first time giving it up, knowing she could finally, finally, let Bertie go too, knowing she had done her very best for the friend she had so loved, continuing *his* legacy; but the truth was she was tired. Christopher, Bertie's brother, the man who had played in the orchestra with her dad, had passed away nearly a decade ago, but he had a daughter, a midwife; Tanzie, who lived in Kent and who had two kids of her own. Lilly didn't know the woman, but they swapped Christmas cards and had met a couple of times. It felt only right to pass it on to her, gifting it in the way dear Bertie had to her. She'd get advice from Denzel Bashington on the best way to make the approach and handle the transfer. It would then be Tanzie's to keep or sell, but she hoped it would be as life-changing for the young woman as it had been for her.

It was as she put her key in the door that Clodagh came down the stairs.

'How did he go in?' she asked, as she stuffed her apron into her tote bag, ready for her later shift at the coffee shop.

'Wonderfully, as usual. May I present today's offering!' Lilly lifted the large and unwieldy branch, which still had leaves attached.

'Oh God, Lilly! It's huge!' Clodagh laughed, gripping the banister rail for support as she chuckled. 'You can't keep all of his sticks! You'd have to move out – even if you weren't being forced to move out, there's no room for you and all of his finds!'

'He asked me today if I was his nan. Didn't know what to say but thought it was a very sweet thing to say to an old woman like me.'

'First, you are not old. You know you are not old!'

'True, I do know this.' Lilly smiled, remembering the woman only six years her senior with the walking frame.

'And second, yes, yes, you are his nan, absolutely, one hundred per cent. And he can call you Nan if wants to and if you don't mind?'

'Mind?' It was, Lilly thought, the most incredible privilege. She tried to respond, but couldn't quite; the lump of emotion in her throat made it impossible. 'Uh-huh,' she managed.

'I got your text: you never need to ask me twice if I fancy a coffee, you know this!'

'Great!' Lilly smiled as the front door buzzer went and none other than Joshua Vaughan came loping up the communal stairs. She watched the way Clodagh tucked her hair behind her ears, as if wanting to look her best.

'There you are. Come on in.'

He looked behind as if confirming it was he that Lilly was talking to with such civility.

'Morning, Miss Cooper, Miss Newman.' He beamed at Clodagh, as if he had forgotten momentarily that he was the enemy. Albeit one that Lilly was, in spite of his questionable associations, rather fond of. 'You want me to come in?' He pointed at Lilly's front door, double-checking. No doubt, like her, remembering the time she forced him to converse through the letterbox.

'Yes, I think you'll find it's still my flat for the time being, Mr Vaughan, and I am inviting you in. We're not to be turfed out just yet.' She narrowed her eyes at him.

He swallowed and nodded, before following Clodagh into Lilly's kitchen.

'Clodagh, could you pop the kettle on?'

''Course!'

'I'll give you a hand,' Joshua offered most gallantly.

It made Lilly smile as she sat in the window in the lounge, looking out at the view, her view. It was strange not to feel the desire to go and paint it. As if she'd completed a puzzle, finished a collection, read the final chapter, won. She stared now at the painting of her mum by the river that hung in pride of place, feeling closer to her than she ever had. As if she understood her a little more, a woman who had been judged, corralled, and who without support had struggled, until she had found love with the man who repaired TVs and lived in a flat on the Tottenham Court Road.

What was it her nan had said? *Brazen, morally slack*. Awful, awful words that Lilly knew had more than likely also been applied to her by the self-righteous medics who had done little to help or support her when she had needed them most. Words that had made her doubt her own self-worth, her own feelings, even her ability to love, but not any more! This was a new era, one where Lilly was not going to be defined by her past or the judgement of others. It was her time to start living!

'I think we were probably more alike than I thought, Mum, and I shall forever regret not reaching out to you, not letting you in, not trying harder to understand and taking Dad's side without question. I understand now that there should have been no side to take.' She spoke to the woman with the red, red lipstick whose letters had given her the insight she had craved, the woman who had loved her!

The sound of Clodagh and Joshua laughing in the kitchen warmed her heart. She had a good feeling about the two of them. The young man who she was confident would show up; after all, Kennington wasn't so very far away.

She rose to answer the knock at the door, and there he stood. The two stared at each other for a beat or two. The quiet was far from uncomfortable. It was instead as if a current of understanding ran through them, a long, lingering look that spoke of connection and attraction.

It was knowing.

It was forgiveness.

It was hope.

'Alfie . . .' No more than a whisper, yet to say his name was lovely, freeing and exciting all at once. 'Thank you for coming over.' It was so wonderful to see him. She felt the girlish thrill of it, yet at the same time was more than a little worried about all the things she had said to him and the way she had said them. Her truths, no doubt, yet still rather harshly delivered.

'Miss Cooper. I was surprised to hear from you, delighted! But surprised.' He gave a slow smile, seemingly very happy to see her too. She felt some of her anxiety fade.

'Come in, come in!' She stood back to allow him access, aware of the closeness of him, the delightful feeling as her body rippled in response to the proximity. A visceral reaction to the man, the scent of him, the sound of him . . . 'Please come in.' She guided him into the lounge, where he, of course, walked straight to the window.

'Wow! I did not expect that!' He shook his head at the wonder of it.

'It's really something, isn't it?' Her smile bittersweet, at the fact that there it was, the river. Old Mother Thames.

'It really is.' He turned to face her now. 'I can't tell you how lovely it was to get your message. I've hardly slept since I saw you last, hardly been able to . . .' He shook his head as the words seemed to run out.

'Well, people change, Alfie, things change, you just have to figure out how to change with it, you have to give life a chance, don't you think?'

'Indeed I do.' He took a step towards her and spoke quietly, as if keeping it between the two of them. It felt nicely conspiratorial, suggesting their story was not done, not quite. 'I want you to know that I tried.'

'You tried what?' She'd lost the thread.

'I spoke to the board and the investors and made an arse of myself. I asked the questions; whether it was possible to build around Waide House, whether it was possible to relocate *The Fortescue* a few feet back, I even asked what was a few million extra between friends? I mean, that's conservatively what it would have cost once we'd worked out how to shoehorn it on to the same parcel of land, shifted it a bit. We would of course have lost the ornamental garden, the water frontage, the space at the rear for parking and deliveries, meaning sales would undoubtedly have been affected too, but I want you to know I tried!'

'Why did you do that?' She stared up at him. It was no small thing, the effort of which was not lost on her, this man who had tried for her, chosen her, showed up. All the very opposite of abandoning her.

'I did it for you, Lilly, just for you.' His gaze was unwavering, his tone sincere, and Lilly felt the pull in her gut of something that felt a lot like excitement.

His words, when they came, were spoken slowly, with consideration.

'It was the thought of you losing your safe space, your haven. I know what it felt like to walk through my nan's front door, as I said, like stepping into a warm hug. I still miss it, even now. And the thought of it still being there and someone coming to knock it down . . .' He sat in the window seat, as if settling in, not planning on going anywhere any time soon. 'I guess your words got to me. Made me think about my legacy.'

'I'm grateful, Alfie, more than grateful.' Her words paved the way for forgiveness, aware as she was that this man was taking something away from her, but also that he just might be giving her something in return.

'I thought maybe we could go for a drink. Hot or cold, I don't mind . . .' He held her gaze.

'Cold, I think.' She smiled up at him, this nice fella, this handsome fella!

'Cold it is.' He closed his eyes briefly, whether giving thanks or offering up a wish, it was impossible to tell; either way, she was here for it.

Clodagh and Joshua came through into the lounge.

'Hey, Joshy!' Alfie smiled at his nephew. 'I was just telling Lilly how I tried to get The Fortescue shifted.'

She saw the way Clodagh's eyes widened in recognition of the gesture.

'And I'm thankful to you.' It meant the world to her, the whole world.

'Well, I wasn't successful, so no thanks required. The consensus was that not only would it set the project back by years, but it would cost too much money, or more accurately, we would lose too much money. Not even I could persuade them to do that.'

The four stood to admire the view, the most amazing secret, a gift for all who entered this little flat.

'The reason I called you all here' – Lilly took her time – 'is because I wanted to say that I am leaving.'

'We know, Lilly!' Clodagh stared at her with a look of concern, as if she might just have lost her reason.

'Yes, but I'm not leaving because some upstart developers with a shiny brochure have harassed me into it, forced my hand!'

Joshua gave a nervous laugh.

'I'm leaving because the time is right for me.' She spoke sincerely, aware of the importance of her words, reclaiming what had been taken from her, choice, and with it her power, control over her life. 'I have decided to stop being a passenger in my own life, I'm grabbing the wheel and steering myself in the direction of happiness!'

She laughed then as she acknowledged this truth and the freedom that came with it. Staring out of the window, taking in the view of the river, her river, just as it had always been and just as it always would be. The sight no doubt similar for all who had gone before, going right back to the Romans who had built that first bridge, and whoever had lived here before that. So many lives, so many people, all with stories of love and loss and change and upheaval and yet that river just carried on flowing, a reminder of the insignificance of those who clung to its shoreline and stared upon it.

'I also wanted to say, not only that I'm leaving' – Lilly took her time, speaking softly and calmly – 'but that someone once told me that life never does quite work out how we think it will, and that's okay.' She swallowed, remembering when Norman had whispered this wisdom, at a time when she had truly needed to hear it. 'Things for us might be changed from now on, and that's okay too. Because life goes on. It has to. And so I go from here, taking all the memories with me, and I am looking forward to my next adventure! Because I am not and never am going to be old!'

Clodagh grabbed Lilly and wrapped her in the tightest hug. '*Our* adventure, Lilly, *our* adventure!'

Lilly smiled at the sweet girl, understanding that she and Apollo were not going anywhere, and this alone filled her with joy, knowing that to be Apollo's nan meant never having to walk through that gateway that led to loneliness. It was, she knew, her greatest privilege, the chance to mother these two most glorious humans.

'I should also say,' Alfie piped up, 'that while I wasn't successful in saving Waide House, I did manage to secure a handsome price for the flat, more than handsome. And the board has agreed that one of the new retail units on the ground floor is yours, Lilly, with a gallery, a studio, whatever you wish.'

'I don't know what to say!' It meant that wherever she ended up, her spot on the towpath was secure. It meant her advice to Apollo stood – he would always be able to follow the river and find her. A studio! A place for her easel, paints, Apollo's stick collection, and her trusty Thermos! It was the most glorious gift, a little spot at the bottom of the stack of Polo mints, *The Waide Gallery* . . . Her mind raced ahead, thinking of all the people who liked to stop and chat as she painted; she was thinking maybe art classes, so they, too, could experience the magic of trying to capture Old Mother Thames . . .

'So where will you move, Lilly? Somewhere close by?' Alfie asked.

'Probably . . .' She smiled at him.

Lilly instinctively knew what the moment needed. Making her way to the racks of vinyl that sat along the wall, she carefully selected an LP and blew on it before placing it on the turntable. With the record player switched on, she very gently lowered the stylus and smiled as the sound of Bill Haley & His Comets filled the room. Alfie removed his jacket and flung it on to the sofa before rolling up the sleeves of his double-cuff shirt. Reaching out, he took her hand into his, as if they had done this a thousand times before and would probably do it a thousand times more. And as the music built, the two shook, rattled and rolled as best as they were able across the parquet flooring. Alfie pulled her in close before twirling her away from him, like she was a spinning top. They laughed loudly like kids, as they moved together, hand in hand, as if they'd practised a lot or as if it came naturally, so in sync were they.

'I think you're incredible, Lilly, tenacious and beautiful, the whole package.'

'It has been said!' She winked at the man who was setting her soul on fire!

'I reckon we might be a couple of odd socks, you and me, what do you reckon?'

'I reckon you might be right.' She beamed, ready for whatever came next.

'You can fly, Lilly, you can fly as high as you want. And if you let me, I'd like to be right by your side, I'll catch you if you fall.'

No reply was needed as she felt his words bind her to him, feeling that this man might just be the great adventure she had been waiting for all her life, and understanding in that moment that it had been worth the wait.

She couldn't wait to introduce him to Glenda and Norman, knowing her friend would of course have something negative to say about his flashy watch, but how she loved her. It was a sadness that Bertie would never get to meet him; he would have adored everything about the man. It was still impossible to think about Bertie without a flash of sadness at the loss of him. But if he had taught her one thing, it was to be bold!

Clodagh and Joshua jumped forward and, doing their best, which was poor by anyone's standards, the two youngsters hopelessly bumped into each other as they chuckled and spun. The four of them jived and danced across the parquet flooring, dancing to the echo of others who had done the same a long, long time ago. As the music played, the whole flat and the people in it were transformed, no longer living under the shadow of redevelopment in Vauxhall, instead somewhere warm and sunny, living in a world of possibilities and laughter with nothing but good times ahead!

Alfie twirled her towards the magnificent view, and as the two moved with abandon, lost to the music and all it represented, Lilly felt her skin shiver as she got the distinct feeling that someone was watching her from the other side of the river.

Staring out of the window, she closed her eyes slowly, capturing the moment like a photograph at the sight of her mum and dad, arm in arm, his hair falling over his head, burgundy braces hanging down over his skinny hips. Her in a pinny, young, wearing red, red lipstick and with her hair intact, both smiling at her, their little girl, as she stood in the window of their home that was a pearl.

A hidden something right there in plain sight . . .

If you enjoyed *The Way Home*, why not read *Life As Planned*, available now.

Ashleigh and Remy Brett

1972

Aged 10

Ashleigh

Five more minutes . . .

Ashleigh Brett prayed, and screwed her eyes shut at the sound of the bedroom door opening. Lying immobile in her single bed pushed against the wall, she wriggled further under her eiderdown and savoured the last few seconds of warmth, of stillness, knowing that once light had pierced the dark, and people moved about and words were spoken, the day would truly begin, and she would be forced to stir.

Wheels would then be set in motion, driving a machine that would carry her into her future. A machine, the sights and sounds of which she had been dreading since the first mention of the exam, almost a year ago now.

An exam.

Not just a test or a mere quiz, but an exam, a word with so much weight attached to it she could barely say it out loud without wanting to crumple with the effort of holding it on her tongue. This was a new and fearful experience and what scared her the most was how powerful it seemed, taking over each waking thought and wiping all the joy from her usually happy life. Lurking like a dark thing, the monster under the bed, a baddie behind the curtain, ready to pounce the moment she was alone.

A whole year of letting the fear build, of feeling the swirl of nausea in her tummy at the thought. A year of doing her best to bury the worry, and able with relief not to dwell on it *too* much because a year was a long, long way away. Then six months was far in the future, and then a month felt like an age, and then a week, which meant it was creeping closer . . . and now, suddenly, it was today.

Today!

In that moment, it seemed to have arrived in a blink.

'Rise and shine, little doves!'

There it was, the slightly irritating sound of her mother's voice, hollering into the small room she shared with her sister.

The room with the Cindy shelf their dad had built. A sturdy white, bold, bracketed affair, on which they displayed their favourite dolls. All the Cindys looked down at her now, as they stood in front of their caravan, with their bike, grill, dog, and backpacks, everything a Cindy doll might require for a decent weekend in the great outdoors. These just a few of a wide array of accessories from gramophones to ironing boards, even a tiny crib. They really did cover all bases when it came to Cindy's life choices.

They had been avid collectors, she and Remy. Relatives had for years delightedly presented them with new Cindys or Cindy-related items on their birthday and at Christmas. Truth was, however, they didn't play with them anymore, and Ashleigh for one would rather have books on the shelf or her collection of Wade Whimsies, but her dad had built it and it felt like a big deal to ask if they could pack away these treasured things. Her mum had cried when they'd placed their Fisher-Price activity centre and record player into a box destined for the loft; goodness only knew how she'd react to a request for a removal of the dolls.

Ashleigh stared at them, the smiling lookalikes. All seemingly excited to go about their day of adventure. She wished she could be a Cindy, just for a day. More specifically, just for *today.*

Some might think it an odd wish, to sit on a shelf with someone who had the exact same face and physical features as you, but this was not strange to Ashleigh, who stole a glimpse at Remy, her identical twin, on the other side of the room. Identical in looks, build, size, shape, everything, but very different people this morning, as Remy was smiling while Ashleigh had to concentrate on not crying.

'One egg split in two, one person really, same genes . . .' her mum liked to remind them. Ashleigh didn't have the heart to say that just the thought of it made her feel a bit sick. Who wanted to be *half* an egg? Who wanted to feel like a person *split* in two?

Not her, that was for sure.

With her head still resting in the satisfying dent in the pillow, she opened one eye fully as her mum, Ruthie Brett, drew back the orange-and-brown swirl-patterned curtains to let the yellow glow of the streetlight fill their room. The window, always an indicator of the weather, carried small icy patches in the corners which, close up, looked like snowflakes. She sank down further on to the mattress, feeling the caress of the striped brushed-cotton sheet on her downy legs.

Remy, she noticed, was already sitting up, happily. This irritated her too, the fact that her sister seemed to be taking it all in her stride, as she did everything. She wondered, not for the first time, if that egg had been split equally, fairly, because it seemed to her entirely possible that her sister got more of the happy genes, the ones that made you care a bit less. It wasn't Remy's fault, but still Ashleigh had to smother the flames of jealousy that leapt inside her, wishing she could be more like her sister, who didn't seem to sweat things in quite the same way.

'Seven eights?' her mum yelled.

'Fifty-six!' Remy responded.

'Okay, this one is for you, Ashleigh, sleepyhead, what's the capital of Iceland?'

'Reykjavik,' she mumbled. *Duh! Everyone knew that.*

'My clever babies!' Her mum, in her lilac housecoat and quilted slippers, danced in the small channel between their beds, her excitement crackling from her like electricity. 'My clever, clever babies!'

She did this, spoke about them as if she had won a prize, as pride and delight dripped from every syllable. It was nice, sometimes, but not today.

'I don't think it's going to be that kind of exam, Mummy.' Remy caught her sister's eye and subtly pulled a face. Ashleigh smiled back. Aged ten, they were already proficient in humouring their mother and understanding the need for it.

'Well, it's still good to get your brains warmed up!'

The woman was both relentless and undaunted.

'What's heavier, a kilo of feathers or a kilo of tar?'

'They're the same.' Ashleigh sat up and rubbed her eyes, wishing she could turn back the clock to last night and sleep all over again, meaning this day would never come. Or better still, turn back the clock to when she had started school, when she now knew it would be wiser not to be so smart, instead to sit at the back and hang out with the gigglers, the slowcoaches, and the dumdums, who seemed to have much more fun than she did. It wasn't fair, how much she cared, how hard she worked and how she now had to sit the stupid exam.

'Ah, I can't fool you!' Her mum lowered her voice and pointed out of the window. 'This is an important day, and I want to talk to you about Mrs Jenkins who lives in that house on the corner, you know the one, don't you?'

They both nodded.

'She's got three spare bedrooms, *three*! And you, my little doves, will pass this exam and get a place at St. Jude's Academy, a full academic scholarship, where you will get the very best education, and that will get you the best job, which will pay you the best money, and you can buy the best house, with four spare bedrooms if you choose, *four*!'

'I don't think I'd like four spare bedrooms,' Remy piped up.

'Why not?' Her mum stared at her sister as if she just didn't get it.

'It just seems like more to clean, all that hoovering and dusting, more rooms to worry about.'

This time Ashleigh caught her mum's eye, and *they* exchanged a slow, conspiratorial look. Remy was right: she *didn't* get it. Ashleigh knew that if you could afford four spare bedrooms then the chances were you could also afford a cleaner or housekeeper to do all that stuff for you.

She wondered if Mrs Jenkins had a cleaner and tried to imagine a life like that. The big question was, what would you do in your house while your cleaner was in it? Her mum was always busy, constantly polishing, cleaning or scrubbing something with her Marigolds pulled up to her elbows and her hips shifting from side to side beneath the bow of her pinny. And if she wasn't doing that she was peeling, chopping, stewing, simmering, or mixing, preparing food for the family.

Ashleigh wasn't sure she wanted a life like her mum's when she grew up, and she had heard Nancy, who worked in the library, say that her boyfriend had cooked their tea! *Her boyfriend had cooked their tea!* It was so shocking she had mentioned it to Remy, who had been just as surprised. It had stuck in her mind; she was quite unable to imagine her dad doing anything in the kitchen, let alone cooking tea! It was an idea so far removed from their little life here in Church Lane it made her laugh, like suggesting her mum go out in the car every day to do her dad's job and come home expecting *her* tea to be on the table!

This wasn't what mums did.

But maybe to have a cleaner would be the answer, someone to do all those chores, while she had time to read! Yes, that was what she'd do if she had a cleaner in the house. She'd sit on the sofa and read book after book. It sounded lovely, a life like that, sitting around while someone else did all the work. A life that would probably not be hers if she didn't pass the exam. And just like that her stomach folded with nerves and she felt like she might be sick.

Remy

Remy was excited for the day ahead – a change in routine and missing lessons was always a novelty on a school day. Plus, she had a trip in the minibus to look forward to and a chance to look around St. Jude's. Oh, and the exam, which she had no doubt they would ace! But it was definitely the minibus trip that felt like the most exciting thing.

'Right, up and at 'em, little doves! See you downstairs in five!'

Her mum clapped as she left the room. Remy stared at Ashleigh, who looked less than keen to rise and shine.

'Did you have any sweet dreams?' Remy asked, as she arranged her soft toys on the pillow. They had an order and a rank that she liked to follow: Little Pigeon in the arms of Blue Cat, Mousey on the foot of Josephine the duck. And Mr Ted and Maureen the hedgehog behind her soft Holly Hobbie 'Heather' doll. It all made sense to her. She kissed the tip of her finger and touched each one, like someone of the cloth issuing blessings.

'No. I didn't dream anything.' Ashleigh was yet to leave her bed, and Remy sensed her reticence. 'I kept waking up.'

Remy had slept soundly, as she always did, knowing her sister was right there and her parents were in the room next door along the hallway. It was even nicer when she heard their voices chattering or the sound of music floating up the stairs from the radio, or their laughter coming from the kitchen, or the click of her dad's wedding ring on the banister rail as he gripped it to walk up or down the stairs. She might be ten, but still, at the sound of this background noise she felt the calming of her pulse, and the settling of her bones, happy to know her mum was within reach. Not that she'd be sharing this with Ashleigh, who would only think her a baby, or worse, a scaredy baby.

Ashleigh was braver than her, more adventurous; she liked to go out and about on her bike alone, or to wander up to the Old Sarum hillfort for a trek and a mooch, whereas Remy preferred to be in the kitchen, watching her mum whip up a Victoria sponge, or helping her peel spuds for tea. She liked to feel useful and liked it even more when her mum put her hand on her face and said, 'Such a good girl.'

There was nowhere Remy would rather be than inside, where everything she needed and everything she could possibly want was right there under the roof of their little house, the one without a spare bedroom. Her parents slept in the double, while she and Ashleigh shared their room, with the smallest room currently full of boxes, her mum's sewing machine and Christmas decorations, ready for one of them to move into *when they were ready* . . . this the vague timeline her mum had attached to the event. Remy couldn't imagine falling asleep without her sister, who she had slept next to since they shared the snug space inside their mum's tum, close by. Together before they even knew how to think, or how to be.

One egg, split in two . . .

She certainly wasn't yet ready to move her bed into the littlest room and, in truth, couldn't imagine a time when she might be.

'Are you worried about the exam?' She tried to guess at the reason for her sister's lack of enthusiasm to get the day started.

'No!' Ashleigh fired, and Remy knew her well enough to understand that this might actually mean *yes*.

'Because it'll be okay. You'll have me there, and even if you don't finish, Miss Delaney said that you can get enough points from the first three parts to pass, so we don't need to rush.'

'I don't care what Miss Delaney said! I told you, I don't care about the stupid exam! Or the stupid scholarship!'

Remy stared as her sister finally jumped out of bed, grabbed her towel, and headed for the bathroom to have her bath, choosing to say nothing rather than say the wrong thing.

Ashleigh got this way sometimes, a little snappy, a little mean.

She had learned it was best to ignore her until the storm passed.

'You all need to be good today. I don't want any naughtiness while I'm gone!' Remy spoke sternly to her stuffies lined up on her pillow. Instantly she felt bad for raising her voice a little, and sat down, running her fingers over their soft faces. 'What can we do to help Ashleigh? She seems a bit upset, don't you think?' As usual, they didn't reply.

Ashleigh

Ashleigh pulled her school jumper over her head and took a seat at the square kitchen table, disliking the uncomfortable feeling of her thick, curly locks trapped inside the neck of her polyester sweater. It made her itch. Her mum stood behind her and gently eased her mop from its woolly confines. The touch of her fingertips to the back of Ashleigh's neck made her shiver and jump, yet more irritation on this day that was already proving tricky.

'I hate my hair!'

'No, you don't.' Her mum did this, dismissed her views as if she could easily transform them with no more than a gentle steer. 'Your hair is beautiful, everybody says so. Besides that's the same as saying you hate Remy's hair, and you don't want to upset your sister, do you?'

Ashleigh shook her head. No, she didn't want to upset her sister. But she also didn't want to look exactly like her, finding nothing funny in the question, *'Now, which one are you?'* that she was asked countless times a day, by their neighbours, her mum's friends, parents at the school, teachers, even her dad, once or twice, although he did so quietly, as if wary of her mum hearing.

She also didn't want to discuss it anymore, knowing that this morning it would take more energy than she had spare to explain that it was not how her hair looked that bothered her, but rather the way it felt, like there was too much of it, and she wanted it to be neater, flatter, less in the way.

Remy, she noticed, was already tucking into toast and jam and glugging from a tumbler full of milk. Ashleigh wished it were dinner time, wished it were possible to blink and the day be done, and they'd be back here eating their tea, instead of breakfast. No doubt they would be quizzed about the exam and what exactly they'd written, and asked numerous questions about what St. Jude's had been like, but it'd be preferable, all of it, as it meant it would be over.

'Brain food!' her mum trilled. 'You have to eat. And talking of eating, I've got you a treat of a tea, all your favourites: toad in the hole, mash, onion gravy, and' – she paused, letting the tension build – 'a special pudding.'

'Yes!' Remy, who sported a large milk moustache, did a fist pump, and her mum's face lit up.

The truth was, Ashleigh barely had an appetite, but knew better than to let on, as this would only encourage her mother to give a half-baked monologue on the importance of breakfast on a day like this. Everything, it seemed, was geared towards keeping her brain in tip-top condition so she could identify shapes and match them on a page, find missing words hidden in code, fill in the blanks of numeric sequences, and circle answers to a passage of writing to show she comprehended it.

Easy enough.

She had done tons of practice tests. All four pupils who were to sit the entrance exam had spent hours doing just this. And she had passed every single one, sometimes finishing with so much time to spare she'd been allowed to take out her book and read, getting lost in the world Noel Streatfeild had created, while the other three continued to scribble furiously.

This felt different. There were three scholarships available and kids from all over the county were vying for them.

But it was more than the exam itself, much more, and she wasn't sure how she could explain it. It was a feeling of pressure, of something heavy on her shoulders and rocks in her stomach, a physical thing that was as new as it was scary. Supposing she didn't pass, supposing she fainted, supposing she couldn't remember a thing, or needed the loo, or her pencil broke, or she actually threw up.

'Ashleigh!' Her mother clapped, and again she jumped. 'Where were you? I've been asking you for the last minute if you want milk or orange squash?'

'I don't mind,' she whispered, trying to find a voice that was steady, trying to control the desire to vomit, as Remy chomped merrily on her toast, and even hummed. Ashleigh didn't want to be the one who wavered, the one who let the side down. The weakest.

'You have to mind!' Her mum laughed loudly, a noise that was an irritation, an upset. 'Milk or orange? Which one would you like best, which would you *prefer*?'

'Orange.'

'And while we are on the subject of fruit, can you name me three different varieties of apple?' her mother asked as she topped up the vibrant cordial with tap water.

'No.' Ashleigh blinked and reached for the glass, knowing the woman wouldn't be satisfied until she had sunk the lot. 'I can't.'

'Oh dear!' Her mum pulled a face that would have been more appropriate for the very worst kind of news. 'What about you, Remy? Three varieties of apple?'

'Nope.' Her sister kept eye contact, letting her know that she was there, and that she understood. Remy offered a small smile telling Ashleigh that it would all be okay. 'No clue.'

'Well, that's not very good, is it?' Her mum tutted.

'Maybe we should have spent more time on apple varieties and not worried about fractions and long multiplication,' Remy whispered sweetly as she bit her toast.

And for the first time that day, Ashleigh felt a smile forming on her lips. It was her sister's gift: she was funny.

'What are you two smiling at?' their mum asked, hands on hips.

'Nothing.'

'Nothing.'

They replied in unison. It was that way with twins. In sync, in tune and always having each other's back.

Remy

Remy was worried about her sister, knowing her well enough to recognise when she was struggling. This was the trouble with Ashleigh, she cared too much about . . . about everything!

Her dad walked into the kitchen, whistling, as was his way. He looked smart in his white shirt and company tie, which was red with a small gold logo on it. Her dad sold concrete. People always made the same jokes when they found this out: '*How does he carry his samples around?*' Or, '*Now there's a job you can really get stuck in to . . .*' He had explained to her in great, great detail that he sold concrete to companies who built things and it was probably the most important part of any project, getting the concrete right. Without it, the whole shebang could tumble down, literally.

Her dad took concrete very seriously. And as he liked to remind them, his smile gone, eyes blinking, 'There's a million people unemployed in this country. One million. I can't even picture that many of anything, fellas who can't put food on the table or shoes on their kids' feet. There'll always be a need for concrete, and for that I am thankful.' His tone and manner hinted that he was not only thankful but fearful too, the slow rise and fall of his Adam's apple suggesting that he was only one wrong move or one pay cheque away from being a fella like that.

She didn't like to think of kids with no shoes.

'How are we all doing?' He always said this, as if he were addressing a crowd. She suspected it was because there were moments when he couldn't tell them apart and was happier with this catch-all, often addressing them directly as 'sweetie' or 'love'.

'Mum's getting us a special pudding.' This, the thing that stuck in her thoughts from their earlier conversation. Remy had a very sweet tooth and was unashamedly motivated by the prospect of sugar.

'Not Arctic Roll, is it? What are we, made of money?'

'Don't be an old grump, Dennis, this is a big day for our little doves, and they deserve a treat!'

'Well, I'm going to work all day, so can I have some?' He winked at her, her lovely dad; she knew he'd never take their ice cream, spoil their treat.

'It's a home-made pud, actually, but I'm not going to say more than that!' Her mum beamed and gave a little wiggle. Excited, it seemed, at no more than the promise of her family around the table, all sampling her special pud.

'How are we all feeling about the exam?' Her dad got straight to it as he slathered marmalade over his toast.

'Well, Mum's excited.' Ashleigh spoke quietly, eyes fixed on Remy. It made them both laugh; there she was, beneath the frosty exterior, her smart sister.

'You'll do great.' Whether he hadn't heard, wasn't paying attention or simply chose to ignore Ashleigh, it was impossible to tell. 'I'll tell you something' – he paused, using his marmalade knife as a pointer as he aimed it at them in turn, verbally ladling on the expectation she knew would do nothing to help ease Ashleigh's nerves – 'when I drive past St. Jude's, do you know what I see?'

She shook her head, knowing he didn't really want her to guess the answer. Ashleigh rolled her eyes and took a deep breath.

'I see fancy cars, and fancy people. Drove past the other week and one bloke was in one of them new Ford Granadas. Cor, I'd give my left nut for one of them.'

'Dennis!' her mum shouted. Her dad was not allowed to say 'nut' in front of them. Unless it was of the pea, wal, or hazel variety.

'And the thought that my daughters will be right there among it.' He shook his head, his voice quavering with emotion. 'It's something I could never have dreamed of. I can't imagine what my old mum would say if she were still alive. She'd not believe it.'

Her mum came up behind him and squeezed his shoulder. It occurred to her then how she, certainly, might be taking the exam in her stride, but for her parents, and Ashleigh too, it was kind of a big deal.

'If we don't pass, don't get the scholarships . . .' She spoke as thoughts formed.

'It doesn't matter!'

'Doesn't matter a jot!'

Her parents replied simultaneously before she had finished the question. They shook their heads, held up their palms and spoke with gusto and false grins, as if they might be able to convince her this was the case. She, however, caught the way they shared a brief but meaningful, wide-eyed glance, as if it *did* matter. As if it mattered a lot.

The colour, she noticed, had drained from Ashleigh's face. Her sister placed her buttered toast on her plate, seemingly unable to take another bite.

'Five eights?' her mum yelled, obviously trying to change the atmosphere as she headed towards the sink.

'Forty-four!' Remy shouted.

'Forty-four?' Her dad pulled a face.

'Goodness me, Remy! Do we need to go over our eight times table in the car?' her mum asked nervously.

Remy smiled at Ashleigh, hoping to make her laugh, knowing her sister was well aware that she could recite all of the times tables perfectly in her sleep.

'I don't know, Ruthie, do we?'

This did the trick, and Ashleigh laughed loudly; the glass of orange squash shook in her hand, spilling over the wipe-clean tablecloth, and Remy's tummy felt warmed.

It was all going to be okay.

Ashleigh

'Here we are then, girls! We need to get a wiggle on as your dad needs the car back pronto. He's heading up to Bristol and won't thank me if he's late. But I wanted to drive you in – no bus for my little smarty-pants, not today.'

Ashleigh gave a brief nod of understanding, although why all the fuss she wasn't sure. She liked getting the bus, liked sitting with

Tony, their friend, swapping their news, not that they had much news, and more often than not spoke about what they'd had for their tea. She looked out of the window on her side of the car, the right. She always sat on the right. Remy did likewise on the left.

'Now' – her mum adjusted the rear-view mirror, and spoke into it – 'don't forget, you are to have an early lunch – your form teacher is aware – then Miss Delaney will meet you by the minibus at the front of the school and she will wait *in* the minibus while you take the exam.'

That word, again . . .

It did little to help her nerves, hearing the plan, the schedule. Her mum pulled out the choke, turned the key, and the car juddered as the engine sputtered into life. Ashleigh wondered how badly she would be injured if she jumped out of the moving car. This wasn't a suicide mission, nothing like that! What she was after was the kind of injury that could mean a few hours in the casualty department, long enough to miss the trip to St. Jude's, and maybe a cast on her arm, to show authenticity and commitment to the cause. Yes, a broken arm would do it. Her writing arm! That would be perfect, but would it hurt? She wasn't very good with pain, and how awful if she sustained something horribly damaging or permanent. It felt risky, too risky. Maybe a faint might be better when they arrived? A graceful fall on to the playground floor, or, or . . . vomiting! That would be easy! She again felt nausea rise in her throat. A quick but meaningful vomit, all over her skirt and T-bar shoes, thus guaranteeing a trip home to get changed, suggesting enough of a bug that might mean isolation from all of her classmates and peers. This felt like the only option.

'Then she'll drive you all back,' her mum continued, 'and I will collect you from school as normal, only it won't be as normal, as I'll be driving you home, and it will all be done and you, my clever babies, will have taken the first step on the wonderful path that means so many great things!'

Four spare bedrooms! her sister mouthed at her, and rolled her eyes, before returning her gaze to the window.

Ashleigh felt her legs tense.

'I've checked your bags, and you've got pencil cases, an apple, and a little note each, not to be read until you are in the minibus. A kind of good luck and go-get-'em note!'

It felt like there was little point in reading it, now her mother had revealed the contents.

'You are both very quiet in the back there, little doves!'

'Why do you call us doves?' she had asked once.

Her mum had explained with her hand at her throat and tears in her eyes.

'On the day you were born, I remember sitting on the side of the bed in the ward, I was tired, so tired, but I couldn't sleep. I wanted to stare at those two perfect little babies who slept holding hands, always within reach of each other. I thought my heart might explode! I'd never felt love like it, not before, not since. You were both so beautiful – miracles! Two babies from one egg, rare and special. I was overwhelmed and just to think of it now makes me cry.' She had wiped her eyes as if to prove the point. *'And then, I heard a sound on the windowsill and when I looked there were two white doves, pretty things with keen eyes and beautiful feathers, and they were looking right at me, looking right at you two! And so I called you my own little doves, and that was that.'*

Ashleigh thought of it now and wished she were a little dove, an actual bird, who could, just for today, simply fly away.

ABOUT THE AUTHOR

Photo © 2023 Paul Smith @paulsmithpics

Amanda Prowse is a multimillion-copy bestselling author who has published more than thirty novels and is one of the most prolific writers of contemporary fiction in the UK today.

Crowned 'the queen of family drama' by the *Daily Mail*, she writes about life's challenges – from heartbreak and loss to dysfunctional family dynamics – but also about the pockets of delight that can be found in our relationships with others, often when we need them most.

Amanda is known for her relatable characters, emotionally compelling plots, and the sense of connection that readers feel with her stories.

She is an ambassador for The Reading Agency and feels passionately about supporting other women, spending as much time as possible outdoors (preferably by the sea!), and her family.

Follow the Author on Amazon

If you enjoyed this book, follow Amanda Prowse on Amazon to be notified when the author releases a new book!
To do this, please follow these instructions:

Desktop:

1) Search for the author's name on Amazon or in the Amazon App.
2) Click on the author's name to arrive on their Amazon page.
3) Click the 'Follow' button.

Mobile and Tablet:

1) Search for the author's name on Amazon or in the Amazon App.
2) Click on one of the author's books.
3) Click on the author's name to arrive on their Amazon page.
4) Click the 'Follow' button.

Kindle eReader and Kindle App:

If you enjoyed this book on a Kindle eReader or in the Kindle App, you will find the author 'Follow' button after the last page.